Trained as ████████████████████████████ ████ental
health serv████████████████████████ London, ███ now writes
full time and has been a visitor to Turkey for over twenty years.
She ████████ the C████ ██████ ████████████████████████ or
her novel *Deadly Web* and the Swedish Flintax Prize for historical crime fiction for her first Francis Hancock novel *Last Rights*.

Praise for Barbara Nadel:

'[İkmen's] unconventional character has been strikingly
established . . . The vividly realised Turkish locales are a particular pleasure of the series'   *Good Book Guide*

'The delight of Nadel's books is the sense of being taken beneath
the surface of an ancient city which most visitors see for a few
days at most. We look into the alleyways and curious dark
quarters of Istanbul, full of complex characters and louche
atmosphere'   *Independent*

'Nadel's evocation of the shady underbelly of modern Turkey
is one of the perennial joys of crime fiction'   *Mail on Sunday*

'Gripping and unusual detective story, vivid and poignant'
                                                Literary Review

'Particularly interesting for its discussion of Turkish customs
and beliefs'   *Sunday Telegraph*

By Barbara Nadel

BARBARA NADEL

LAND of the BLIND

First published in Great Britain in 2015
by HEADLINE PUBLISHING GROUP

First published in Great Britain in paperback in 201
by HEADLINE PUBLISHING GROUP

Apart from any use permitted under UK copyright law, this
publication may only be reproduced, stored, or transmitted, in
any form, or by any means, with prior permission in writing of
the publishers or, in the case of reprographic production, in
accordance with the terms of licences issued by the
Copyright Licensing Agency.

All characters in this publication are fictitious and any resemblance to real persons,
living or dead, is purely coincidental.

Cataloguing in Publication Data is available from the British Library

ISBN 978 1 4722 1378 5

Typeset in Times New Roman by Palimpsest Book Production Limited,
Falkirk, Stirlingshire
Printed and bound in Great Britain by Clays Ltd, St Ives plc

MIX
Paper from
responsible sources
FSC® C104740

HEADLINE PUBLISHING GROUP
An Hachette UK Company
Carmelite House
50 Victoria Embankment
London EC4Y 0DZ

www.headline.co.uk
www.hachette.co.uk

To Ruth, Jeyda, Pat and Elsie.
Also thanks go to Flora Rees and Darcy Nicholson at Headline.

Cast List

Çetin İkmen – Istanbul police detective
Fatma İkmen – his wife
Kemal İkmen – his youngest son
Samsun Bajraktar – his cousin
Arto Sarkissian – Armenian police pathologist
Hürrem Teker – Istanbul police commissioncr
Mehmet Süleyman – Istanbul police detective
Gonca Şekeroğlu – his mistress
Ömer Mungun – Suleyman's sergeant
Peri Mungun – Omer's sister, a nurse
Kerim Gürsel – İkmen's sergeant
Sinem Gürsel – Kerim's wife
Pembe Hanım – Kerim's lover
Dr Ariadne Savva – a Greek archeologist
Meltem Doğan – her assistant
Demitrios Savva – Dr Savva's father
Professor Ramazan Bozdağ – head archeologist at Istanbul Archeological Museum
Dr Aylın Akyıldız – archeological pathologist
Ahmet Öden – property developer
Semih Öden – his younger brother

Kelime Öden – Ahmet's daughter

Mary Cox – Kelime's English nanny

Ayşel Ocal (Gulizar) – Ahmet Öden's mistress

Dr İnçi – a dentist

Madam Anastasia Negroponte – an Istanbul Greek

Yiannis Negroponte – her son

Hakkı Atasu – Madam Negroponte's retainer

Lokman Atasu – Hakkı's son

Nar Hanım – Gezi protester

Madonna – Gezi protester

Madame Edith – Gezi protester

Iris – Gezi protester

Melda Erol – Gezi protester

Fatima Erol – Gezi protester

Özgür Koç – Gezi protester

He could only stand. A slight bend of the knees was all he could do and if he leaned forward his head touched the wall. Just out of reach, on the dirt floor, was a candle. It was wide and tall and if he put his left leg too near it his trousers began to crackle. His chest felt as if it was enclosed in the coils of a snake. The air, stale and thick with dust, irritated his lungs, forcing him to breathe consciously against the pollutants as well as the embrace of the imaginary serpent. On a ledge, just beside his left arm, was a tall jug of water. Within his reach, it must have been put there for him and at first he appreciated it. His mouth was dry and the first sip tasted delicious. The second, bitter.

He forced himself to put the jug down. Why was the jug there, really? And what did it contain? If it was poison and he died, did it count as suicide if he hadn't put it in the water himself? And if it was clean why had it been left there? To prolong his torment? To make him eke it out like a common prisoner? There was nowhere for him to pee except on the floor. He'd have to concentrate to get his arms down to unzip his fly. It wouldn't be easy. He wanted to weep. But men didn't.

'Who is there?' he called out. 'Is anyone there?'

He hadn't expected an answer and he didn't get one.

The water shone in the candlelight. Entirely clear and pure. How could it be poisoned? Did he feel unwell? How could he tell? He was in a cavity about two metres tall by two metres long, the width he could only guess. Was it one metre or less? It meant he couldn't sit unless he almost folded himself in half, or lay. When he thought about it, he could only just breathe. His heart began to pick up its beat and he prayed. Not properly because he couldn't prostrate himself. Would God listen? Of course He would! Where had *that* thought come from? He always listened and provided.

Except maybe now? The thought had insinuated itself into his head almost before he'd noticed. Sin could be so easily fallen into. And he had just plummeted. Now he began to cry. There was fear. Doubt was a terrible sin and to sin meant that when death came he would not walk in the gardens of Paradise. He begged and begged for forgiveness, his voice slicing the silence, the power of his words causing the candle flame to gutter and twist. Afraid he'd blow it out by accident, he stopped. The flame became stable again and he prayed in his head.

God was listening and He did care. All his life he'd done exactly what those more educated in the words of the Koran had told him. Not one request had he ever denied. Bar that moment of doubt, his soul was pure. His mind said, *And your body?*

A noise came out of his mouth. Like a squeal. Then he began to shake. 'Oh, God,' he said. 'Oh God!'

Hearing his own voice tremble was not a comfortable thing. He begged. 'Please, please help me. I'll never do it again. Never.'

And he waited and he waited. But no help came. He wanted and didn't want water and the candle flame guttered again in time to his sobs. Still no relief came, no rest from the reality that he had been buried alive. Which he had been.

Chapter 1

'Porphyry,' Çetin İkmen said.

'What?' His colleague, a rotund Armenian pathologist, continued to look into the deceased's eyes.

'The piece of stone in her left hand,' İkmen said. 'It's porphyry.'

'Is it.' The pathologist, Dr Arto Sarkissian, looked at İkmen. 'Forgive me, I'm rather more concerned that this woman has not long given birth. I can't get excited about stone.'

'There's no porphyry in here,' İkmen said. To prove his point he flashed the light from his torch around the darkened space. He'd never been there before. Although less than five minutes from his apartment, the sphendone or curved back edge of İstanbul's Hippodrome was unknown to him. Or rather the interior of the ancient monument was. Thousands of tourists explored what remained of the Byzantine structure above ground every day, but Inspector Çetin İkmen and his friend and colleague Arto Sarkissian were underground. In what remained of a ruined gallery they were where the charioteers used to robe before the Games commenced and where wild animals – lions, tigers and bears – would wait their turn to fight each other to the death for the entertainment of the baying crowd in the arena. It was a place already soaked in blood. Now it was absorbing some more.

'There's trauma to the back of the head,' Arto said.

'Was that why she died?'

'I don't know. Won't know until I can examine her properly.'

It was impossible to stand up straight in that place. Earthquakes plus thousands of years had transformed what had been a double galleried Roman hippodrome into a crumbling, squashed wreck. The doctor could see that the woman was dead and even the non-medically trained police inspector could work out that the blood between her legs together with the severed umbilical cord meant that she'd given birth not long before. But beyond those facts, investigation became difficult.

İkmen looked around again. When he'd first seen the woman and realised she'd just had a baby he'd run, hunched up against the sagging galleries above, looking for it. But he'd soon come up against spaces so small not even he could squeeze through them. He'd also feared he'd get lost.

When he'd spoken to the two young men who had found the body – 'urban explorers' they'd called themselves – they'd told him they hadn't seen or even heard any baby.

Bilal, the smaller of the two, had said, 'We opened the door and there she was. Alone. We called you immediately.'

His friend, a lanky youngster in tight Lycra, said nothing.

Bilal had told İkmen that they'd got permission to go underneath the Hippodrome from the local authority, Fatih, as well as from the holders of the key to the monument, the Archaeological Museum. And to İkmen's surprise there had only been one key required to open the small green door that led into the back of the ancient site. Heavy and clearly old, the urban explorers' key looked like something that might unlock a castle. It was also identical to a key the dead woman held in her right hand.

'It's possible she's only been dead for an hour,' Arto said. 'There's no sign of rigor. Mind you, it's hot in here.'

In spite of it being five o'clock in the morning, the city of İstanbul and especially the cramped cavities underneath the

Hippodrome sweated in the heat. When summer arrived in the great metropolis on the Bosphorus it really made an impact.

A photographer, a man even portlier than the doctor, came through the small green door and looked at Sarkissian expectantly. Clearly he didn't want to have to squash his considerable stomach by bending for too long. The Armenian said, 'I want all the usual shots, Ali. Pay special attention to the head and the sexual organs.'

'Yes, Doctor.'

Çetin İkmen had to get out. He couldn't breathe and he was beginning to feel nauseous. Outside, a gaggle of uniformed officers stood with the awkward looking urban explorers. One of the constables offered İkmen a cigarette which he took and lit up.

'Thank you, Yıldız,' he said.

Constable Yıldız, a slim man in his mid-thirties, mumbled that it was nothing.

The sun, coming up over the Asian side of the city, sent a ray directly into İkmen's face and he winced. Bastard! Not only had he been wrenched from his bed by death, now the sun had it in for him too. If he'd had four hours sleep before his mobile phone had clattered in his ear at four fifteen, he'd been lucky. And now he had a missing baby to worry about too. Had the child died with its mother or had someone taken the baby away? Arto said the woman had a head wound. Had someone hit her deliberately with child stealing in mind? And who had cut the woman's umbilical cord? There had been no sign of a knife or scissors. There'd been no ID either. Women usually carried handbags, but this one hadn't. Then again, she had been giving birth. But she'd done that wearing what had looked to İkmen like an ordinary summer dress.

'God help me, I can't stay in there any longer,' Arto Sarkissian said. Getting out through the tiny green door had been a challenge and the Armenian's face was red from exertion.

İkmen told one of his uniformed officers to share his bottle of water with the doctor.

'Thank you.' Arto Sarkissian shook his head. 'What on earth was she doing giving birth in a place like that?'

İkmen shrugged. 'How old do you reckon she was?'

'Mid to late thirties.' The doctor drank some more water and then splashed a handful over his face. 'From her general condition and her clothes I'd say she was urban, educated, secular. This is no little country girl raped by her uncle. Which makes one wonder why she gave birth in a place like that.'

'She had a key,' İkmen said.

'She did.'

İkmen tipped his head at the two urban explorers. 'They got theirs from the Archaeological Museum. They hold some and so do the Municipality.'

'So it's fusty archaeologists and slimy local government officials for you then,' Arto said.

'Seems like it.'

İkmen always looked disappointed even when he wasn't, and dealing with government either national or local always made him depressed. Politicians were evasive, even when they didn't need to be. It was a habit they all got into as soon as they attained office. Maybe it was mandatory.

'I'll determine cause of death and hopefully a more precise time as soon as I can,' Arto said.

İkmen nodded.

A van arrived containing five white-clad individuals. The forensic team would investigate the corpse and the site and take samples before the doctor would be able to take the dead woman to his laboratory. He walked over to liaise with the team leader leaving İkmen alone with his thoughts. It was always reassuring to work with his friend Arto Sarkissian. They'd known each other

6

all their lives and each trusted the other completely. But if this woman's death was a murder then someone was missing from İkmen's team and he felt that lack like a knife to the soul. He looked up into the sky and wondered whether the religious people had something when they talked about souls and Paradise. And against every secular atom in his body he hoped that they had something because he didn't want Ayşe Farsakoğlu to be nowhere.

Commissioner Hürrem Teker knew what they called her. She'd known the name they'd given her when she worked in Antep. The policemen of İstanbul were no less subtle. Whereas in Antep she'd been *The Stormtrooper*, in the city on the Bosphorus they called her *The Iron Virgin*. If only they knew.

Hürrem looked at the report of a suspicious death in Sultanahmet. A woman's body had been discovered inside the back of the Hippodrome. She didn't know it even had an inside. Çetin İkmen, one of her older and more interesting officers, was at the scene. Him, she liked. Life-scarred, cynical and given to some of the bad habits and addictions she had, İkmen was also, according to her predecessor, Ardıç, the most trustworthy police inspector in İstanbul.

There was a knock on her door. However, this man she was about to see was another matter. 'Come.'

Inspector Mehmet Süleyman was a handsome man in his early forties. An immaculate dresser, he belonged to one of those old Ottoman families distantly related to the Sultans. Consequently he had the kind of naturally arrogant allure that a lot of women, Hürrem included, found very attractive. But he wasn't always to be trusted. Commissioner Ardıç had told her so but Hürrem also knew it by instinct. Handsome men had always been her weakness, in the past, and they had consistently let her down.

The door opened.

Hürrem smiled at him. 'Sit down, Süleyman.' She pointed to a chair in front of her desk. She preferred using surnames as people did in the West rather than using the Ottoman appellation, 'bey'. She considered it an anachronism in the twenty-first century; she also felt that if she called a man like this 'Mehmet Bey' she was colluding with the view some had of him as an 'Ottoman gentleman'. The last thing Hürrem wanted to encourage in her officers was any sort of hierarchy that was not police-related.

Süleyman sat down.

Hürrem got straight to the point. Süleyman might not be entirely trustworthy, but he didn't deserve the rebuke she was about to deliver. So he fucked some gypsy women? So what. That wasn't her business. But there were some, both inferior and superior to Hürrem, who felt that it was very much their concern. A few were people she couldn't ignore. 'I've called you in because I've had complaints,' she said.

'About me?'

'Yes. Although I should hasten to add these complaints are not about your work. They concern the company you keep, namely a gypsy woman you visit in Balat.'

'Oh.' He looked crushed.

Hürrem hated herself. What this man did in bed was his affair. Except that in some people's eyes – those she called the 'Morality Police' – his life was not his own, but needed to be lived according to their standards. And there were a lot of people like them.

'Be discreet,' she said. 'I'm not going to lecture you about your personal life, especially in view of the tragedy that befell this department only a few months ago.'

İkmen's sergeant, Ayşe Farsakoğlu, had been shot and killed in the line of duty and many of her colleagues still felt her loss keenly. Principal amongst those who suffered was Çetin İkmen, who had been her immediate superior, and Mehmet Süleyman, who at one time had been her lover.

'Personally I don't care who you associate with provided they don't have a criminal record,' Hürrem continued. 'But you know as well as I just how influential those of a highly moralistic tenor are in our society right now, and I don't want you to get caught out by them. The bottom line is that I don't want to lose a good officer. I don't think I have to tell you that such people can affect careers and lives, and there's not a lot someone like me can do about it.'

The current government and some of their allies were religiously inspired in their opinions. Their resultant moral standards, particularly when it came to sex, were high. More and more of them had entered the police in recent years.

'I see.' Now he looked defiant – and arrogant, and very attractive.

Hürrem cleared her throat. 'I'm not going to say you must stop seeing this woman, Gonca Şekeroğlu,' she said. 'I'm not saying that you should marry her. Who knows what those of a moralistic nature would make of a gypsy as a policeman's wife. But leave your car somewhere other than outside her house. I know where she lives is up a monstrous hill that I wouldn't want to climb. You smoke, I smoke; I know the problem. But your last medical showed you to be fit. Walk there.'

Now he put his head down. 'Yes, madam.'

'And when you arrive it would be better if this woman's vast tribe of children and grandchildren didn't spill out on to the streets to see what sweets you've brought for them.' She shook her head. 'I'm sorry, Süleyman, truly . . .'

'I know these words are not yours, madam,' he said.

'In instances like this I have to act on the words of others,' she said. 'And I'm sorry.' Then she smiled. 'Discreet. Yes?'

After a moment he smiled too. 'Discreet. Absolutely.'

'Thank you.'

After he left she berated herself for giving in to pressure and telling Süleyman he had to be more careful, but also congratulated herself on a job well done. She hadn't forbidden him from seeing Turkey's most famous gypsy artist, Gonca Şekeroğlu, which was what she was supposed to have done. Hopefully she'd made him behave as if he was being watched by an enemy, which he was.

Everything about the 'Morality Police' stuck in Hürrem's craw. Her father and grandfather had been professional soldiers who passionately believed in Ataturk's secular republic. They would have been horrified at her interference in Süleyman's personal life. Admittedly, they would also have been horrified by the amount of power the military had taken for themselves prior to the coming of the Islamically based AKP government. The army's rigidity and cruelty had helped to bring the AKP into power just as surely as the party's promise to break the military's iron grip on the country. But even in her wildest imaginings, Hürrem had never considered the kind of moral bullying she and many others were being subjected to.

She opened her office window, stuck her head out into the torrid İstanbul air and lit a cigarette. In a moment of rebellion, she hoped that some 'morality policeman' in the street below saw her. After all, she could get away with the cigarette by arguing that her head was outside the building. What she would be able to say should either of her two latest lovers be identified, she really didn't know.

If Kerim Gürsel had been a young man, İkmen would have expected him to bound across open ground like a gazelle. But he was in his early forties, which made his rapid gambol look a little awkward.

10

'Don't know where the fire is, Sergeant Gürsel,' İkmen said as his deputy approached.

Gürsel, whose face was slim and dark and forever mildly amused, said, 'We've got a murder, sir. Can't afford to waste time.'

'No, but I'm not sure that Professor Bozdağ will share your enthusiasm. When he gets here,' İkmen said.

He'd been sitting outside Dr Sarkissian's pathology laboratory for over an hour. For the past ten minutes he'd been waiting for this Professor Bozdağ. When he'd first stepped out of the Armenian's lab he'd done so to smoke and also to get away from the inevitable smell of blood and preserving fluid that pervaded the building. He'd found out what he needed to know, which was that the woman from the Hippodrome had been killed by a blow to the back of the head. She had possibly fallen, although some of the indentations in her skull seemed to suggest that she could also have been hit with an instrument of some sort. Then he'd got a call from the station about this Professor Bozdağ.

'If he's an archaeologist a dead body won't upset him,' Kerim Gürsel said. 'They deal with them all the time.'

'When they're thousands of years old, yes,' İkmen said. 'I doubt very much whether Professor Bozdağ has seen many fresh corpses.'

'He offered to come.'

'Because one of his colleagues has gone missing,' İkmen said.

Kerim continued to smile, which was annoying. He did a few things that wound İkmen up. He made puerile jokes sometimes, did far too much running and didn't smoke. But he was a good soul who talked about his wife, whom he seemed to adore, and he liked animals, which was a plus in İkmen's book. His main

11

fault was that he wasn't Ayşe Farsakoğlu. He, poor man, had been given the impossible task of replacing a dead officer most people had liked and everyone had trusted. Luckily he was an İstanbullu, which was a plus in most people's eyes, but he still wasn't Ayşe and he never would be.

A yellow taxi with a pair of Türkcell bug antennae on the roof stopped in front of the laboratory and an elderly, grey-haired man got out.

'Inspector İkmen?'

İkmen threw his latest cigarette butt to one side and stood up. 'Yes.'

The man paid the driver and then walked up the steps towards the police officers. 'God but it's hot!' He put a hand out. 'Ramazan Bozdağ,' he said.

İkmen shook his hand and then introduced Sergeant Gürsel.

'I'm really hoping that this visit is going to be a waste of time, from my point of view,' the professor said. 'When our Dr Savva didn't arrive for work this morning, I thought she might just be late. But then when Meltem Hanım came to me and said she'd not seen Dr Savva return to her apartment last night I became concerned. I tried to ring her but she didn't pick up. And then of course I heard the news about the woman inside the sphendone.'

'The back of the Hippodrome.'

'Yes. Dr Savva is a specialist in Byzantine art, she has a key to the structure.'

İkmen looked meaningfully at Gürsel. Then he said, 'Let me take you through, Professor Bozdağ.'

The older man wiped his brow. 'I imagine it will at least be cool in there . . .'

When Arto Sarkissian exposed the dead woman's face, the professor didn't look shocked or horrified, just sad.

'Oh God, what has happened here?' he said.

İkmen could see that Kerim Gürsel was champing at the bit to know whether the body was the professor's colleague or not, so he put a calming hand on his shoulder. Moments that felt like minutes passed.

Professor Bozdağ took in a deep breath. 'It's her, gentlemen. My colleague, Dr Ariadne Savva. She was a Greek national, so you'll have to inform the consulate.' Then he leaned forwards to get closer to her. 'Oh Ariadne, what on earth has happened to you?'

They let him have a few moments with her and then Arto Sarkissian said, 'Professor, when we found Dr Savva she had just given birth to a child.'

The archaeologist straightened up. 'A child? In the sphendone?'

'Did you not know she was pregnant?'

All the colour disappeared from his face. İkmen, afraid that the professor might be about to faint, got him a chair. As he sat down Bozdağ said, 'No.'

A lot of men, especially older ones, could be notoriously unobservant when it came to what women looked like and what they wore. İkmen always relied on his daughters to tell him when his wife had a new dress or a manicure.

'Was she married?' İkmen asked. 'Or did she have a partner?'

'No,' the professor said, 'to both. Ariadne was married to her job. She had friends, at the museum, and she was involved in some sort of voluntary social work . . .'

'Do you know what?'

Arto Sarkissian covered the body's face and wheeled it out of the viewing room.

'No,' Bozdağ said. 'But I believe she got some of her colleagues at the museum involved. I assume you'll want to interview everyone . . .'

13

'Yes.'

There was silence for a while. The professor began to shiver, and when Arto Sarkissian returned he got him a blanket which he draped around his shoulders.

The archaeologist thanked him and then said, 'What about Ariadne's child? What is it? A boy or a girl?'

'We don't know,' İkmen said. 'When we found her the baby had gone.'

'Gone where?'

'We don't know. We've been searching the immediate vicinity ever since we found the body of the mother. Now we know who she was we'll search her apartment. Commissioner Teker is giving a press conference this afternoon where she'll appeal for information.'

'What was Dr Savva doing having a child in the sphendone?' He looked up at İkmen. 'It's filthy in there. And dark. Did she have a light with her?'

'No. No handbag, no light, just the key to the monument.' İkmen kept the other detail, the porphyry stone, to himself. Holding back certain pieces of information about a crime scene often proved useful when suspects began to emerge.

'The museum will do whatever we can to assist your investigation, Inspector İkmen,' the professor said. 'Especially with a baby out there somewhere. Do you think that maybe its father took it?'

'It's possible. But if he did,' İkmen said, 'he also, possibly, killed Dr Savva first. Because it's very possible she was murdered, Professor Bozdağ. I think she gave birth and then either she fell, was pushed or someone smashed her skull in. And that someone could have her baby.'

The old archaeologist closed his eyes and shook his head.

Chapter 2

He finished for the day at one and headed straight for Gonca's house, but he left his car right down by the Golden Horn. Then it was hill climbing and crumbling staircases all the way up to where she lived, which was behind the Greek School. Technically Gonca and her vast family lived in the old Greek quarter of Fener but it was on the border with Balat, which was its postal address.

The climb in the fierce afternoon heat was tough. But Mehmet Süleyman was determined to do what he wanted in spite of what unnamed moralisers in the department might think. Ever since Ayşe had been killed he'd found he needed Gonca even more. Not just for sex, although that was part of it, but because he could talk to her about how he felt. Gonca was way too old and way too wise to be threatened by the spectre of a dead woman.

When he arrived all the kids were out and she was alone, painting in her studio. When she saw him sweating and panting in her doorway she smiled. 'You're eager,' she said.

'Yes – and no,' he said. He sat down and told her what Commissioner Teker had spoken to him about. He also pointed to his car, which was a tiny white dot beside the water. She got him a large glass of water.

When he'd finished she said, 'Bastards! What business is it of theirs who you have sex with? Or give presents to?'

He shook his head. 'The children will have to wait in the house for their sweets. It's a reality we have to deal with now.'

'We don't have to like it!'

She looked even more magnificent when she was angry. Tall and curvaceous, Gonca had to be at least sixty even if she didn't look it. And she loved sex.

'Nobody's going to tell me I can't have you!' she said. 'I don't care how religious they might think they are!'

He smiled. Now he'd caught his breath he was aroused. She was only wearing a skirt and a bra which barely covered her breasts. He stood up, cupped her breasts with his hands and then kissed them. It was as if he'd set her on fire.

She undressed herself and him where they stood. Then she sank to her knees and took him in her mouth. He put his fingers in her hair and closed his eyes. The studio window was open but he didn't care. Later when she was on top of him he said, 'I'll never give you up, Gonca, never!'

He buried his head in her breasts.

'Try to leave me and I'll kill you,' she said. And he knew that she meant it.

'Our overriding concern is for the safety of the child. The woman gave birth before she died and we have no reason to believe that it wasn't a live birth.'

Commissioner Hürrem Teker, on a raised platform above the press pack below, was flanked by the İstanbul Police Department's Press Officer as well as by the investigating officer, Çetin İkmen.

Camera flashes went off and newsmen and women jostled for position, shouting out questions.

'Was the woman a prostitute?'

Teker shook her head. She knew the querent, from a right-wing anti-feminist rag.

'No, she wasn't,' she said. 'As if it matters. The İstanbul Police Force is tasked with protecting the people of this city. All the people. If you can't ask sensible questions, don't ask any. The fact is, we need to find this child as soon as possible. Without its mother it may not survive. We also need to catch whoever may have killed and abandoned the woman.'

The Greek consul had only just been informed of the tragedy and wanted to contact the Savva family in Thessaloniki before any public statement was released.

'Inspector Çetin İkmen is in charge of the investigation,' she gestured towards him. 'Anyone with any information should contact him or a member of his team here at police headquarters. At the end of this briefing we will be announcing a dedicated telephone number just for this incident. And if people want to remain anonymous then that's up to them. We just need to find this child. That is our number one priority.'

Hands flew up in the air again and Teker pointed to a female left-wing reporter.

'Hürrem Hanım,' she said, 'what do you think about what İstanbul police officers are doing right now in Gezi Park? I don't see burning tents down and using tear gas against a peaceful protest by environmentalists as the act of a caring organisation, do you?'

Hürrem should have expected it. Environmentalists had been camping out in Gezi Park for some time. Angry at the government's decision to build on the last green space in the central Taksim area of the city, those opposed to the plan had been making their feelings apparent for some time. The encampment had taken the protest one stage further and now that the police were involved the situation was escalating. Hürrem knew that Gezi could potentially be a catalyst for unrest related to other issues people had with the government. Like the restrictions on the sale of alcohol, the government's opposition to a proposed extension to gay, lesbian and transgender rights and the naming of the proposed new Bosphorus Bridge after a sultan, Selim 1, who had massacred thousands of the country's Alevi citizens back in the sixteenth century.

'All the protesters want is to preserve a green space,' the reporter said. 'They're not hurting anyone. But they're being hurt, women as well as men, Hürrem Hanım. And all because they don't want yet another shopping mall in what is fast becoming a city of shopping malls.'

Hürrem hesitated. She'd sent officers to Taksim in full riot gear on orders that had come directly from the Chief of Police. She knew at least one woman had been sprayed with water by police and everyone was aware that tents had been burned. She hated it. Like she hated the people who had busied themselves in Mehmet Süleyman's private life. But for the moment they represented the state she had sworn to protect, even if some of her officers' zeal for the Gezi job had sickened her.

She smiled at the reporter. 'Sabıha Hanım, this briefing is intended to inform the media about the dead woman who was discovered last night in the Hippodrome and to put out a call to find her baby. Any other matters are beyond the remit of this briefing.'

'Hürrem Hanım, with respect—'

'I'm sorry,' she held up a hand. 'That is all I have to say for the time being. Let us all find this child as quickly as we can.'

As she left, the pack followed her, and by the time Hürrem got back to her office she felt as if she'd been in a riot of her own. She had her head out of the window, smoking a cigarette, when there was a knock at her door.

She knew there were other 'sinners' in the department and she'd only just lit up so she said, 'Who is it?'

'İkmen.'

She relaxed. 'Come in, Inspector. Shut the door behind you.'
He entered, saw what she was doing and said, 'Oh.'

'Join me,' she said. 'I've had three smokers at this window in the past and neither of us is a giant.'

He smiled, walked over to the window and lit up. Outside the air was thick with heat. It was almost June and summer was once again threatening to stifle the golden city on the Bosphorus.

'I've just had a call from the Greek consul,' İkmen said. 'He's spoken to the Savva family, the father's on his way.'

She shook her head.

'They want the child,' he continued.

'I can understand that. Do you think it's alive, Inspector?'

'I don't know. I hope so.' He paused. 'I also hope that the victim's nationality isn't a significant feature of this crime.'

'Because she's Greek?'

'Greek and a specialist in Byzantine art,' he said. 'Madam, if I may speak frankly I don't think that those who are at this moment protesting in Gezi Park are as much of a threat to state security as some of those who claim to be acting solely in the interests of the nation.'

She narrowed her eyes. She knew he knew she was secular, just like him, but she wondered what he was going to say.

'For example,' he said, 'believing it would be a good idea to turn Aya Sofya, the greatest Byzantine building in the world, back into a mosque.'

'Not a good idea,' she said. 'In my opinion. But I don't think there is a lot of anti-Greek sentiment here any more. Last time we scrapped, over Cyprus, was back in the 1970s. Look into it, İkmen, by all means, but I'd be surprised if it was a factor.'

İkmen finished his cigarette and put it out on the window ledge. 'I can see that, but with respect, madam,' he said, 'you are too young to remember the events of September 1955. I do.'

And then he left. Hürrem suddenly felt cold. Although she hadn't been born in 1955, she knew what had happened in İstanbul in the September of that year. Turkish mobs enraged by a supposed attack on the house of Ataturk in Thessaloniki had attacked the local Greek population over the course of a nine-hour rampage. Thirty-seven İstanbul Greeks had been killed while the police just stood back and let it happen. Of course the real reason had been because of the bitterness that still remained over the ethnically split island of Cyprus. But by recalling 1955 İkmen had made Hürrem think. The people of İstanbul were in turmoil. Those who wanted a more pious government and those who wanted more secular governance could not find any common ground. And one group, or so it appeared, were riding roughshod over the wishes of the other.

Ariadne Savva's small apartment in Kadıköy was in a slightly crumbling apartment block with very distant views of the Sea of Marmara. She certainly had a lot of books, mostly in Greek, which Kerim Gürsel couldn't understand. But the place was neat and clean and, more significantly, entirely child free.

Weirdly there weren't even any baby clothes or equipment anywhere. Had Ariadne Savva known she was pregnant? Kerim shook his head. She must have done. She had a doctorate, she was no fool. But if that was the case then why hadn't she made any preparations?

If she hadn't wanted the child it made sense. But if she hadn't wanted it then why hadn't she had an abortion? As far as Kerim knew, just as in Turkey, abortion was legal in Greece. Maybe Ariadne had possessed personal objections to the practice? Then again possibly she had decided to have the child with the intention of giving it away. Some childless couples even paid pregnant women for their babies. Usually poor women, not educated doctors. And besides, if it had just been business then why hadn't Ariadne given birth in a nice discreet private hospital? But then maybe she had. There had been very little post-partum blood in those collapsed rooms under the Hippodrome.

Kerim's father had been born and brought up in Sultanahmet and liked to tell spooky stories about the old Hippodrome, Aya Sofya and water cisterns under the streets. He claimed that one night he'd even seen chariots racing around the circus, driven by Byzantine princes in full armour. Kerim reckoned that his dad's vision had rather more to do with too much rakı than ghosts. But Pembe Hanım had seen the ghost of the Empress Theodora in Aya Sofya and she was no fool. Kerim didn't know what to think.

His mobile rang. He looked at the screen. It was Sinem.

'Hi, honey,' he said.

'Kerim.' Her voice was weak and exhausted. 'Can you pick my medication up from the pharmacy on your way home?'

He'd thought she had enough.

'I called Dr Sorak,' she said. 'I had to. Kerim?'

He shook his head. 'Sorry. Just a bit – surprised.'

'Can you do it?'

'Of course.'

'Where are you?'

'Over in Kadıköy,' he said.

'Oh God. You know there are people in Taksim and all down İstiklal.'

They lived above an electrical shop on Tarlabaşı Bulvarı. The pharmacy she wanted him to go to was about ten minutes away from their flat, on İstiklal Caddesi. He'd heard that people were protesting in and around Taksim Square about the proposed destruction of Gezi Park.

'Are there more protesters?' he asked her.

'I can see them out of the window,' she said. 'They seem to be coming from everywhere. Not that I don't applaud what they're doing—'

'I'll leave as quickly as I can.' He ended the call.

Kerim sat on Ariadne Savva's one kitchen chair and indulged in a moment of self-pity. Getting back to Beyoğlu when the streets were even more heaving with humanity than usual was going to be tough. Witnessing his colleagues dealing with the protesters was going to be harder. He'd heard what orders had been given. Gezi Park's new incarnation as a shopping mall wasn't up for debate; it was happening. Kerim didn't want to see the park go. He certainly didn't want another shopping mall put up in its place. And then there were other, wider considerations to be taken into account too. His country was changing and in ways that could further limit his personal freedom. He was boxed in as it was.

He looked out of the window. The sky was still blue and the air remained thick with heat but he knew that night would fall before he got back to Beyoğlu. With any luck Rafik Bey the pharmacist would take Sinem's medication to her when he closed his shop. It wouldn't be the first time. But then maybe the crowds would put him off . . .

Kerim looked through Ariadne Savva's wardrobe and chest of drawers and then left. Beyond her clothes and a few light-weight novels she kept very few personal things in her apartment. According to her boss Professor Bozdağ, she lived almost entirely at her place of work. It was there that she kept all her academic research, her source books and photographs, and it was there that she socialised. Her baby wasn't at her apartment and neither was her soul. Kerim left and ran downstairs to his car.

'I thought that Gizlitepe was reduced to rubble months ago,' İkmen said. Although he very rarely ventured across the Bosphorus to the Asian side of town, so what did he know?

'In large part, yes,' the small, timid looking woman in front of him said. Called Meltem Doğan, she had been Ariadne Savva's assistant. 'Much of it is just – rubble. But people still live there, Inspector. Rubbish pickers, mainly. Unlike a lot of Gizlitepe people they didn't own their homes, and so when the developers moved into the area they didn't get any compensation. That went to their landlords. Now many of them are destitute. Ariadne wanted to help them. She told me she used to see them walking past our apartment block with their little carts full of empty plastic bottles and she felt so sorry for them. One day she spoke to one of them. It went from there.'

'What did?'

İkmen didn't know whether marble had a smell but if it did, it was like the odour in Professor Bozdağ's office. The archaeologist had lent it to him so he could interview Ariadne Savva's colleagues in peace. Also one of the first things he'd noticed when he'd entered had been a portion of a brown skull on a shelf above his head. Ignoring it wasn't easy.

Meltem Doğan cleared her throat. 'Dr Savva, Ariadne, became friendly with them. Where I live, where she lived, is only a short walk from Gizlitepe. At first she took them food.'

İkmen looked down at the notes he'd taken from another of Ariadne Savva's colleagues, Ali Pamuk. He, so he'd said, had joined Ariadne when she'd made representation to the local authority and the developers on behalf of the rubbish pickers. He, like her, had been laughed at.

'Then she began to spend a lot of time away from her apartment,' Meltem said.

'With the rubbish pickers?'

'I think so. She was always talking about them.' She shook her head. 'The people at the local authority were horrible to her. They said that as a foreigner she had no right to criticise what they did. But the developers were worse.'

Öden Holdings was owned by a man called Ahmet Öden who had become rich off the back of the government's İstanbul building boom. He was well known and admired by many. He was also despised by even more. According to Ali Pamuk, Ahmet Öden had threatened to 'hurt' Ariadne if she didn't stop helping the rubbish pickers to squat on 'his' land.

'For a while four of us from the museum used to go to Gizlitepe with Ariadne after work and sometimes at weekends,' Meltem continued. 'But the developers threw things at us and then one day they chased Dr İşbilen into an alleyway and beat him.'

'Did any of you report it to the police?'

She blushed. 'No.'

'Why not?'

'Dr Savva wanted to but the rest of us were scared. I was scared,' she said. 'I am no political radical, Inspector İkmen, but I am not blind either. If certain developers want to knock down old city neighbourhoods they can and nobody can stop them. Dr İşbilen is one of this city's foremost archaeologists. But put up against a rich builder . . .' She shrugged.

İkmen could not only hear the sadness in her voice, he could sympathise with it too. A lot of his colleagues were behind the redevelopment of the city. Some of them even said they saw it as a sacred duty to support what they called 'regeneration'. İkmen preferred to call it 'urban cleansing', because when the

24

developers moved in the traditional residents – gypsies, immigrants, prostitutes, transsexuals – moved out and he didn't like that. And what he disliked almost as much was the destruction of his city's history.

'Meltem Hanım, I have yet to speak to Dr İşbilen, but please be reassured that when I do I will make a point of asking him whether he wishes to make a complaint against Öden Holdings.'

'He won't,' she said. 'No one does.'

'Maybe not,' İkmen said. 'But if Dr İşbilen has a legitimate complaint which he can prove, I will take that to Öden Holdings. And they will have to listen to me.'

She looked into his eyes. He could see that she didn't believe him. But why should she? Öden was all but untouchable and they both knew it. What she didn't know was that Çetin İkmen didn't approve of that state of affairs.

'Meltem Hanım, did you know that Ariadne Savva was pregnant?' he asked.

'No. The first I heard about it was when Professor Bozdağ told us that Ariadne had died,' she said. 'I couldn't believe it. Still can't.'

'Why not?'

'She wasn't seeing anyone. No one ever came back to her apartment and she was always at work. And she didn't look pregnant. In retrospect I suppose she had put a little weight on in the last year . . .'

. 'Did she get close to any of the male rubbish pickers?'

'No. She felt sorry for them and wanted to help, but that was all. They're a poor, shabby group, Inspector. Ariadne was all for the little guy, you know? The pickers get abused by everyone – the developers, the local authority, even the local police take their little carts away from them and then charge them when they try to get them back.' Then, realising what she'd just said, she added, 'So I hear. I didn't mean to speak out of turn—'

'Oh I know that these things go on,' İkmen said. 'Sadly. I know that some of my colleagues are far from perfect. All I can do is give you my assurance that I will do what I can. Meltem Hanım, it saddens me to think that certain elements within my organisation are behaving badly and are not giving the respect they should to those who seek to preserve our great city's history.' He looked down at his notes. 'Professor Bozdağ has told me that you were working more closely with Ariadne Savva than anyone else. Can you tell me about that?'

'Sort of. Ariadne kept a lot of what she did to herself. She was particularly interested in the connections that existed between ancient Rome and the Byzantine Empire.'

'Which it preceded.'

'Yes. Byzantium was the new Rome, which was why it had a hippodrome and games even after the empire was converted to Christianity in the third century AD.'

'Dr Savva had a key to the back of the Hippodrome.'

'The sphendone, yes,' she said. 'She spent a lot of time in there, photographing and measuring. Although the Hippodrome collapsed centuries ago, what remains can tell us a lot about how the games were performed and which parts of the building served which purpose.'

'Her main field of study was the Hippodrome?'

'No. Her academic playground was the whole of Byzantium. Recently she spent a lot of time in the Aya Sofya.' She frowned. 'I expect you know that some people want it to be turned back into a mosque. Ariadne was keen to catalogue every aspect of the building before that happened.'

'What did you do?'

'I was just her assistant.'

'Just?'

She smiled and then she looked tense again. 'I have a lot of passion for history, but my qualifications are not of the best, Inspector. But Ariadne liked me and was very good to me. Everyone liked her. In common with all academics she had an ego, but we talked about so many things—'

'What *didn't* you talk about, Meltem Hanım?'

She shook her head. 'I'm not really sure, but sometimes I'd come into the office, she'd be writing something, and then she'd stop. She'd close up the notebook she was writing in and put it away.'

'She kept this notebook here at the museum?'

'Yes,' she said. 'I think it's green. Whenever I saw her with it she always put it away in the top drawer of her desk and then locked it.'

'I'll need to see it,' İkmen said.

Sergeant Ömer Mungun sat outside his favourite bar in Sultanahmet, the Mozaik, and drank his beer in silence. At the top of Ticarethane Sokak he saw a group of his uniformed colleagues walk past dressed in riot gear. From the direction they were travelling he assumed they were coming from Gezi Park. Peri had said that she'd seen what had looked like hundreds of them in the streets when she got on the tram at Karaköy. He looked at his watch. She should have arrived by this time. He wondered whether he should call her but then decided to leave it another five minutes.

He looked around. His fellow drinkers were tourists plus a couple of guys he knew worked in a local carpet shop. One of them, a Kurd called Şeymus, came from the town of Midyat which was in the same south-eastern province as Mardin, Ömer's home city. Whenever they saw each other and they were alone,

Ömer and Şeymus spoke in the Aramaic they had both grown up learning. But his friend was with his boss on this occasion and so Ömer just smiled. Across the road from the bar was the back of an apartment block he'd been told was where Inspector İkmen lived. Opposite the Blue Mosque and the Hippodrome, it had to be worth a fortune, although Ömer doubted that it had been when İkmen had bought it. He'd lived there since well before Ömer was born. And İkmen was sixty, although it was hard to relate his age to his enthusiasm and passion for his job, even if he did look as lined as an old piece of leather. There were definite pluses to being a thin, ugly man with a police badge. Very attractive men like Ömer's boss Mehmet Süleyman seemed to be constantly batting away advances from both women and men. Rumour had it that he was in trouble again for his liaison with that gypsy artist up in Balat. And he'd broken Sergeant Ayşe Farsakoğlu's heart just before she died. İkmen and Süleyman had been friends ever since Süleyman had been İkmen's sergeant many years before, but İkmen had been close to Farsakoğlu too and word was that his relationship with Süleyman was under strain. From Ömer's point of view the two men were cordial but he'd noticed that İkmen rarely came into Süleyman's office just to chat any more.

'That was hell!'

Ömer looked up into Peri's clear, slanted eyes. He stood up and kissed her on both cheeks. 'You took your time,' he said. 'Drink?'

His sister let herself fall back into the chair opposite and said, 'Gin and tonic. And the tram was held up by great roaming ranks of policemen, if you must know.'

He went inside the bar and returned a few minutes later with a long, tall glass decorated with ice and mint. Peri put it to her lips and drank. 'That is marvellous,' she said.

Ömer sat down. 'If you're very good you can have another one,' he said.

She smiled. Her little brother had blossomed in İstanbul, as she had known he would. If only he hadn't joined the police. She switched languages to Aramaic. 'Your brothers in arms are kicking and beating innocent people in Gezi Park. One of our doctors went out to see what was happening and came back with two injured men.'

'I can't condone it,' Ömer said. 'But the protesters should go home. There's nothing they can do. The decision is made.'

Peri's face reddened. 'You say this?' she said. 'You who hated what the developers did in Tarlabaşı to the gypsies, the black people, our own? They moved them out, Ömer, so that they could make themselves rich. Believe me, this going in like a pack of Robocops will backfire.' She finished her drink.

Ömer went inside the bar and got her another. When he returned she was smoking a cigarette. Peri had been a nurse at the German Hospital in Beyoğlu for almost ten years and so she knew what cigarettes did to the human body. Her brother knew that she only smoked them when she was stressed.

'The people here don't want any more shopping malls,' Peri said. 'In fact, if my colleagues are to be believed they don't want anyone telling them what they want any more. They have decided they want this park, why shouldn't they fight for it?'

'Because the State knows best?'

'Oh, come on, you don't believe that any more than I do!' She puffed heavily on her cigarette, which disturbingly reminded Ömer of Inspector İkmen. 'What do they know? Eh? They certainly don't know much about us, do they?'

Ömer turned his head away. He'd taken an oath to protect the Turkish Republic which he took very seriously. But he also knew that in one sense he was at odds with his country. Back in the days of the old hard-line secular Kemalist republic, anyone with any religion was an oddity. In recent years the current government had made it plain they would prefer people to be Muslims. Ömer and Peri were not secular nor were they Muslims.

'Remember all those battles the army had with the PKK in our streets?' Peri said. 'Then Hezbollah. Remember how all sides turned against our people whenever they found us? They say we worship idols, Ömer. They are ignorant. Let these people have their park is what I say. Those two men who were brought in by Dr Schell, one had a rainbow flag, you know, the symbol that gay people use. The other one told me that he was an environmentalist. He just wanted a green space for people to go to and relax. Is that too much to ask? Is it so wrong to want that as opposed to endless shopping?'

He looked at her but said nothing.

'I know you agree with me, Ömer,' she said. 'But I also know that you're in a difficult position.'

'What can I say?' He shrugged.

'You're not likely to be called out to the park if this continues, are you?' Peri asked.

'No,' he said and then he smiled. 'It's very unlikely.'

Unless of course the authorities wanted detectives to mingle with the protesters under cover. But Ömer didn't tell his sister that and he didn't think about it either, because the prospect frightened him. He had another beer and as darkness fell he and Peri talked of other things. They even, once they'd had enough to drink, laughed.

Chapter 3

Rat Boy said that he found the bag of empty water bottles first. But One-Legged Nurettin said that they were his.

'I saw that man throw the bag from his car,' he said.

'Where from? You were lying down in your own piss,' Rat Boy said. 'Anyway, I picked it up, so it's mine!'

Nurettin made a dive for the bag and fell over. But Rat Boy, laughing, ran away. 'You're out of control, you little bastard!' Nurettin shouted after the kid.

'Oh, he's just trying to make a living.'

Nurettin looked up and saw Emine. She was Rat Boy's aunt and the sister of Nurettin's wife, Beliz. She put one of her arms around his shoulders and lifted him up on to his one foot. She gave him back the stick he had dropped.

'The boy is out of control and I'm sorry,' she said. 'But the fault isn't with him.'

'I know.'

He shuffled forwards. Behind him, Emine scoured the ground for anything worth picking up.

'Mustafa Bey just deserted us,' she said.

'Because that son of a pig Öden gave him money.'

'Mustafa Bey is a landlord, what do you expect? Honesty?'

'I'd say that even amongst landlords honesty should be a given.' The voice Nurettin heard was deeper than Emine's and it was male. He looked up. The speaker was a small, thin man with a smoke-dried face and thick black and grey hair. He held out a police badge.

'Inspector Çetin İkmen,' he said. 'I'm investigating the death of a woman called Ariadne Savva. I understand she used to come down here.'

The Greek woman, dead? Was she really, or was this just some sort of police trick to get them to move on or give up their carts?

'I don't know what you're talking about,' Nurettin said.

'She was an archaeologist,' İkmen said. 'A Greek.'

Nurettin shrugged.

'She used to come here sometimes with her friends and distribute food.'

'We don't know anything about her,' Nurettin said.

He saw İkmen look at Emine. Then he heard him say, 'She'd just given birth to a child when she died. It's in this city somewhere. We need to find it – soon.'

Emine put a hand up to her face. 'A baby?'

'Do you know where Ariadne's baby might be?' İkmen asked. 'Just newborn . . .'

'Oh Allah, I didn't know she was pregnant!' Emine said.

Nurettin was furious that she'd fallen for the policeman's lies. 'Shut up, woman. You don't know what you're talking about.' He turned to İkmen. 'We don't know of any such woman.'

'Yes, we do,' Emine insisted.

'The woman is delusional,' he said. 'She talks nonsense.'

Emine hit him. 'Delusional? Me?' She turned to İkmen. 'I apologise for him, Beyefendi,' she said. 'He's old and crazy and he's missing a leg. Ariadne Hanım is very dear to us. She has tried to help people here. Why is she dead? What has happened to her?'

'We think she may have been murdered,' İkmen said.

Emine began to weep. 'Oh the monster!' she said. She hit Nurettin again and then crouched down on her haunches to cry.

Accusatory black eyes powered into Nurettin's soul. 'All right, all right, we knew her,' he admitted.

'Ariadne Savva.'

'Yes. We live by picking up rubbish, we always have,' he said. 'There's no dishonour in that. At least there wasn't until we all got evicted from our homes and the bulldozers moved in. When you are homeless you cease to exist. You become a squatter and a pariah. But that Greek lady knew better. She knew that when the police arrested us for vagrancy they were going to take our carts and then make us pay to get them back. You know about that, do you?'

'I do.'

'Huh. She argued with the police and with the bastard who created all this mess here in Gizlitepe. And I don't mean our landlord.'

'He means Ahmet Öden,' Emine said.

Was it wise for her to tell an unknown policeman about that? Nurettin wondered. But then, did it really matter now? Öden had taken their homes and had them chased from pillar to post; what was there left for him to do? And Nurettin was sad about Ariadne. She'd been a nice lady.

'Ahmet Öden threatened Ariadne if she kept on helping us,' Emine said.

'Threatened her how?'

'He said that if she carried on coming here he'd make her sorry. He's capable of anything. He even beats his own men. If you're looking for Ariadne's baby you'd better start searching his house. Are you sure that Ariadne was pregnant? She—'

'Yes.'

Nurettin shook his head. 'That such things can happen . . .'

33

And then he saw that İkmen was being joined by two more, this time uniformed, police officers. Nurettin narrowed his eyes. 'What's this?' he said.

'We'll need to search the area,' İkmen said.

He offered Nurettin a cigarette which he thought about taking and then refused.

'Why do you need to search?' Nurettin said.

'For the baby.'

'Then why look here?' he said. 'We told you, we didn't know that Ariadne was pregnant. Why would we have her baby here in all this filth we have to live in anyway?'

'I don't know,' İkmen said. 'But you knew her and so we have to do it.'

He ordered the two uniformed constables into the rubble and dirt that represented all that was left of old Gizlitepe.

'That bastard Ahmet Öden knew her too!' Emine yelled. 'But you won't search his great mansion out at Bebek, will you?'

'I will if it's necessary,' İkmen said. 'I am aware, madam, that the worst villains in the world live in nice clean houses and wear suits. I may be many things, but I'm nobody's fool.'

Not sleeping didn't work for Kerim Gürsel. First he'd had to watch Sinem when she took her medication and then he'd been distracted by the comings and goings to and from Gezi Park in the early hours of the morning. More people had arrived and then more police.

Sinem had never taken such a high dose of pain control before. Her doctor had left instructions at the pharmacy to call him if her breathing became laboured. It hadn't but Kerim had been worried. She was only thirty-eight and already the arthritis he'd always known her to have was threatening to push her over into a drug dependency he knew she'd hate.

Now he was with a man he suspected felt just as helpless as he. Mr Abdülhamid Akar was a senior official at the offices of Kadıköy Municipality. But he was a man who clearly knew the limits of his power.

'When developers move in, single municipalities have limited power over firstly what they buy and secondly what they build,' he said. 'Privately owned land, such as that in the Gizlitepe district, can be bought and sold freely.'

'But surely you as the local authority have the power to enforce local planning regulations,' Kerim said.

'Indeed.' he adjusted his glasses. 'We will oversee new development. The plans submitted conform to our regulations – so far.'

'And yet a proportion of the population of Gizlitepe have been made homeless.'

'Sadly, yes.' There was an awkward pause and then he said, 'Sergeant, it is a sad fact of life that when a municipality is subject to the higher authority of a city government we cannot always get what we want or fulfil the expectations of our residents.'

'So—'

'A great many people in Kadıköy do not want our famous Haydarpaşa Railway Station to be developed into a hotel,' Akar said. 'The city of İstanbul, on the other hand, thinks that it is an excellent idea. If I am being realistic, and in light of our redevelopment plans that have come to fruition in the city, I imagine that the many people of Kadıköy will be disappointed. Do you understand what I mean?'

'Yes.' Kerim knew there was a political dimension too, Kadıköy being under the auspices of one party, while the city of İstanbul was under that of another.

'However, I take your point about the rubbish pickers of Gizlitepe. Provision has not been—'

'Mr Akar, did you ever come across the woman who, we believe, became their advocate?' Kerim asked. 'Ariadne Savva?'

'Not personally. But I knew of her,' Akar said.

'How?'

He smiled. 'Via the complaints of colleagues,' he said. 'This lady was making some legitimate points about issues we could do nothing about. You know the rubbish collectors are few in number and they choose to stay where they are?'

'Where else can they go?'

'Unless they try to find somewhere, how will they know?'

'Maybe they've tried to find somewhere and failed.'

Mr Akar smiled. Suddenly Kerim didn't like him as much as he'd thought he did. 'You know, Sergeant,' he said, 'between the demands of the very rich and the cries of the poor we find ourselves between a rock and a hard place. We do our best. But if people will not move along gracefully . . .' He opened his arms in a helpless gesture. 'Unfortunately we cannot always have what we want.'

Kerim didn't feel that having somewhere to live was an unreasonable 'want' but he said nothing. Mr Akar was a man under pressure, which meant he was like ninety per cent of local government officials. He wondered what he made of the Gezi Park situation and decided that he would probably be very non-committal on the subject.

Both French windows were open so he could make the most of the breeze coming in from the Bosphorus. Out on the balcony he watched Kelime play with her dolls. Ahmet Öden smiled. He knew people wondered how he coped with her on his own but she was such a good girl. And he had Mary for the more unpleasant tasks.

He looked again at the plans the architect had submitted for a radical new apartment block in Kadıköy. He'd thought it was very innovative until the English nanny had seen it.

'Oh Mr Öden,' Mary had said, 'that looks just like the Shard of Glass in London.'

She'd Googled it for him, his well-spoken English nanny, and he'd seen that what she'd told him was quite true. His architect's building looked almost identical to what was now apparently the tallest building in London. Why did people always try to cheat him? Did they think he was a fool?

Ahmet Öden was an İstanbullu born and bred. His family, who had lived in Eminönü for generations, had been poor. For fifteen years after he'd left primary school, he'd worked mainly with his father in every low waged, manual job he could find. The city had offered many temptations and he could have turned to crime on several occasions, but he hadn't. His father, Taha, whom some had called a bigot, had been a religious man, and so Ahmet had known that the pious life was the only option for him from an early age. He'd accepted his lot, married a pious Muslim girl, Kelime's mother, and busied himself promoting the notion of moderate Islamic government. He'd never imagined that his beliefs would become mainstream. But in 2002, when the Islamically rooted AK Parti had come to power, Ahmet's political dreams came true. In the three years that followed that victory, he got in with a group of like-minded Islamic movers and shakers and eventually he managed to start a small building company of his own. He'd worked on building sites for years, he was eloquent and pious, and so it wasn't hard for him to persuade people to invest. Also, then, he had wanted to build low-cost, decent housing for poor but observant people, like his parents.

And then, finally, Lale his wife had got pregnant and for the first time in his life Ahmet felt content. The memory of it made Ahmet's smile fade. It had been obvious that Kelime had not been right from the moment of her birth. Tiny and limp, her mouth had been fat and her eyes had slanted upwards like, as Ahmet had put it, 'a Chinese person'. One of his new friends got the couple an appointment with a paediatrician who told them that Kelime had Down's syndrome. She was 'bad', apparently, and would need twenty-four-hour care. Lale had just cried but Ahmet had been like stone. Unwilling to allow himself to feel, he'd poured all of his energies into finding ways he could make the money he would need to give his daughter everything a 'normal' child would want. And more.

He watched her play and then when she looked up, he waved. Kelime had every Barbie doll that could be bought in Turkey. She loved them all and never tired of making up stories about them. He heard her chattering, holding each doll up to her face and smiling. At twelve Kelime was overweight in spite of Nanny Mary's efforts to make her walk more. She loved ice cream and so he gave her every flavour that existed. Just because he couldn't have it didn't mean his daughter should be denied. Mary had, gently, told him off. Apparently the diabetes he suffered from could be inherited. And eating lots of high-fat, sugary food made that more likely. But Ahmet had told Mary that she was a nanny, not a nurse, and he didn't pay her such a huge salary to criticise him. Mary had shut up. When he finally decided to take a new wife, distant though that was, Ahmet had promised himself that he would sack the English nanny and get a cheaper, local woman. She wouldn't have the same cachet as the English woman, but Ahmet had already made his point about his wealth to anyone who mattered years before.

Kelime's condition had only crystallised a greed Ahmet had always known he had. Once he'd completed the social housing project, he'd looked for other clients of a different sort. As his developments became more and more elaborate so his charges increased. His influence grew. There were elaborate dinners (men only, no alcohol) and charitable activities around education and support for the poor. Lale had been left alone with Kelime during that time. Ahmet knew she found it hard; he watched her get thin, fall into silence and wander the house at night talking to herself like a sad ghost. One day when her mother took Kelime out in her buggy for a few hours, Lale drank a bottle of disinfectant. And as soon as he'd buried his wife, Ahmet worked even harder. Now he was a multi-millionaire, which meant that he and Kelime could have whatever they wanted.

A much younger version of Ahmet walked into the room and said, 'You've heard about these protests in Beyoğlu?'

'Yes.'

'What do you think?'

Semih Öden was fifteen years younger than his brother. Dressed in tight jeans and a designer tee shirt, he looked a lot like some of the young environmentalists who were still, in spite of police efforts, gathering in Gezi Park.

'I think it will pass,' Ahmet said. 'People want to shop. Look at all the malls in this city. Of course they do. What use is a park?'

'I don't know. Some of them look a bit crazy. But maybe they have a point—'

'Like what? This country will never go back to what it was before,' Ahmet said. 'They're just making a fuss because they're not at the top of the tree any more. Forget it. We've got more important things to think about.'

Semih looked at Kelime absorbed in her dolls.

Ahmet nudged him and gave him an envelope.

'What's this?'

'My latest offer to the Negropontes,' Ahmet said. 'Returned unopened.'

'You know they don't want to sell. I don't know why you bother with it.'

'You know exactly why.'

Semih turned away.

'And that plot could be very lucrative,' Ahmet said. 'Right in the middle of Sultanahmet. I could build a hotel to rival the Four Seasons.'

'Couldn't you do that using the existing building? It seems to me it's a nice house and—'

'No! Why do you even ask? You know why!'

Semih shrugged.

Ahmet said, 'I can make something new and individual. Those old houses are a fire risk and they cost a fortune to equip with the kind of technology billionaire guests will expect.'

'But space is so limited in that area,' Semih said. 'I don't know why you don't build something here or in Yeniköy. Give them Bosphorus views. They can moor their yachts—'

'Semih, you disapprove,' Ahmet said. 'I've got that. But you're young, you don't really remember your father. Trust me and the memory of our father on this. This was his dream. It's my job to fulfil that. Be my brother, do your job and I will always take care of you.'

His brother said nothing. It was his way of backing down and Ahmet knew it.

Ahmet Öden stood up and took back the envelope he'd given to his brother. 'I'm going to have that site whether the Negropontes like it or not,' he said. 'The man says his family have been in this city for over a thousand years. Well, that's long enough. It's now time for them to leave.'

A knock on Ahmet's office door was followed by the appearance of a small, headscarfed woman.

'Ahmet Bey, there is a policeman here to see you,' the maid said.

'A policeman? Why?'

'He says he needs to speak to you, Beyefendi.'

Ahmet waved a hand. 'Tell him I'm out,' he said. 'Tell him if he wants to speak to me he'll have to wait.'

The girl left.

'Police?' Semih queried. 'What have you been doing, brother? Anything I should know?'

'No. I live a good life, Semih, as well you know. If I won't or can't talk to the police then that is because I choose not to. The days of jumping to attention every time one of my "betters" calls me are over. I'll complain. Now I do what I want, what I think is best and what it is written I must do.'

Çetin İkmen felt as if he was back at school. He wondered whether Kerim Gürsel, shuffling uneasily from foot to foot and knitting his own fingers, felt the same.

'You have to make an appointment to see Mr Öden,' Commissioner Teker said. 'You can't just arrive.'

İkmen and Gürsel had only just returned to the station from Ahmet Öden's house in Bebek.

'So if he wasn't in, how come he's complaining to you now?' İkmen asked. 'How did he know I went to his house if he was, as I was told, out?'

'His staff told him, apparently,' Teker said. Then she shook her head. 'Listen, İkmen, Gürsel, we all know what Mr Öden is—'

'An arrogant—'

'A man of some force,' she said. 'And also someone who is very powerful. If, as you say, İkmen, he had a run-in with the late Ariadne Savva then he may well have wished her harm. I do not buy into his holy image so don't worry about that. But would he kill her? Over a few derelicts in Kadıköy?'

'No, of course not,' İkmen said. 'But that child is still missing—'

'Or dead.'

'Or dead,' he said. 'And Öden has a connection. I'm only doing my job, madam.'

Hürrem Teker sat down behind her desk. İkmen could still see her predecessor Ardıç sitting there sometimes. Fat, sweaty and world-weary, he'd always tried to do his best and Teker, thankfully, seemed to be the same.

'I know, İkmen,' she said. 'And I commend you for it. But we have to tread carefully with people like Öden. Especially at the moment.'

'Gezi . . .'

She looked up at Gürsel.

'The park is quiet now, but people are still gathering and I fear it may all start up again if the authorities don't back down over this mall – which they won't,' she said. 'And we are on their side, which means that by extension we are on the side of Mr Öden.'

'Sides are irrelevant, we have to find that baby,' İkmen said.

'I completely agree, but—'

'But what?' İkmen said. 'We find the baby and we find out how Ariadne Savva died. That's all that matters.' He leaned on her desk. 'Madam, Ariadne's father will be here tomorrow. The man has lost his daughter. If I can't put his grandchild in his arms . . .'

Teker sighed. 'İkmen, we've been through Sultanahmet and we've found nothing. How far do you think this infant has travelled? And how realistic is it to think you'll put the child in its grandfather's arms? Whoever killed the woman, if she was killed by someone, probably killed the child too.'

'Then why wasn't it with its mother?'

'I have no idea.'

'I only have theories,' İkmen said. 'One of which is that the killer was the child's father.'

The room went quiet for a moment.

'We don't know who got Ariadne pregnant,' İkmen said. 'She kept that a secret. And nobody has come forward to say they were her lover. Assuming he didn't kill her, why not?'

'Because that person might be married?' Teker suggested.

'Or embarrassed,' İkmen said. 'Ariadne moved in limited circles, madam. The men in her life were few. But Öden, albeit as an enemy, was one of them and so I need to speak to him. And I need to do that as soon as possible and without, if I can, being subjected to a load of arrogant point-scoring and rank-pulling.'

She looked up at him, 'I'll do what I can.'

And then she told them both to go.

İkmen, with Gürsel in tow, marched down to the station car park and lit a cigarette. Once he'd calmed down enough to speak he said, 'You know, Kerim, Mr Öden's refusal to see me has really made me suspicious. I know in all probability he is just asserting himself over me for his own pleasure, but I'm finding it hard to shake the idea that something else is going on too.'

Chapter 4

They watched, Süleyman leaning against a lamp post, smoking, while Ömer Mungun ate a corncob. They could have been any two businessmen taking a break from their office. In stark contrast to the uniformed Robocops stalking the park and the people who continued to gather there, they were also much more invisible than the two undercover officers Süleyman had spotted in the crowd. He tipped his head at one of them. 'Him,' he said. 'See? Looks like a refugee from San Francisco in the 1960s.'

'Sir?'

'He looks like an old hippy,' Süleyman explained. 'It's too much. You see any other men wearing flowers and dancing to a tune in their own head? And her.' He waved a hand towards a girl wearing a long dress and smoking what looked like a joint. 'If that's cannabis she's puffing I'm a Persian.'

'No smell,' Ömer said.

'We'd smell dope from here. And she'd be stoned. I'm surprised the people around her haven't noticed. She might as well have "cop" written in neon above her head.'

They were standing at the end of İstiklal Caddesi casually, and unofficially, looking at a scene that was, so far, quiet and colourful. The weather was warm, people sat outside tents, some playing flutes or recorders, while pretty girls walked past holding rainbow flags in support of lesbians, gays, bisexual and transgendered citizens. There was a tension that could sometimes be

44

seen on the faces of some of the younger men but in general the atmosphere was calm. An older man walking hand in hand with a woman held up a placard which said, 'Architects Say No to Taksim Redevelopment'.

'Do you think we might have to get directly involved in this, sir?' Ömer asked once he'd finished his corn.

'It should be unlikely, but I don't know,' Süleyman said. 'If this protest grows then we'll be involved whether we like it or not. The whole city will be.'

Ömer wanted to ask his superior what he thought about the protests, but he didn't. Officially they both had a duty to uphold the rule of law, which protests of any sort clearly threatened. He surmised that Süleyman didn't like the idea of the Ottoman-style shopping mall which was meant to replace the park. He knew he hated the new faux Ottoman housing developments that had been built all over the city in the last few years because he'd said so. He was, after all, the real thing. Grandson of an Ottoman prince and scion of one of the old empire's most prestigious dynasties, Mehmet Süleyman came from old money. He had real class, which even a country boy like Ömer could see. He'd met his boss's parents once. Living in genteel poverty in Arnavutköy, the old woman had looked heartbreakingly sad while the old man, who had dementia, talked to himself in French about his father's eunuchs and the family's long-dead Greek physician.

Süleyman put his cigarette out. 'Well, Ömer, let's go and see these bones.'

An incomplete skeleton had been found in the grounds of the Galatasaray Lisesi, one of the most prestigious schools in Turkey. Housed in a large nineteenth-century building on İstiklal Caddesi, it was also Süleyman's old alma mater.

He began walking. 'I think it's probably a job for the archaeologists, but I imagine the students must be excited,' he said.

Ömer followed him, silently wondering whether Süleyman was going to meet up with any of his old teachers.

Sitting outside when the weather was warm was one of the few real pleasures Anastasia Negroponte had left. Eighty-seven years of life had stripped most of the meat from her bones and even her wonderful black hair, which had retained its colour until her seventies, had now turned white.

From the street beyond her gates, a young man looked at her as if she was an exhibit in a museum. She knew what he thought. It was the same as most people: that her mind didn't work, that she was an idiot, a living tragedy, only notionally alive.

But although her face moved only with difficulty, Anastasia was still there. On days like this, Hakkı would put her chair in the garden and she would drink mint tea through a straw while he, her last remaining servant, tended to the plants. Years before there had been the cook too, the driver, Yılmaz, and later on Hakkı's wife Sırma and their two children. But Sırma had died, the children had gone and the cook and Yılmaz were just distant memories. Now there was just Hakkı – and Yiannis. If she moved her neck as far to the left as she could manage she could see him standing outside the front gate. With his long legs apart, he looked substantial and, knowing Yiannis, a little fierce. But he'd be useless against a bulldozer.

Anastasia looked away. Seeing that Hakkı was watching her she called him over.

He bent low so that he could hear her. Between her weak voice and his poor hearing communication was not always easy. 'T-tell Yianni come inside,' she said.

Her own voice had irritated her for over fifty years. She still wasn't used to it.

Hakkı bowed. 'Yes, Madam Anastasia,' he said.

He left some sort of flower on her table when he went. It was red and round but she didn't know what it was. She couldn't remember. Apart from those things she could never forget, her memory was random. In that sense she was an idiot. But the passers-by she sometimes heard who said that she didn't know who she was were wrong. Anastasia Negroponte knew exactly who she was. She knew where she lived, because her ancestors had lived in the same place for over a thousand years, and she also knew that she was in danger of losing it all.

And Anastasia Negroponte, for all her age and her disabilities, was not about to let that happen.

'Mr Ahmet Öden?'

İkmen held his police ID up to the window of Öden's Range Rover Evoque.

Öden leaned his head out and took off his dark glasses.

İkmen smiled. 'Inspector Çetin İkmen,' he said. 'I tried to contact you at your home yesterday but you were out.'

'I'm out now,' Öden said. 'What do you want? How did you find me?'

İkmen hadn't waited for Commissioner Teker to gently ask Ahmet Öden for an appointment. Having Kerim stake out his house from early that morning had been much more effective. And they'd ended up almost on İkmen's doorstep, in Sultanahmet.

'I need to speak to you about a woman called Ariadne Savva,' İkmen said. 'She was an archaeologist up at the museum and—'

'She that woman who's died?'

'She is dead, yes, sir,' İkmen said.

Ahmet Öden had kept his engine running ever since İkmen had first seen his car pull up in front of the old Negroponte mansion. People like him often claimed to be 'green', but if this behaviour was anything to go by then conspicuous consumption was probably more his thing. İkmen didn't like it but he made himself ignore it.

'We're trying to trace all Dr Savva's contacts in the city,' he continued. 'Of which I believe you were one, Mr Öden.'

'Why would I know an archaeologist?'

İkmen lit a cigarette. He saw Öden bridle.

'Do you have to do that, Inspector?' he said.

İkmen smiled. 'No law, as yet, against it out in the open air, sir,' he said. 'Now about Dr Savva, I believe you knew her due to her philanthropic activities with the rubbish pickers in the Gizlitepe district of Kadıköy—'

'Her what?'

'Dr Savva tried to help the rubbish pickers made homeless by your redevelopment project in Gizlitepe.'

'Their landlords made them homeless, not me,' Öden said. 'Carry on saying I did it and I'll have my lawyer on you.'

These modern urban developers liked litigation. İkmen ignored it. 'Back to Dr Savva . . .'

'Oh yes, I remember her,' Öden said. 'Kept on about how I should do something about the rubbish people. I told her what I told you, "it's the landlords". But she wouldn't listen. She had this agenda about the buildings, which I think were more important to her than the people. All this talk about how valuable old, filthy buildings are supposed to be. What's that? I build nice, modern homes that are clean. Gizlitepe was just old gecekondu property. What was the point?'

İkmen wondered where Ahmet Öden wanted him to start. But of course he couldn't. If he got into his stride about preserving the past and the value of traditional neighbourhoods he would never stop. Instead he said, 'Whatever Dr Savva's motives might be, she disagreed with you over the fate of the rubbish pickers.'

'Yes.'

'You even threatened her over it.' As he watched Öden's face darken, İkmen added, 'Allegedly.'

'Who told you I threatened her? I didn't! It was those rubbish pickers, wasn't it?' He wagged a finger in İkmen's face. 'If you're looking for the woman's killer then don't come to me! I live my life according to my faith, which means I can't kill.'

'I never said she was killed—'

'Those down-and-outs are drunk most of the time. Anything could have happened when she was with them. I warned her. I didn't threaten her but I warned her about them.'

'What did you think those Dr Savva only wanted to help might do to her, Mr Öden?'

'I don't know. What do I know of such people? But I said it would end badly and it has.'

'Not in Gizlitepe. Her body wasn't found there,' İkmen said. 'It was actually found here.'

'Where? In that house?' He pointed.

İkmen looked over his shoulder. The Negroponte house had all but disappeared behind its old trees and twisting plants in recent years. As a small child Çetin and his brother Halıl had often been invited into that garden with their mother, Ayşe. Madam Anastasia liked to have her fortune told and İkmen's mother had been a well-known witch who read the cards and the coffee grounds. Back then Anastasia had been a young woman with a young husband who owned a very successful tailoring business on İstiklal Caddesi. The Negropontes were Byzantine Greeks who had been living in the city since it wasn't much more than a village. Even as a small child İkmen had found them fascinating. But then in 1955 they had, along with most of their community, suffered the most horrific violence at the hands of their Turkish neighbours. Anastasia's husband was killed and she was left brain damaged. Her newly born child suffered another fate, depending upon whose story one believed.

'Why do you ask about that house?' İkmen said.

'I have an interest in it,' Öden said.

İkmen felt the back of his neck tingle. Although he would never have described himself as a witch like his mother, he had inherited a sensitivity to what people said and did and what it might mean. Some of his colleagues called it second sight. He just accepted it was what it was.

'And that interest is—'

'None of your business,' Öden said. 'Was the foreign woman's body found in that house or not?'

'If you'd read whatever paper you take yesterday you would have seen that the body of a woman was found in the ruins at the back of the Hippodrome,' İkmen said. 'So no. A short walk from here, but not here.'

'I can't help you with this,' Öden said. He got out of his car. Two men İkmen hadn't noticed before walked towards him. 'I've got work to do. As I said before, if you want to know who killed that woman, go and speak to those drunken rubbish pickers.'

'Sir.' İkmen put a hand on Öden's arm and felt him cringe.

'Don't touch me.'

The two men with him didn't look as if they approved either. İkmen took his hand away. 'For legal reasons you will have to make a statement about your involvement with Ariadne Savva even if we do have to make an appointment with you to do it,' he said.

Öden shrugged. 'Then do it. Call my office in Üsküdar. Make your appointment and then come and see what a modern friend of the people looks like. You know they call my offices "the soup kitchen" over there because I feed all of Üsküdar's good

50

poor people.' Briefly he moved in close to İkmen. 'Don't take that foreign woman's word over mine,' he said. 'I do everything I can for the needy in this city, everything.'

Then he and his companions walked away. İkmen wondered what, if anything, Mr Öden did for the bad poor of Üsküdar. He was about to leave and go back to the station but he saw Öden knock on the great gates outside the Negropontes' house and he was intrigued.

He heard him call out 'Yiannis!'

But no one answered him and so he called again. When no reply was forthcoming this time, one of Öden's men tried the door. But it was locked. The three of them stood around talking for a while and then they moved off. But not back to their cars.

Öden wanted the house. Alone now, İkmen couldn't think of any other business he might wish to do with Anastasia, her servant and the man alleged to be her son. Yiannis Negroponte, a baby barely three months old, had disappeared in the anti-Greek riots of September 1955. Everyone had assumed he had died. But then in 1997 a forty-two-year-old man had arrived at the Negroponte house claiming to be Yiannis. He'd come with a story about being rescued from the back of the Negropontes' shop in Beyoğlu by a childless Turkish woman. She and her husband had taken him with them when they moved to Germany for work which was why, when he'd arrived, he'd had such a strong German accent. That had been the story, but few people had accepted it. Except for Anastasia Negroponte. Whether her old servant, Hakkı, believed Yiannis was genuine was not known. A dour man in his mid-eighties, he, like his mistress, rarely left the house.

Yiannis on the other hand was often out. He liked to entertain with magic tricks and would trawl the streets, the tea gardens and coffee houses for an audience. He was an odd man, whoever he was. İkmen looked at the house and lit another cigarette. If Ahmet Öden was trying to buy the Negroponte house, he wondered whether he was doing so at Yiannis' behest. Anastasia was as old as wood and would die soon and the site had to be worth a fortune. Yiannis wasn't a young man but he could still have a very comfortable life if he cashed in his mother's property. And, at least since he'd moved into the Negroponte house, he'd not had a comfortable life, locked in with only the old woman and her retainer for company. Even back in the 1950s when İkmen used to go to the house as a child, the place had been damp, and he still remembered their old store rooms with a shudder. Spiders as big as his hand had clambered over the Negropontes' wine racks and there were spooky arches, blackened with age, which dripped with stale smelling water. Much as he'd always loved going there, İkmen had sometimes suffered nightmares over that house when he was young.

The skeleton, which was very dark brown, was hidden from view. Attached to the palm tree underneath which the body had been found, a tent concealed Dr Arto Sarkissian and his many instruments of investigation.

One of the Lise's students had found what he had thought was a joke skeleton hand coming out of the ground by the tree. It was only when one of his teachers took it away from him when he was playing with it in class that further investigations had been made. The hand had been part of a whole skeleton that had been entwined around the roots of the palm tree.

'Doctor.'

Sarkissian looked up. 'Ah, Inspector Süleyman,' he said. He nodded at Ömer Mungun. 'Sergeant.'

'So tell me about it,' Süleyman said.

The doctor crossed his arms. 'Well, our body is that of a

man. He has some quite elaborate dental work in his mouth and so it's reasonable to deduce that he wasn't poor. He's adult but I can't tell how old yet. I don't know how he died. What I can say with some certainty though is that even if he died unlawfully, that happened a long time ago.'

'What do you mean by a long time?'

'Decades,' he said. 'Look at how degraded the skeleton is.'

'If it's so old why wasn't it discovered before?' Ömer Mungun asked.

'There can be various reasons,' the doctor said, 'but mainly it's because the earth beneath our feet, much as we don't like to think about it, is very rarely static. Even if we didn't live on a seismic fault this would be the case. But because İstanbul is in an area of earthquake activity this phenomenon is even more pronounced. He just rose to the surface one day. Enmeshed in palm roots.'

Süleyman moved closer to the skeleton. 'Have they damaged it?'

'Not much, no. Palm roots are not as deep or as hardy as, say, mature olive roots. It's time that has caused the most damage. He died a long time ago. I've called a friend to help me determine when that might have been.'

'Who's that?'

'Dr Akyıldız. She's one of our few archaeological pathologists. Although I may well be able to determine this man's age and how he died, she is more expert than I at pinpointing when. For all I know he could have been here for twenty years or seventy.'

Süleyman nodded. 'OK.'

'We've already had the press sniffing around,' the doctor said. 'I believe at least one of the students at the Lise has a media mogul in the family. So this will be in the papers and on the

53

TV news. But do I think this is a job for the police? No. If our friend here was poisoned with strychnine sixty years ago there's no need for urgency.'

'Unless his killer is still alive,' Süleyman said.

The doctor shrugged. 'I'll let you know as soon as Dr Akyıldız and myself have got any news.'

Süleyman sighed. 'And in the meantime I will have to tell the Commissioner . . . What?'

'Tell her that we've found an historical skeleton in the grounds of the Galatasaray Lise, cause of death unknown,' Sarkissian said. 'In all seriousness, this is a story that will soon get lost in today's climate. Have you been up to Gezi Park?'

'Yes,' Süleyman said. 'All quiet.'

'For now.'

'You think it's going to kick off again, Doctor?' Ömer Mungun asked.

The Armenian looked down at the ground. 'I do.'

'Any particular reason?' Süleyman asked.

For a moment the doctor said nothing. Then he leaned towards the two officers. 'People can't take much more redevelopment. You know what I mean? I know you know Tarlabaşı neighbourhood, Inspector.' Süleyman and Mungun had worked on a case in that area the year before. It was where Gonca's father had lived. 'The poor move out of picturesque slums, the developers knock the slums down and build hideous tower blocks which the rich move into. The poor live on the streets because they've nowhere else to go.'

'It's like this in every major European city. It's the free market economy,' Süleyman said.

'It's wrong,' Sarkissian said. His red face showed his passion. 'Those people in the park know it. And so do all the thousands who will join them.'

Süleyman shifted uncomfortably from one foot to the other. 'We'll see. Now, Doctor, do you have any idea when you and your colleague will be able to tell us more about this skeleton?'

Clearly any sharing of opinions about Gezi Park was over. Sarkissian cleared his throat. 'Three days, maybe less. Three to be on the safe side.'

'Good.'

By the time Süleyman and Mungun left through the vast metal school gates, İstiklal Caddesi was full of young people wearing face paint and brightly coloured hats. They carried banners that had slogans on them saying, 'Hands Off Gezi Park,' and 'Another Shopping Mall? No, Thanks!'

'I used to sometimes get out of school at lunchtime and buy kokoreç from a stall in the Balık Pazar,' Süleyman said. 'That was before İstiklal was pedestrianised. I can't tell you how thick with fumes the air was.' He lit a cigarette. 'This street has changed a lot over the years. Not all of it for the better.'

'It's good the fumes have gone, sir,' Ömer said.

'Oh yes, they were bad,' Süleyman said. 'But the boy who used to sell me the kokoreç my parents so disapproved of, I wish was still in business.'

'Why isn't he, sir?'

Süleyman took a deep drag from his cigarette. 'Because he fell through the cracks, Ömer. He lost his home to the developers, his wife took his children away to live with her parents in Mersin. Working's difficult if you're homeless. He slept underneath his stall for months until it all got too much for him. One night he drank half a bottle of cognac and then cut his own throat.'

Chapter 5

'Çetin! Çetin!'

Hands grabbed at his pyjama top. It was dark and he was disorientated. 'What?'

'He's only just come in! Kemal!'

'Kemal?' İkmen turned his head to look at his bedside clock. 'It's four thirty,' he said. 'In the morning.'

'Yes! Yes! And that boy has only just got in.'

'He's not a boy, he's twenty-one.'

His wife, Fatma, put her bedside lamp on.

'God!' İkmen screwed up his eyes and buried his face in his pillow. 'When I was twenty-one I had a son of my own and another one on the way. He's a man.'

Fatma İkmen shook her long grey hair. 'In law, he may be,' she said. 'But you know how silly he can be. Easily led. He'll've been up to that park in Beyoğlu.' She pushed her husband to the edge of the bed. 'Go and talk to him.'

İkmen swung his legs down on the floor and stood up. He felt groggy and his mouth tasted indescribable.

'Go on!'

He walked to the bedroom door. 'Only if you don't follow and keep putting your contribution in. If you want me to talk to Kemal then I will, but not with you censoring me.'

'I won't.'

'Make sure you don't,' he said.

Pausing only to find a cigarette in his jacket pocket and then light it, İkmen knocked on his son's bedroom door. The youngest of the nine İkmen children, Kemal was the only one still living at home. 'Kemal?'

There was no answer. İkmen didn't know when the boy had got in but it couldn't have been long before. 'Kemal!'

There was a sort of snorting sound and then a voice said, 'What is it?'

İkmen opened the door to a room he didn't want to illuminate. Even in the dark he could see that it was a chaos of clothes, books, computers and dirty tea glasses. Something in the middle of the mess reared up. 'What do you want, Dad?'

'Your mother says I'm to tell you not to go to Gezi Park,' İkmen said. 'Have you been to Gezi Park, Kemal? Tell me the truth.'

There was a pause and then Kemal said, 'Yes. And I'm going to go tomorrow too. I haven't got any lectures so why not? Why? Going to try and stop me?'

'No,' İkmen said. 'On the contrary I applaud your commitment.'

'So why are you telling me off?'

'I'm not, but your mother's worried. She asked me to speak to you. So I'm speaking.'

'I don't understand. Do you want me to go to Gezi or not?'

'I want you to do what your conscience tells you to do whilst keeping safe and avoiding confrontation. And I want you to call me and most definitely not your mother if anything goes wrong.'

'Dad, are you saying that you support what people are protesting about in Gezi?'

There was a pause before İkmen spoke. 'My job is to uphold the law and protect the people of this city from harm. My opinions don't matter. Things that do matter are people's lives, their homes and their liberty.'

'So you do—'

'I support no one,' he said. 'And I support everyone. Policemen are not supposed to be political. Now go to sleep and remember what I told you. Oh, and try not to be so late next time, Kemal. Your mother is a trial when you're out beyond one a.m.'

'OK.'

İkmen left the boy, finished his cigarette and then went back to bed.

Fatma was sitting up, knitting. Nervously. One of their daughters, Gül, had just had her first baby and Fatma was producing whole new woollen wardrobes for it every week.

'Well?' she said. 'Had he been to the park?'

İkmen got into bed beside her. 'He had.'

'Well did you tell him not to?'

İkmen lay down. 'I told him to be careful and not to come home so late,' he said.

'But did you tell him not to go to that park?'

He looked her in the eyes. 'No, I didn't.'

'Why? I—'

'Yes, Fatma, I know what you told me to tell him,' he said. 'But I couldn't do that and you shouldn't have asked me.'

'But you went—'

'To shut you up, yes,' he said. He put a hand on her arm. She didn't pull away. 'Fatma, you know that I love you more than life. You know, I hope, that I respect the way you live the religious life with every part of your being. I know that—'

'Çetin, I don't want another shopping mall to be built where Gezi Park is,' she interrupted. 'Just because some of the people who do want it are religious too, doesn't mean I have to agree with them. I just don't want Kemal to get hurt. Some of your colleagues in the park have been . . . zealous . . .'

'Bastards,' he said. 'Don't get me started.' He put his arms out to her. 'Come on, we need to sleep.'

Fatma put her knitting down beside the bed and slid down into his embrace. 'Oh, Çetin,' she said, 'if anything were to happen to Kemal I'd never forgive myself.'

'For what? Being his mother?' He hugged her.

'You know. Just look after him, Çetin. Do that for me.'

'I will have as many eyes trained in Kemal's direction as I can,' İkmen said. And then he kissed her. 'Don't worry.'

Fatma closed her eyes and soon she was asleep. But Çetin was awake now and thinking, about Ariadne Savva and her unknown, lost child. Where was it? Hospitals and doctors' surgeries in every part of the city had been contacted, it was all over the media. There had even been yet another press conference. Every day he saw hundreds of people walking along holding small babies or pushing them in prams. At the very periphery of his consciousness most of the time, they passed him by like ghosts. It could be any one of them or none.

And had Ariadne even known she was pregnant? Nobody around her seemed to have noticed her expanding girth very much, but had that included Ariadne herself? Had her first intimation of pregnancy been as she was passing the Hippodrome? Had labour pains forced her to hide herself away in the sphendone? But there had been so little blood there. And wouldn't she rather have got help? Or did she maybe think that 'the Turks' wouldn't help her? Surely she'd lived in the city long enough to know that was very unlikely? But then whether she knew she was pregnant or not wasn't really the point. Who, if anyone, had killed her and may have taken her baby, was.

Mehmet Süleyman walked down the hill to where he'd parked his car. He'd hardly slept, but not because he was having passionate sex with Gonca. At almost midnight large sections of her extended family had arrived at the house. He had recognised three of her brothers, a sister and her eldest son, but all the others had been unknown to him. A colourful mob passing around bottles of cognac and rakı, they had settled themselves into Gonca's studio and then talked at the tops of their voices until dawn. He'd gone to bed, but their noise had kept him awake. And when they had finally gone and Gonca had joined him in bed she'd had the temerity to ask him why he was still awake! Noise didn't seem to affect gypsies. Why was that?

And now he knew all their business. They'd all got together to talk about what had been going on in Gezi Park, who they knew was taking part and how they could maybe use the protests to draw attention to the way their traditional neighbourhoods had been developed. There had been a lot of talk about the police. None of the gypsies so much as hinted at any fear of the authorities. Rather they expressed their anxieties through their fears for others.

One had said, 'The people they beat are like the hippies from the 1960s. Peace lovers, they just let them kick them.'

'And transsexuals,' another said. 'Pulling their hair and shouting filthy insults at them.'

An old voice put in, 'All the transsexuals I know carry weapons. None of them would hesitate to defend their honour. What kind of weak transsexuals did you see, Metin?'

People had laughed and then there had been more drinking. They'd all wanted to go to Gezi Park and that had included Gonca. But in the end the young people were chosen. Some nephews and nieces, students who would blend with the crowd.

Süleyman passed a heavily bearded man and his wife, whose face was covered by a niqab. Beyond the Greek school, over the hill, was the district of Çarşamba where a lot of pious Muslims like this couple lived. Süleyman was not convinced that outward appearance necessarily reflected inner piety but he didn't know how else to describe such people.

In the very earliest days of the twenty-first century some artists, young intellectuals and gypsies had moved into the Fener/Balat area with the idea that they'd build a vibrant community of like-minded people. To an extent that had happened, but the pious presented what, to Gonca at least, felt like a dour presence. She talked about them looking down their noses at those who were not like them and mouthing bad words at her daughters. Süleyman didn't know whether they did such things or not. The people who had complained about his relationship with Gonca were much less obvious than the men and women of Çarşamba. They were his colleagues. Anonymous and hidden in the vastness of the department, they could be anyone. They could even be someone he knew well. The only thing he did know was that it couldn't be İkmen or Ömer Mungun. If İkmen had a problem with Gonca he would have told Süleyman to his face, but he liked the gypsy, who was closer to İkmen's age than Süleyman's. And Ömer Mungun wasn't going to draw attention to himself unless he had to.

Süleyman opened his car door with his remote control. As the BMW bleeped in response, some children who were picking through rubbish on the pavement ran up to him and asked for money. He gave them one lira each then got in his car and drove away.

When Yiannis pulled the cotton thread he'd put in his mouth out of his eye all the children screamed and pulled faces. One little girl held her baby brother up high so he could see. But he was so young he could barely focus.

'There you see, magic,' Yiannis said. 'Anyone want to see a kitten come out of this box?'

'Yeah!'

'I do, but my mum does say you're evil,' one boy said.

Yiannis Negroponte put the small box on the ground in front of him and then covered it with a silk scarf.

'Oh? Why does your mum say that?'

'Because magic is evil,' the boy said.

'Where'd your mum get that from?'

The boy shrugged.

A girl said, 'Kitten! Come on! Let's see the kitten!'

Yiannis waved a thin, dark hand over the silk scarf and mumbled some words the children strained to hear, but couldn't. There was a pause. Then he flicked the scarf away to reveal a tiny black kitten.

'Aaahhh!'

The girl with the baby brother said, 'Can I have it?'

Yiannis picked the kitten up. 'No,' he said. 'But you can stroke him if you like.'

The children treated the kitten gently, even the boys. The sons and daughters of shopkeepers and pansiyon owners, they were not street urchins who had little regard for animals or rich kids who found anything not on a computer screen boring. These kids were the ideal audience and Yiannis made a point of always having some new tricks for them whenever they gathered outside the gates of the Negroponte house.

Once all the children had stroked the kitten, Yiannis said that was the end of the show for the day and went back through his gates. Hakkı was in the garden and Yiannis gave him the kitten as he passed.

'He can go back to his mother now,' he said.

'As you wish.'

Yiannis walked into the house via the French windows. Anastasia was asleep on one of the couches in front of the television, which was blaring out football scores. He turned it off but she didn't wake. Then he looked at her. In sleep she looked almost serene. But he knew she couldn't be. Peace of mind, under the circumstances, was impossible for any of them. He looked again at the figure Ahmet Öden had offered him for the house. He'd written it down on the back of one of his business cards. At the time, Yiannis had just shoved it in his pocket. Now he looked at it and wondered how the man had the gall to think they'd even consider such an insulting sum. But then Öden could afford gall. He had never and would never pay the going rate for the land he developed. Mostly he bought from the poor and ignorant or from people who would get some sort of kickback once he'd built his tower blocks. Öden had made it abundantly clear to Yiannis that he was doing an old Byzantine family who were a bit strapped for cash a big favour. What he didn't know was that there was actually no price he could offer that would buy the Negroponte house.

When Anastasia opened her eyes and looked at him he said, 'Don't worry, Mama, everything is going to be all right.'

She smiled.

The contents of Ariadne Savva's desk at the museum arrived at İkmen's office just before the archaeologist's father, Demitrios. He put them away quickly.

An elderly, frail man, Demitrios Savva spoke Turkish fluently. 'Our family lived in this city and then later in Anatolia for centuries,' he told İkmen when he commented on his language skills. 'We were "exchanged" for Turks from Salonika in 1923.'

The population exchanges between Greece and Turkey in the 1920s still left a bitter taste.

'I was born in Athens,' Savva said, 'but my parents still spoke Turkish. I taught it to my children. You can never know enough languages, whatever they are.'

He looked around the room as if he had a bad smell under his nose. İkmen was polite. He tried to converse about the daughter Savva had lost but the old man wouldn't be drawn. 'I've come to see my daughter's body and take her home, Inspector,' he said. 'And the child. What of that? Do you have it? Do you know who its father is?'

'No, we don't have the child and neither do we know the identity of its father.'

'If you don't have the child by this time—'

'We must not lose hope,' İkmen said. 'On the positive side we have not found the dead body of a child. The father could have it—'

'Or paedophiles,' Demitrios Savva said. 'Or maybe the father was a paedophile.'

İkmen took in a deep breath and then let it out slowly. 'Sir, your daughter was an intelligent woman. Do you honestly think that she'd have a relationship with a pervert?'

The old man shuffled in his chair. 'I don't know. I never wanted her to come to this country.'

'She was a scholar of the Byzantine Empire. She had to come here,' İkmen said. 'Like it or not, Mr Savva, İstanbul is the centre of Byzantine inquiry. And by your own admission, you taught your daughter Turkish—'

'Don't be clever with me!'

İkmen looked down. 'I'm sorry. I thought—'

'You thought nothing. I've lost a child. My only daughter. And I have to come to this place where my family were treated like cattle . . .' He began to cry.

İkmen wondered whether he should tell Mr Savva that he too had lost a child but he decided against it. What good would knowing that he had lost a son do for this man? He let him cry.

When he'd finished the old man looked up. He still had fury in his eyes.

İkmen said, 'What I can do is take you to see your daughter.'

'Where is she? Here?'

'No, she is still at the pathology laboratory. As you can understand, we had to find out what had caused Ariadne's death.'

'Which was?'

'Trauma to the head,' İkmen said. 'After she had given birth.'

'I see.' His eyes began to water and swell again. 'Animals!' he muttered. 'Animals!'

'Whether the trauma was accidental or deliberate is uncertain. Our pathologist, a Christian—'

'You think you do me some sort of favour by having my daughter cut open by a Christian? Do you?'

İkmen didn't know what to say. Dealing with bereaved relatives was something he usually did well, but this time he felt entirely wrong-footed. Greeks in Turkey were one thing but Greeks from Greece were something else. A proud people, they now lived in a bankrupt country next to a neighbour, Turkey, which seemed to be living the economic dream. It had to appear, İkmen thought, as if the clock had turned back five hundred years to when Turkey had been an empire and Greece a starving backwater.

Demitrios Savva appeared to collect himself and then he said, 'I apologise. Of course it is thoughtful that you assign a Christian pathologist to my daughter.'

'He is our most senior doctor,' İkmen said.

'I appreciate that. And again, I apologise, it's . . .'

'Your daughter is dead,' İkmen said. 'You are naturally distraught. I am just so sorry that I can't give you any more positive information. I too think of the child. I think of it day and night and I . . . I can't believe I haven't found it.' He shook his head. 'But Mr Savva, if the child is out there I will find it and I will provide justice for your daughter. Now, shall we go?'

The Greek nodded his head. His anger spent, he sat quietly while İkmen gathered what he needed for the journey to Arto Sarkissian's laboratory and then they left.

Süleyman didn't usually put people he spoke to on the phone on speaker. Had he done it this time to impress him?

Ömer Mungun didn't know. Understanding his superior was not something he could claim to have ticked off his mental list of life skills.

Süleyman smiled into the phone. 'And the English Club, Professor Bekdil, how are your numbers there?'

'Oh, always high, Mehmet Bey,' an elderly voice replied. 'Lessons are one thing, but conversational practice . . .'

'I wish I'd spent more time at Club,' Süleyman said. 'I understand English perfectly but sometimes my spoken English does leave something to be desired.'

'I do hope you're coming to Pilav Day,' the professor said. 'It's next Sunday, the second. It would be wonderful to see you in a social milieu. That is if we can have Pilav Day this year.'

'Why wouldn't you? Pilav Day has been an annual celebration of the school and its achievements since its inception.'

There was a pause. Süleyman had telephoned his old English teacher to tell him the latest news on the skeleton that had been found in the grounds of Galatasaray Lise. Dr Sarkissian had found what he thought could be stab wounds on the dead man's sternum and ribs. Bekdil had been liaison between the school and the police ever since the body had been found.

'These protests,' Bekdil said. 'There are thousands of people on İstiklal Caddesi, all moving down towards Gezi Park. It's all very colourful and they're all carrying very bright banners and flags, but when Monsieur Lamartaine went out at lunchtime he said that something in the air made his eyes sting. Are the police using tear gas, do you know, Mehmet Bey?'

Süleyman looked at Ömer, who shrugged. He didn't know the latest from the park any more than his boss.

'I don't know,' Süleyman said. 'But of course if things have become violent, then it's possible.'

'The people in the streets seem very peaceful.'

'I'm not there, Professor, I wouldn't know.'

'Of course not,' he said. 'I apologise, Mehmet Bey. Of course you are not involved in street disturbances.'

Süleyman said nothing. Ömer felt the professor's last statement was obsequious. But then he imagined that the staff at the Lise did have to crawl, to some extent, to their often exalted students, especially when they grew up. His teachers back in Mardin had smacked him around the ear when he talked in class or failed to attend to a sufficient degree. Money bought lack of pain in so many ways.

'Does Dr Sarkissian have any idea about the age of the skeleton?' The professor had changed the subject, which was what, Ömer had observed, elite people did when they had made some sort of social gaffe.

'Not yet,' Süleyman said. 'He's working with a forensic archaeologist so the assumption is that the body is old. I will let you know when we have an approximate date.'

'Do. As you may recall, Mehmet Bey, every so often at the Lise, kitchen and cleaning staff have just left without giving notice over the years. It's a common thing amongst domestic workers. And back in the 1970s there was Dr Deliveli.'

'Was he the mathematics teacher?'

'Yes. Just before your time, I think. He disappeared on Pilav Day, I seem to remember, in 1972. At the time there were rumours of homosexuality. It was said that he fell in love with a young male prostitute in Karaköy. But I don't know.'

Süleyman frowned. 'Was there a police investigation?'

'I think so, but not like these days,' the professor said. 'I remember a detective coming and interviewing all the teaching staff but I can recall no resolution.'

People had gone missing back in the 1970s. It had been a time of political strife with socialist supporters pitched against conservative groups. In the middle, a succession of governments had tried to exercise control. Finally the military had staged a coup in 1980.

'It is a name to bear in mind, Mehmet Bey,' the professor said.

'Indeed. I will.'

They talked for a few minutes more and then Süleyman ended the conversation. Ömer watched him lean back in his chair. 'Like all institutions, the Lise has its own life, its legends and its rumours,' he said. 'Schools have much in common with hospitals and prisons.'

'Total institutions.'

'Yes. And my status as an ex-student at the Lise could prove useful. As an "old boy" people like Professor Bekdil will speak freely to me. He may also seek to co-opt me into some sort of alliance with the school, should what we have found prove embarrassing for the Lise. Therefore I will include you, in your capacity as disinterested observer, in my conversations with the school.'

'You want me to listen in again?'

'If possible whenever I have any contact with the Lise,' Süleyman said. 'I'm not saying they will or even may seek to influence me in any way, but my old school is a special place and I wouldn't like to do anything that may harm its reputation.

But I will do if I have to, and I want you, Ömer, to remind me of that from time to time.'

'Yes, sir.' But if he were truthful Ömer's mind wasn't really on the Galatasaray Lise. The body they'd found there had been dead a long time and so it was unlikely the murderer was still stalking any street, in İstanbul or anywhere else. He was thinking about the thousands of people who had gathered in İstiklal and about tear gas.

'Sir, do you know what's happening in İstiklal and in Gezi Park today?' he asked.

'Not really.' Süleyman paused. 'Ömer, we have a job to do. What others are assigned to isn't our business. This is a huge city. You need to realise that we can't be everywhere or know everything. In fact, sometimes it's best if we don't know anything. Do you understand?'

He was saying that they shouldn't get involved. Which, on one level, suited Ömer, but on another it really didn't. Some of the new legislation the government wanted to pass restricting the sale of alcohol offended him, and he believed that suspending the extension of lesbian and gay rights was a step backwards. He felt conflicted. Just then a text came to his phone from Peri: 'Gezi Park is erupting. A hell of tear gas and water cannon. Tell your colleagues to stop it, Ömer.'

Chapter 6

Fatma had told him that she could hear the crowd in Gezi Park from their apartment in Sultanahmet.

'Roaring and screaming like mad people,' she'd said. 'Thanks be to God that Kemal is in tonight. Good sense must have prevailed.'

Fatma disapproved of protesting, especially against government policies that she found sensible. 'What's wrong with restricting the sale of alcohol?' she'd said. 'Mr Prime Minister doesn't want people to become alcoholics.'

He'd tried to explain about choice but she'd thrown Sharia law at him and so İkmen had put the phone down on her. Now, alone with Ariadne Savva's personal effects from her office, he turned again to a small notebook which had been found in her drawer. It was the only document that was not in Turkish. He could make out a few words of the Greek handwriting but he'd have to send it for translation.

One word he did recognise, however. When Ariadne's body had been found there had been a small piece of porphyry stone in her left hand. Almost purple in colour, porphyry had been the building material favoured by Byzantine emperors. There was loads of it in Aya Sofya. But none in the sphendone of the Hippodrome. Now here it was in Ariadne's notebook.

Mr Savva had broken down again when he'd seen his daughter's body. That happened a lot. Loved ones could often hold

70

themselves together until they actually saw the reality of a dead body in front of them. Mehmet Süleyman's ex-wife, Zelfa, a psychiatrist, used to say that until a father or a partner actually saw the corpse of their relative they didn't quite believe that they had died. It was self-delusion but he could understand it. Not that it always worked that way. When Sergeant Ayşe Farsakoğlu had died in the garden of Professor Cem Atay, she'd passed as soon as she'd been shot. İkmen had run to her, cradled her in his arms, but she'd already died. In spite of the prohibition on smoking indoors, İkmen lit a cigarette. It was late and that memory always upset him. That Atay was now in prison for the rest of his life didn't make İkmen feel any better. When he'd held Ayşe's body to his chest, she'd still been warm, and he'd clung on to that fact as proof of some sort of life for as long as he could. It had only been when Arto Sarkissian had taken her away from him that the spell her body had exerted over him had been broken. After that he could see that she was dead. He would never forget it. However successful Kerim Gürsel's appointment as his sergeant turned out to be, he could never be Ayşe.

'What do they think they're doing?'

Ahmet Öden had a good view of Gezi Park from his brother's apartment on Cumhuriyet Caddesi.

Semih brought him a cup of coffee. 'They're protesting,' he said. 'Against laws on alcohol, restrictions on perverts, all sorts of things they feel do not conform to their middle-class liberal agenda. They're spoilt, secular rich kids.'

'They also demonstrate against us,' Ahmet said. 'Because they're middle-class and privileged. They want these grim old parts of the city to be preserved because they're "historic". But they don't have to live in them. Developers are doing people like the folk in Gizlitepe and Tarlabaşı a favour. Look at what's been achieved in Sulukule. Once a slum full of criminals, now a place where families can live in peace and security.'

Ahmet was fifteen years older than his brother and he could remember Sulukule when it had been the place to go to watch gypsy dancers and have your fortune told. As a teenager, he'd often sloped off for some guilty pleasures in Sulukule, away from the prying eyes of his covered mother. Down in the park, Turkish flags waved side by side with rainbow flags which, someone had told him, denoted gay pride. Ahmet turned back into the vast, gilt-encrusted living room. He'd ensured that Semih had done well and it made him happy. Property development had made them both rich. They'd cleaned up slums in the process, which had had the effect of limiting the instances of immoral behaviour in those areas. That was a good thing.

Ahmet sat down. So, if slum clearance was a good thing, then why did so many people, middle-class or otherwise, oppose it? He'd heard that the gypsies of Sulukule had first been sent to live in tower blocks outside the city, which they hadn't liked. Then thousands of them had moved back, mainly into other slums like Tarlabaşı. Now that was being demolished a lot of them lived and begged on the streets. Often the police picked them up for vagrancy and threw them in the cells. And yet there were nice houses, houses the developer could be proud of, in Sulukule. Quiet, pious families had bought them and the whole area had completely changed character. Undoubtedly this had been for the better. Nonetheless, at the back of his mind, usually when he slept, Ahmet wasn't so sure. Gypsies particularly were loud and irreligious, and most of the men drank, but did that mean that they didn't deserve to live somewhere decent?

'All this will blow over,' Semih said. 'Those people down

there are in a minority; they always have been, really. Now we're officially in charge there's nothing they can do.'

'No.' But he wasn't sure. The government was furious about Gezi and the police were all over the area, but those in the 'minority' still came, and silently Ahmet found them frightening. Mobs like that could do things. His father had told him. And those things were not always to the benefit of people like them. He felt a sense of urgency he hadn't experienced before.

The front door opened and closed, quietly. Kerim got up from the kitchen table and went to greet his guest, silently. Sinem had finally got to sleep and neither of them wanted to wake her. Kerim took Pembe Hanım through to his small lounge and shut the door behind him.

'It's madness out there,' Pembe said as she threw her large straw hat on the sofa beside her. 'But brilliant. Everybody's had enough. It's a big "fuck you" to all the politicians and developers. Now they'll have to listen.'

'You think so?' He went over to a small cabinet in the corner of the room and took out two glasses and a bottle. 'Whisky?'

'To celebrate? Why not?' she said. 'Mind you, for you I suppose all this is worrying, isn't it?'

'Gezi?' He poured the whisky, gave her a glass and sat down. 'Officially I'm dead against it. Unofficially . . . I don't have to tell you.'

She smiled. She was a tall woman with very long tanned legs made to look even more impressive by sky-high heels. Pembe was slim and blonde, albeit out of a bottle, and handsome rather than beautiful. 'Going to be difficult for you to be on the right side of history, boy,' she said. She frowned. 'Why did you join the police?'

He smiled. 'I needed a job and I'm good in a scrap, as you

know. It was this or work with Dad, and even this is better than that.'

'You got lucky when you got the job with İkmen.'

He watched her light a cigarette and wished that she would offer him one. But she wouldn't. He'd given up. 'I'd rather someone hadn't had to die for me to get my opportunity,' he said. 'You know the old man still mourns Farsakoğlu.'

Pembe shrugged. 'And yet it was Süleyman who was fucking her,' she said. 'Then he went back to Gonca Şekeroğlu the gypsy. He broke Farsakoğlu's heart. She didn't care whether she lived or died. Her friend Nar Hanım – you know, the great big tall trans girl who worked with the police sometimes . . .'

'Sort of, yes.'

'She told her to ditch him, but she wouldn't.'

Kerim shook his head. 'It's his business,' he said. 'I don't have to work with him.'

Pembe drank. 'Sounds like you don't like him.'

'I'm indifferent.'

She shrugged.

He changed the subject. 'Sinem had a bad day,' he said. 'I think the pain together with the noise from the street wore her out. She's asleep now.'

'Poor kid.'

'Are you staying over or . . .?'

'If she'd like that.'

'To see you in the morning? You know she'd love it,' he said.

'And you?' She raised an eyebrow.

'I'm working my way through the contacts of a possible murder victim,' he said.

'Oh, the one found in the Hippodrome.'

'Yes. I've got to make an early start in the morning. If you slip in bed beside her later, you won't wake her. She's drugged.'

When he said it, he looked sad. Pembe leaned across his lap and took one of his hands in hers. 'She has to be,' she said. 'It's not your fault.'

And then she kissed him. It was a long, deep kiss that aroused him. When it was over, Pembe said, 'Do you want it?'

He didn't even bother to reply. He didn't have to. Her long, manicured fingers unzipped his fly and she took him in her hand. He sighed.

He'd been in early middle-age at the time of his death which, she reckoned by experience and by eye, had to be at least forty years ago. He'd also suffered a lot with his teeth, but he'd had some complicated dentistry too. He had crowns and bridges and there was evidence that at least four teeth had been root filled. He'd not just been 'anyone'; he'd had money and maybe even position too.

Dr Sarkissian had told the police but they wouldn't open their files until they had a more accurate date than 'about forty years ago'. They, like Dr Aylın Akyıldız, were waiting for the carbon fourteen dating tests to be completed.

Aylın covered the male skeleton and turned to the remains that, for the last six months, had become her passion. This was incomplete – just a skull, some vertebrae, a pelvis and one femur – but it was when it had been dated and what it had been found with that fascinated her.

Carbon-dated to between the 1450s and '60s, it came from the era of the Turkish Conquest, which had taken place in 1453. When Mehmet the Conqueror had finally entered the city of Constantinople on 29 May 1453 this man could very well have been alive. However, if the sword that had been found at his side was anything to go by then he wasn't a Turk. The fact that it was crested with the double-headed eagle of the Byzantines

75

meant that he was probably a Christian and of some standing. Not only that, but the sword was lacking what had been a considerable cluster of jewels on the hilt. It was still possible to see where the gems had been hacked and smashed out of their settings and in one case an emerald had left a few slivers of itself behind. If the sword had belonged to the middle-aged man it had been found lying beside, then who had he been?

Suddenly deflated, Aylın sat down. The skeleton had been found in one of the few gardens that remained at the foot of the city walls in Edirnekapı. The archaeologist who had discovered it had asked her to date it and Aylın had become close to her. And although Dr Ariadne Savva had views on the body that Aylın found fanciful, she had liked her and had been horrified to learn of her death. She hadn't known anything about Ariadne's pregnancy. They had simply spent time together with the skeleton which had absorbed many days and nights of their lives. Aylın believed that he was probably a Byzantine soldier, many of whom had died at the walls in defence of the city. But because of the jewelled sword and, possibly, because she was a Greek herself, Ariadne had speculated that perhaps 'he' was Constantine XI Palaiologos, last emperor of the Byzantines. Legend had it that he had died fighting the Turks at the city walls although his body and, more significantly for the Turks at the time, his fantastically valuable crown had never been found. Greek nationalists were fond of the legend that Constantine had not died but been turned into a marble statue that was buried underneath the Golden Gate awaiting the day when the city was recaptured by Christians again.

Aylın had tried to curtail Ariadne's excitement. She only shared her thoughts with her, or so she said. But it had been difficult to calm Ariadne down. Although she wouldn't go into detail, she was convinced that 'Byzantium is coming back to life'. She was thrilled, and although Aylın couldn't get her to go into any sort of detail, she suspected that this belief was based on more than just one incomplete skeleton from Edirnekapı.

In the morning she'd have to tell the police all about Ariadne's beliefs and assertions, such as they had been. Eventually she'd have to share Ariadne's find with the Archaeological Museum.

Yiannis puffed on his cigarette and then handed it to Hakkı. They stood outside the gates to the Negroponte house in what would usually have been the quiet of the night, but the sound of car horns and voices were drifting across the city that night. They both knew where they were coming from, but neither of them spoke about it.

Yiannis looked up at the stars. 'Ahmet Öden will never get this house,' he said.

'He mustn't,' the old man said. 'But I fear he will.'

'We're never leaving.'

'Wouldn't *you* like to leave?'

Yiannis looked into Hakkı's watery brown eyes. 'Why would I?' he said. 'Nothing has changed. Not with the house.'

Hakkı smoked and said nothing.

Yiannis said, 'You still doubt me, don't you? Don't try to say that you don't.'

'I won't.'

Yiannis turned his head away.

'Remember what happened to Madam,' Hakkı said. 'And what didn't happen to me. They beat her until she passed out. Smashed her head in. Nikos Bey they kicked and stabbed to death. How could a child escape a mob like that?'

'I did.'

'Because a Turkish couple saved you? Why would they do that? I was there in 1955, and the Turks' blood was up—'

77

'Yours wasn't.'

'Only because I knew my duty to this family,' Hakkı said. He finished his cigarette. 'Who you are, I don't know, but you have a fight on your hands with Ahmet Öden and his kind. They run the world these days and there's nothing your magic tricks can do to change that.'

'He's offered me a ridiculous price that no one in his right mind would accept. Not that I'd accept any price,' Yiannis said.

'Well don't expect any price,' Hakkı said. 'Because his offer is his offer and that will be that.'

'People are protesting about redevelopment,' Yiannis said.

'Yes, and they will live to regret it.'

'Why?'

'Because, as I told you, those people like Ahmet Öden run everything. The people in the park, do they have guns? No. Öden and his people have the guns because they have the police. But to be honest I don't care. I'm too old to care. All I live for now are my family and Madam Anastasia. All the doctors may say her brain is damaged but I know her better. I know that if she lost this house it would kill her.'

'She's not going to lose the house. I told you, I—'

'No, I will save it!' Hakkı raised a finger up to Yiannis' face. 'When all is done and there is no light at the end of the tunnel, I will save the Negroponte house.'

Yiannis shook his head, finally tired of being put down. 'Without me? You'll be able to do nothing, old man,' he said. 'You've been able to do nothing.' He walked back through the gates and into the house.

Chapter 7

Peri Mungun had to go around the park to get to work but she couldn't pass by. The police had moved in on the demonstrators some time before she arrived and were using tear gas and water cannon. People were everywhere. Some were soaking wet and unconscious while others stumbled around coughing, their eyes streaming from the effects of the tear gas. She helped a young woman in a headscarf get out of the immediate area and then bathed her eyes with water from her drinking bottle.

'Who are you?' the woman asked as she tried to open her eyes.

'I'm a nurse,' Peri said. 'Let me open your eyes, don't try to do it yourself. Who are you with?'

Peri held the woman's eyes open and poured. The woman whimpered.

'You're doing really well,' Peri said. 'Look, howl if you need to. It's OK. What are you doing here?'

'I'm with Muslims against Capitalism,' she said. For a moment she panted. Then she continued, 'We don't want this park or any other park to disappear. We don't want any more shopping malls.'

Peri pulled the woman to the top of İstiklal Caddesi and sat her down on the ground.

'You'll be all right now,' she said.

A young girl with her hair in dreadlocks appeared. She squatted down beside the woman in the headscarf then she looked up at Peri. 'Tear gas.'

'Yes. I've bathed her eyes,' Peri said. 'I'm a nurse.'

'A nurse? Shit, we need you,' the girl said.

'I'm on my way to work.'

'Work? This is the biggest social demonstration in this country for decades and you're worried about going to work?'

'I've got patients who need me,' Peri said.

'Where'd you work? At the Taksim?'

'No, at the German Hospital.'

The girl snorted. 'Where all the rich people go? Fuck them.'

'That's easy for you to say, but I need that job,' Peri said.

The girl, all dreadlocks and Goth gear, was beginning to irritate her. She spoke well, dressed and swore as she pleased. She probably came from one of those elite secular families the current government were so hacked off by. Now, for different reasons, Peri was too.

'You might not need a job, but I do,' she said.

'So lie,' the girl said. 'Call in sick. Look, if you're a nurse—'

'Please do it,' the woman on the ground said. 'This young lady is so right. We're all here together because we oppose the exploitation of our city. Doesn't matter if we're Muslims, Christians, secular people, Socialists, gay people, gypsies. Nurse, you're not rich, you can't be happy about all the money these property developers are making out of ordinary folk. If we want to change things we have to make an effort to do something.'

'I do something every day,' Peri said. 'I look after sick people.'

She began to walk away.

She heard the girl say, 'You'll regret this.'

But it had no effect on her. Someone with designer dreadlocks was not going to put her on a guilt trip.

Then she heard the woman's voice. 'There are people still in the park, being gassed.'

And Peri knew it was true. Looking over towards Gezi she

could see a vast plume of smoke rising out of the trees. She also heard people screaming. Without help they could fall over and cause untold damage to themselves. Even distant proximity to tear gas was making her eyes sting. But if she could be there for people when they came out of the epicentre at least she'd be able to help. Peri turned back, soaked her headband in water and put it over her mouth.

Yiannis didn't hear a thing until Hakkı burst into his bedroom, his face white, his eyes staring.

'Look out of the window!' he yelled. 'Look out now!'

With a flourish he pulled Yiannis' bedroom curtains to one side and said, 'Come and look, man!'

Yiannis Negroponte wasn't an early riser. He looked at his clock – it was seven a.m. – before he staggered out of bed and went to the window.

'What is it?'

'There! There!'

Hakkı pointed but he hadn't needed to. The bulldozer outside the front gates was one of the biggest Yiannis had ever seen and, although it clearly wasn't going anywhere, it was surrounded by a group of men who looked as if they wanted to get it on the move.

'Fuck! Is that—'

'Öden! I told you he wouldn't give up,' Hakkı said.

Yiannis threw a pair of trousers on over his pyjamas and ran down the stairs and out of the house. Arriving at the front gate he saw Ahmet Öden at the back of the crowd of men around the bulldozer and he called him out.

'Öden! What do you think you're doing?'

The developer, resplendent in a fine Italian suit, came forward and smiled. 'Merely making the point that if you take my offer I am ready to take possession of this land immediately,' he said.

'Oh really? I've told you I don't want to sell.'

'In case you've changed your mind.'

'I haven't and I won't.'

Yiannis noticed that a few police officers stood behind Öden's men and he began to feel afraid. In some other parts of the city where residents had 'resisted change' they had been forcibly evicted. Was that going to happen here? Surely it couldn't. He hadn't agreed to sell the house.

'Well, we're here. Ready.'

Yiannis looked at the men and vehicles outside his house. On the right side of the Negroponte house was an empty piece of land and then another house that was almost identical. To the left was a smaller building on a larger plot of land.

'Why do you want this house so much, Öden?' Yiannis asked. 'Why not this one, or this?'

He pointed to his neighbours. He hadn't thought about this before but now that he did it made him wonder whether Öden somehow knew more than he was letting on about the property.

'I want to build a hotel,' Öden said. 'I've explained this. The best hotel in the city.'

'So why not build it where the Alans' place is on the corner?' Hakkı said. 'It's more prominent and it will be easier for taxis and buses to park down the side of the building.'

Öden's face reddened. 'I don't want the Alans' place, I want this one!' he said.

'Why?'

'Because it's perfect for . . . Because I do! I want the Negroponte House, all right? Now, money. What will it take . . .?'

'You're wasting your time,' Yiannis said. 'We're not selling. I've told you before and I'm telling you again.'

Ahmet Öden, his fist up to his mouth, paused for a moment

and then he said, 'Then we'll have to wait until you do choose to sell, won't we?'

'We won't sell.'

'Yes, but if you do—'

'This is intimidation,' Hakkı said. 'Come, Mr Negroponte, we must call the police.'

Öden laughed. 'What for? I've got the police here if you want to speak to them.'

Hakkı looked at the uniformed officers standing behind Öden and said, 'Those? Some kids in blue? No, I mean the real police.'

'These are the—'

'No, they're not.'

Hakkı pulled Yiannis inside the house and picked up the phone. 'We can't have the police here! We can't! And how can we call the police when we've got them supporting Öden on our doorstep?' Yiannis wasn't hysterical but he was close.

Hakkı dialled. 'Because we are calling Inspector İkmen,' he said.

Yiannis shook his head. 'Who?'

'Fatma Hanım's husband from Ticarethane Sokak,' Hakkı said. Then, seeing that Yiannis still didn't get it, he said, 'Çetin Bey, the homicide detective.'

'Oh. Oh, yes, I know but . . . Oh no! Ah, but isn't he the one who—'

Hakkı held a hand up to silence him. Then he said into the phone, 'Can I speak to Inspector İkmen, please?' There was a pause and then he said, 'Yes, I'll hold.'

Yiannis sat down, shaking a little. İkmen. They'd conversed once in the street just after one of Yiannis' magic shows. Before Yiannis had been born, İkmen and his brother had visited the Negroponte house with their mother. She'd been some sort of seer who Anastasia had consulted to read tarot cards for her.

İkmen had talked about his visits with great affection and Yiannis had wondered if he'd been trying to get an invitation into the house. He had wondered sometimes what the policeman remembered from those days. What he did know was that he worked in homicide. He was working on a case that was all over the media. Quite rightly.

He heard Hakkı say into the phone, 'OK, I'll call back later.'

Then, when he'd put the phone down, Yiannis said, 'But if we get İkmen to visit, does it mean he'll have to come inside the house?'

'It would be rude not to invite him in,' the old man said. 'But we can manage a short visit, can't we?'

'Maybe.' Yiannis bit his lip.

'Well, we have to.'

The small notebook that had been in Ariadne Savva's desk drawer was now with a translator but İkmen had Kerim Gürsel on the phone and he had news. He was also awfully lively by the sound of his voice. İkmen had to make a big effort not to bring him down.

'Dr Akyıldız is also working on that skeleton found at the Galatasaray Lise.'

'Inspector Süleyman's—'

'Yes, no news there. But for us, sir, it's good. Dr Akyıldız knew Ariadne Savva and she's actually working on a skeleton that she dug up in Edirnekapı. It's Byzantine and Dr Akyıldız thinks it might have been a defender of the city, you know back in 1453 . . .'

He was gabbling, which was annoying, but İkmen just put up with it. Then he said something that did make him listen.

'Dr Savva however believed that the body was the last Byzantine emperor.'

'Constantine Palaiologos?'

'If that was his name, yes.'

Legend had it that at one point the victorious Turks had paraded the head of someone they believed was the emperor but it had turned out not to be him.

'Why did Dr Savva think that this body was the last emperor?'

'Dr Akyıldız says it's because of a sword that was found with the body. It bears the crest of the Byzantines, you know, the eagle thing . . .'

İkmen rolled his eyes. 'The eagle thing, yes the two-headed eagle.'

'That's it, but it also had jewels in the hilt. Lots of them. They're all gone now, stolen years ago.'

'So Dr Savva thought that the body was that of Constantine Palaiologos because of a jewelled sword.'

'Kings have jewelled swords, don't they?'

'Kerim, the Byzantines were a very opulent civilisation,' İkmen said. 'I don't think only the emperor would have had a jewelled sword. I'd be interested to know what her colleagues at the museum felt about this.'

'Not a lot,' Kerim said.

'Why?'

'Dr Savva was keeping the skeleton very much to herself and Dr Akyıldız. It's at the forensic laboratory. Dr Savva's colleagues at the Archaeological Museum don't know about it.'

'At all?'

'Not according to Dr Akyıldız,' Kerim said. 'She says she was never comfortable with the situation but she's also fascinated by this skeleton herself.'

'Does she think it's the body of Palaiologos?' İkmen asked.

'I don't know. I think she's undecided. The only way to really find out would be to compare DNA from the skeleton to that of any living descendants of the Byzantine royal family. And this is where it gets interesting because Dr Savva asked Dr Akyıldız if she would do this.'

'When?'

'Two weeks ago.'

'Using whom?' İkmen asked. 'As far as I know, which isn't very far, all the Palaiologi are dead.'

'Don't know,' Kerim said. 'It never happened, of course, and Dr Akyıldız has no idea whose tissue Dr Savva was going to bring to her. There are still old Greek families in the city, though, aren't there?'

'Yes, but they're not royalty,' İkmen said. 'Some of the Byzantine nobles and priests escaped the worst excesses of the conquest, but the royal family all died.'

'I don't know then,' Kerim said. 'I've got my next appointment in half an hour and the traffic's insane, so I have to go.'

'OK. This is the priest at the Aya Triada, yes?'

'Yes. Although how close I'll be able to get in the car I don't know.'

İkmen put the phone down. The Greek church of Aya Triada was on Meşelik Sokak just off İstiklal Caddesi at the top end, nearest Taksim Square and Gezi Park. From what he'd been told by other officers, that whole area was chaos. In the early hours of the morning hundreds of police had moved in on the protesters with tear gas and water cannon. Now, so he'd heard, rather than disperse the protesters, the police action had brought more people on to the streets in support of them. Kemal had still been in bed when he'd left for work that morning. İkmen hoped his son was still there and not getting a face full of tear gas. Why the police had been ordered to break up the protest so violently, he didn't know and couldn't condone. What was happening had been coming for a long time. Why such a knee-jerk reaction?

His phone rang.

'İkmen.'

'Çetin Bey, this is Hakkı Bey from the Negroponte House.' The voice was old and breathless. Hakkı Bey was Madam Anastasia Negroponte's last surviving retainer. He was one of the few people still living who could remember Çetin İkmen's mother.

'Hakkı Bey, are you in trouble?' İkmen said. 'How can I help?'

'It is Ahmet Öden,' he said. 'He has a bulldozer and police outside Madam's house. It has not been sold to him. This is intimidation, Çetin Bey!'

İkmen felt his face flush with fury. 'I'm on my way,' he said as he put his jacket on. 'Do nothing, Hakkı Bey, and don't let them into the property.'

'I would never do that,' the old man said.

'Good.' İkmen put the phone down.

This time a developer had gone too far. Öden didn't even own the site and he was preparing to knock it down. Why was he so dead set on that one particular house anyway? It was hardly the biggest and best site for a hotel in the area.

'Inspector Süleyman?'

'Yes.' He held the phone in the crook of his neck as he attempted to type into his computer at the same time as taking the call.

'It's Aylın Akyıldız. I have the result from the carbon fourteen test performed on your Galatasaray skeleton.'

'Oh, yes. What have you discovered?'

He watched Ömer Mungun eat two portions of börek at his desk. Earlier he'd been too anxious to eat because he'd been worried about his sister. Now he knew she'd called in sick and

87

so wasn't anywhere near Taksim he'd regained his usual good spirits and appetite.

'Any carbon dating technique used on material post 1945 does have to be regarded as slightly open to error because of the atomic bombs that fell on Japan in that year,' she said.

Süleyman widened his eyes. 'Really?'

'The whole world suffered in one way or another,' she said. 'But anyway, the tests have shown that your dead man was buried some time in the 1950s. Mid-fifties is most likely.'

'Mid-fifties.' That successfully ruled out the maths teacher from the 1970s, who would have just been a child at the time.

Ömer looked up from his börek. Süleyman said, 'Our man at the Lise dates from the mid-1950s.'

Ömer nodded.

'So not a recent death, but Dr Sarkissian and I both agree that it was a violent one,' Dr Akyıldız said. 'I hope you like historical research, Inspector.'

He said he didn't – much – and put the phone down.

'So it's unsolved murders of the 1950s,' Ömer said as he finished his börek and brushed the crumbs off his shirt.

'In part, yes,' Süleyman said. 'But the 1950s were a complex time in Turkey.'

'What they call the Cold War?'

'Oh, we were very anti-communist in those days and Russia was most definitely the enemy,' Süleyman said. 'We were also governed by a prime minister the nation later executed called Adnan Menderes. He allowed more Islam in public life than had been seen in the early days of the Republic. But he was executed for violating the constitution and also for allowing a terrible series of anti-Greek riots to take place here in İstanbul. Like the 1970s, the 1950s were a time of great political turmoil. Our man could be a Russian spy, an American spy, a supporter of Menderes or one of his enemies. Or maybe he's even a Greek. I don't know whether all the Greeks killed in the 1955 riots were accounted for or not. I think they were. But look it up, Ömer, and try to find out the names of any missing persons during that time. Concentrate on the well off.'

Chapter 8

'What are you doing here?' Çetin İkmen asked the group of uniformed constables slumped against some trees outside the Negroponte house.

The one with the most agreeable expression on his face stood up a little straighter and said, 'Supporting this demolition.'

'Who told you to do this?' İkmen said. 'Where are you boys from?'

'Ayakapı.'

'You were ordered here from Ayakapı?'

'Yes.'

The bulldozer was massive and it was surrounded by a group of workmen who looked as if they meant business. Ahmet Öden, however, was nowhere to be seen.

'So where's Öden?' İkmen asked the slumping officers.

'Dunno.'

İkmen was irritated by their attitude. 'Dunno, *sir,* to you, boy.'

'Sir.'

İkmen walked through the crowd of workmen towards the house. He could see Yiannis Negroponte standing behind the gates of his house, his face white. Beside him, the small, shrunken form of Hakkı.

'Ah, Inspector, you have come!' the old man said as Yiannis opened the gate and let İkmen in.

Hakkı bent down to kiss İkmen's hands and, although he

wasn't keen on this old custom of respect that dated from the Ottoman Empire, he let him do it. Hakkı came from a different time and such traditions provided comfort to him.

'Çetin Bey, this Öden man persecutes us with his demands to have this house,' Hakkı said. 'I called you because I know you are a good man. Maybe one of very few now. And because Öden has police.'

'Öden has a few young constables who know as much about the law as I do about rock climbing,' İkmen said.

The two men led him into the house. Although İkmen couldn't recall the Negropontes' living room in detail he remembered enough about it to know that it hadn't changed. The Louis Quatorze furniture was still overstuffed, its gilding scuffed and faded, and the carpet was dull and covered in dust. Yiannis offered him a glass of home-made lemonade which he took; it was hot. There was no sign of Madam Anastasia anywhere.

İkmen asked if he could smoke, was told that he could, and then he sat down. 'Tell me about Öden,' he said. 'How long has he been offering to buy this house?'

'Since the new year,' Yiannis said. 'He telephoned in January. I told him I wasn't interested.'

'Did he offer you a good price?'

'I've been offered better. Sometimes I get talking to tourists and when they see where I live they want to buy.'

'Yes, but with respect,' İkmen said, 'tourists don't know the local market. And they tend to be well off. Was Öden's offer reasonable?'

Yiannis shrugged. 'It was OK. But it was irrelevant. I don't want to sell. My mother is old and a move now could kill her. And this is her home.'

'So you turned him down?'

'Yes, and I've been turning him down periodically ever since,' he said. 'It's only in the last week it's really escalated. We've never had bulldozers before. I don't understand why he wants this house so much. He only wants to knock it down to build a hotel. Why here? There are far better places for a hotel. There's lots of empty land down towards Cankurtaran railway station.'

'But you're in the midst of all the monuments here,' İkmen said. 'Right on your doorstep.'

'So why not choose the Alans' house on the corner? It's got a bigger plot and there's more space for buses and taxis to park.' He shook his head. 'I don't understand and it's worrying me. What if Öden forces us out? Now he's got police backup and the world seems to have disappeared over to Gezi Park. What if he breaks in here? My mother could die from the shock.'

İkmen put his hand in his pocket and took out a card. 'This has my mobile number,' he said. 'If anything like that happens, call me, day or night.'

'But aren't you working—'

'Doesn't matter.' İkmen gave him the card. 'I'm local, you're local, we need to look after our neighbours. And Öden can't do this. He doesn't own this property and if you don't want to sell then that is up to you.'

'The gypsies didn't want to sell in Sulukule,' Yiannis said. 'Or the people of Gizlitepe.'

'That was slum clearance. This is an historic building. It's different.'

Yiannis stood up. 'Is it?' he said. 'I know that you mean well, Inspector, but you know as well as I do that if these developers want something then they get it one way or another. What do they care about heritage? I'm sorry, I need to give my mother her medication now.'

He left. Alone with the old man, İkmen said, 'And what do you think, Hakkı Bey?'

92

He sighed. 'I think that Ahmet Öden comes from a family with an unfortunate history.'

'Unfortunate how?' İkmen lit another cigarette and offered one to Hakkı, who took it but put it in his pocket.

'I know you were only a child in 1955 but I remember that year well,' Hakkı said. 'It was a terrible one for this family. Nikos Bey was murdered and Madam was beaten so badly by those nationalistic animals it damaged her for life. That rumour the Menderes government spread about Greeks attacking Ataturk's old house in Salonika was a lie. I knew it and so did they. It was just an excuse to loot, rape and kill. And you know who was one of the people at the head of that mob? Taha Öden, Ahmet Öden's father.'

'You know this? For sure?'

'I knew Taha's father, Resat the carpenter. He was a decent man. The Ödens were a good family, except for Taha. A bully, a religious fanatic and corrupt,' Hakkı said. 'He pretended to be a carpenter like his father but he was just a cowboy. He took people's money but whatever he made fell down. When I heard about the attacks on the Greeks on the morning of the sixth of September, I went to İstiklal to Madam and Nikos Bey's shop. But I was too late. Nikos Bey was dead, Madam was badly injured and the baby, Yiannis, had gone. As I carried Madam out of there, I had to beat off men who wanted me to prove I was a Muslim. I stabbed one in the arm. I admit it and I will never regret it. But I also saw Taha Öden in the crowd. Yelling "Death to the Infidels!" he had a priest on the ground and he was pulling out his beard. If I hadn't had Madam in my arms I would have attacked him. I knew the priest and he died in those riots. I still feel ashamed I did nothing to help him.'

'You saved Madam Anastasia's life,' İkmen said.

'What life?' he shrugged. 'Haunted by ghosts from the past, always in pain.'

'She got her son Yiannis back.'

Hakkı said nothing.

'Didn't she?'

'I don't know whether Taha Öden brought his son up to have his opinions,' the old man said. 'But Çetin Bey, he is one of those who has stated publicly that he wants the Aya Sofya to be turned back into a mosque. Now I try to be a good Muslim. Most of the time I fail but I try. What I don't do is pick fights with people of other religions. It's wrong. Aya Sofya was a church, then a mosque, then Ataturk stopped any more religious argument by making it into a museum. He did that for a good reason. It works as a museum, it's right.'

'My opinion entirely,' İkmen said.

'And some of those who want it to be a mosque are of a type I cannot take to,' Hakkı said. 'I find them bigoted. I also observe that a lot of those who have made their money in development of housing and office space are amongst their number. I think they dream of a new empire and I also think they use religion as a weapon. Ahmet Öden is one of these, as I am sure you know, Çetin Bey. But I also think that hate is in his blood too. What his father did to that priest will remain with me forever, and if he has passed that down to his son then we are dealing with something evil. Ahmet Öden wants this house because it is owned by Greeks. That's why he wants it so much and that is why he can't wait to knock it down.'

By the time İkmen left the Negroponte house, Ahmet Öden had returned. When he saw İkmen he frowned.

'What do you want?' he said. 'Don't you have some woman's death to investigate?'

'And don't you have some other, real building projects to work on?' İkmen countered. 'Mr Öden, you don't own the Negroponte House and the owners have told you, and me, that

94

they don't want to sell. You need to take your bulldozer and your workmen away. You have no business here.'

'And what business do you have telling me what to do?' He moved his face close to İkmen's. 'The old woman is a vegetable and the so-called son isn't even related to her.'

'Madam Anastasia has recognised him as her son, Yiannis,' İkmen said.

'Oh, and do you think that he'd submit to a DNA test if she suddenly asked him to take one?'

'That is irrelevant,' İkmen said. 'In law she has recognised him as her heir and that is all that matters. And he doesn't want to sell his house to you, Mr Öden. That is his right.'

'I have police—'

'Some idiot has allowed you to co-opt a few half-civilised constables,' İkmen said. 'Now get your equipment and your men off the public highway. I'll give you until six o'clock this evening.'

'Oh? And then what will you do?'

İkmen began to walk away. 'Make sure you don't find out,' he said. 'What you're doing here, Mr Öden, is intimidation and that is against the law.'

As he turned his head away he heard Ahmet Öden laugh.

As he'd suspected, Kerim Gürsel hadn't been able to get his car anywhere near Taksim Square or the Aya Triada Greek Orthodox church. It was mid-afternoon and the whole area was covered with a layer of smoke. The atmosphere was strange. Part menacing, with police officers stalking the streets in riot helmets and carrying shields, and part carnival with singing and people in bright clothes.

On the face of it the Aya Triada was the same as it always had been. There were chickens running about in the garden and the old custodian who lived on the site was doing his car up outside his flat. The only thing that was different was a tall, thin woman who was sitting on the grass looking exhausted. He walked up to her. 'Is everything all right?'

When she looked up he saw a strong, angular, mannish face that was slightly familiar. 'Just shattered,' she said. 'Do you have any idea why the police are firing tear gas canisters at people? I've treated two people rendered unconscious by canisters in the last hour. They're not supposed to do that, are they?'

For a moment Kerim didn't know what to say. He knew that firing at people was strictly forbidden but he'd seen it happen. That it was occurring here was not something that pleased him, but it didn't surprise him either. Not all of his colleagues were like Çetin İkmen.

'You say you treated people, are you a doctor?' he asked.

'I'm a nurse,' she said. 'Are you going to the church?'

'Yes,' he said. 'But are you all right? Is there anything I can do for you?'

'Not unless you can stop the police hurting people. The irony of it is that my brother is a police officer.' She laughed, but without humour.

Then Kerim knew who she was. He sat down beside her. 'You're Ömer Mungun's sister,' he said.

She widened her eyes. 'How do you know that?'

'You have the same laugh,' Kerim said. 'I too am a detective.' He offered her his hand. 'Kerim Gürsel.'

She took it. 'Peri Mungun. You don't know if my brother is involved in any of this, do you, Detective Gürsel?'

'I believe he's working on an historical murder,' he said. 'So no.'

She shook her head. 'I know you probably can't say anything about what is happening here, but I think that if the authorities want to assert some real control they ought to listen to the people. They can't keep on smashing their way through people's concerns and telling them they're wrong all the time. They need to listen. I go and eat my lunch in Gezi Park every day in the summer. I look forward to it. What am I going to do with a shopping mall? Or a mosque?'

'People need somewhere to pray,' he said.

'I know that but I need somewhere to eat. I'm sorry if that offends your religious sensibilities . . .'

'Oh, if people need to pray they can always find somewhere.'

They both looked at the man who had come to sit with them. Wearing black robes and with a long, brownish ginger beard, he was a Greek priest and he was probably only just thirty.

'Are you folk all right?' he asked. 'You're welcome to sit in the garden or the church if you want to. In view of what's going on . . . well . . .'

'I'm here to see Father Diogenes,' Kerim said.

The priest, whose face was rather pudgy and gnome-like said, 'Detective Gürsel?'

'Yes.'

He held out his hand. 'I am Father Diogenes.'

They shook hands.

'And the young lady . . .'

'Oh, we're not together,' Peri said. 'I'm a nurse. I've just been trying to help people with tear gas injuries.'

'Bless you for that,' the priest said.

Peri stood up. 'I don't know about that,' she said, 'I lied to my employers so I could do it.'

'Then you lied in a good cause. God will understand.'

'Maybe.' Peri left.

'So, Detective Mungun,' Diogenes said, 'you want to know about Ariadne Savva.'

'Yes.'

'Then let's go into my office in the church. This smoke makes my eyes sting.'

His office wasn't much more than a cupboard. It was somewhat chaotic and reminded Kerim of İkmen's lair at Police Headquarters. Not that İkmen had a chicken under his chair. Diogenes shooed it out.

'Our custodian Ali Bey keeps them for eggs,' he said. 'Somehow they get in.' He waved his hands at Kerim. 'Find a seat if you can. Move the books.'

Every surface was covered with books in Greek and the two chairs in front of Diogenes' desk were no exception. Kerim moved two piles on to the floor and sat down.

Diogenes leaned on his desk and said, 'So, Ariadne Savva. What can I say? When she came to work at the museum she joined our congregation here at the Aya Triada. Don't misunderstand me, Detective, we have some very nice congregants here, but nobody like Ariadne. Our people talk about the Byzantine past, but Ariadne lived it. It was everything to her.'

'It was her job.'

'And more.'

There was a pause and then Kerim said, 'Father Diogenes, did you know that Ariadne was pregnant?'

'Ah.' He looked down. 'Yes, I did. But if you're going to ask me who the father was, then I'm going to have to disappoint you because I don't know.'

'Did you ask?'

'I did, she wouldn't say. But she was happy about being pregnant. She seemed relaxed and so I didn't press her. She was an adult woman, after all. I told her that when the child was born she could count on the church for support. She seemed happy about that.'

'When we searched her apartment we found no clothes or equipment for a baby,' Kerim said.

Father Diogenes sighed. 'Ah well, some people believe, you see, that it is bad luck to buy anything for an expected baby until the child is born.'

'But she was alone, in a foreign country. Her parents didn't even know she was pregnant.'

'Then I don't know, Detective,' he said.

'Do you think that the father of the child could have been a member of your congregation?'

'Our congregants are mainly over seventy,' the priest said. 'And Ariadne wasn't close to any of them. She was aloof. She came to church, sometimes she talked to me and then she left. I think that the father of the child, God willing the little one is still alive, is more likely to be a work colleague or maybe even a man she left behind in Greece. I don't know if such a person even exists. I will speak to my congregants on Sunday and try to find out if anyone knows anything. I don't know everything, after all. I'm not the Pope.' And then he laughed. 'How could I be? They don't take Greeks, do they, the Catholics?' His face dropped. 'Nobody takes Greeks, not these days.'

Turkey's neighbour was in a terrible financial mess and Kerim left the priest to absorb his own obvious disappointment for a moment before he spoke again. 'Father Diogenes, do you know if any of the old Greek families in the city are related to the last Byzantine dynasty?'

'The Palaiologi?'

'Yes.'

He smiled. 'I could ask you why you want to know such a thing, but I won't, because I imagine you won't tell me,' he said. 'And because the answer is absolutely no. They all died during the conquest, and those who were abroad at the time died out not much later. Rumours of Byzantium's demise, Sergeant, are not exaggerated.'

Only the details involving spies were alien to Ömer. What had happened to the Greeks in 1955 was like the stories he'd heard whispered in his grandparents' house in Mardin round the fire in winter. Stories about people who were 'other', and how that had worked against them. Started in response to a rumour that Greeks had attacked Ataturk's old house in Salonika in Greece, hunting the 'other' had become the thing to do on İstiklal Caddesi for two insane days in September 1955. Businesses had been looted, women raped and people killed. Accounts of priests being forcibly circumcised made Ömer's stomach muscles tighten. In the scheme of things, this had only happened a short time ago and there were people still living who remembered it.

In a way he wanted to share these old, yellowing records with one person and one person alone, Peri. But he knew he wasn't allowed to do that and he also knew that she was much more volatile than he. If Peri read these papers she'd want to go and shout at people in the street. She'd grab hold of every man over seventy and ask him if he'd been involved.

Just one example was that of the Mavroyeni family. They'd had a jeweller's shop almost opposite the Galatasaray Lise. On the first day of the riots two of the female assistants had been raped, the owner Konstantine Mavroyeni had died of a heart attack and the shop had been stripped. However, because all the incidents had been witnessed by Turks who tried to help their Greek neighbours as well as by foreigners, everything that had happened was well documented. And when, in 1961, the Prime Minister at the time of the riots, Adnan Menderes, had been put on trial for violating the constitution as well as instituting actions against the İstanbul Greeks, every detail had been pored over. This included who had been injured by the mob, who had died and who was missing. The last category contained no names except that of a child under one year old. Yiannis Negroponte had disappeared from the back of his parents' tailoring shop. But Yiannis wasn't the man in the Lise garden. Nor was his father, Nikos, who had been killed and whose body lay in Şişli Greek Orthodox cemetery.

Ömer felt a twinge of disappointment. If the body wasn't Greek then identifying it was going to be difficult. So far, old murder cases from the time had also yielded bodies that had been identified. A spy had to be a possibility, which had a frisson about it, but which was almost impossible to follow up. Some spies had been in the country legally, but under false names, others had got in illegally. The author of the James Bond novels, Ian Fleming, had been in the city at the time and he had worked for British Intelligence. But the body wasn't his. Whose was it?

Only a Cem Atasu, a man of around the right age who had been reported missing in 1954, even remotely fitted the profile. But he'd had rickets and so it wasn't him. In spite of everything, Ömer held on to the idea that the body in the Lise had to be Greek. Was it possible that the body was that of a Greek man who had no family? There weren't many Greeks living in İstanbul any more; most had moved out post-1955. But they existed and Ömer knew he could track them down. If no one else, then Inspector İkmen would know where they were. He knew everyone. But it was tricky. Not only was İkmen busy with the death of, coincidentally, a Greek, he and Ömer's boss Mehmet Süleyman were not really communicating. Speaking to İkmen would have to be something Ömer did when he was alone.

As his men began to drive their vehicles away from the front of the Negroponte house, Ahmet Öden seethed. In retrospect he should have gone higher than Commissioner Teker. It was well known that she was no friend to people like him. But he had imagined that his name would frighten her. It hadn't. Now he'd have to do something else. The idea had crystallised when he'd been talking to Çetin İkmen. Although he hadn't imagined he'd have to actually use it.

The first part was relatively easy. He'd wait for the retainer to go out and then he'd speak to Negroponte through his gates if necessary. He'd be awfully conciliatory. Getting to the old woman, however, would be another matter. That would take planning.

Chapter 9

Gezi was exploding. Nar Hanım and Madonna had been there all day and Nar had phoned to tell her all about it.

'Pembe Hanım, you have to come here,' she'd said. 'They're giving out gas masks and everyone you can think of is in Gezi. There are some gorgeous young men . . .'

But Pembe hadn't been able to leave Sinem. When she'd woken that morning, just after Kerim left for work, she'd been in a bad way. Although she'd slept all night, it had been a drugged sleep which had left her feeling sick. She hadn't eaten all day. Kerim wouldn't be pleased.

Pembe poured herself a glass of wine and sat in front of the television.

'Why isn't there anything on the news about Gezi?' Sinem said.

She was even paler than usual and her cheeks were dark and hollow.

'You know who controls the media,' Pembe said. 'Why do you even have to ask?'

'Because I hoped that maybe I was having a bad dream.' She shrugged. 'Do you think that these protests will change things?'

In districts like Şişli and Cihangir people had started coming out at night in support of the protesters. Housewives banging pots and pans, old men waving pictures of Ataturk. There were rumours of other protests in other parts of the city, and extra police were being drafted in from all over the country. But they were up against the State, a freely elected and legitimate government.

'I don't know,' Pembe said. 'I hope so.'

'They might draft Kerim in. That's what worries me. He will feel torn.'

'Kerim Bey knew what he was doing when he joined the police,' Pembe said. 'Even if he does get drafted to Gezi, he'll do what's right. You know that. But he's working on the death of that woman who was pregnant.'

'What woman?'

'Some Greek.'

'Did he tell you that?'

'Yes.' She lit a cigarette.

Sinem looked sad. It was more than the pain. She had that all the time.

'He cares for you more than anyone, you know that, don't you, Sinem?'

As her face lost weight Sinem's eyes were beginning to look huge. She had the appearance of someone young and yet very old at the same time. Pembe often found it hard to look at her these days.

'Yes,' she said. 'But you know it's not enough.'

'If you mean what I think you mean then that could be taken care of. Easily.'

There was some kids' programme on TV involving weird, brightly coloured balls of fur.

'I'd like to be in love,' Sinem said. A red fur ball screamed and a yellow one laughed. 'I'd like to know how that feels.'

And before she could stop herself, Pembe said, 'Wouldn't we all, darling.' And then she realised what she'd said and she lowered her head.

* * *

104

'I knew nothing of this,' Professor Bozdağ said.

Sitting in İkmen's office he looked far less venerable than he had when they'd first met at Arto Sarkissian's laboratory. He was also tired – it was late – and he was upset.

'Constantine Palaiologos died with his troops when Mehmet the Conqueror took the city,' he continued. 'His body was never found. Why would Dr Savva suddenly and miraculously dig it up and have DNA she could compare it with? It's a fantasy.'

'Not according to Dr Akyıldız, the forensic archaeologist,' İkmen said.

'And what was she doing concealing what Savva had found? That isn't professional. What did she have to say for herself?'

'Only what I told you,' İkmen said. 'Dr Savva believed that the body she had found was that of the last Byzantine emperor. But she wanted to be absolutely sure about that before she presented her evidence to you and the rest of the department.'

'Akyıldız should have come to me as soon as Savva approached her.'

'This meant a lot to Ariadne Savva.'

'Of course! And she was trying to keep all the glory for herself!' He shook his head.

İkmen's late father had been an academic. As a child Çetin had seen his father's colleagues figuratively stab each other in the back many times. He recognised the form that the professor's rage was taking. Ariadne Savva had tried to hold on to what would have become Bozdağ's 'find' had she told him. And by doing a DNA comparison to boot she had clearly been planning to present him with a fait accompli. She may even have gone on to publish a paper if the body had proved to be that of Constantine Palaiologos. But how could that be?

'All the Palaiologi died.' Bozdağ's words mirrored İkmen's thoughts.

'Yes,' İkmen said. 'Although I imagine there must be descendants somewhere. You probably heard about the case of that English king where a relative was discovered in Australia or somewhere . . .'

'Richard III, yes,' the professor said. 'Mmm. That was a long shot. But is it the exception that proves the rule? As far as we know the last Palaiologos died in Barbados in the seventeenth century, without issue.'

'Perhaps Ariadne Savva knew different.'

'Well if she did then she should have shared that information with her colleagues.' His face reddened. 'Her particular interest had always been expanding knowledge about the life of the Empress Zoe, as far as I was concerned. Had I known I couldn't trust the wretched woman I would never have employed her.'

'Well, we will never know,' İkmen said. 'But Professor, I will have to re-interview your staff in light of this new information. It's possible someone else knew about Ariadne's find.'

'Whoever made her pregnant!' he snapped.

'That could be the case, yes.'

What sounded like the march of a Roman battalion out in the corridor made speech temporarily impossible. It went on: the scraping of riot shields against the walls, the clicking sound of plastic bullets being loaded. İkmen watched the professor shudder and only just managed to conceal his own antipathy.

When the many boots had passed he said, 'I am told they are reinforcements from Mersin.'

'For Gezi?'

'That is my understanding,' İkmen said.

The professor was looking into his eyes and İkmen returned his gaze. They both knew what the other was thinking although neither of them acknowledged it. But when the professor left, İkmen did offer him an escort back to his home in Nişantaşı.

106

'You have to go past Gezi,' he said, 'it may be dangerous.'

'In what way?' Bozdağ said. 'You think kids and fellow academics are going to have at me with knives?'

'No . . .'

'No, I didn't think so either,' he said. 'I think I would be at far greater risk from your men from Mersin, don't you?'

Peri was soaked. But, unlike the woman she'd seen lifted off her feet by a jet of water from the TOMA cannon, she wasn't bruised. And it was preferable to the tear gas which had made her fear her eyes might melt.

When she'd left Kerim Gürsel at the Aya Triada, she'd had no other intention than to go home. But when she'd reached Gezi she just couldn't. Iris, the girl with the dreadlocks, had taken her to a man who had fallen over and cut his leg. Amazingly there'd been a ready supply of cleaning materials and Steri-Strips.

'Medicine we can get,' Iris had told her. 'It's people who know what to do with it that we lack.'

Pharmacists had to be helping them, or doctors. Iris kept Peri busy well into the dark hours. More police arrived with yet more TOMA vehicles. People got hurt and yet there was also a carnival atmosphere too. Two headscarfed women smiled and laughed as they handed out simit and drinks, while a man on stilts juggled with flaming batons. What came as a shock to Peri were all the pictures of Ataturk that seemed to suddenly be everywhere. When she'd been a child such pictures had been common, but in recent years their numbers had started to dwindle, and it was only now that she had noticed. Had the present government been trying to cut the founder of the Republic out of everyday life, or was that just her paranoia speaking? The darkened facade of the Ataturk Cultural Centre seemed to point towards the former. Once it had been a hub of artistic life but now the government wanted to replace it with an opera house and a mosque. But then, was that a bad thing? It was, to Peri's way of thinking, just another ugly 1960s block. It was what it symbolised – cultural exchange – that mattered. So was cultural exchange under attack here?

A little girl carrying half dead flowers in a basket gave Peri one and said, 'Wear it for the park, abla.'

She was ragged and a bit dirty and Peri thought that she was probably a little Roma girl. She expected to be charged for the flower but she took it anyway and stuck it in a buttonhole in her cardigan.

'That's it,' the little girl said and then she was gone. Peri chided herself for thinking that the kid was trying to make money but she smiled. If the girl had made a few kuruş out of the situation then who could blame her?

Peri looked at her watch. It was almost midnight. She should go home. She had to get up for work in the morning, she couldn't just take another day off. But she wanted to.

'You know what he's calling us now, that man who runs this country?'

Iris was at her side eating börek, her face curled into a sneer. 'Hooligans and looters,' she said. 'Have you seen anyone looting? Seen any bad behaviour except by the fucking police? His police?'

She hadn't. 'No.'

'We're politically engaged is all,' the girl said. 'Finally. Just because we've had enough of his developers and his cronies ruining our neighbourhoods and our parks. Enough of the rhetoric dividing people. I don't give a shit if someone's Christian, atheist, Muslim or queer and I won't be told I have to give a shit.'

Peri looked away. Was the girl saying things she knew someone like Peri would want to hear? But how did she know who she was? How could she?

108

And then the sound of marching cut across the laughter and the conversation that had sprung up around makeshift homes in tents and under trees.

'Oh, no!'

Peri stood on tiptoe to see over Iris's head. A mass of dark figures marching in time signalled what her brother always called 'boots on the ground'. The police had called up reinforcements. Just outside what had become the Gezi encampment, they stopped. Inside the camp everyone stopped to look at them.

Under her breath, Iris said, 'Bastards.'

But the officers didn't move. Their faces hidden behind visors, they could have been anyone or anything. Peri's phone rang.

'Hello?'

Her voice sounded loud in the almost silence. She lowered it. 'Yes?'

'Where are you?' her brother said. 'You should have finished work hours ago.'

The men behind the visors moved forwards slightly. The crowd in front of her moved, almost, to meet them.

'I'm in Gezi,' she said. 'I've been here all day.'

'*What!*'

'People were injured, Ömer,' she said. 'What was I supposed to do? Leave them?'

'You didn't go to work?'

'I called in sick.'

He didn't answer.

She said, 'This was more important. I know you know that, Ömer.'

For a moment he was silent, then he said, 'I know that the situation is very dangerous. They've just sent in reinforcements.'

'I know. I can see them.'

'Then you . . .'

109

Peri held the phone away from her ear as people around her jostled to see what was happening.

'Ömer, they're surrounding the park,' she said. For the first time she felt a twinge of real fear.

'Then I will have to come and get you,' her brother said. 'Stay—'

'No!' The word came out loudly and violently and Peri noticed that people were looking at her. She dropped her gaze.

'No? What?'

She put her head down and whispered into her phone. 'Ömer,' she said, 'do you remember all those times when we were at school and we couldn't say what we really believed? Couldn't be who we really were in spite of everyone knowing exactly what we were because it gave them a licence to bully us? These people here are done with that. They're done with developers and hate speech and they are standing up for their rights.'

The visored men put their riot shields up. Peri felt her body shake but she said, 'So don't you dare come and get me. I'm here, now, because I want to be. And if you came here and mixed with these people you'd feel like that too.'

The reinforcements began beating their shields with their batons. Peri ended Ömer's call.

He sat in front of the gates he usually hid behind – doing things with his hands. Making things disappear, reappear, manifest out of nothing. He called it magic but it was just a load of tricks.

As he walked towards the Negroponte house, Ahmet Öden could hear the wall of sound from Taksim. Arseholes! What were they getting themselves so worked up about a park for? It was just a few trees and a bit of grass. It wasn't as if it was even a nice park. In the winter it was a lake of mud while in the summer it was dry and lifeless.

Yiannis Negroponte looked up and, for a moment, while he thought he was alone, he smiled. But then he saw Ahmet.

His face dropped. 'You're not supposed to be here,' he said.

'I come empty-handed and alone,' Ahmet said. 'A man out for a walk, that's all.'

'Men don't go for walks in cities that are as dangerous as this one is,' Yiannis said.

Ahmet looked around. 'There's no danger here in Sultanahmet that I can see. And you are out of your house.'

'I'm on my threshold,' said Yiannis. 'I live here. You live out on the Bosphorus. What do you want? Or need I ask?'

'Your house?' Ahmet hunkered down opposite Yiannis, who put a hand on his gate, clearly so he felt he could go inside at any time. 'No, not this time. I'd just like to talk if that's OK.'

'What about?'

'About what you want out of life.'

'Oh, so we're back to the several million lira you have offered me for this house. I told you, I don't want to sell. I won't sell. Bring your bulldozers back and I will die in this house together with my mother. Ahmet Bey, you either leave us alone or you get blood on your hands. There is no middle ground.'

Ahmet thought. What Negroponte had said was probably true, although, if he did have to kill the old woman and her son to get it, then so be it. Their deaths would complicate what he wanted to achieve, and people would ask questions which could hold up the work, but he wasn't where he was to even think about that.

'Yiannis—'

'Mr Negroponte.'

'Mr Negroponte. Look, I accept that you don't want to sell your house now.'

'Or ever.'

'OK, or ever,' Ahmet said. 'But I need to acquire property

in this area and so, if you're staying here, I'd like to be on good terms with you.'

'So I can help you to persuade some other poor bastard to sell to you?' He shook his head. 'I don't think so.'

Ahmet remained quiet for a moment and then he said, 'I don't want any of your neighbours' houses.'

'That's not what you just implied.'

Did Negroponte know why he wanted his house? He had to. He was no fool. But should Ahmet allude to it? He hadn't been planning to take that line.

He leaned in close and felt Yiannis cringe away from him. 'You know why I have to have your house, Mr Negroponte,' he said.

'No, I don't.'

'Yes, you do. You know what's *there* . . .'

Yiannis began to stand up but Ahmet dug his fingernails into the flesh on his hand.

'I've been into your house,' Ahmet said. 'Many years ago. Before you came from Germany. When I was just a builder on a job . . .'

He looked into Yiannis' eyes. A steady gaze met his and Ahmet was almost tempted to look away. What held him was the need to try and read what was in Yiannis' soul. But he came up with nothing. Ahmet dug his fingers still further into Yiannis' flesh.

'Take your hands off me.'

'Yiannis, Mr Negroponte—'

'That policeman, İkmen, he may be a Turk but he has a fair mind and this is assault.'

They looked down at their unnaturally conjoined hands at the same time. Blood had seeped on to Ahmet's fingers and behind his nails.

112

'If I show İkmen this—'

'Then you'll have to prove that I did it,' Ahmet said. 'You'll also have to prove I didn't do it while defending myself.'

The end of a scream funnelled up from Taksim and then what sounded like drumming began. Ahmet looked at Yiannis' blood on his fingers and felt excited.

'Take your hand off mine,' Yiannis said. 'I tell you this one more time or—'

'Or what?'

But Ahmet let him go.

Yiannis jumped to his feet. 'Get off my property, Mr Öden,' he said. 'Get off it and don't come back. I don't know why you want my house and I can't imagine why you would think that I would know. I don't know whether you've ever been inside the Negroponte House or not but I can assure you it is an ordinary, if shabby, house.'

'Then let me see it.'

'Had you not bullied me and my family, I gladly would,' Yiannis said. 'I don't know what fantasies you have about this place, but they have no foundation in reality. You may have seen my house many years ago, I don't know. But what you remember now is flawed. Go home, Mr Öden, and wash my dirty Greek blood from your hands before it taints your soul.'

When he got back to his car, Ahmet very carefully scraped the fragments of Yiannis Negroponte's flesh and blood into the sterile container he had acquired from the Internet. There was more than one way to get that 'Greek' out of his house. Ahmet knew what he'd seen all those years ago and, as soon as he got into that house, he'd see it again, whatever Yiannis Negroponte said.

İkmen got as far as his car before his phone rang.

'Sir, it's Ömer Mungun.'

'Ömer?'

He got behind the steering wheel and put the key in the ignition without turning it.

'Çetin Bey, I have a delicate situation,' he said.

'You also have a superior who is not me.'

There was a pause. Then Ömer said, 'Sir, my sister Peri is in Gezi Park. Reinforcements have recently gone out there.'

İkmen leaned back on his car's tattered headrest. He really wanted to go home and sleep.

'Where are you, Ömer?'

'I'm looking at you,' he said. 'Out of my office window.'

İkmen looked up and saw that the light was on in Süleyman's office. No Süleyman, of course, but then he was with Gonca if he wasn't being unfaithful to her somewhere. İkmen chided himself for being so fucking judgemental while at the same time feeling entirely justified in his opinions.

'Çetin Bey, if I try to get through our lines on my own, I doubt I'll make it. But if you come . . . I'd heard of you when I was back in Mardin,' he said. 'Everyone has heard of you. I must make sure that Peri doesn't get hurt.'

İkmen took a breath. He'd met Peri Mungun once. A tall, spare young woman, handsome rather than beautiful, who had that eastern Turkish dreaminess in her eyes. He suspected her religious beliefs were as obscure and unknowable as her brother's. To İkmen's consternation, most cops in recent years talked about faith. Ömer Mungun never did. İkmen let his breath out.

'Come and get in the car and we'll go there,' he said.

'To Taksim?'

'That's where Peri is, isn't it?'

In less than five minutes they were on their way.

Chapter 10

The two women behind her had turned out to be transsexuals. They'd also had their small tent burnt down by the police.

'They only let you join if you're a thug,' Peri heard one of them say to the other.

'And stupid,' the other replied.

'Oh, stupid's essential! If you're not stupid they don't give you a gun. Why would they?'

Peri knew that Ömer wasn't like that and felt that she should say something to them. But she'd also seen the police do some cruel, unnecessary and ridiculous things since she'd come to the park. And the more they tried to impose their will, the more the park people just dug their heels in. Slogans had begun to appear on the sides of the tents that remained. They said 'At least three beers' in reference to the Prime Minister's statement about good citizens having at 'at least' three children. There were some good cartoons of him too.

The expected push from the police hadn't come. No one knew why. Some people feared they were awaiting yet more reinforcements while others, of a more optimistic type, reckoned the protesters had them scared. Peri didn't know.

Iris and her dreadlocks walked over and said, 'Hi.'

'Hi.'

'You staying with us, Peri?' she asked. 'You've been great, we really appreciate it.'

She wanted her to commit and Peri didn't know that she could. It wasn't that she didn't want to, but she had responsibilities – and her brother – to consider. His phone call had made her think. 'I've got my job,' she said.

Iris shrugged. 'Nursing rich people.'

Peri had been able to tell immediately that Iris was from a wealthy family. Even without the dreadlocks and the tattoos, she reeked of the kind of privilege that had clung to the secular elites for generations. Now, pushed on to the back foot by the conservative majority from the countryside, they nevertheless still possessed a huge sense of entitlement. This protest came as much from them as it did from the transsexuals, the Roma and the Muslims who didn't approve of the current status quo.

'Blow it out,' Iris said. 'Some fat businessman who prays five times a day and has mistresses all over the city can afford to get himself another nurse.'

'Yes, but I can't afford to lose my job!'

They looked at each other and Peri felt Iris's disapproval.

'God, you want to be here when we change EVERYTHING, don't you?'

'Yes, but—'

'You'll get another job, you're a nurse!'

Some women started dancing accompanied by other women on bongo drums. Small fires had been lit and she could smell the delicious aroma of cooking meat. It made her empty stomach growl. She ignored it. A gulf had opened up between Peri and Iris and it was one that she resented.

'Look,' she said, 'I'm just an ordinary—'

'No, you're not, you're amazing!' Iris said. She put her hands on Peri's shoulders. 'You've done amazing things here today!'

Peri looked into her eyes and, although she could still see the gulf between them, she could also see Iris's sincerity. And everything around her underlined what she'd said about this being the point at which things changed. Peri knew she wanted them to, probably even more than Iris did. 'I—'

'Peri!'

One of Ömer's bony hands gripped her arm.

A baby had been found in a dustbin in Tarlabaşı but it wasn't Ariadne Savva's. The child, who had been taken to the Taksim Hospital, had been black. Somalis and some Ethiopians lived in the bedsits and damp flats of Tarlabaşı, refugees from the never-ending problems of Africa.

Kerim had considered the possibility that Ariadne Savva had maybe had an affair with a black man and had been to see the child. But the doctor who showed him the girl had said she would be surprised if the baby had any non-African blood. Kerim could only concur. He lifted the child's dead face up to his own and he could see no sign of Ariadne's features on it.

'I don't think that Pembe will be back tonight,' Sinem said.

He had thought that she was asleep, resting in his arms.

'Pembe does as Pembe wants,' he said.

The sound from the television, a nature programme about elephant seals, failed to drown out the music and the voices from Gezi. Earlier, some local residents had come out in support of the protesters, banging pots and pans together in the street.

'Do you think that all this will change anything, Kerim?'

'I don't know,' he said. It had taken him over an hour to push his way through the crowds on İstiklal and get to the hospital. That was crazy for such a short journey. There were a lot of people on the streets. If they all wanted the government to go then maybe change would come.

'I'd like to see that happen in my lifetime,' she said.

Kerim didn't say anything. When she was in this sort of mood there was no point in trying to cheer her. All he could do was change the subject.

'Have you got enough to read?' he asked. 'The crowds on İstiklal move so slowly at the moment I can easily go into Simurg or Pandora and pick up something for you.'

She didn't answer at first, apparently fixated on elephant seal mating rituals. Then she said, 'If you can find anything by Josephine Tey that would be nice.'

Kerim had never heard of her. 'Who?'

'Josephine Tey. An English crime writer from the sort of Second World War time. I think you'll have to get it in English.'

'Is that OK?'

'I read one book of hers, *The Franchise Affair*, in English and it was slow going but OK.'

'How did you find out about her?'

'That American friend of Pembe's, Rita.'

The image of a small, thin woman with close-cropped hair came into his head.

'I expect Rita's at Gezi,' Sinem said. 'I wish I could go.'

'You can.'

As soon as he'd said it, Kerim regretted it.

Sinem sat up. 'How can I go, Kerim?'

'I can take you,' he said. 'If you really want to . . .' He stopped. Her eyes were cold and he had to look away.

'I'm dying, I can't go anywhere,' she said. 'Why do you taunt me with things I can't do?'

The elephant seals on the TV bellowed in anger. Kerim was so close to telling her, but he didn't. What good would it do? She believed what she believed, he was fond of her, always had been, and she was his wife.

He smiled. 'I'm sorry, Sinem, sometimes I forget.'

She got up slowly. 'Doesn't matter.'

'It does.'

She left the room. Kerim turned the TV off and then the light. He'd wait until he was sure she was asleep before he went to bed. Alone in the darkness he wondered, not for the first time, what it was like to be Sinem. Most people he knew, maybe even that dead baby he'd seen earlier, clung to life with every atom of their souls. How could Sinem, and those like her, break that pattern? Was it just the pain that made her like that, or was it also what she was too? That he did understand, but it didn't make him want to die.

'Çetin Bey!'

One of the transsexuals opened her arms wide.

İkmen, smoking, bowed. 'Nar Hanım.'

Nar Sözen snaked an arm around his waist. 'What are you doing here? You're not going to threaten people, are you? That's not really your style.'

'No . . .'

'I was devastated when I heard that Sergeant Farsakoğlu had died. Devastated! She was such a good friend to—'

'Yes.'

Peri Mungun knew that Çetin İkmen had the reputation for being a man of the people but she hadn't realised that it meant people quite as diverse as these.

He looked at her, Nar Hanım and her friend with their arms draped around him and said, 'Miss Mungun, it's your choice but if you want to come with your brother and me now we can get you out of here safely.'

Ömer leaned forward and said, 'Please.'

His eyes pleaded and because she loved her brother, it touched her heart. She knew what he was thinking. If their parents found out where she was they'd be horrified. But Iris, for all her privilege, had had a point too.

119

'Ömer, Çetin Bey,' she said. 'It's very good of you to come but—'

'You can't stay here, Peri, you can't!'

He looked terrified. She took his arm and led him a little away from the others. Some children rushed past covered in brightly coloured face paints, laughing.

Peri had thought it through. When Iris had challenged her, when she'd watched the transsexuals' tent burn down and when she'd thought about her job in İstanbul and her life back in Mardin, she'd weighed the pros and the cons of everything that had happened and could happen very carefully. She'd decided what was important. To her.

'Ömer,' she said, 'whether we like it or not our lives have been dominated by what other people think of us and those who share our beliefs. Back home, to some extent, we were accepted, but here and in the rest of the country . . . And it's getting harder. Like these transsexuals, we are being told, albeit not always directly, to hide ourselves away still more and I don't want to do that. Why should I? Why should I or you have to deny the existence of our beliefs? It's not right, and if this protest is about anything it's about stopping things that aren't right.'

'They want to build a shopping mall.'

'And they want to cut down trees and kill off a green space to do it,' Peri said. 'Ömer, if our faith teaches us anything, isn't it that the natural world is sacred? Everyone I've talked to here just wants what we want – equality, peace, respect for the natural world and an end to this mad development that is making a few people rich at the expense of many more who have become poorer.'

'Peri, the government won't have it; they—'

'If this is the moment, then, to challenge them, that is what I must do,' she said.

'You have to go back to work tomorrow.'

'Do I? Yes, I know that logically I do,' she said. 'But I'm going to call in sick again tomorrow.'

'You'll lose your job!'

'Maybe.'

'You will! Nurses queue up to work in that hospital. You know that. *You* did.'

Peri looked down at the ground. What he was saying was sensible and accurate and in a moment he'd invoke the image of their ageing parents.

'Mum and Dad—'

'Mum and Dad should be able to be who they really are too,' Peri said. She looked up at him. For a moment the fear she saw on his face almost made her crumble, but then she took a deep breath and said, 'Ömer, I have to do this, for all of us.'

Yiannis watched Anastasia sleep. She always looked peaceful. That was the drugs. Awake she was tortured by her own inadequacies and by the past. What had she seen on that day in 1955 when her husband had died and her son had vanished?

They'd never spoken of it. She'd just accepted him and then they'd started what had been a quiet life together. He'd learned a little from Hakkı Bey. The mob had torn Nikos Negroponte to pieces and smashed Anastasia's head against the floor of their shop until, as Hakkı had put it, 'her brain had died'.

But it was possible to have a conversation with her, albeit of a frequently one-sided variety. She didn't speak for weeks sometimes and then, suddenly, she would almost chat. What she understood was not always clear. Yiannis felt she knew what went on around her, which was why, when she woke up, they had to speak.

Ahmet Öden and his development plans had been worrying

and upsetting. Now they had achieved a different level. Had he really been in the house years and years ago? He had been a builder when he was young and so it was possible. Hakkı would possibly remember, although he'd never mentioned it, but he had gone home. Would Anastasia recall such a thing? She spluttered in her sleep, turned over on to her side and began breathing normally again.

Had Öden been bluffing? Yiannis looked at the cruel stripes that the property developer had dug into the back of his hand. It was undeniable he was passionate. But about what? If he'd really been into the house and explored its every corner it was possible he knew. But why would that interest him? And if he didn't know, then what had his threats actually meant?

Yiannis went over to his mother's bedroom window and looked up at the sky. Dawn was just discernible as a thinning of the darkness over the great monuments of Sultanahmet. Although he hadn't slept he wasn't tired, but his body ached. He looked back at the old woman asleep in her bed and wondered what she was dreaming.

Chapter 11

İkmen looked at the e-mail again. The translator of Ariadne's notebook was very specific. She talked about two massive finds in the city. The body of Constantine Palaiologos had to be one and then there was something else. Described as a 'structure' by the translator, it had dimensions and, significantly, it was categorised as a 'red' building.

Constantine didn't feature; it was all about the structure. But where was it and what was it? İkmen had called the translator, who'd said he didn't know. All he could say was that from Dr Savva's descriptions of it, allied to her enthusiasm, it had to be Byzantine. Some of the less well-known Byzantine structures had been demolished in recent years, some in the last few months. Was this building even extant?

'The entire text is a minutely observed description of every part of this structure,' the translator had said. 'For instance, there is a red block with a flat red slab on top in the middle of this building. She measured every dimension and observed where the "red" had been damaged in any way. I've found measurements of windows, doors, arches, carvings. Again and again she states how unbelievable and precious this place is.'

'Could the "red" be stone?' İkmen had asked.

'Yes. Probably porphyry if the building was Byzantine. They used it all the time.'

Just as in the case of the body of Constantine Palaiologos,

there had been no photographs. Had Ariadne Savva been too cautious, too worried about keeping her finds to herself to risk taking pictures? And if the structure she had found had been made of porphyry, when had she been there last? They'd found a piece of porphyry in her hand when her body had been discovered. Had she visited this building within hours of giving birth? And where was it – somewhere near the sphendone?

The city was littered with Byzantine buildings and fragments. If, as her journal claimed, she'd found an entirely new structure, then where could it be? A lot of the city's Byzantine heritage had been discovered underground, but the existence of windows in this one seemed to imply that it was above ground. In any western European city the notion of a valuable historic building hiding for centuries behind more recent structures was probably laughable; in İstanbul İkmen knew that it was possible. He'd grown up playing in abandoned hamams, empty Greek houses and what remained of Byzantine cisterns. But the city was changing fast. Rampant development meant that the past was being unearthed every day and it was having to compete with the present, which sometimes relegated it to loser status.

Where was this place? As far as he knew Ariadne Savva's social and work route took her to her apartment, Gizlitepe, the Museum, Aya Sofya and the Hippodrome. So basically Kadıköy district and Sultanahmet. All the latest Byzantine finds in Sultanahmet had been underground and the area was so well documented he couldn't believe that researchers hadn't found whatever remained. Of course parts of the Great Palace of the Byzantines were still hidden and so it was possible Dr Savva had found part of that. But how? And where? Were there any significant Byzantine structures in Kadıköy? He didn't know the area well. But then he remembered something he'd once been told by an old Greek priest about Aya Sofya.

124

So it wasn't a structure, as such, but it was, if it existed, most definitely Byzantine. It was also, at least in part, almost certainly made of porphyry too.

Süleyman peered over Ömer's shoulder. The younger man felt his skin creep. He'd hoped he wouldn't see it.

'That's Inspector İkmen's handwriting,' he said.

'Yes, sir.'

'Are those Greek names?'

'Yes, sir. Inspector İkmen knows some of the old Greek families in the city.'

'He knows everyone.' Süleyman returned to his desk.

'I asked him about families he thought might have been caught up in the 1955 riots,' Ömer said. 'And he gave me these names.'

'Good idea.' He didn't look exactly overjoyed but at least he hadn't shouted.

A family called Gabras had owned a high-class bakery on İstiklal. An Alexis Gabras, a direct descendant, still lived in Şişli. But then all the bodies back in 1955 had been accounted for. Surely if someone had been unaccounted for, there would have been a record of it? Unless some of the Greeks had simply cut their losses. Most of the families who had lost members had left the city after 1955. A few had stayed, like the Diogenes, the Vatatzes and the Negropontes. Their dead, buried in the Greek cemetery at Şişli, had been quietly consigned to a history neither Greeks nor Turks could forget.

Dr Akyıldız, the forensic archaeologist, was still waiting for further results on the Galatasaray skeleton that might give some indication as to ethnicity, which would help. But she was also taken up with another skeleton that was much more exalted. What if the body found in Edirnekapı did turn out to be that of the last Byzantine emperor? Ömer suspected the Greeks would probably want to rebury him with a religious ceremony, most likely in Aya Sofya. That would be contentious, especially if it was going to be converted back to being a mosque.

If he were honest, Ömer wasn't up to being at work. He hadn't slept and was still in the clothes he'd worn the previous day, which Süleyman had noticed with a wry raise of an eyebrow. Ömer imagined he thought that he'd been with a woman all night. And in a way he had. She'd been his sister.

Peri had flatly refused to leave Gezi. In spite of appealing to her responsibilities as a dutiful daughter, Ömer had failed to persuade her to give up on what had been developing into an almost carnival atmosphere. That was the problem. Since last night the police had pulled back and there were reports of people setting up facilities for the protesters including food, drink and clothes.

The enthusiasm had been compelling. People dancing in the night around fires where they were cooking meat and vegetables, the music and the atmosphere of brotherhood was something he wouldn't forget in a hurry. Floridly 'out' gay boys standing shoulder to shoulder with bearded Muslims was an image that wouldn't fade quickly either. He could see why Peri was there but that didn't stop him worrying about her. The Prime Minister was due to go on a foreign trip in a few days and Ömer couldn't see that he'd leave the situation in Gezi as it was now and just go. The government was furious about the protest. Ömer looked across at Süleyman who was smoking out of his window, and wondered what he thought. He was a distant member of the deposed royal family and so he had to approve of what some were calling the 'new Ottomanism' that was sweeping the national consciousness. The government were actively promoting the notion of being proud to be Turkish and doing things in a uniquely Turkish way with pride. This was all good. But much of the new Ottomanism rhetoric was also connected to religion and also, perversely, to a type of consumerism that would seem to be completely opposed to the tenets of Islam. People were better off. But what the Gezi protestors were asking was, 'At what cost?'

Süleyman was bored. While his old friend İkmen was engaged in a race against time to find a newborn child, he was stuck with an historical case involving a skeleton that was over fifty years old. He wasn't involving himself in it any more than he had to, which meant that Ömer was really on his own.

The body could have been that of a homeless man – enough of them died violently every year and always had – except for the complicated dentistry. How had a man with expensive teeth come to be buried under a tree in the grounds of a posh kids' school? Galatasaray had been very co-operative and had sent over whatever they had about missing teachers or pupils over the years, very quickly. But that left nothing unexplained.

On the one hand, the dead man was a nobody, and yet on the other he couldn't be. And then it came to Ömer. What was key to this conundrum was, of course, teeth.

'I would never say that anything was impossible, Inspector,' Professor Bozdağ said. 'But it is unlikely that a tunnel exists underneath Aya Sofya leading to the church of St Mary of the Mongols in Fener. I accept, however, that the story has been around for many centuries.'

Although he was listening to the academic, İkmen couldn't help looking up into the great dome, flanked by mosaic angels, their wings decorated with gold leaf.

'We know that tunnels do exist under this building,' Bozdağ continued. 'One that leads in the direction of the Topkapı Palace and another that goes off towards the Sultanahmet Square. Which makes sense. The emperors were often at risk from their people and so it would have been of great benefit to them to be able to travel to the Great Palace and to the Hippodrome, unobserved. The last time the cavities underneath this building were explored was in 2009. But it's very difficult because everything down there is flooded.'

İkmen looked down.

'Not only is there a reservoir down there, but seismic activity over the centuries has damaged the foundations and the passages and rooms they may conceal. I cannot see how even one as passionate as Dr Savva would have been able to explore such an environment, particularly on her own.'

'But you said there were tunnels and that one led to Sultanahmet Square. Could that not extend up to St Mary's?' İkmen asked.

'Theoretically, yes,' the professor said. 'But even if it does exist it is probably very damaged. From here to St Mary's is about three kilometres, and when you think of all the earthquakes the city has suffered over the centuries . . .'

'True.'

A group of people in what İkmen still considered 'country' clothes – the men in battered suit jackets, the women in long dresses, their heads and faces covered – walked into the great building in silence. They were probably from one of the migrant communities along the Golden Horn, city dwellers, but they were all affected by the place.

'What about evidence from the other end?' İkmen said.

'St Mary's?' The professor shrugged. 'As the only Byzantine church to remain in Christian hands after the Conquest it has always guarded its secrets jealously. Or rather the Greek Orthodox Patriarchate has always protected it, I should say. I don't know of any research into its foundations. What it may be built upon,

I have no idea. Archaeologists have never been permitted to conduct research inside its walls. As an officer of the law, though, I imagine that you wouldn't have any problems gaining access. You are, after all, investigating a murder. Whether it will be worth your time or not, I don't know.'

İkmen didn't either. What he was really looking for was a building, but not even the professor could come up with one of those.

'Are you sure that Dr Savva's notebook referred to a real place?' Bozdağ asked.

İkmen had explained why he wanted to know about a tunnel under the Aya Sofya.

'I don't know for sure,' İkmen said. 'But why record the dimensions and details of a place that doesn't exist?'

'Maybe it was somewhere she read about?'

'Maybe. All I can say is that, in the translation we've been given, her enthusiasm and her joy shine through. You know Greek, you might think differently if you read the original, but at the moment of course I can't show that to you. Professor, was Dr Savva in any way a fantasist?'

He frowned. 'She was wildly enthusiastic about her subject but I never caught her out in a lie of any sort. So I'd have to say no. Until this business with Constantine Palaiologos came to light, I always thought that she was trustworthy. But then academic selfishness is a trait people in our profession all share to some extent.' He smiled. 'I've got over the shock, Inspector. And if that body Dr Akyıldız has been investigating is Palaiologos, nobody will be more delighted than me. To find him after so many centuries would be amazing, although now that Dr Savva is no longer with us, quite how we do that, I don't know.'

'We haven't been able to find anything on her system or amongst her papers that suggests who she might have been comparing that skeleton's DNA to,' İkmen said. 'I don't suppose you would—'

'No.'

The group of 'country' people moved on to be replaced by a deluge of excited middle-aged Italians. The two men got a little jostled and so the professor suggested they move out of the main building and in to the narthex or entrance hall. The entire structure was lined with varying shades of red porphyry stone ranging from pink to dark purple, but the narthex in particular was very obviously and gloomily maroon.

'Unless Dr Savva had found another genuine Palaiologi corpse to compare the Edirnekapı bones to then she must have had a living relative in mind,' the professor said. 'And that I don't think is possible. I think she may have been duped by someone who wanted her to believe that, which may be why she died. The Palaiologi are extinct. As far as I am aware, not even the patriarchate have any of their bones in their reliquaries. They are a dead end. Literally.' He paused, then said abruptly, 'Any news of the child?'

İkmen sighed. 'My sergeant went out last night, into the maelstrom of Beyoğlu, to look at a dead child. But it was African. So no, Professor. The child remains enigmatic and I feel I have failed with each passing day.'

İkmen didn't often share his innermost feelings with members of the public, but Professor Bozdağ reminded him a little of his father. And as his father would have done, Bozdağ put a hand on his shoulder. 'Getting around this city at the moment, in these circumstances, is hell, Inspector,' he said. 'And you have very little to work with. I am right, I assume, in saying that nobody saw or heard anything unusual around the sphendone on the night that Dr Savva died?'

'No.' He shrugged. 'Logically the child is either dead or

something terrible has happened to it. Although I can't allow myself to dwell on that.'

'No.'

'Instead I must concentrate on what I know about Dr Savva and her interests, and so I think I will go up to St Mary's.'

'They have a sacred spring there,' Professor Bozdağ said, 'so maybe it will bring you good fortune.'

Having information and using it were two different things. Yiannis told Anastasia nothing about his latest spat with Ahmet Öden but instead asked Hakkı whether he could remember whether Öden had ever been in the house. Hakkı told him that he had.

'Why didn't you tell me this before?' Yiannis said.

He knew that Hakkı didn't like him, but the house was at stake here.

'He came to put in a new window frame in Madam's bedroom. Back in the 1980s. You weren't here,' Hakkı said. 'But I watched him. He didn't go anywhere he shouldn't.'

'And did you watch him in the toilet? Did he go to the kitchen?'

'I watched him all the time,' Hakkı said. 'He didn't work for his father at that time and I didn't know that he would be the workman who came to fix the window. If I had I would have barred him. You know what I know about his family. He was not left alone.'

'So when he spoke to me he was bluffing?'

'Or he's heard a rumour.'

'Are there any?'

'There are always stories about old places,' Hakkı said. 'Maybe Nikos Bey said something as he was dying? Who knows what has been said over the years.'

'I can take him around the house but, apart from the fact I

131

don't want him in here, what if he doesn't see what he remembers? Because he won't.'

'Then he remembered in error,' Hakkı said.

Yiannis sat down. It was a beautiful day in the sunshine but he felt sick. Ahmet Öden had been so passionate about the house that when he'd held his hand, he'd injured him. But more importantly he had him worried. He looked up at the old man. 'Hakkı, can I tell you something?'

Hakkı sat down beside him and lit a cigarette. 'Yes.'

'It must go no further.'

'No.'

'I know something about Öden I could use against him.'

'What's that?'

'But I can't use it because of where I got it from.'

'Which was where?'

Yiannis paused. Hakkı looked at him.

'I can't say.'

'You can to me.'

He had a notion that the old man might be taking pleasure in his discomfort. It stemmed from Hakkı's distrust as well as from what he and Yiannis alone knew.

Yiannis looked at him coldly. 'I can't and I won't. I'd be sick. You know why,' he said. 'But Öden has a mistress. I've seen her.'

'Have you? How?'

'You know who he knew!' he said. 'Don't taunt me. You know! The mistress's name is Gülizar, she's Roma and he keeps her in an apartment in Moda. Can you imagine what his pious backers and his oh-so-clean-living workforce would think about him if they knew? Gülizar is a big, brassy gypsy who used to strip for a living before Ahmet started paying her to do things the faithful would never do.'

'Blackmailing Öden would be risky,' Hakkı said.

132

'I'd do it to save this house, you know I would!' Yiannis said. 'But how do I explain how I know? Why would I ever have gone to Moda? He knows I never leave this house. Someone would have to have taken me. Which was what happened.'

'He'll cover it up. He may even kill you,' Hakkı said. 'Don't speak of it. Not unless there is no other way to stop him.'

'I can't. How would I know where this mistress of his lives unless someone had told me?'

'We must trust in Çetin Bey and hope these young people in Gezi Park make the government rein these developers in.'

'Do you think that will happen? Really?'

Hakkı shrugged. 'I don't know.'

'And if it doesn't and Çetin Bey can't keep Öden away from this house? What then?'

Hakkı rose stiffly to his feet. 'Then we fight,' he said. 'And we use every weapon we have to do that, including what you've just told me. We can invent a reason why you went to Moda. We can invent a person who took you there. Madam will die in this house as she has always wanted and the Negroponte family's legacy will continue.'

The old man went back into the house, leaving Yiannis wondering how any of that might be done. The bottom line was that Öden could just bulldoze the place if he wished. That was what he wanted to do. So why not let him do it?

There had been a time, shortly after he'd arrived in the city, when he hadn't cared. He'd not grown up in the house and there were many days when its dampness and inconvenience had been all he'd noticed. But over that year it had seeped into him.

The sacred spring wasn't so much as a trickle. Dedicated, apparently, to St Anthony, it had dried up years ago according to the custodian.

'There's nothing else there,' he called down the steep stone staircase to Çetin İkmen. That immediately began to make the policeman suspicious and so he looked around. There were definite signs of walls having been excavated.

'You have archaeologists down here?' he asked. 'A woman from the museum?'

'No.'

'Oh.'

The custodian was suddenly at his shoulder. A small, miserable looking man, all he'd wanted to talk about when İkmen arrived was the copy of the irade, or order, signed by Mahmut II guaranteeing the church of St Mary of the Mongols to the Orthodox patriarchate in perpetuity. He'd really wanted to impress on İkmen just how great a concession that had been.

'So why does this place look as if it's being excavated?'

He shrugged. 'The patriarchate do what they want. They can, it's theirs. You saw.'

He was fixated.

'I've heard,' İkmen said, 'that there could be a tunnel that leads from here to the Aya Sofya. Do you know anything about that?'

'A tunnel? No. Why should I?'

'Because when you let me in you proudly told me you'd been custodian here for the last twenty years,' İkmen said. Ignorance irritated him and this man had a lot of it. 'Do you actually know anything about this building apart from the fact that it was protected by an imperial irade?'

'That was a very good—'

'Listen, tunnel, yes or no?'

'No.'

'Right, so ask the patriarchate, yes?'

'Yes.'

İkmen left. He hadn't actually been able to see any sort of

ingress leading elsewhere from underneath the church but that didn't mean that one didn't exist. And maybe the patriarchate had given Ariadne Savva permission to study the building which she had kept from the museum.

İkmen lit a cigarette and looked around. Fener was the old Greek quarter of the city and so there were a few significant Byzantine buildings in the area as well as some that were just shells. Almost opposite the church was what could have either been an old hamam or a Byzantine ruin that had looked like a sort of half dome on top of a wall for years. Now almost completely sunk into the ground, it was a rubbish dump and İkmen, disgusted, spotted bags of used babies' nappies.

'Thinking of buying it?'

He knew the voice. Deep and female and seductive.

'Gonca.'

He looked up at her and smiled. As usual her hair hung down her back like a glossy carpet and her breasts swelled out of the top of her dress. How could she still be so gorgeous after so many years? At times like this it was easy to see why Süleyman was still bewitched by her. The bastard.

İkmen smiled. 'No, no, I'm not buying anything.'

Gonca lived in the neighbouring district of Balat, what had been the old Jewish quarter.

'Well, should you buy property around here you'll either make a killing or get fleeced,' she said.

He sighed. 'Balat and Fener now up for redevelopment?'

'Yes,' she said. 'But I brought my whole family here from Tarlabaşı when they developed that and so we'll stay and fight if it comes to it.'

Before Tarlabaşı, Gonca's people had lived in the centuries old gypsy quarter of Sulukule which had submitted to the bull-dozers years ago.

'Mmm. So I suppose you're hoping this Gezi Park protest will make the authorities listen.'

'Roma are in Gezi in force,' she said. 'Have you been? It's an amazing atmosphere.'

'Yes, I have.'

They began to walk down the hill towards the Golden Horn. His car was parked on a steep slope in front of a few gentrified houses people said belonged to Armenians.

'Mehmet has seen it but he's not been into the park,' she said. 'We don't talk about it.'

İkmen didn't answer.

'You don't talk about it with him either, do you?' she said. 'But then you don't talk at all unless you have to.'

She was right but İkmen didn't want to discuss it.

She put a hand on his arm. 'Çetin Bey, don't be so hard on him,' she said. 'I know you're angry about what he did to Sergeant Farsakoğlu but that was as much my fault as it was his.'

İkmen stopped. 'I know,' he said. 'But you didn't string her along, did you? You took him, because you love him.'

'And he loves me.'

He said nothing. Süleyman was infatuated with the gypsy but whether he loved her or not, he didn't know. Whether he loved anyone except his son Yusuf was a fair question. And what would happen when he either tired of Gonca or some other women inflamed that sexual itch inside him? Would he only stop when he became as old and demented as his own father? Was he ever going to grow up?

'I took him away from her,' Gonca said. 'Deliberately.'

'And he let you.'

He began walking again, sideways and gingerly towards his car.

She walked completely normally, sure-footed in her own terrain. 'I seduced him.'

'Oh, and I imagine that was *such* a difficult seduction.'

'No, it wasn't.'

'Well of course it wasn't!'

'I just can't bear to see your friendship disappear like this,' she said. 'You were so close. That is rare.'

İkmen skidded down a line of cobbles and came to rest, just about upright, leaning against the boot of his car. 'Gonca,' he said, 'it was Mehmet who acted without any thought for anyone but himself.'

'And me.'

He didn't respond. There was a slight desperation in what she was saying that made him wonder how sure she was of Süleyman. Had something gone wrong between them?

'When Mehmet left her for you, my Sergeant Farsakoğlu lost hope and became reckless. It was that recklessness that was the direct cause of her death,' İkmen said. 'If he'd still loved her she wouldn't have put herself at risk.'

'But Mehmet said that she saved you and him and Sergeant Mungun!'

'Maybe, maybe not,' İkmen said. He took his car keys out of his pocket. 'Her killer may have given his gun up to us if she'd not surprised him. He was surrounded.'

Professor Cem Atay had killed Ayşe Farsakoğlu, when he had been holding İkmen and Mungun captive. He had already drugged and almost killed Süleyman. Farsakoğlu's intervention had brought what had been a stalemate to a head. But she'd died for it.

'All I know,' he continued, 'is that had Mehmet still been in her life she would have been more cautious. In my opinion. I can't help the way that I feel, Gonca. It's tough for me to look

Mehmet in the eye, and I don't know what, if anything, I can do about that.'

'But he misses you!'

İkmen doubted whether Süleyman had actually verbalised this, but he didn't doubt it was so. He himself felt the lack of their close friendship in his life and he mourned it.

'You know he will never come to you. You'll have to come to him,' Gonca said. 'It's what he's like. His pride—'

'His pride is not something I miss,' İkmen said. Reference to Süleyman's famous Ottoman gentleman's pride had made him angry. 'And Gonca, he will have to come to me. He was in the wrong. Not me.'

He staggered around to the side of his car and opened the door.

'Çetin Bey, he is so unhappy!'

'That's not my problem, Gonca.'

İkmen got into the driving seat and then looked at her in his rear-view mirror. She wasn't crying but her eyes looked pained. A moody and unhappy Süleyman was not doing much for the gypsy, but that wasn't his problem. Now he had to go to the Greek Orthodox patriarchate at the bottom of the hill and find out what he could about a mythical – or not – tunnel. Süleyman and his woes were not his concern.

Except that they were and he knew it.

Chapter 12

Ahmet Öden would have to wait. The online DNA test was going to take at least week and even then it wouldn't tell him whether or not Yiannis Negroponte was Anastasia's son. For that he had to get some DNA from her, and that was going to be difficult. But at least he'd be able to discover whether Yiannis was Greek.

Ahmet Öden didn't like waiting. Not even playing with his daughter made him feel better. In fact, too much time with Kelime made him feel worse. Food and toys comforted her but the greed he had encouraged in her appalled him. Mary the nanny still occasionally braved his displeasure and complained about how she found it hard to control Kelime because of her addiction to sweets and ice cream. He turned over in bed and looked at Gülizar. *She* made him feel better. Twenty-five and as firm as a drum, her flesh was augmented with implants that he had paid for. He touched her breasts and she moaned. She claimed they'd become more sensitive since she'd had surgery.

He'd never meant to take a mistress. He'd met Gülizar in a cheap strip club and had paid her for what he imagined would be a one-night stand. But then he'd gone back, again and again. Soon he was visiting her every week. Sexy rather than beautiful, Gülizar would do anything to please men. Some activities she claimed to have invented. She'd do anything he wanted and so Ahmet began to explore those areas of his sexuality that religion forbade. Sometimes she would involve other people, men and women, although the men were never allowed to touch her.

As Ahmet grew richer his ability to hide a mistress success-fully grew correspondingly. He put Gülizar in an apartment in Moda and had her breasts made huge. She couldn't sleep on her stomach but they made him want to come every time he looked at them.

'Gülizar.'

He woke her up. He was hard again and he pushed himself roughly inside her. She made noises and rolled her tongue around her lips. Some men, he'd heard, said that it was important for a woman to take pleasure in sex as well as a man. He had never believed in the truth of that, but with Gülizar he wondered. She always seemed aroused and when he'd watched her with another girl she'd become wild. When the two of them had finished she'd fallen on him like a beast. He'd felt terrible about that and about how much he'd wanted to do to Gülizar what that girl had done. But he couldn't.

Thinking about it, though, made for better sex. When he came, and although she was only half awake, Gülizar told him he was a 'lion'. Ahmet threw himself back on the bed and tried to enjoy a moment of post-coital contentment. But he couldn't. He never could. Whenever he visited her it had to be in disguise and always at odd times. Guilt squeezed his heart and he had to fight an urge to beat Gülizar until she died for making him do such things with her. And although he knew that other men like him had mistresses too, it didn't bring him comfort. Gülizar was his sin and he'd have to take his punishment for her in the afterlife. In this life, if anyone found out, he'd suffer a more immediate form of censure. Those opposed to him, and people like him, would eat him alive. He'd be thrown to the Gezi Park mob, which was getting bigger and more vocal every day. If they didn't stop soon he'd have to move to take the Negroponte House while he still could. İkmen or no İkmen.

The central heating fitters were supposed to have arrived but they hadn't. The old wood-burning heater, the soba, had already been taken out and everything was ready for the wonderful new gas central heating. However, because other open spaces across the city were beginning to set up their own mini Gezi Park protests, the traffic was so horrendous the fitters couldn't leave their own district, which was over the Bosphorus in Üsküdar. And Kemal had gone out.

Fatma İkmen fumed. The boy had gone to Gezi because suddenly it had all become a lot of fun. For some reason she couldn't understand, and Çetin wasn't saying, the police had pulled back from the park. As a result even more oddities and malcontents had joined in the protest. Including her youngest son.

Sometimes Fatma despaired. In spite of the country becoming more religious, her own family just went the opposite way. It had to be because of their father. And yet with Çetin she was always and forever conflicted. Unlike a lot of men, when it came to elections, he didn't tell her who to vote for. He had to know that she'd always vote for the ruling AK Parti but he'd never asked her, even though he often referred to them as 'your lot'. When she'd asked him about voting and why he was so uninterested in what she might be doing, he looked at her as if she was insane. He could go on and on about being a democrat and yet she knew that he approved of the Gezi protests, which, in her mind, meant that he was in favour of violent insurrection.

With Kemal out and no gas fitters on the horizon, Fatma went out. There was a small enclosure where people could pray behind the Aya Sofya and she felt the need to perform her prayers with others.

Tourists in Sultanahmet Square were rather less evident than usual. In common with everything except Gezi Park and its offshoots and the traffic, the city was quieter than usual. Holding its breath for what might happen next. Because the area was so clear, Fatma raised her head and looked at the sunlight as it shone through the branches of the trees. It was a beautiful day in spite of everything. Then she saw an old face, which made her smile. Hakkı Bey.

'Peace be upon you, Fatma Hanım,' he said.

'And upon you, Hakkı Bey,' she replied.

He was with a tall, middle-aged man who had a toddler, a little boy, in his arms.

'My son, Lokman,' he said.

Fatma tilted her head in greeting.

'Visiting from Van with his new wife and children,' he said. 'The girl has had three in three years. Imagine! We're very proud. Madam likes to watch the children play. It makes her feel part of the world.'

Fatma recalled that Lokma had always been an expressionless man, and now he didn't disappoint. So what he felt about it was impossible to tell. He had to be in his late fifties, but if he wanted a new family with a new wife, that was fine. It was good to have a lot of children.

'I am very glad for you,' Fatma said. Then she bade the pair farewell and walked towards the Aya Sofya. Hakkı Bey had looked after the old Greek woman, Anastasia Negroponte, for as long as Fatma could remember. Even when that man had turned up from Germany who said he was her son Yiannis, Hakkı Bey had stayed. Long, long ago there had been a rumour that Hakkı Bey loved Anastasia Negroponte. She'd even heard, just the once, a whispered story about him having killed her husband during the anti-Greek riots of 1955. It was said that

142

Anastasia had seen him stabbing her husband and so Hakkı had had to hit her to silence her. As a result she'd become the vegetable people said she was today. Fatma believed none of it. Hakkı was a good man, a pious man.

She watched Hakkı, his son and grandson walk in the direction of the Negroponte house. It was such an awful wreck now – odd that, according to Çetin, someone wanted to buy it.

'There is no tunnel,' İkmen said to Kerim Gürsel. 'A very articulate priest at the patriarchate told me it was an "urban myth".'

'Do you believe him?'

'Not entirely,' İkmen said. 'But most probably, yes. Professor Bozdağ is of the opinion that all is pretty much wrecked and waterlogged underneath Aya Sofya, and we do have earthquakes in this country.'

They hadn't spent time together in their office for some while. Kerim had uncomplainingly gone to view two dead babies that had been found in the city, neither of which could have belonged to Ariadne Savva – one had been black, the other too old. But his dark eyes now looked haunted and İkmen knew that he would have to relieve him of that burden. People with babies all over the old city had been required to show their ID cards and answer questions about their infants, and so far that had yielded nothing. The chances of finding the child alive were diminishing.

'Is Dr Savva's father still in the city, sir?'

'No, he's gone back to Greece,' İkmen said. 'He'll return when the body is released. He wasn't comfortable here. Which is understandable.'

Savva had not been convinced that his daughter's death didn't have a racist motive. But he came from Anatolian Greek stock and so it would be difficult for him to imagine a different explanation. So much hatred between the two nations over the centuries had produced a distortion in some people's minds that always raced to the hated 'other' whenever misfortune came. It wasn't a trait that İkmen shared. He felt fortunate that his father had been an educated man who had abhorred racism of any kind.

İkmen pushed himself back from his desk, opened the office window and lit a cigarette. In common with at least five other people, as far as he could see, he hung his head out into the warm summer air.

'You live near Gezi Park, Kerim,' he said. 'What's the mood in your area?'

'It was tense when we – the police – were going in. But now it's, well, it's almost like a carnival sometimes. People go to Gezi when they leave work. Do you know why the site's not being cleared, sir?'

'No. That's political and I keep well away from that. But I'm puzzled as to why the government hasn't pushed it. The Prime Minister is due to leave for North Africa in a few days and I should imagine he'd want the problem cleared up before he goes. But what do I know?'

He was so disillusioned with politics. To his way of thinking, although Turkey had got richer it had lost much of its soul to profit and shopping. When the five-hundred-year-old gypsy quarter of Sulukule had been demolished to make way for a housing estate he'd felt it like a wound. Not only had his old friend Gonca's family lived there but he'd wandered those historic streets as a boy. Seeing the gypsies leave had made him weep.

İkmen's phone rang. He put his cigarette out on the window sill and answered it.

'İkmen.'

'Çetin Bey, it is Hakkı,' a breathless voice said. 'I have just returned to Madam's and Ahmet Öden is outside the house. He's alone, just sitting in his car. He's not meant to be here. It's making Yiannis very agitated.'

İkmen put his head in his hands. This situation, quite separate from his current investigation, was going to run on until, he feared, Öden got his way. 'Has he spoken to anyone in the house? In person or on the phone?'

'No,' Hakkı said. 'He's just sitting, looking at the house.'

'Doing nothing?'

'Yes.'

'Hakkı Bey, if he's not doing anything there's not much I can do,' İkmen said. 'There are no traffic restrictions, as you know, and so he has a perfect right to sit in his car doing nothing for as long as he likes.'

'But it's intimidation!'

'If you interpret it that way.'

'How else, given what's gone before, can we interpret it, Çetin Bey?'

'I agree, intimidation is the most likely motive,' İkmen said. 'But his defence to that will be that he just wanted to sit in his car and enjoy the sunshine. Hakkı Bey, he is playing mind games with you and it is unpleasant, but if you want to defeat him then you have to remain calm.'

'I fear Yiannis will collapse. Every minute he's looking out of the window at the car, drinking and smoking himself into an early grave. Madam will not survive if anything happens to him.'

İkmen accepted that he had no choice. 'OK, Hakkı Bey, I will come out as soon as I can. But it will be as an act of solidarity rather than anything else. I won't confront or even speak to Ahmet Öden. Standing on shaky legal ground with someone like him and his lawyers is not a healthy place to be. I'll come, we'll talk, I'll try to calm Yiannis down and then I will go.'

'I know you do this, Çetin Bey, when you are so busy and—'

'Let's just see if my visit can give Öden something to think about,' İkmen said. 'You don't know what he's doing. Now he won't know what *you're* up to.'

'But why is it a game, Çetin Bey?' Hakkı asked. 'This place is a home. Why has it become someone's sport?'

'Because it's worth more money than we have ever seen in our lives,' İkmen said. Then he put the phone down.

Kerim looked at him questioningly.

'We should go back to the sphendone and see if anything more has been found in there,' İkmen said. 'And then we'll make a little detour.'

'To?'

'That house I told you about, the Negroponte place. Apparently the developer who wants it is indulging in a little light-hearted intimidation. And so I think we should go and spoil his fun.'

The sound of the drill made Ömer wince. Knowing that he wasn't going to have dental treatment himself didn't make him feel better. He'd only ever had one filling in his life but that had been when he'd been very young and it had hurt. What also didn't help was the way patients in the waiting room kept looking at trashy magazines, throwing them aside and then biting their lips.

'Sergeant Mungun?'

He looked up. It was a nurse and half her face was covered by a surgical mask. A man at her side scuttled round her, holding the side of his face.

'Yes?'

'Dr İnçi will see you now,' she said. 'Follow me.'

Ömer got shakily to his feet and followed her down a short corridor to a treatment room that looked rather more like something from a *Star Trek* film than a dentist's surgery. The old practice he had visited in Mardin had been behind a butcher's shop and had smelt of meat and looked like a torture chamber. But then this was one of Beyoğlu's foremost practices, right on İstiklal Caddesi.

A stout woman, who had been bending over a stack of papers when he entered, turned and said, 'So what can we do to help the police?'

She was about fifty, rather plain and, Ömer felt, a little hostile.

'As I explained to your receptionist on the phone, I've come here because I understand that this is an old, family practice,' Ömer said. 'Here since the 1950s.'

'Yes. We are a dynasty of dentists. My father and my grand-father, now me,' she said. 'What of it?'

'I'm trying to trace the identity of a body we found in this area recently—'

'The one in the Lise?'

'Yes.'

'OK.' He felt she thawed slightly, particularly when she offered him a seat. 'That's all it's about?'

Had she been afraid that he was going to ask her to do some-thing to help the police break up Gezi, maybe? It was just a guess, but she didn't look as if she was the sort of person who would be entirely in favour of the current administration.

'Yes.'

'So how can I help?' she asked.

'The body we found dates from the mid-1950s,' he said. 'What's unusual about it is that it's had complicated dentistry, especially for that time. Crowns and bridges.'

'Crowns and bridges have been around for a long time for those who can afford them,' she said.

'Exactly. This man had to have had money to be able to have

his teeth so well maintained,' Ömer said. 'From this we deduce he wasn't a vagrant or a person of low status. And yet we're struggling to identify him.'

'What about the anti-Greek riots of 1955?'

She just came out with it and Ömer was a little shocked.

'My father hid as many as he could find in here,' she said. 'Then he and my grandfather stood in the doorway with pistols raised.'

'Oh, that was very—'

'They were brave men and they did the right thing and I'm proud of them,' she said.

Was it just Ömer's imagination or did Dr İnçi raise her head a little higher as she spoke?

'Well, I have some X-rays and photographs of what remains of this man's teeth and dental work,' Ömer said. He took an envelope out of his pocket.

'I can look, but—'

'I don't know whether you have kept dental records from so long ago, but because I know this is a family business I'm hoping there may be a chance.'

She put her hand out for the envelope and he gave it to her. She looked at the photographs and put the X-rays up on her light box. For what seemed like a long time, she was silent. Then she said, 'We do have some old records. But from the 1950s I really don't know. My father was in the habit of keeping very detailed accounts of work he performed that was either difficult or unusual in any way. As I said, if you could pay, even in the fifties you could get crowns and bridges fitted. But this was a poor country then and so those who had such work done would have been few. What about the Greeks?'

'You mean the people who died in 1955?'

'Who were murdered, yes.'

148

'They were all accounted for,' he said. 'This body may well be Greek but we don't think that he was killed in the riots of 1955.'

'Maybe his family didn't report him.'

'Maybe. But those events have been well documented,' he said. 'Dr İnçi, this man died violently, and although it is unlikely we will be able to bring his killer to justice after all this time, if we can give him a name at least we will be able to know where to bury him.'

She thought for a moment. 'I'll do my best,' she said. 'But it will take time. Some records are kept here, upstairs, and others at our summer house in Tarabiya. I can't give you any idea how long this may take.'

'I understand. And I appreciate it.'

She smiled, which made her look quite attractive.

When he left, she took Ömer's hand and shook it. Her grip was firm and dry, like a man's.

Peri had had lahmacun for breakfast and now she was eating some honeyed figs which had been given to her by a transsexual who called herself Madonna. Music was playing, the sun was shining, the man lying on the grass next to her was reading James Joyce and Iris was smoking a cigarette and talking to a group of gay boys. If this was protest then it was all rather pleasant. But should it be?

Peri looked at her watch and realised that her shift for that day would start in forty-five minutes. Surely rather than lying about in the sunshine she should be tending to her patients? The hospital had taken her excuse for the previous day without question but if she didn't turn up again there could be problems. Besides, her patients, rich or otherwise, were sick and they needed her. Peri stood up. Her uniform was filthy and smoke dried, but she had another one in her locker and if she moved herself she would have time for a shower before the start of her shift.

'Where are you going?'

Peri looked down at Iris. 'To work.'

'To work? I thought you'd made your decision to join the protest.'

'I have. I did. But at the moment there's nothing to do,' Peri said.

'Yeah. But the police could come back any time. The prime ministerial trip's in only a couple of days. We could be under attack any minute.'

'Then I'll come back,' Peri said. 'But at the moment there's nothing going on here and my patients need me.'

Iris shrugged, said, 'Whatever,' and then returned to her conversation.

Peri walked out of the park towards İstanbul's German Hospital.

'It's over fifty years since I was in this house,' İkmen said. He wanted to continue and say that it hadn't changed a bit – unless you included the degradation of almost everything about it. But he didn't.

Hakkı said, 'I told Madam you were coming and she insisted on seeing you.'

'I'd be delighted to see her.'

'But alone, Çetin Bey,' the old man continued. 'Not your er, your . . .' He looked at Kerim Gürsel.

'I'll go and sit in the kitchen if you like,' Kerim said.

It had been an uncomfortable morning with the crime scene officers in the sphendone. With the help of the Archaeological Museum they were investigating the further reaches of the cavities underneath the Hippodrome, looking for possible clues and maybe even more bodies. It was a good place to hide a body or two, out of sight and difficult to access. Many of the rooms and other cavities were almost completely collapsed and so one had to crouch for much of the time. Then there was the water, which had seeped in to almost every part of the building except the area where the body had been found.

'No, no, no,' the old man said. 'Yiannis will entertain you in the salon.'

As if on cue, Yiannis Negroponte appeared. 'Of course,' he said. 'If you'd like to follow me, officer . . .'

'Gürsel.'

'We have home-made lemonade and iced tea,' Yiannis said.

Hakkı led İkmen up the wide, mirrored staircase he had once run up and down with his brother when they were children while his mother read Madam Anastasia's cards out in the garden. Now he was trudging up the same, if more worn, staircase, to get to the old woman's bedroom.

'Madam doesn't leave her bed often these days,' Hakkı said. 'And her speech has been bad since the events of 1955. But at least she can speak a little now. For a good decade afterwards she was mute.'

İkmen shook his head. 'You have done well to look after her so diligently, Hakkı Bey.'

'I did what needed to be done.'

İkmen vaguely remembered sneaking into the bedrooms in the Negroponte house. They were all roccoco gilt-fests complete with Venetian putti floating around the ceilings and *trompe-l'œil* paintings of fat women with long blond hair and bearded men in loincloths. All the beds were huge and heavily laden with faded blankets and counterpanes. This one was no different, except that it also contained a tiny figure.

Almost completely bald, Anastasia Negroponte had the look of a tiny, delicate baby bird. Her skin, which was a grey-purple colour, appeared to be just lightly draped over her skeleton, while the nails on her toes looked not unlike the talons of a pigeon. Only the eyes were familiar to him. They alone hinted at the slightly plump, white-skinned woman he had known as a child. In those days Madam Anastasia's hair, which had been as black as licorice, had reached down to her waist.

İkmen bowed. 'Good morning, Madam Anastasia,' he said. 'It's very kind of you to see me at such short notice.'

She smiled and he saw that, brown and broken though they were, she still had teeth. She beckoned him forwards with one arthritis-knotted hand.

'Go to her. Sit on the bed,' Hakkı said.

İkmen moved. 'Is that right, Madam?' he said.

There was a pause. She swallowed and then said, 'Sit.'

Her voice, not much more than a whisper, was hoarse and he wondered whether it had always been like that or whether time had ruined it. He couldn't remember her speaking, only laughing – with his mother.

'Kind . . . child,' she said. ' . . .you.'

'My parents wouldn't have cruel children, Madam,' he said.

She held one finger up. 'Ayşe . . . Timur . . . İkmen.'

'Yes, Ayşe and Timur,' İkmen smiled. 'And my brother Halil. You used to give us home-made lemonade and chocolate and let us run about all over this lovely house while my mother read your cards. You were very kind too. I'm not sure I'd allow a couple of little boys with too much energy to run all over my home unsupervised.'

Tears fell from her eyes. 'Ayşe died?'

'Yes, sadly,' İkmen said. His mother had been Albanian and had died as a result of a blood feud. 'My father too, but much later.'

She nodded and closed her eyes, which still appeared to weep. Hakkı put a hand on İkmen's shoulder and said, 'Come, Çetin Bey, Madam is tired now.'

They left the bedroom, İkmen feeling saddened. Surely the old woman couldn't live long in such a weakened state? It was a miracle she was still alive at all. When they got to the ground floor, İkmen told Hakkı that he needed the bathroom. He remembered where it was – in the basement, across the corridor from the kitchen. He began to make his way to the stairs.

'Ah, let me show you, Çetin Bey,' Hakkı said.

'I remember,' İkmen said.

But the old man insisted on accompanying him. He even opened the toilet door. However, once İkmen had finished the old man had disappeared to be replaced by Yiannis, who stood in the doorway to the kitchen. It had never had a door to İkmen's recollection and had always smelt of sugar. That had now gone, as had, apparently, the old decor. Over Yiannis' shoulder he saw a white, rather than a brown stone kitchen, which, unsurprisingly, given the number of years that had passed, looked a lot smaller than he remembered.

'Öden's still out there, in his car,' Yiannis said.

'Of course. He's playing a game. The fact that Sergeant Gürsel and myself are here is probably a challenge to someone like Öden.'

Yiannis put a hand on İkmen's shoulder and led him upstairs. In the salon, Kerim Gürsel was drinking lemonade with Hakkı. The old man offered İkmen a drink.

'Thank you.'

That taste took him back. Madam Anastasia's lemonade had been one of the stand-out flavours of his youth. What he was drinking was exactly the same. Whoever was making it now was using Anastasia's recipe.

But in spite of so much being just as he had remembered, a lot of things had changed. The house was older, more degraded and shabby. And then there were the people. Yiannis had come after İkmen's time and Hakkı and Madam were of course old. There was something else too: this thing about being escorted in the house. When he'd been a child he'd roamed free, as he'd told Anastasia. Why was he not apparently trusted to find his way around as an adult?

Chapter 13

Gezi Park had suddenly become a wonderland of opportunity for the likes of Nurettin the rubbish picker and his associate, the Rat Boy. The two Gizlitepe residents had all but taken up positions by a bin that, however quickly they emptied it, kept on filling up with plastic drinking bottles. Other İstanbullus on the margins had the same idea and so keeping their bin to themselves wasn't easy. After much discussion and a few fights they came to the conclusion that the old man should guard the bin while the boy took the bottles to be sold, and then they'd reverse the duties. That way they both had a stake in the bin and the temptation to just make off with money earned was replaced by the desire to obtain more cash in the future.

As far as Nurettin could see, most of the protesters were weirdos – people with coloured hair and tattoos wearing strange clothes that often didn't cover their bodies properly. There were gays and drag queens too, and women he felt had to be prostitutes. Nurettin didn't approve. These were the people the government didn't approve of either, so it was said, and he agreed with them on that count. But on the other hand it was the same government who were supporting the redevelopment of the city and Nurettin didn't like that.

The Rat Boy had gone to sell the latest two sackfuls. It was still early, but if it continued at this rate, they'd be rich by the evening. Although he knew it was wrong to drink alcohol, Nurettin had promised himself a drinking session in Nevezade Sokak. The bars down there would take his money even if he smelt like an old toilet. Admittedly they might make him stand outside, but Nurettin didn't mind that. It was summer. Rat Boy would go and score heroin, but that was his business. Soon it would be winter again and they'd both be cold and hungry, so now they just had to make what money they could and enjoy themselves while they could. What good was saving when you had no home? Some bastard just robbed you. Better to be broke and have some good memories than in funds with money that could be taken away in a heartbeat.

Nurettin looked out across the tents of Gezi Park and smiled as he watched the protesters get ready for another day. He was going to make some big money and by midnight, if all went well, he'd be drunk and happy.

The world had become irrational and had been going that way for some time now, it seemed. Why, Aylın Akyıldız wondered, had she not noticed? Was it because she had been so deeply engrossed in her work that life had passed her by? Or had she just deliberately closed her mind to things she felt were irrelevant?

Somehow, and she couldn't help but suspect museum staff, word about the body of Constantine Palaiologos had got out. She'd received one death threat through the post and the lab had been bombarded by similar e-mails. Consequently the remains had been moved, in the dead of night, to the museum under the care of Professor Bozdağ. In a way Aylın was relieved but she was also anxious. Now the professor had Palaiologos all to himself and she couldn't shake a very small voice in her head that told her he'd set the whole death threat thing up. Intellectual jealousy was very real, as Ariadne had known. Had her pregnancy actually been irrelevant? Or had she been killed because of what someone had discovered she had found?

Aylın wished she'd called the police when the first e-mails arrived. But then over the years she'd become a bit inured to the opinions of the 'what you're doing is ungodly' lobby. The difference here had been that these e-mails had mentioned a dead infidel king. How had they known? She'd feared that they might have emanated from inside the police force, which was why she'd called Bozdağ. His solution had been immediate and to his own advantage. Or was it?

She'd never discussed with Ariadne who she'd had in mind when she'd talked about a DNA comparison between the remains and a living descendant. Had that person lived in İstanbul or in Greece? Like most people, Aylın had always believed that the Palaiologi had no descendants. But what if they did? With half the population demonstrating about too much religion in public life while the other half wanted more and, further, were demanding that the great Byzantine church the Aya Sofya be turned back into a mosque, now was not the time for Constantine Palaiologos to make an appearance. Religious Greeks would see his discovery as a sign that Aya Sofya should be theirs once again while conservative Muslims could be roused to fury. Maybe the professor had taken possession of the body to keep it under wraps while things were so tense? But then possibly he had found out who Ariadne had in mind for the comparison and had made contact with that person himself. But it was useless speculating. She had no proof for any of her theories and, on top it all, she was feeling bad about herself.

Her husband, Burak, had abandoned his architectural practice and was living in a tent in Gezi Park. The protest had been just what he'd been waiting for. When it had started he'd said, 'Maybe now we'll be able to get out from under all these ghastly, unimaginative shopping malls that have grown up like tumours all over the city.'

Burak particularly hated the faux Ottoman style that was so favoured by developers like that odious man Ahmet Öden. Supposed to be so pious and proper, he knocked people's homes down with impunity and replaced them with Ottoman style buildings that Burak said were about as earthquake-proof as a stack of empty boxes. Still, Aylın couldn't help but feel a little respect for him. He had a daughter who had Down's syndrome, but he was really proud of her, always had photographs taken with her and gave her everything. A man like that surely couldn't be all bad?

Aylın had told Burak that she did want to join him in Gezi, although this wasn't strictly true. In spite of any hopes she may have, she couldn't convince herself that the protest was going to achieve anything, even though it was spreading beyond İstanbul. All she could do – what she'd always done – was to disappear into her work. There was still the skeleton from Galatasaray Lise, plus two that had come in from a site just outside Edirne. She had things to do.

'I can't stand it any longer! What's he doing just sitting there day after day? I've got to tell him to fuck off!'

Yiannis Negroponte was trembling with fury.

Hakkı put a hand on his arm and pulled him back from the front gate. 'You'll do so over my dead body, you stupid bastard!' he hissed. 'As Çetin Bey said, he's playing a game with us. Mainly with you. He just sits in his car. Let him.'

Yiannis sat down. Then he stood up. 'I can't. I can't!' he said. 'Get Çetin Bey. He has to see that Öden is still doing this!'

'No, I will not,' Hakkı said. 'Çetin Bey has other things to do. And we don't want him here too often either. Remember?'

Yiannis walked back from the front gate with his eyes closed, shaking his head.

'Öden cannot buy this house unless you sell it to him,' Hakkı said. 'He wants to wear you down. Don't let him. Eventually something will come along that will take his attention away from this house.'

'Nothing has so far!'

'But it . . .'

Yiannis put his face close to the old man's. 'He knows,' he whispered. 'He all but told me that night he sat beside me in — front of the gate. He remembers.'

'How? I told you, I watched him every moment when he was in this house as a young man.'

'Well I don't know, do I?' Yiannis sneered. 'I was still in Germany being someone I wasn't! You tell me! You were here! Somehow he knows, and if word gets out in times like these they'll put all their power behind him and force us out.'

'Who will?'

'The state, the ruling party, I don't know! But if he doesn't back off and he starts to blab about this house to people in power then we don't stand a chance. You talked about some sort of distraction? Well, we need that now. When the authorities crush Gezi they'll be so buoyed up they'll go for everyone and anyone they see as an enemy.'

Çetin İkmen was trying to work from home. He needed peace and quiet to re-read the translation of Ariadne Savva's notebook and he also wanted to Google some of her interests. Namely Constantine XI Palaiologos and the ninth-century Empress, Zoe. But it wasn't easy. To İkmen's horror and his wife's delight, the central heating engineers had made it in from Üsküdar and were making a terrible noise. They had also switched off the electricity.

İkmen went to see the man in charge, who was in the kitchen drinking tea. He did very little except smoke, drink tea and smack his 'boys' round their heads when they did anything wrong.

'How long is the electricity going to be off?' he asked.

'Ah, that I can't tell you, Çetin Bey,' the man said. 'Depends how long it takes those sons of dogs to put in the pump for your new boiler.'

Although tempted to ask why he employed 'sons of dogs' who he clearly felt were not up to the job, İkmen didn't. Instead he said, 'I'm trying to look up something on my son's computer. It's important.'

The man shook his head. 'Sorry, can't help you. These things take as long as they take.'

Fatma, who was standing by the cooker, looked furiously at her husband and then smiled at the gas fitter. 'Well, Ali Bey, I understand,' she said. 'And I think that you're all doing a wonderful job.'

'Ah, thank you, Fatma Hanım,' he said with a bow.

Çetin İkmen rolled his eyes. Both his wife and the gas fitter saw him.

Fatma pursed her mouth. 'Don't you roll your eyes at me, Çetin İkmen,' she said. 'You're the one who shouldn't be here, not this gentleman. If you want to work, go to work, don't stay here and get under everyone's feet.'

Amazed at how vehement this woman was being with her husband and fearful of witnessing a 'domestic', the gas fitter left the kitchen quickly.

'Whatever happens you're getting your precious central heating, Fatma,' İkmen said. 'It's summer, in case you've not noticed, and so there's no urgency, is there?'

She moved towards him like a small, grey-haired fury. 'You've never wanted this central heating, have you?' she said. 'Rather stick with that disgusting old wood-burning soba.'

'Well, it—'

'It nearly broke my back last year,' she said. 'We're having

160

it and we're having it now.' Then she whispered, 'Do you know how difficult it is to first get and then keep workmen these days? They all want to work for the big developers now. They look down on small jobs like this.'

'Yes, yes, I know all about that,' he said. He lit a cigarette. She wasn't wrong but that didn't make his situation any easier. 'And so I suppose I'll have to try and work in my noisy, hideously smoke-free, infuriating office.'

'That has secure Internet access,' Fatma said. She shook her head. 'I went to the prayer area behind Aya Sofya yesterday and look how I have been rewarded now. These workmen coming are a gift.'

İkmen shook his head. 'I wish you wouldn't pray at Aya Sofya,' he said. 'It's a museum.'

'Maybe not for much longer.'

'You want another war with Greece, do you, Fatma?' İkmen said. 'Remember your cousin Hüsnü died in Cyprus in 1974.'

'Yes, but we won that war, didn't we?' she said. 'The Greeks won't do anything, Çetin. Not now. Anyway, you should be glad that I went out.'

He was always telling her that she didn't get out enough. He feared that being indoors all the time was a sign of increasing religiosity.

'I even met a man when I was on my way to the prayer area yesterday,' she said proudly.

İkmen rolled his eyes again. She made it sound like bungee jumping – unusual and exotic. 'Who was that then?'

'Old Hakkı Bey. You know, who looks after the Greek woman.' İkmen's ears pricked up.

'He was with his son, Lokman, and a grandchild. They were visiting. You know, Lokman's new wife has had three children in three years,' Fatma said. 'I wish our daughters were more

161

keen to have babies. None of them more than two. What can you do?'

İkmen hadn't seen Lokman when he'd gone out to the Negroponte House. But then maybe he and the child had gone back to Hakkı's own home, wherever that was. Because he had always spent so much time at the Negroponte House it was easy to forget that Hakkı had a place of his own.

What Fatma said to him then, İkmen didn't know. He only caught the last bit: 'Well are you going to go to your office or not?'

He went. As he left, he said, 'I'll be back when I'm back.'

Fatma didn't answer.

Ahmet Öden put his phone down on the passenger seat of his car and put his head in his hands. He knew it was cowardly and selfish but all he could think about was fucking Gülizar. In the car it could take him hours to get over the Bosphorus to Moda. He needed her now!

He put a hand on his chest and tried to control his breathing so that he could think clearly. If he drove down to Karaköy he could put the car in a parking garage and get a ferry, then a taxi to somewhere near Gülizar's apartment. That way he could be over there within the hour. And the sooner he was over there the sooner he was back on the European side again – to his real life. In the meantime, he realised he needed to eat. If he didn't eat he couldn't inject himself and that could prove fatal.

By four p.m. Nurettin and the Rat Boy had enough money for their various entertainments and the kid had scooted off to see his dealer. Nurettin, at a rather more leisurely pace, made for the bars on Nevezade Sokak, a small but lively alleyway branching off from the ancient Beyoğlu fish market on İstiklal Caddesi. Hidden in even smaller courts and alleys in the twisted streets round about, Nurettin occasionally caught sight of a church, Greek or Armenian, silent reminders of the communities who had once lived in that area.

If he'd wanted to, he could have had something to eat. There were some nice small restaurants in the area. But that wasn't the mission for Nurettin. He found a bar that was a bit more down at heel than the others, sat outside on a stool and when the waiter came, he ordered a bottle of rakı. The slightly harsh aniseed spirit, mixed with just enough water to make it cloudy, went down like silk. He'd bought a packet of cigarettes on the way up İstiklal too and so Nurettin was entirely at peace with himself and his fellow man for many happy hours.

However, at some point a sort of time shift happened and Nurettin went from being contented on his stool in the late afternoon sunshine to being in a puddle of his own vomit in neon-punctuated darkness. The bar had gone and all he could smell, apart from vomit, was fish. As he attempted to sit up, his hand slid about on slime and scales which seemed to be all over the rough pavement beneath him. Then a cat came along and sniffed his feet. He told it to 'Fuck off!'

A man, a fish vendor by the look of his apron, said, 'You'd best move along, brother. The police'll be here in a minute picking up people like you.'

'What do you mean by that?' Nurettin said. 'People like what?'

'People who've had too much to drink,' the fish vendor said.

'I haven't had too—'

'Brother, you were brawling with a man, which was why they threw you out of the Afrodite Bar.'

Nurettin didn't remember any brawling. He didn't remember leaving the bar or even what its name had been. Had any of that happened? Or was this man just delighting in obliquely calling him an alcoholic?

163

Nurettin got up shakily. 'I'm no alcoholic,' he said. 'I'm a true believer. I just have problems.'

'We all have those,' the man said. 'Not all of us try to solve them by drinking a bottle of rakı and then trying to smash glasses in people's faces.'

'What do you mean? I didn't do that.'

'Yes, you did,' the man said. 'Luckily the man you ended up fighting was even drunker than you were and so he just reeled away. Now you need to go home.'

Nurettin flared. 'Don't tell lies!' he said. 'You're only picking on me because I'm poor. It's all right for you with your own business and your nice home to go to and your wife and—'

'Will you just leave?' the fish man said. 'I mean you no ill will.'

He put a hand on Nurettin's shoulder.

It proved to be a mistake.

'Don't you touch me, you bastard!' Nurettin pushed the man's hand away from him and then slapped his face. 'Don't you dare, you little shit!'

For a moment the fish man just stood and looked at him. Had Nurettin not followed through with a punch to the man's mouth, he would probably have let the slap go. But the punch was too much. The fish man hit back and Nurettin socked him in the stomach.

Equally matched, one small and weak, while the other was as drunk as a sailor, they fought in almost silence, sometimes not even making contact with each other. But it was enough to alert the fish man's neighbours, who went and got the police who were standing at the bottom of the market.

When an officer finally pulled Nurettin off the fish man, the rubbish picker hardly knew what his own name was, let alone what he'd done or where he was.

Chapter 14

Pembe Hanım had been insistent.

'Come on,' she'd said to Sinem when she'd got her out of bed that morning. 'I've cleared it with Kerim, we're going to Gezi.'

Sinem had looked confused. She'd had a lot of pain in the night and had only managed to get through it by reading the book, by Josephine Tey as requested, that Kerim had bought her. Consequently the skin underneath her eyes was black and her face was as pale as the moon.

'Our glorious leader has gone on his foreign trip and so nothing will happen until he gets back,' Pembe said. 'The police won't make a move without his say-so and there are rumours that the President is ready to make concessions. If you don't come now, you'll regret it.'

They went, Sinem in a wheelchair pushed by Pembe which had a rainbow flag tied to the back. When they arrived they were greeted by Pembe's very effusive American friend Rita as well as by a very heavily made up elderly woman.

The American, whose Turkish wasn't bad after ten years as a hostess in İstanbul, introduced her friend. 'This is Samsun,' she said. 'She knows everyone. Samsun, this is Pembe and Sinem.'

The older woman held out her hand to the younger ones as if she might want them to kiss it.

'Sinem is married,' Rita made speech marks with her fingers, 'to a policeman and so we're pretty safe around her. He'd call you if anything bad was going to go down, wouldn't he, honey?'

'Yes.'

There was more noise than Sinem was used to. Loud music, people's voices and even, when they'd first come into the park, a woman belly dancing while people clapped. She was overwhelmed and found it hard to be anything more than monosyllabic. Later, Pembe would tell her off. She'd say, 'There's no need for you to be like that. You need to have more confidence in yourself.'

It wouldn't change a thing.

'My cousin is a *senior* police officer,' Samsun said. 'So I have no worries.'

Whoever she was, she was playing the Grand Dame, which got up Pembe's nose. Who did the old girl think she was?'

'Inspector Çetin İkmen is my cousin,' Samsun said.

The name made Sinem look up.

'What? Kerim's boss?' Pembe said.

'Kerim?'

'He's Sinem's husband,' Pembe said. 'Kerim Gürsel, İkmen's sergeant.'

'Oh,' Samsun said. 'Ah, so does Çetin Bey know that you are—'

'No, of course he doesn't!' Pembe said. 'Why would he?'

Samsun shrugged. Her paste jewellery jingled in the sunlight. 'Well, he and I are friends,' Samsun said. 'He walks with me on World Aids Day every year in memory of my late partner.' She looked at Pembe. 'And although he might not quite get who his sergeant's wife really is, he'd know you, dear. As a chick with a dick myself, I can tell you that İkmen knows his way around the world of the trans.'

'Is that so,' Pembe said.

'Yes.'

'Well, Kerim Bey would rather keep his associations outside his work to himself. Know what I mean?' Pembe said. 'So no telling İkmen—'

'That his sergeant is married to a woman whose friends are transsexuals? Why would I?' Samsun said.

'Just make sure that you don't,' Pembe said.

Samsun raised her hands in submission. 'I won't,' she said. 'But I can assure you that my cousin is not the sort of man who—'

'Just do as we tell you, eh?' Pembe said.

Rita, who was sweating, rubbed her neck with a handkerchief and adjusted her choker to cover her Adam's apple. She didn't like scenes of any kind. She had thought that Pembe might like someone with so much trans life experience like Samsun, but she hadn't reckoned on the shared connection via Pembe's lover, Kerim. Awkward.

'She's running a temperature and she wants her father,' Nanny Mary said in that clipped, superior English of hers.

Ahmet Öden rubbed his thumbs together, a nervous tick left over from childhood. 'You have called the doctor?' he said.

'Of course. He prescribed antibiotics. It's a relatively mild infection but it's in her intestines and Kelime is in some pain. She does want you, Mr Öden.'

The Prime Minister had left the country and there were insane rumours going about that the President might accede to some of the Gezi lunatics' demands. He wanted to get over to Sultanahmet. He'd seen Yiannis Negroponte's face through one of the windows and he was ready to crack. İkmen's visit hadn't increased his confidence one iota. If he could just be leaned on for one or two more days . . .

'Mr Öden, I must—'

'All right! All right!' He stood up.

'I'm sorry, but when a child is sick only her parents will do,' Mary said.

'Yes. Yes.'

He knew that. He loved Kelime with all his heart, she was his world. But spending time with her was hard. What conversation she had was about Barbie dolls and there was a limit to the amount of time he could talk about those. She also repeated herself. And sometimes there were continence issues, usually when she wasn't well. He employed the Englishwoman to deal with these things. He wanted the best for Kelime, the girl who ate everything she wanted and loved her daddy so very, very much.

But he followed Mary to Kelime's little pink bedroom. Usually it smelt of whatever perfume she liked but this time there was an acidic twist of sickness on the air.

'Daddy!'

She put her fat, pink arms out towards him. Her face was flushed and her long black hair was stuck to her head in thin, wet ribbons.

Mary whispered. 'Dr Koç also said that Kelime must have a change of diet. More roughage and—'

'Yes. Yes.'

He sat down next to his daughter's pink bed and then kissed her.

Kelime smiled. 'Daddy.'

Of course the child needed a change of diet. She lived on ice cream, sweets and little else. But what was he supposed to do? She wouldn't eat anything else, and if he tried to make her, she became so unhappy he couldn't bear it. Mary, he knew, tried to get her to take fruit and vegetables but the tantrums she had to put up with were epic. He didn't want Kelime to hate him.

'How are you, my princess?' he asked.

'Got a sore tummy.'

He squeezed her hand. It was clammy. He needed to be in Sultanahmet and then he wanted to be in Moda with Gülizar for the night.

'Don't go,' Kelime said.

Those eyes he found so strange and almost frightening at times, stared down his soul.

'Dr Koç said that Kelime can't be left today,' Mary said. 'It will take twenty-four hours for the antibiotics to work.'

Which was one of the many reasons why Ahmet Öden employed Miss Mary Cox, he thought. But that wasn't the point. Kelime wanted him and so she was going to have him.

He smiled at his daughter and kissed her again. 'Well then, I'd better have a little bed made up for me in here, hadn't I?'

His daughter giggled and shook with excitement. He hugged her. Once she was asleep he'd leave.

The Byzantine Empress Zoe had lived in the ninth century and had been 'born to the purple'. This meant she had been a true daughter of a Byzantine emperor. In common with the Ottoman dynasty, the Byzantines had suffered from occasional outbreaks of pretenders to the throne as well as heirs that lacked legitimacy in some way. But Zoe was not one of them. Beautiful and clever, Zoe ruled alongside three husbands and her sister, Theodora, who she hated. Her first marriage didn't take place until she was fifty and in her final marriage, to Constantine IX, Zoe had been part of a *ménage à trois* with her husband's mistress. As she aged, so she sought to look younger, and the elderly Zoe was well known to brew up fertility potions and skin creams in order to remain beautiful. Some of her subjects called her a witch. No wonder Ariadne Savva had been fascinated by this woman.

İkmen rubbed his eyes and looked away from his computer

screen. According to her colleagues, Ariadne Savva's greatest ambition had always been to write a book about Zoe. But as far as he could see she hadn't even made a start. There had been copious notes on her system but no sign of any coming together of ideas. And her notebook had been silent on the subject of Zoe. That had been about this unknown building and Constantine Palaiologos. She'd been knocked off course and she hadn't told anyone.

'Breakfast! Don't I get breakfast?'

İkmen raised his eyes to the ceiling. By the sound of it they were dragging some drunk along the corridor outside his office.

'You know that food's the best thing to have after a lot of drink!'

There were scuffles and something thudded against his door. He hoped it wasn't the man's head. Some of his colleagues could be less than gentle with drunks. He decided to check the situation.

When he opened his office door he saw two young constables holding up a man whose feet, one real and one false, dragged uselessly on the floor. One of the officers had a fist raised, ready to hit the man.

'Ah, don't be a mindless moron!' İkmen said to the lad. 'Just because he's drunk don't use that as an excuse to—'

'Çetin Bey!'

The voice of the drunk wasn't familiar but the face, even through the bruising and the cuts, was.

'It's me, Nurettin, from Gizlitepe!' he said. And then he smiled, revealing more broken teeth than he'd had when İkmen had first seen him.

'Ah, Nurettin Bey,' İkmen said. 'What are you doing here with us this fine morning?' Then he turned back to the officers, 'Bring him into my office.'

'He's been fighting, sir,' one of the young men said.

'Yes, alcoholics do that sometimes, and he's homeless, so things happen,' İkmen said.

The constables reluctantly took him into İkmen's office and pushed him into a chair.

'So,' İkmen repeated, 'Nurettin Bey, what have you been doing?'

'Oh, I had a few drinks . . .'

The constables left, one of them with some reluctance, İkmen noticed. Everyone was anxious about street unrest in the light of Gezi.

İkmen closed his office door. 'What happened?' he said.

Nurettin shrugged. 'I got arrested fighting a fish seller in the Balık Pazar last night.'

'Because you'd had more rakı than was good for you?'

He shrugged again. 'Because the fish man told lies about me,' he said. 'That I'd been smashing glasses into people's faces. It wasn't true. I didn't do that and I'm fed up with people telling lies about me.'

İkmen locked his office door, opened his window and offered the man a cigarette. Nurettin took it and they both lit up.

'Who tells lies about you, Nurettin?' İkmen asked.

'Well, Cebrail Bey for a start,' he said.

'Cebrail Bey?'

'Our landlord. Told that pig Ahmet Öden that none of us tenants had paid our rent for months and that he could just evict us whenever he wanted to. It was convenient for Öden to believe him and so we all had to go. But Cebrail Bey saved his worst spite for me. He told Öden that I was an alcoholic and an unbeliever. So every time he or his men saw me they chased me away like a mad dog.' He shook his head. 'I have a problem with drink from time to time, Çetin Bey. I'm human, I sin. But I am no atheist and with me, for all my faults, what you see is what you get.'

171

İkmen smiled. Ariadne Savva had been fond of Nurettin and his colleagues from Gizlitepe and he could see why.

Nurettin leaned across İkmen's desk, flicking ash into the old, old saucer the policeman used as an ashtray. 'Ahmet Öden has a mistress,' he said. 'A prostitute.'

İkmen wasn't surprised; he was never surprised when someone who set him- or herself up as a paragon of virtue had feet of clay, but he was very interested. 'Really? How do you know?'

'Ariadne,' he said.

İkmen sat up straight.

'Dr Savva?'

'Yes.'

'How did she know?'

Nurettin shrugged. 'People know. This is İstanbul. No secret can be buried here forever.'

'Did Dr Savva tell you anything about Öden's mistress? Who she is? Where she lives?'

'No, she wouldn't. Said the less we knew the better.'

'So how—'

'I think she was maybe trying to use what she knew about his mistress to get Öden to rehouse us,' Nurettin said.

'Blackmail him.'

'Call it what you like. But that was a long time ago. Months. And she never showed me any proof, so it may be true, it may not be.'

'But you believe it?'

'Yes. Why not? People like him with money to burn, why not have a mistress? He gives money to all sorts of charities. He probably thinks God won't notice. I don't know. But Çetin Bey, I have no proof and Ariadne never showed me any. I've thought that maybe he killed her to silence her. But why would he do that? People like him are untouchable whatever they've

172

done these days. Why take the risk of killing her? Just to call her a liar would have been enough.'

He was right. But İkmen was still intrigued. Being as corrupt as a mass grave and treating your workmen like slaves was one thing, but getting embroiled in sexual misadventures, to many of the conservatively minded, was something else. That was 'dirty' and could taint Öden's image as the sad widower and saintly father of a damaged child which he had so carefully cultivated. But could he have killed to preserve that image? And was İkmen's own view of Öden being coloured by the cruel mind games played at the Negroponte family's expense?

It was hot. Midday, and the more empty than usual streets of Sultanahmet oscillated in the heat haze. Even so, the Negroponte house was locked, shuttered and had its windows closed. Behind one, hidden by a thick, dusty net curtain, Yiannis sat on a wooden chair, looking out into the street.

For what seemed like hours, he didn't so much as twitch. Then he said, 'He's not coming. Not now. Why not?'

Hakkı, halfway through darning a sock, looked up. 'I don't know. Maybe he'll come later.'

'No, he always comes before midday,' Yiannis said. 'Has he given up?'

'How should I know? Will you give it a rest?' Men like Ahmet Öden didn't give up. He was simply doing something else. That was the only reason he wasn't sitting outside in his car.

'What do you think Inspector İkmen thought of the house?' Yiannis said.

'Madam always allowed the children who visited to have the run of the house,' Hakkı said. 'Nikos Bey and Madam had to wait for a child of their own for some years, but in the meantime

173

she filled the house with other people's children. Çetin Bey's mother was her seer. A strange woman, but she knew things.'

'What?'

'I don't know. What passed between Ayşe Hanım and Madam was for them alone. But the Albanian predicted the tragedy of 1955, that I do know.'

Yiannis shook his head and then went back to looking out of the window again.

The call to prayer broke the silence. It was loud in the old city these days, the numerous muezzins' calls amplified through high-volume loud speakers. Yiannis watched as people began to walk towards the Blue Mosque and the prayer area behind Aya Sofya. He still remembered what you had to do. In grey mosques in Hannover and in the small prayer room at the Volkswagen plant. It had been second nature. Now it made him shudder.

Hakkı said, 'In answer to your question, I imagine Çetin Bey would have found being escorted in this house different, but not odd. He is no longer a child and he is a policeman; he wouldn't expect to wander at will. Who would?'

'I thought I discerned shock on his face when I took him from the bathroom back to the salon. I saw him look past me into the kitchen.'

'And so the kitchen is different,' Hakkı said. 'After all these years he would be expecting that. You over-think everything.'

'Yes, but no other part of the house has changed.'

Hakkı shrugged. 'So what?'

Yiannis turned away from the window. 'If Öden gets in here what do you think he will see?'

'Only you can really know that,' Hakkı said. 'But while he isn't here, you should go and entertain the children with your tricks. I saw some boys at the gate this morning. When the weather has cooled later this afternoon, you can go out.'

174

'What if Öden comes back? Who will look after my mother? Aren't you at the doctor's today?'

'Later, yes. But you need to get out. You're going mad. Do your tricks by the gate. Then if Öden arrives you can slip back in and lock up,' Hakkı said. 'The little ones, if no one else, like what you do.'

But Yiannis didn't know. He did enjoy performing tricks and illusions for the local children, but ever since Öden had put pressure on, the joy seemed to have gone out of everything in his life, including even that. Eventually he said, 'We'll see.' And then he turned back to the window and looked out at the baking street.

Iris was talking very intensely to a plain, middle-aged woman in a headscarf about 'the Kurds'.

'You see, that deputy from the BDP was right,' she was saying. 'It's not about just individual rights, not now. It's about Kurdish rights and identity, yeah, but it's also about the rights of the lesbians and gays, young people, religious people, Christians, Jews – everybody in this country. We don't want to be *told* stuff. You know what I mean? We don't need to be *told* anything. We're adults. Yeah?'

The woman just nodded. Peri smiled. Back in Gezi now that her shift had ended, she could see how much the protest had grown in just one day. Now people were coming from all over İstanbul to visit the tent city and to thank the protesters for standing up for the park. Some of the opposition political parties had tents, as well as Greenpeace. Some people reckoned that the protest had swollen to 100,000 people, and yet underneath all the carnival was a threat that was all too obvious. One man was selling gas masks, and others were selling 'Guy' masks like the ones in that film, *V for Vendetta*. Lots of people were running around wearing them, looking creepy. And then there was the immediate vicinity outside the park. Beyond the tents were barricades, TOMA water cannon and more police than could be counted. She'd seen some when she'd arrived, staggering around the edge of Gezi looking sleep deprived. It was said that some of the protesters were giving them water and that they were sleeping on their riot shields. A few, it was rumoured, had expressed sympathy with the protest. But all the shops in the area had been boarded up and Peri knew that it could all kick off again at any moment.

She bought herself a can of peach juice and sat on the grass. At least Ömer was happier now she was back at work. But he still didn't like her visiting the park, even though he agreed with everything Gezi stood for. How couldn't he? Maybe this was finally the chance for all marginalised groups to get a real say. Even, perhaps, their own people.

Everyone in Mardin knew about the snake goddess, the Sharmeran. Some of the Christians openly worshipped her alongside their own deities, but only a few had dedicated their lives just to her. The Munguns were one such family, as well as the father of a high-ranking local police inspector. But in spite of their successes and respectability, inequalities still remained, especially outside the walls of Mardin and away from the plains of Mesopotamia where the Sharmeran lived in a deep, deep cave.

Night began to draw in almost before Peri knew. She had to decide whether to go home – she was on an early shift the following day – or stay and listen to a group of young boys singing in Armenian. She decided to stay.

Chapter 15

Mehmet Süleyman's mobile phone rang just once before he answered it. It was almost morning and he hadn't slept all night. But Gonca was asleep and he wanted her to stay that way. He'd picked a fight with her the previous evening because he was bored and he didn't want it to start all over again. He put the phone to his ear, got out of bed and took the call in the bathroom.

'Süleyman.'

'Inspector.'

He recognised the voice: Commissioner Teker. What did she want at this hour?

'Madam.'

'Süleyman, we have a situation that may or may not be suspicious,' she said. 'An apparent suicide.'

He felt his heart sink. He wanted to have a case he could get his teeth into. Lack of meaningful work, beyond the identity of a 1950s skeleton, was making him crazy – and turning his eyes towards women who were not Gonca.

'Apparent?'

'Looks like a suicide but the attending officer isn't so sure.'

'Why not?'

'You'll have to let him explain,' she said. 'I'd like you to go there. Dr Sarkissian is already on his way.'

'Madam.'

'It's in Moda, I'm afraid,' she said. 'So you'll have to catch a ferry. The local constabulary will pick you up from Kadıköy pier-head.'

Against every feeling of disgust that rose up in his mind, he hoped the local officer was right and it wasn't a suicide.

'Get back to me,' Teker said.

'Of course.'

She ended the call. Beyond Gonca's bedroom door he could hear the rest of her family waking up and beginning to move about. Soon, all but her father and an old maid aunt would be off to Gezi Park in their brightest summer clothes, and that included Gonca. Not that he knew everything they did when they were there. Gonca, he knew, collected material for her collage art, but he suspected the others danced for money or sold flowers from the garden. He knew he was probably misjudging them, falling into every possible cliché that existed about Roma. But he didn't see Gonca's family as particularly politically engaged in spite of their bad experiences with property developers.

He had a quick shower, dressed and went out into the cool morning air. The day was young, Balat looked shabbily beautiful and for a moment he almost felt optimistic. If only he could have shared that feeling with his friend Çetin İkmen.

'Come on, get up!' Fatma said. 'The workmen are here.'

İkmen had to struggle to get out of his dream. As soon as she'd consummated her first marriage, when she was fifty, the Byzantine Empress Zoe had spent the next decade trying to get pregnant. She'd been to doctors, seers and sorcerers, visited the shrines of saints and created potions and aphrodisiacs in the seclusion of her own bedchamber. All to no avail – except in İkmen's dream. In that she'd had a child, the son she'd always dreamed about, child of a ruling empress, born 'to the purple'. Why the child had looked like his own son, Kemal, was prob-

178

ably because Fatma had spent much of the previous evening trying to persuade the boy to leave Gezi Park and come home. But he hadn't.

'Come on! Come on!' Fatma said as she shooed him into the shower. 'They want to turn the water off.'

He got out of his apartment as soon as he could and wandered down to the old Pudding Shop for coffee and a cigarette outside in the weak early morning sunshine.

Ever since he'd spoken to Nurettin the rubbish picker, he'd been unable to think about much except the possible existence of Ahmet Öden's mistress. It made absolute sense that a good-looking, rich and powerful widower like him should have a woman in his life. İkmen couldn't and wouldn't condemn him for it, but he knew that some of those who had put Öden where he was today would. Was it really possible he had killed Ariadne Savva to silence her about this woman? And how had Savva found out about her?

It seemed to İkmen that Ariadne Savva had been a woman ruled by great passions: for her work, her heritage, even for the rubbish pickers of Gizlitepe. But would she have put her life on the line for them? Considering the professional breakthroughs she seemed to have been making, this didn't make sense. Had Öden reacted in a way she hadn't anticipated? And if he had done so, why had he taken her child? If he'd taken it.

İkmen went inside the Pudding Shop, got another coffee and returned to his chair in the sunshine and the third cigarette of the day. Öden was well known to have a disabled daughter. Occasionally he displayed this girl in public with an expression on his face, İkmen always thought, that looked halfway between pride and constipation. He obviously loved her and would probably do anything he could to make her life pleasant and wealthy. And if Ariadne Savva had threatened that . . . Then why hadn't

179

Öden just given the rubbish pickers some cheap, shonky old flats to live in and shut her up that way? That was what, according to Nurettin, she had wanted. But then that was bypassing the issue of Öden's character, which didn't allow for defeat. The Negropontes knew all about that.

İkmen wanted to confront Öden, but knew he couldn't. Where was his proof for this mistress outside the mind of a bitter alcoholic?

Arto Sarkissian stood back from the bathtub and narrowed his eyes.

'It isn't right,' he said to Süleyman, 'because I would expect far more blood.'

'There's blood in the water,' Süleyman said.

'Not enough. Remember, a small amount of blood goes a long way, and while I accept she was probably put in the water while she was still alive, she didn't survive for very long.'

A scene redolent of ancient Rome had greeted Kadıköy Sergeant Tuncel when he'd been called in the early hours of the morning to an apartment on Rıza Paşa Sokak in the pretty waterfront district of Moda. A man en route to Ataturk Airport had found a neighbour's front door open. Fearing it had been broken into, he'd gone inside, where he'd found his neighbour, a Mrs Ayşel Ocal, dead in her bath. Both wrists had been slit.

'And then of course we come to the cuts, which are equally as deep on both arms. That's difficult to pull off with the first arm weakened by the first cut,' the Armenian said. 'They run vertically up the arm as opposed to horizontally, which shows that the cutter knew what he or she was doing. But her heart had all but stopped when she entered the water.'

'So she didn't cut her wrists in the bath?'

'No. Her heart was already beating its last by then,' he said. 'What killed her? Did she kill herself? I won't know until I can get her on the table. But I can see no sign of head injury or any other marks on the body apart from the cuts to the arms.'

'Poison?'

'Maybe. Toxicology as ever is on my "to do" list,' he said.

Sergeant Tuncel, a uniformed officer in his forties, joined them.

'Er, Inspector . . .'

'Yes?'

Arto Sarkissian saw the man flinch. Süleyman's manner had always been arrogant but as he was getting older it was becoming more exaggerated. But he was unhappy, which wasn't helping. Arto would have to have a word with İkmen and get him to end this feud between them. Hell would freeze over before Süleyman would make it up with him.

'Neighbours say the woman was a bit of a lively sort,' Tuncel said. 'Dressed very loud, if you know what I mean. Never covered her head.'

'Managed to rouse the kapıcı?' Süleyman asked, referring to the building's concierge. Kapıcıs usually knew just about everything about the people they served, including details of their private lives.

'Gone,' Tuncel said.

'Gone? Where?'

'Gezi, the neighbours think. Went about three days ago,' Tuncel said.

'Then we'll need to find him.' He turned to the Armenian. 'How long do you think she's been dead, Doctor?'

'Given her condition and when she was discovered, a few hours ago at the most,' he said.

'Did Mrs Ocal live alone?' Süleyman asked Tuncel.

'Yes, but a man visited.'

'Always the same man?'

He shrugged.

'Find out.'

'Yes, sir.'

He went to leave but Süleyman called him back. 'And find out what Mrs Ocal did for a living, will you?'

'Sir.'

'And I want this place searched. Specifically looking for this woman's contacts. So computer systems, phones, address books, diaries, photographs.'

'Yes, sir.'

He left. They both looked at the body in its pool of red-tinged water. Mrs Ocal had been a large woman with wide hips and a narrow waist. Her breasts, which were also large, were very obviously enhanced by silicone implants. Naturally honey-brown skinned, she had long, thick, dyed dark red hair. She looked either eastern or foreign. As to her age, Arto had to say over twenty, but how much over he really wouldn't know until he examined her properly.

Then Süleyman said, 'So, Doctor, would you concur with Sergeant Tuncel?'

'That this is a suicide? No,' he said. 'Given what we can see here, I'd say murder is the most likely scenario.'

'OK. Thank you.'

Süleyman turned away. But as he moved, Arto Sarkissian was horrified to catch sight of a smile on his face.

He'd been there when Kelime had woken, which had been the main thing. But now Semih had called him and he had to go.

Ahmet Öden kissed his daughter on the head and left the house. Some bastards in Gizlitepe had attacked the site overnight and he had to go and assess the damage. Animals! Why did they fail to realise that it was people like him who were turning their İstanbul into a world city? Why did they want to live in hideous old slums?

182

He drove south to the Bosphorus Bridge, which was at a standstill, and then just moved forwards centimetre by centimetre until he got to the Asian side. Why all the crazies had come out to oppose a new, third Bosphorus Bridge he just couldn't fathom. So it had been decided to name it after a particularly punitive sultan? So a few hectares of trees would have to be sacrificed? If nothing was done the city would come to a standstill.

He turned right towards Kadıköy and Gizlitepe. He had wanted to get to the Negroponte House but his brother had insisted he look at the Gizlitepe damage first.

'It's a disgrace,' he'd said. 'All the windows in the lower part of one tower have been broken and what looks like faeces smeared all over the equipment.'

He'd called the police, such as they were. Most of them were up at Gezi Park and, apparently, there'd been a murder too. The dregs of the police world had turned up according to Semih. How could second-rate old men hope to catch anything other than a cold?

Öden put his hand on the briefcase on the passenger seat. He'd had his lawyer draw up a contract for the Negropontes which, although it was for far more money than he had wanted to pay, had to be for an amount that would finally impress them. But if that didn't work, he'd take Yiannis to one side and tell him what he'd done after he'd scratched his hand, with Yiannis' blood and skin.

That would be a gamble, because there was always a chance that Yiannis really was who he claimed to be. But Ahmet doubted it. He'd heard the way the old man Hakkı spoke to him, seen how he looked at him too. With suspicion.

There were, it was said, over a hundred thousand people in Gezi Park, and the politicians the Prime Minister had left behind when he went on his North African trip appeared to be trying to appease them. There were now protests similar to Gezi in Ankara, Izmir, Adana – all over the country. If they brought the government down, they'd bring him down with them and then he'd never get the Negroponte house. He'd never be able to fulfil his promise to his father.

It wasn't easy trying to second guess where a disgruntled kapıcı would be in a crowd of over a 100,000 people. Cafer Ayan was a small man in late middle-age with grey hair and a thick moustache. How many millions of those were in the city?

All Ömer Mungun really had to distinguish the kapıcı of Ayşel Ocal's apartment in Moda from the common herd of disappointed middle-aged Turkish men was that he had a limp. He'd lost his right leg in the Cyprus war of 1974. What had replaced it was apparently made of metal.

None of the residents had known anything more about Mr Ayan. Divorced and childless, apparently he was a miserable man addicted to daytime television and, some speculated, pornography. According to Süleyman, Ayşel Ocal had been a handsome woman. Had Ayan decided to murder her after she had rebuffed his advances? If he'd ever made any advances.

Ayan's story, according to his residents, was that he'd left the apartment block three days before after having a row with a man on the fourth floor known for his piety. It had started because Ayan had wanted to have the radio on when he washed the apartment's staircases. The man on floor four had said he found the music offensive. They'd argued, Ayan had told the man to 'fuck off' and then he'd yelled that he was off to Gezi and fuck them all at the top of his voice.

The woman Süleyman and Dr Sarkissian had found with her wrists slit in her bath had died, the pathologist reckoned, at the earliest at ten p.m. the previous evening. Well after Ayan had left the building. But had he gone back at some point? And if so, why? There was no evidence at all to suggest that Ayan had ever had designs on Ayşel Ocal. In fact, one resident had said that it was only Ayan who ever spoke to the man who sometimes came to visit Mrs Ocal. That was why they needed to find him.

Ömer looked down at the one picture he had of Ayan and found himself thinking that he looked like his father.

'Ömer? Who's that?' Peri pointed at the photograph. They had met, as agreed, by the Greenpeace tent.

'Someone we need to question,' he said. 'Shouldn't you be at work?'

'Just finished. I was on an early. You know, Ömer, nobody's going to help you find anyone here.'

He frowned.

'I mean, how many officers are lurking like death outside this park with their gas canisters and water cannon?'

'I'm not here to arrest this man, only to talk to him,' Ömer said.

'Yes. Right.'

'No, really!' He took her arm and led her off the path and over to a more secluded area. He showed her the photograph again. 'A woman was found murdered in her apartment this morning in Moda,' he said. 'This man is the kapıcı of her building. Three days ago he left to come and camp out here.'

'Oh, so he can't . . .'

'We don't think he killed her, not at the moment,' Ömer said. 'But the woman had a lover. Nobody in the building knew who he was or ever spoke to him. Except this kapıcı, Cafer Ayan. We need to find this boyfriend, as you can imagine, and this man Ayan is the only lead we have.'

'So what are you doing?' Peri said.

'Just looking around. There's three of us, including Inspector İkmen's sergeant.'

'Kerim Gürsel?'

'He'll be flattered you remembered his name. But Peri, he is married.'

She waved a dismissive hand. 'I don't need man trouble in my life, I've enough problems with a little brother.'

'If I could I'd ID check every man here,' Ömer said. 'But given the situation and the mood . . .'

'That would not go down well,' she said.

'So hence the stupid sneaking about after a man who has no friends, no family and whose only distinguishing characteristic is a limp.'

Peri crossed her arms over her chest and looked at her younger brother. He was clearly tired and looked crushed. She got the impression that his boss used him badly and hard much of the time. And although Süleyman had always been the soul of gallantry to her, she didn't like him because she didn't like it when Ömer looked like a whipped dog.

'Well, you know what you need, don't you, Ömer?' she said.

'What's that? Divine intervention?'

'Failing that.'

'No.'

'You need allies,' she said. 'You need people who can walk through these crowds looking for a man with a limp without sticking out like you do in your suit and tie and shiny shoes. Ömer, I have made friends here. Some of them are very colourful and flamboyant and some are not. But they all fit here and when I tell them that you need their eyes and ears to help you solve a murder I'm sure they'll forgive you for being part of an establishment that wants to cut down innocent trees.' She smiled. 'Maybe.'

Then Ömer's phone rang.

*　　*　　*

A junior researcher in a white coat, a kid by the look of him, brought tea for them both. When he'd gone Aylın Akyıldız closed her office door.

'Ariadne and I worked together,' she said. 'But I never knew what she did in her leisure time.'

'She never mentioned her work with the rubbish pickers of Gizlitepe or the name Ahmet Öden to you?' İkmen said.

'No. And believe me, I would have known if she had talked about Öden. My husband is an architect and he goes on about his buildings all the time.'

'In what sense?'

'He hates them,' she said. 'Says they're unimaginative and poorly constructed. How does Öden come into the rubbish pickers of Gizlitepe? I thought he knocked their homes down to build some tower blocks.'

'He did,' İkmen said. 'Which was why Dr Savva had issues with him.'

She frowned.

'Dr Savva befriended the rubbish pickers and tried to get Öden, who had thrown them out of their homes, to rehouse them,' İkmen said. 'Because they were only ever tenants as opposed to owner occupiers, he didn't strictly owe them anything. But they were and are homeless and Dr Savva felt sorry for them. She made representation to Öden on their behalf which he apparently took badly.'

Aylın Akyıldız drank some tea. 'In what way?'

'It is alleged that he threatened her. With what, I don't know. That's why I am speaking to her colleagues and friends,' İkmen said.

She shook her head. 'I wish I could help you, but I don't know anything.' She sighed. 'And now they have taken Constantine Palaiologos to the museum . . .'

187

'Oh?'

She looked very unhappy. Had Professor Bozdağ's very apparent anger at what Savva and Akyıldız had been doing without him finally resulted in his taking over the entire project?

'I knew I'd have to surrender him to the museum eventually, but my researches were not complete,' she said. 'What can you do? Ariadne should have shared her find with the museum, I know that. And anyway, there were other factors involved.'

'What other factors?'

She looked as if she was struggling with something. Then she said, 'Look, I know that maybe I should have told you, but for the last week I've been getting death threats.'

'If you've been getting death threats you should definitely have told me,' İkmen said. 'What kind of death threats?'

'Relating to the body,' she said. 'Palaiologos. Post and e-mails about how if I don't stop working on the body I will be killed. Religious nonsense about how the body of an infidel king should be destroyed. What scared me the most was how they knew. As far as I know, it's only myself, you and Professor Bozdağ's team at the museum who know that the alleged emperor even exists.'

'Unless Dr Savva told someone. Her lover? The father of her child? If we could locate him, then maybe we could find the baby. We've got uniformed officers interviewing men convicted of child abuse. I've even spoken to a woman who stole a baby from Yeşilköy thirty-five years ago. Nothing! Are you sure you never saw her with a man, Dr Akyıldız?'

She shook her head. 'I've wracked my brains but I can't think of anyone,' she said. 'I knew so little about her.'

And yet her child had to have had a father. What also passed through İkmen's mind was that maybe Professor Bozdağ or someone in his team had sent the death threats to get hold of the body for themselves. But they hadn't needed to do that. As Dr

Akyıldız had said, Ariadne should have shared the body with them when she'd first found it. They had a right to study those bones.

'I'd like to see those e-mails and letters if you still have them,' İkmen said.

'I do. But our IT guy said that it was impossible to trace the e-mails.'

'Well, let's let our IT people have a look at them,' İkmen said. 'And with the letter maybe we can get some fingerprints or DNA.'

'OK,' she said.

He left with two word-processed letters and a stack of printed e-mails. They were standard religious fanatic fare, littered with words like 'infidel', 'unbelievers' and 'unclean'. They could have come from almost any monomaniac. Or not. Although Dr Akyıldız had been wrong not to take these documents straight to the police, she had been right to be scared. Nobody at the museum would have spoken to anyone outside the institution about Palaiologos. If he was who Dr Savva thought he was, then he could be a jewel in their academic crown. And they all cared about what they did.

What was particularly worrying was why Dr Akyıldız had only received death threats since Dr Savva's death. Did that mean anything? One scenario that İkmen couldn't shift from his mind was that Ariadne Savva had told her killer about her find to try and save her own and her baby's lives. But that assumed that he or she would be interested in Palaiologos.

Maybe, if she had been murdered, it was so that her killer could gain access to the body. Maybe that had been his or her plan all along? But then why kill Savva when Akyıldız was the one who actually had Palaiologos in her possession?

Chapter 16

It was after midnight, and although the vast, ugly house was shut up for the night, a row of pink and green fairy lights around the front door merrily flashed on and off. Hürrem Teker pushed the doorbell again and tried to imagine what would be inside this house which looked like a frosted wedding cake. Vast gilded sofas sitting on expensively cheap-looking carpets and more leather than a herd of bulls, probably. At her side, she heard Mehmet Süleyman clear his throat.

There were five of them outside Ahmet Öden's Bebek house: Teker, Süleyman, Ömer Mungun and two uniforms. A ridiculously overblown display of manpower for just one person. It seemed stupid that someone of her seniority was there at all. But Öden, whatever he had or hadn't done, was powerful, and that, if nothing else, had to be taken into account and respected.

A young man, bleary eyed and wearing old-man style candy-striped pyjamas, opened the door.

Teker held up her ID. 'Police,' she said. 'We want to speak to Mr Ahmet Öden.'

'He's in bed. What—'

'Who are you?' Teker asked.

'I'm his brother.'

'Get him up then, Mr Öden,' Teker said. 'Tell him we need to speak to him.' She looked at the two uniforms. 'You, round the back.'

'What do you want to speak to him for?'

'That's between us and your brother. Now are you going to get him up or am I?' Teker said.

The young man, who had to be Semih Öden by Teker's reckoning, let the three of them into the house and took them through to a large, modern lounge. They all took their shoes off. Then the young man went to fetch his brother.

Teker, Süleyman and Ömer Mungun stood on a shocking-pink carpet the size of a swimming pool and tried to look anywhere that wasn't lurid. Eventually Süleyman said, 'I'm speechless,' but then they all stayed silent until Ahmet Öden appeared.

Although clearly just roused, he looked alert and even groomed in his faux karate suit pyjamas. 'What do you want?'

He addressed Teker and only her, as she had known he would.

'We'd like to know where you were last night between nine p.m. and two a.m.,' she said.

'I was here,' he said. 'Why?'

'Can anyone corroborate that?'

'What, that I was here? I imagine so,' he said. 'My daughter was sick yesterday and so I stayed here at home all day and all night.'

'I trust your daughter is better now.'

'Yes. Much.'

'However, she is a minor.' Teker smiled. 'Were any adults in the house last night? Your brother?'

Semih Öden had not returned with his brother.

'No. But my daughter's English nanny, Mary Cox, was here.'

'Then we'll need to speak to her,' Teker said. 'Is she here now?'

'Yes. What's this about?' he said. 'Why do you want to know where I was last night? What's happened?'

'Mr Öden, would you please go and wake Mary Cox,' Teker

said. She looked at Ömer Mungun. 'Sergeant, would you please accompany Mr Öden.'

'Yes, madam.'

'Accompany me!' Ahmet Öden's face flushed. 'What do I need him with me for?' He moved towards Teker and pushed his face into hers. 'What's this about, Commissioner? Have you come to arrest me? What for? I am a law-abiding citizen whose sole focus is to improve this city. Not some hooligan sitting down on the grass in Gezi Park smoking drugs and drinking beer!'

Teker remained calm. She'd been expecting this. Either he was a good actor or he hadn't seen the news.

'A woman we believe has a connection to you has been found dead in an apartment in Moda,' she said.

He stood, his mouth slightly open. Silent.

'The woman's name hasn't as yet been released to the media,' Teker said. 'But she was called Mrs Ayşel Ocal.'

'Known as "Gülizar" when she used to strip for a living,' Süleyman said.

'I believe so.' Teker smiled. 'Twenty-five years old, originally from Sulukule . . .'

'How on earth would I know anyone like that!' Öden said. 'How?'

She shrugged. 'Don't know, sir. But she had a lot of photographs of you on her computer and you weren't just drinking coffee and making polite conversation, if you know what I mean.'

'No, I don't actually, I—'

'In one you were naked and in a state of arousal,' Süleyman said. 'Another, one of many, was what I believe is called a "selfie" of you and Mrs Ocal where you are both naked and you have a hand on—'

'This is monstrous!' He ran a hand through his hair. 'Why would someone like me know some foul, indecent gypsy?'

'I never said she was a gypsy,' Süleyman said.

'You said she came from Sulukule!' he bellowed. 'They were all dirty gypsies there!'

'Gypsies, mainly, dirty—'

'I don't know this woman! The photographs are fakes! Composites! People can do such things on computers now,' he said. 'Show them to me!'

'The computer is being examined by forensic investigators. They're part of a crime scene. I can't.'

'Well, they have to be composites anyway!' he said. 'Have to be!'

'Why? Why would Mrs Ocal make composite sex pictures of you?' Teker said. 'Unless of course you do know about this because she was trying to blackmail you. Gypsies can't like people like you, Mr Öden, can they? Developers who destroy their homes.'

Suddenly deflated, he sat down on one of his many pink sofas and put his chin in his hands.

'Quite honestly, if you were having an affair with this woman, I couldn't give a damn,' Teker said. 'Even if you bought that Moda apartment for her, it's none of my business.'

The kapıcı of the Moda building still hadn't been found, and so far all that had come to light had been a large set of photographs of Öden, with Ayşel Ocal or alone, often asleep on her bed. He'd been to that apartment. He'd certainly had sex with her. That no one in the building had recognised him meant either that he always went to Moda in disguise or that no one in the block knew who he was.

'The reason we're here,' Teker continued, 'is to find out where you were between the hours of nine a.m. last night and two p.m. this morning. If you had an affair with her, I really don't care. I want to know if you killed her.'

* * *

193

Yiannis Negroponte couldn't sleep. A twenty-five-year-old woman had been found dead in her apartment at Moda. Although the police had not released her name to the media, he wondered whether it could be Gülizar the gypsy. And, although he had never borne her any ill will, he hoped that it was her. The police suspected foul play and so whether her lover Ahmet Öden had killed her or not was almost irrelevant. Somehow his connection to her would come up and then his reputation as an upright, moral man would be ruined. Then he'd leave them alone.

He read the news item in *Cumhuriyet* again. The woman had been found in a third-floor apartment in a block that overlooked the Sea of Marmara. That described Gülizar the gypsy's accommodation exactly. Yiannis breathed raggedly. Did he dare to hope that it was her? Did he further dare to dream that Öden had killed her?

But if he had, he couldn't think why. Unless it had been an accident. Although she was very obviously sexy, Gülizar was discreet and she was his only mistress, which implied that he had to be attached to her. But had she been attached to him?

He was good-looking and rich but other than that – if one needed any more than that – he was an odious bigot. As a gypsy, Gülizar must have been affected by developers like Öden, if not Öden himself. They bought sites in gypsy areas with impunity. Or so it seemed to Yiannis. Had she finally argued with him about it and he'd killed her in a fight?

He heard Anastasia cough upstairs and breathed shallowly so that he could hear her. If she suddenly gagged he might have to go up and make sure that she was all right. But she didn't and he went back to his newspaper again. In the morning, when Hakkı came in, he'd ask him if he'd heard any more about the killing in Moda. He knew Çetin İkmen well and so the inspector might have told him something.

*   *   *

'The last time I went in to see Kelime last night was eight o'clock,' Mary said. 'Mr Semih Öden had left to go back to his own apartment, and because Kelime was ill, it was decided that we would all have an early night.'

Although Mary spoke reasonable Turkish, Teker had decided to conduct her interview in English. It was the middle of the night and the woman was clearly scared – it made sense and would hopefully reduce misunderstanding.

'When I went in this morning at seven, Mr Öden was lying on top of the bed I'd made up for him in Kelime's room,' Mary said.

'Was he in his night clothes or dressed?' Teker asked. 'I ask because you said that he was on top of the bed and not inside.'

'He was in his night clothes. But it was hot.'

'Do you know whether Mr Öden left his daughter's room at all during the night?'

Süleyman had asked the question. Mary turned her attention to him. 'No,' she said. 'I certainly didn't hear anyone moving around in the night and I sleep in the room next door to Kelime. Not that I did sleep.'

'And yet I noticed a bottle of sleeping pills on your nightstand, Miss Cox.'

She turned back to Teker.

'If you were having trouble sleeping, why didn't you take one?' the Commissioner asked.

'I don't take them often.' Mary looked down. 'Usually I have to stay alert in case Kelime needs me in the night. But whenever I have a night off or, like last night when Mr Öden was with her, I do take pills to help me sleep. Generally.'

'Why didn't you on this occasion?'

'I wanted to be alert in case Mr Öden needed me. Kelime was very sick.'

'Does your employer know about your pill habit?'

'I don't know.'

'You've not told him.'

'No.' She coloured a little. 'Mr Öden is a very moral man. He doesn't drink, smoke or take drugs. Maybe I should have told him but I just didn't know how. Will you tell him?'

Teker said, 'No. If you didn't take them last night then they're irrelevant to this investigation. But if this situation becomes more serious then maybe that subject will have to be addressed. I suggest you tell him yourself now, Miss Cox.'

Mary nodded, but she looked extremely anxious. While Ömer Mungun sat with Öden in his lounge, Teker and Süleyman were with Mary in the kitchen. Small, pale and older than she looked, Mary Cox was a career nanny who had been all over the world with 'her' children. She'd never married and probably never would.

Teker and Süleyman had, so far, told Mary nothing about why they needed to know where Öden had been the previous night. But now Teker said, 'Miss Cox, do you know whether your employer is in a relationship at the moment?'

Mary looked flustered.

'You may answer without fear and truthfully,' Teker said. 'Your employer cannot discipline you for that. They don't do that.'

Teker knew that was a lie but she said it anyway. Hundreds of domestic workers were dismissed every year because they gossiped about their employers' sex lives. But Mary Cox's continued employment wasn't her problem.

Mary, however, shook her head. 'Mr Öden is a very moral man,' she said. 'I have never seen him with any woman apart from the servants and his secretary.'

'And what of them?' Süleyman asked. 'Has he . . .'

'Oh, he would never abuse his staff!' Mary was horrified. 'No, no, no, no, no!'

196

And yet it was well known that on his building sites he was a harsh boss who dismissed men he felt didn't work hard enough and, it was said, was not above physically abusing them. It was possible he didn't bring that into his home and also possible that he didn't prey on his female domestic staff.

'Mr Öden has always said that he will never marry anyone while Kelime is still at home,' Mary said.

Teker frowned. 'Will Kelime ever leave home?' she said.

'With support she could have her own flat, er, apartment, one day,' Mary said. 'I know what a lot of people think about Down's syndrome individuals but a lot of them can cope. I knew a married couple with Down's back in England.'

'Did you.'

When Teker and Süleyman walked back into the salon, Öden said, 'Well?'

'Miss Cox says that you slept in your daughter's room last night, Mr Öden,' Teker said.

He stuck his chin in the air. 'I told you so. Why didn't you believe me?'

Ömer Mungun drove Teker and Süleyman back to police headquarters. The two uniformed officers followed on behind.

As they drove through the pretty Bosphorus village of Ortaköy, Teker said to Süleyman, 'Well, even with my gloves on, I don't suppose Mr Öden is happy with the treatment I meted out to him. I imagine his lawyer will be on the phone to me in a few hours' time.'

'Madam, do you think that it's possible those photographs of him with Mrs Ocal are composites?' Süleyman said.

'No, of course not! Whether he killed her or not is open to question and we'll have to wait for forensics to guide us on that,' Teker said. 'But he was having sex with her. No question! He was worried and he was guilty.'

197

'When you both left the room he didn't say a word to me,' Ömer said.

'No?'

'Nothing. I got the feeling he was embarrassed,' Ömer said.

'If he's been caught out in an affair, particularly with an ex-stripper, he probably is embarrassed,' Teker said. 'What I want to know is whether he murdered her or not. His political allies can all wring their hands in false shock at his liaison with a "filthy whore", but we have to catch her killer, and if that is him . . .'

A group of what looked like young boys in Guy Fawkes masks ran into the road in front of the car carrying an anarchy banner. Ömer slammed on the brakes. The boys stopped, laughed and then ran away. Nobody in the car said anything.

Semih Öden looked across at his brother with disgust. 'How could you?' he said. 'With a whore! How many people do we know who would have matched you with a clean, pious girl you could have married and had more children with?'

'How could I?' Ahmet Öden said. 'With Kelime? How could I bring her a stepmother who might hate her?'

'If the woman hated Kelime, you could divorce her!'

'Or what if we had children, this woman and I, normal children? Would I love them more than Kelime because they are normal? Would I love them more because their mother was not a selfish slut like her mother? Would Kelime just fade into the background of my life and die without my noticing? That is not the right way of things. That is not the Islamic thing to do.'

'And buying an apartment for a cheap gypsy and having sex with her is?' Semih shook his head. 'You delude yourself because you want this woman!'

'Who is dead!' Ahmet stood up and paced the salon. 'How

198

can she be? I saw her three days ago. Nothing had changed. She didn't complain about being followed or leered at.'

'She probably liked it.'

'No she didn't!' Ahmet bent down to shout into his brother's face. 'Gülizar gave herself to me, alone. I did everything for her. Bought her an apartment, her clothes, surgery, I loved her. And before you say anything, my brother, I have built this business, I have given you a job, an apartment and a life of ease. Put this about, tell our friends about this and all that will go.'

Semih shook his head. 'I won't tell anyone, Ahmet, and you know it,' he said. 'I just need to understand why because you are my brother.'

'Why what?'

'Why you went with her. I know you didn't kill her,' Semih said.

'Good! I just wish the police did.' Ahmet sat down again. 'I'd never find anyone as loyal and discreet as Gülizar. Why would I kill her? I know you are a man of the world, Semih. She would do anything sexual. No headaches, no not feeling well. Every time I went to the apartment I left satisfied. And she was beautiful. For as long as she gave me love like that, I would love her, old and wrinkled as she may have become in the end.'

'Ugh.'

'Don't sneer! You don't know what she was like!'

'Then why aren't you crying?' Semih asked. 'If you loved her so much?'

Ahmet knitted his fingers underneath his chin. 'I don't know. Maybe I'm in shock?' He thought for a while, then said, 'I was always discreet when I went there. I wore a hat and a coat and I kept my head down. Occasionally I spoke to the kapıcı, but only to pass the time of day.'

'Did you know she was taking photographs of you?'

'I knew she had some. She really wanted them. We were apart so often.'

'And yet you deny that you're in them,' Semih said.

'I can't own up to an affair with someone like Gülizar! It would ruin my reputation!'

Semih leaned in towards his brother. 'But if you don't and they prove those photographs are genuine they will think that you killed her.'

'They think I killed her anyway! That woman, Commissioner Teker, is from the east. She's a devil-worshipping Yezidi.' His teeth ground and his face contorted. 'She'll do anything to stop people like us. Did you see her at Gezi, giving those hooligans hell? No. She likes them! She's a commissioner of police and she isn't doing her duty!'

Semih said nothing. His brother often had strange ideas about people who opposed him. He'd thought the Greek archaeologist who'd tried to get him to rehouse the rubbish pickers of Gizlitepe was a spy. Now she was dead.

Ahmet shook his head. 'So much going on but I can't let any of this distract me,' he said. 'The Negroponte house still has its secret intact and we must take it and destroy it. When the sun comes up you must go to Kadıköy and begin moving some of the larger bulldozers across the Bosphorus. Why leave them there to be destroyed by vandals anyway?'

'But you still haven't bought the Negroponte house!'

Ahmet waved a hand dismissively. 'I don't care,' he said. 'Tomorrow I will get into that house and make that man sign it over to me. Even if I have to break his gates and his front door down.'

Chapter 17

'Mehmet Bey?'

Süleyman looked up.

'I apologise if I'm disturbing your work,' İkmen said.

'You're not.' Ömer Mungun had gone to Dr Sarkissian's laboratory to get the Armenian's preliminary findings on the body of Ayşel Ocal. He pointed to Ömer's chair. 'Please have a seat, Çetin Bey.'

İkmen entered what had once been an office almost as familiar to him as his own. They had spoken since the previous autumn, after Ayşe Farsakoğlu's death, but only when it had been strictly necessary and usually by telephone. This visit was unusual. Mehmet Süleyman tried not to feel joy or hope. But he smiled.

'How can I help you?' he asked.

İkmen took a deep breath. 'I know that you're working on the Moda death,' he said.

'Ayşel Ocal, yes.'

İkmen took another deep breath. Either he was nervous, or didn't really want to be there – or both. 'I've heard that last night you interviewed the property developer, Ahmet Öden,' he said.

Süleyman sat back in his chair. 'What if I did?'

'I have an interest in him,' İkmen said. 'In relation to the Hippodrome body. He had a dispute with my victim.'

'What about?'

'Mehmet, did you interview Öden last night or not?'

Was he being evasive with İkmen just for the sport or had he been told to keep Öden close to his chest? Teker hadn't wanted Öden brought in – yet – but if she knew that İkmen had an interest too, surely they could discuss the property developer, however 'sensitive' his position was.

Süleyman got up, closed and locked his door, opened his window and offered İkmen a cigarette. He saw İkmen almost refuse and then capitulate. Süleyman sat down and they both lit up.

'We think that Ayşel Öden, otherwise known as Gülizar, was Öden's mistress,' Süleyman said. 'She owned that apartment outright, paid for with cash, and I've not met many twenty-something strippers who can do that.'

He saw İkmen smile.

'Can't prove, yet, that Öden bought it for her, but photographs of him with her, without her and in various compromising positions were all over her computer and her phone,' Süleyman went on.

'So much for the saintly among us.'

'He claims that the photographs are composites, created on computer, but he's clutching at thin air,' Süleyman said. 'However, they don't prove that he killed her. Ömer has just gone to the lab to get Dr Sarkissian's preliminary report on the body.'

'Found in the bath?'

'Yes, wrists slit, but Dr Sarkissian thinks that she was almost dead when that was done. He's looking for blows, toxins. What about your own involvement with Öden?'

İkmen drew on his cigarette. 'Twofold. One to do with this dispute he had with Dr Ariadne Savva, who set herself up as protector of the rubbish pickers he evicted in Gizlitepe, and another one centred round the old Negroponte House.'

'Is that what some people called the Greek House on Kabasakal Caddesi?'

'Yes. Owned by Madam Anastasia Negroponte, proper old Byzantine, and her son Yiannis.'

Süleyman frowned. 'Wasn't he the one who came back from Germany after forty years or something?'

'That's him,' İkmen said. 'Always been questions about Yiannis. But his mother, if she's his mother, loves him and that's all that matters. Öden wants the Negroponte house and he's been sending his men to rev up bulldozers outside the front door and playing mind games with Yiannis.'

'Has he offered the Negropontes money?'

'Yes.'

'Lots?'

'It sounds like a lot to me and I expect it would to you as well. But the point is that neither Madam Anastasia nor her son Yiannis want to sell.'

'Well then, Öden can't—'

'Oh now come on, Mehmet Bey, you know that these developers can do as they please now,' İkmen said. 'With the help of compliant advocates, they twist and torture the law into shapes where it's possible for them to get what they want. And if that fails, they use force. And with the word "progress" on their side, well . . .'

'Öden isn't going to tear the Negroponte House down, is he?' Süleyman said.

'He wants to.'

'Why? It's an historic—'

'He wants to build the best and most luxurious hotel on the Sultanahmet peninsula,' İkmen said. 'Make the Four Seasons look like a gecekondu.'

Süleyman shook his head. If he was honest, he did like some of the new build apartments that were springing up across the city. Provided they weren't in faux Ottoman style. But he didn't like them when they were built at the expense of lovely old structures or made already poor people homeless. In his experience that just led to vagrancy, drug abuse and alcoholism.

'How did you get involved with the Negroponte house?' he asked.

'Their old servant Hakkı Bey called me in. He knows me because I used to go there as a child. My mother would read Madam Anastasia's cards. Then Mother died and then we had 1955,' İkmen said. 'And I know something else you've been working on which may relate to that year.'

'You've been speaking to Ömer.'

İkmen shrugged.

'A body found in the Galatasaray Lise gardens,' Süleyman said. 'He may date from the awful events of 1955 or he may not. What we do know is that all the fatalities connected with the anti-Greek riots were accounted for long ago. The unusual thing about this unknown man is that his teeth have been extensively capped and filled using high-class materials and with a lot of skill. He wasn't poor.'

'So he was more likely to be Greek.'

'But all the Greeks have been accounted for,' Süleyman said.

'A foreign visitor?'

'Ömer has made contact with a dentist whose father was practising in Beyoğlu at the time. He did complicated remedial work for those who could pay. But it was a long time ago and the dentist's father is dead. She told Ömer she'd try to find what remains of his records from that year if she can.'

'Mmm. Madam Anastasia was badly beaten during the anti-Greek riots,' İkmen said. 'Never been the same since. Her husband Nikos was killed. Torn to pieces by the mob.'

Süleyman shook his head. 'I must've seen his name on a list of the dead. I don't know whether we'll ever know who the

204

Galatasaray man was. It may not be possible now. The forensic archaeologist Dr Akyıldız—'

'Ah yes, she worked with my Hippodrome victim on a rather older skeleton,' İkmen said.

'Oh?'

He told Süleyman about Ariadne Savva's find.

'But if no Palaiologi descendants exist then how was she ever going to prove that particular skeleton was that of the last emperor?' Süleyman asked.

'I don't know and nor, more significantly, does Dr Akyıldız. Savva didn't tell her.'

'Frustrating.'

'Like so many things in life,' İkmen said.

Süleyman wondered if he was referring to him and his behaviour towards women. But he said nothing.

'The main reason I came here this morning was to alert you about my interest in Ahmet Öden,' İkmen said. 'And to tell you that if you want to speak to him and he isn't at home he will in all likelihood be sitting in his car outside the Negroponte House. As you know there are no parking restrictions on the street and so theoretically he can sit there as long as he likes. I know he's messing with Yiannis' head, and it's working. Yiannis is becoming hysterical and, much as I know he is committed to keeping that house, I fear he may sell just to get Öden out of his life. I wish I could do more to help him. But I must tread carefully.'

'We all have to tread carefully with big businessmen,' Süleyman said. 'Did you know that when I went out to Öden's place last night Commissioner Teker came too? In fact she led.'

İkmen shook his head.

'Apparently I'm not exalted enough to interview a builder on my own.' Süleyman smiled.

'Makes me want to weep,' İkmen said. 'And on top of that

I have to be extra careful because I'm also investigating the death of Ariadne Savva, with whom Öden had some issues. I've no proof he killed her and, given the fact that her newborn baby was taken from her before she died, I can't imagine that it was Öden. Why would he want someone else's baby?'

'Unless it was his.'

'I doubt that,' İkmen said. 'Dr Savva was Greek and Mr Öden, I am reliably informed by the Negropontes' servant Hakkı, comes from one of those families who attacked the Greeks in 'fifty-five. Back to that again. He's also very vocal about his support for turning Aya Sofya into a mosque. He's everything the people in Gezi Park hate. And I imagine he's feeling threatened by what's happening there.'

'You think so?'

'Yes. Not that I've given it too much thought. My Kemal spends most of his time in Gezi these days while his mother rails against everything it stands for. I'll be honest, I care, I understand. But I'm more concerned that any moment now I am going to discover a dead baby, because it has to be dead now. And then I'm going to have to tell Mr Savva that on top of the death of his daughter he's going to have to absorb the death of his grandchild too.'

They sat in silence, looking at each other. In spite of the grim subject matter, Süleyman had missed conversations like this. He'd missed İkmen.

'Oh, and another thing,' İkmen said.

'Yes.'

'One of the rubbish pickers Ariadne Savva was trying to help claims she knew that Ahmet Öden had a mistress. He didn't know who she was or where she lived but he did describe her as a prostitute.'

'Some would describe Ayşel Ocal so.'

İkmen shrugged. 'Don't know if it's true or if it will be of any use to you.'

'Intelligence is always useful,' Süleyman said. 'Particularly from you.'

'Right.' İkmen was embarrassed. 'I have to go.' He stood up. 'Do you?'

Süleyman imagined the needy look on his own face and felt as if he should be ashamed but he wasn't. 'Çetin, I have missed you,' he said.

İkmen looked down at him and shook his head. 'I can't take it any more, Mehmet,' he said. 'I saw Gonca. Did she tell you?'

'No.'

'She begged me to make peace with you because you are so unhappy. She said you'd never come to me—'

'I—'

'Mehmet, no,' İkmen said. 'I am just not ready to do that. I know you. I know what's happening. You're unhappy and you're making Gonca unhappy and so your eyes are wandering in the direction of other women. I've known you for over twenty years. But when you did it to Sergeant Farsakoğlu you crossed a line and it's going to take me a long time to forgive you.'

He walked towards the office door.

Süleyman put his head in his hands.

'Just don't compound what you've already done by breaking Gonca's heart,' İkmen said. 'She loves you and she's a good woman. Throw her away and you'll be setting yourself up for a very lonely and miserable old age. You may be a handsome prince but nobody will care when you're sixty-five unless you have money. Now let's keep each other informed regarding Ahmet Öden.'

'Yes, Çetin Bey.'

İkmen left.

Mehmet Süleyman, alone at his desk, felt as if he'd just been told off by his old class teacher back at the Lise.

'Mr Öden.'

He was just about to leave and get over to the Negroponte House. What did Mary want now? They'd already spoken about what had happened with the police.

'Can I have a word with you, please?' she said.

'What about?'

'About the police. About something that happened the night before last, something I haven't told you.'

He took her into his office.

'What?' he said.

He hadn't even offered her a seat.

'When the police came last night, I lied to them about something,' Mary said.

He was unable to fathom this woman. Maybe it was because she was a foreigner or maybe it was just her. He didn't know and hadn't cared, because he'd always intended to replace her with a cheaper Turkish version as soon as he could.

Mary, without being asked, sat down.

Unnerved by her boldness, Ahmet said, 'I have a lot to do. I can't—'

'You went out the night that woman in Moda died,' Mary said. 'I heard you leave Kelime's room and then I looked out of my window and saw you get into the MX5. She slept the whole time but I didn't take a sleeping pill; I stayed awake in case she needed help. You came back at just gone three.'

Ahmet Öden pulled his chair out from behind his desk and sat down.

'How could you leave her like that, Mr Öden? After you'd promised her you'd stay with her?'

He didn't answer because there was no answer.

'Did you think that I'd just take a sleeping pill when I knew that Kelime was ill?'

'You generally do,' he said. 'Take pills, I mean.'

'Not when I know I can't.'

He lowered his gaze from her eyes.

'So what did you tell the police, Mary?'

'What I told you I told them, Mr Öden,' she said. 'That I was awake all night and heard no one leave the house. I told them you didn't know that sometimes I took sleeping tablets but that I would tell you in due course.'

'But I know you take tablets.'

'Yes, and I imagine you thought I'd taken one the night before last, didn't you?'

'Until I learned you had been awake, yes . . .'

'Now I know that you didn't kill that woman because you are a good man, Mr Öden. Which was why I withheld that information from the police.'

'Your confidence in me is very pleasing,' he said.

'But I knew the police wouldn't see it that way,' she said. 'Which was why I lied. That said, I do feel, Mr Öden, sir, that in order to feel right with myself, I do need to know where you did go.'

She looked at him very steadily, which was unnerving. Apart from knowing where he went, what else did she want? She had to want something for herself. Otherwise why lie to the police?

'I went to look at a new site I'm considering developing in the Belgrade Forest,' he said.

'Oh.'

She didn't believe him.

He embellished. 'You have to look at prospective investments at night as well as in the day. I wanted to see what could be seen of the cityscape from that vantage point and also whether the area is used by vagrants or drug addicts. I have to think of the security of my men when I purchase a new site.'

'Of course.'

The Belgrade Forest wasn't far from Bebek. He knew she knew this. He also knew she'd be wondering what he'd been doing there for four plus hours. He had no words.

But then Mary spoke. 'Mr Öden, all I've ever wanted from this job has been security. I love Kelime and I do hope that you will be able to continue to employ me as her companion for many years to come. I require neither big pay rises nor long holidays. Just stability.'

So that was it. Ahmet tried to remember whether he'd talked about getting rid of the nanny to anyone, talk she could have overheard. He'd mentioned it to Semih several times. It was possible. But was it also possible that was all Mary Cox really wanted to buy her silence?

Ahmet Öden looked at her and forced himself to smile.

'She was strangled?'

Ömer Mungun put the doctor's report back on his desk.

'Yes,' Arto Sarkissian said.

'I don't remember any marks on her neck.'

'There aren't always any. And she'd been submerged in water for some hours, which had discoloured and deformed the tissues.'

'So it was strangulation that killed her?'

'Yes and no,' the doctor said. 'She was strangled from behind and I would say with hands or in the crook of an arm, crushing the larynx as pressure was exerted. Whoever killed Ayşel Ocal wanted it to look like suicide. He didn't realise that once dead, blood-letting isn't possible. As I said to Inspector Süleyman when I first saw her, I think that she was still just alive when she entered the water. But then she very quickly drowned, leading to the minimal loss of blood I recorded at the crime scene.'

'She was strangled and drowned.'

'Yes. A total botch, in my opinion,' the doctor said. 'If the intention was to make Mrs Ocal's death look like suicide, whoever did it knew very little about the subtleties and mechanics of death. Have you managed to contact any family members?'

'A brother, but he lives in Germany,' Ömer said. 'When the family were pushed out of Sulukule, they scattered. Like a lot of them. The brother told me that Ayşel was always a bit on the wild side. Parents are dead. The brother, Ali, has got no idea where their other siblings are. He was quite interested when I told him his sister owned her own apartment.'

'Does he know how she got it?'

'He says not.'

'Mmm.' Arto Sarkissian nodded his head. 'Who would have thought taking one's clothes off could be so lucrative?'

Ömer smiled.

'But then we know there is a man behind this, don't we?'

'Yes,' Ömer said. He didn't use Ahmet Öden's name. Süleyman had told him they had to be careful who they shared that information with, even within the department and its supporting organisations.

'Forensic have retrieved various samples from the apartment that may belong to people other than Mrs Ocal,' the doctor said. 'From my point of view, I can tell you that Mrs Ocal's stomach was not full when she died, but she had recently snacked on sour plums, ayran and a very small amount of cognac. She was a smoker and she wasn't a virgin, although she hadn't had sex anytime close to her death.'

'Her assailant didn't sexually abuse her.'

'No. In my opinion she was first strangled from behind, then her wrists were slit, then she was drowned in the bath. Forensic tell me there was no sign of forced entry into the apartment, so she may well have known her attacker. Did the neighbours see or hear anything?'

'They say not,' Ömer said. 'And what with the kapıcı being over at Gezi Park . . .' He sighed. 'He's still missing.'

'Which has to put him on whatever list of suspects you have,' Arto said.

Kapıcıs always had keys to all the apartments under their care, so Cafer Ayan, the kapıcı of the dead woman's block, could have let himself into her apartment at any time. There was no reason to suppose he had killed her – Ayan was, according to the neighbours, an almost silent man who clearly hated his job and took very little notice of the residents. But Ömer knew that appearances could be deceptive.

When he left the doctor's office he walked up to Gezi Park and looked at the tens of thousands gathered in the sunshine.

'Look.'

Yiannis handed Hakkı the document that Ahmet Öden had flung on to his front path, and then he sat down. Looking at it had exhausted him. He wasn't sleeping any more and so it didn't take much.

Hakkı registered the vast figure at the bottom of the document. 'That's a huge amount of money.'

'A thirty per cent increase.' Yiannis shrugged. 'Meaningless! It could be a million times that, I still wouldn't sell.'

'I've told you before, ignore it,' Hakkı said. He gave it back.

'How can I?'

'He's getting desperate. At the moment you have the whip hand.'

'Oh, and if Öden uses his influence to go for compulsory

212

purchase? This area is littered with the rubble of buildings that have been bought and knocked down.'

'This isn't a slum and it's an historic building,' Hakkı said.

'The others weren't slums either!'

Hakkı let him fulminate impotently. He was good at that. Then he said, 'If the Gezi people win then people like Öden will become a thing of the past.'

'Oh, and how realistic—'

'I know it's not likely, but even if they don't win, Öden is desperate and in his desperation he will make a mistake. He may have already made one,' Hakkı said. 'You said yourself that a woman who may be his mistress has been found dead in Moda.'

'I don't know for certain it's her.'

'Maybe, maybe not,' Hakkı said. 'But whatever is happening, you need to calm down. You've got no self-control! A man your age should be able to master his emotions. I know he's out there now and it is unpleasant but, as Çetin Bey said, it's only a game. There is nothing he can do at this point. He—'

'I should show him round the house,' Yiannis said. 'Everywhere.'

'Why?'

'Because I know and you know I'll be able to control it,' Yiannis said.

'When you can't even control yourself! Don't be ridiculous!'

'Yes. It's what I do!' Yiannis said. 'Prove to him that what he thinks is here, isn't. That is why he wants this house. He wants to please his God by destroying the trappings of a past he envies. That's what fanatics do.'

'Yes, and you are being just as much of a fanatic as Öden,' Hakkı said.

'No, I'm not!'

213

'Yes, you are. You want to prove that you can master him, outwit him and prove him wrong. Who do you think you are, eh? And what if you fail?'

'I . . .'

'You may.' Hakkı held up a warning finger. 'You are not invincible. And you don't need to do this. Do nothing. Öden is sweating, leave him in his filth. Let him sit out there day after day adding yet more noughts to that figure and forget about him. I know it's hard, but Madam gets distressed every time there is a commotion or a bad atmosphere in the house. We must think of her health. You know I don't give a damn about you. But we both care about her. She is all that matters.'

'I know.'

They sat in silence for a while. It was very pleasant and shady in the plant-filled garden and under normal circumstances they would both have enjoyed just drinking lemonade and smoking. But Yiannis could see Ahmet Öden's car from where he was sitting and it stuck in his brain like a splinter.

Eventually, unable to contain himself any longer, he said, 'No, I'll end this.'

'What?'

'I'll invite him in, tomorrow. That should give me enough time to prepare.' And then, seeing that Hakkı was about to speak again, he held up a hand. 'I don't want to know what you think. My mind is made up. The only way that Öden and anyone else who may have theories about this house is going to go away is if I prove them wrong. And I know I can do it. And so do you.'

Gezi was creating such odd bedfellows. Peri Mungun hadn't had an easy time getting into the park that afternoon. The police were getting rough again and were preventing people from entering by force. Even those in nurses' uniforms. But luckily

214

for Peri a very tall, slim transsexual had come to her aid.

When an officer had pushed Peri, she'd raced out of the park and said, 'Hey! You! Leave that woman alone! She's a nurse!'

He'd said something not too complimentary under his breath.

'Ah don't swear at me, boy!' the transsexual had said. And then she'd pulled Peri towards her and they'd run together back to the park.

Peri had thanked her rescuer, who she discovered was called Pembe, and had joined her and her friends, who were making tea on a small camping stove. They were an odd little group. There was one other transsexual, called Madame Edith, who apparently had a cabaret act based on the songs of the legendary Edith Piaf. Then there were two young girls and a baby. Completely covered, the girls were part of the Muslims against Capitalism group.

'Now who would like tea?' Madame Edith asked.

Pembe declined in favour of another cigarette, while the girls said yes, and Peri was very glad of a glass. She'd had to pander to the whims of a woman who'd had an elective caesarean section for most of the day and she was tired. As soon as the woman's baby had arrived she'd lost interest in it. Unlike these two girls. She asked them what the baby's name was and there was a slight and rather awkward pause before one of them said, 'Ali.'

'Is he your little brother?' Peri asked.

This time they both spoke at once.

'Yes.'

'We're looking after him for a friend.'

Peri looked at Pembe and Madame Edith, neither of whom seemed perturbed by what the girls had said. Madame Edith, still on the tea, said, 'So does the baby want some tea? I don't know about these things. Do babies drink tea?'

'No,' one of the girls said. She took a bottle out of a bag. 'I've got milk.'

'OK.'

She fed the baby, whose clothes were – unlike the girls' clothes – dirty. There were new and used nappies in the bag the girls had brought with them but they didn't once put a new vest on him even when he dribbled milk down his front.

Once Madame Edith had finished her tea she lay down for a nap in the sunshine. Pembe looked at her and shook her head. 'Napping like a grandma! I'm going to find some food.'

She left. Madame Edith snored and Peri looked at the baby. Not newborn, although not far off, he was a fractious little thing who nevertheless drank his milk. But his limbs were thin. Peri put her fingers around the top of one of his arms and she could feel his bones.

'This is a friend's baby?' she said.

Both girls' eyes were big, but they both said, 'Yes.'

'Where is she? Your friend?'

'Working,' the girl on the left said.

Her companion nodded.

'Oh. What does she do?'

'She—'

'Why do you want to know?' the girl on the right said. 'What's it to you?'

Pembe knew she'd have to proceed carefully. She wasn't convinced of their story. How could she be when they hadn't initially agreed on the child's identity?

She said, 'I'm a nurse and so I can't help noticing when things aren't right, especially with children. Little Ali is very thin.'

'His mother's poor,' the girl on the right said. 'That's why she works.'

'I accept that,' Peri said. 'And I'm sure she's doing the best that she can for him.'

'Her husband ran away.'

'That's really unfortunate,' Peri said. 'But the little one's clothes are very dirty. I'm sure she could wash them from time to time. I see she's given you lots of nappies and so she must have some money.'

Neither of the girls said anything, but their eyes wouldn't meet hers. With Madame Edith asleep and Pembe off who knew where, Peri knew she only had a limited amount of time on her own with the girls. At any moment they could disappear off into the Gezi crowds and be lost forever and, although she didn't know that they'd done anything wrong, she knew she couldn't live with herself if they had and she'd done nothing.

She glanced around to see if anyone was watching. 'Look,' she said, 'you're bright girls. You've got your own opinions on what is going on in the world and you keep yourselves informed. You must know about this baby that's missing—'

'This baby is a friend's,' the girl on the right said. 'She has to work.'

'What does she do?'

They looked at each other again. Was Peri mistaken or did the one on the left look as if she might be about to cry?

'She is a prostitute,' the one on the right said. 'A bad thing to be but we don't judge. The real Muslim way is to care and to understand.'

Peri was sure that she was sincere. And in her experience, sincere religious people of all kinds didn't judge. They were nice girls.

'That's a very fine sentiment,' Peri said.

The girl on the right began to stand up.

'Where are you going?'

'I think we have to go now,' she said as she helped her friend, with the baby in her arms, to her feet.

Peri, quickly, stood too. Then she put a hand on the baby's leg.

'Listen,' she said, 'a baby went missing last week. I know you'll know this. It was all over the news. It happened in Sultanahmet. The baby's mother died.'

'I heard about it, yes.'

'Well, my brother, who is a police officer . . .'

Both girls visibly cringed.

'Yes, I know what they've been doing here, gassing people, beating them. But my brother is a detective,' Peri said. 'He's a good man. And my brother has a colleague, another nice man like him who spends all his time at the moment looking for a baby he fears might be suffering or even dead. Now if you really do have a friend who is a prostitute who is this baby's mother, I'd like you to take me to her, because I think she might need some help looking after the child. I can give her that help. But if there is no friend and you, for every good reason, are looking after this baby because you found him, then you need to talk to my brother's colleague. He won't hurt you and you won't get into trouble, because I'm sure you've been looking after this baby because you care for him.'

'We heard the mother was dead. We feared for him!' the girl on the left blurted.

'Fatima!'

The girl on the left freed a hand and grabbed her friend's arm. 'Melda, we can't go on bringing him here every day! What if he gets gassed?'

Peri's instinct was to grab the baby but she resisted. At least one of the girls was coming to the conclusion that things could not stay as they were.

But the girl on the right began to move away.

'Come on, Fatima,' she said. 'We've got to get little . . . the boy . . . back to his mother.'

But Peri kept her hand on the boy's leg and looked into Fatima's eyes. The girl was close to tears.

'You don't even know this child's name, do you?' Peri said.

Chapter 18

Çetin İkmen only saw the baby for a moment, before he was taken into the care of social services. The only impression he got of him was that he was very small, very loud and he was white.

Together with Kerim Gürsel, he interviewed the two girls, Fatima and Melda Erol, in his office. He knew that they were terrified and that exposure to one of the windowless interview rooms would make them clam up immediately. He'd given them the option of having their father or a brother with them but Fatima said that they didn't want their family to know about the baby. Melda added that they didn't need men.

'Where did you find the baby?' İkmen asked.

'In an outhouse,' Melda said.

'Where?'

'On the street where we live.'

'Which is?'

'Küçük Ayasofya Caddesi, opposite the mosque.'

'So where, in relation to your home, is this outhouse?'

'Towards the Nakilbent Mosque on the right.'

Two minutes from the sphendone. Çetin İkmen began to sweat. Had he, or rather Sergeant Mungun's sister, just found Ariadne Savva's lost baby?

'It's just a shack,' Fatima said. 'Street kids play in there sometimes. But also dogs, some of them fierce. We can take you there.'

220

İkmen turned to Kerim Gürsel. 'Get Küçük Ayasofya cordoned off.'

'Sir.'

Gürsel left the room.

'When did you find the child?' İkmen asked.

'The day after Gezi really started, last week,' Fatima said.

'The twenty-ninth of May.'

'Yes.'

'How did you find the child?'

Melda spoke. 'It was early, six a.m. Fatima and I were taking soup to our grandmother for her breakfast.'

'She lives on Nakilbent Sokak.'

'She's got arthritis,' Melda said. 'Our mother makes her meals every day and does all her laundry. We are always backwards and forwards.'

İkmen said, 'The baby . . .'

'Oh, yes, we heard him crying,' Melda said. 'A very weak cry.'

'We were very cautious when we went into the old outhouse because we thought there might be dogs in there,' Fatima said.

'But there was just a baby. Naked and covered in blood,' Melda said. 'Just lying on the ground.'

'On anything?'

'No.'

Kerim returned and nodded at İkmen. They would have to obtain a basic outline from these girls and then get them over to Küçük Ayasofya as soon as possible.

'I wrapped him in one of the towels Mother had laundered for Grandma,' Fatima said. 'Then we took him with us.'

'To your grandmother's?'

'Yes.'

'What did your grandmother have to say about that?' İkmen asked.

221

'He made her smile,' Fatima said.

'Did you tell your grandmother where you'd found him?'

'Yes.'

'She said that he was probably a prostitute's baby,' Melda said. 'She said they often leave them for people to find and give a decent life.'

This was true although, as İkmen knew, they usually ended up in state orphanages.

'Grandma said we should keep him,' Fatima said.

'At her apartment,' Melda said. 'She told us what milk to buy and where to get some clothes for him.'

'What about your parents?' Kerim asked. 'Did they know about the baby?'

'Oh, no,' Fatima said. 'Mother has a good heart but she is one of those Muslims who judges. She wouldn't have had a prostitute's baby in the house.'

'What were you and your grandmother going to do with the baby in the long term?' İkmen asked.

The two girls looked at each other and then Melda said, 'When we found out that a baby was missing and that its mother had been killed we became even more fearful for him. Grandma said that we had to be careful where we bought milk and clothes and not to get them locally any more. We started taking him to Gezi to give Grandma a rest.'

'And because we believe in Gezi,' Fatima said.

'And so you didn't think that it might be better to let us know you had what could be a dead woman's baby and allow us to call off our search?' İkmen asked. He wasn't exactly angry with the Erol girls but he was resentful of their fearful unworldliness.

Fatima looked down at the floor. But Melda said, 'How could we trust you? Look at Gezi. How can anyone trust the police?'

'And yet here you are . . .'

222

'If Nurse Peri hadn't persuaded us, we wouldn't be,' Melda said.

Her sister put a hand on her shoulder. 'But we weren't coping, were we, Melda?'

There was a pause. Melda too looked down now. Then she said, 'His clothes were dirty. We couldn't take them home to wash. And he was thin.'

She began to cry.

İkmen, though irritated by them, also felt some sympathy for the Erol girls. They'd done what they'd thought was right in the face of what he imagined to be a very strict and judgemental mother.

'You saved the baby's life,' he said. 'That's the main thing.'

Yiannis' hand shook as he knocked on the car window. Ahmet Öden, who hadn't seen him leave his house, rolled the window down.

'I don't know what you think is in my house, Öden,' Yiannis said, 'but—'

'I'm sure that you do.' Öden smiled and Yiannis had to look away.

'You can come inside and look for yourself tomorrow morning,' Yiannis said.

There was a pause. Ahmet Öden hadn't been expecting that. However, he retained his composure. 'Why tomorrow? Why not now?'

Yiannis wanted to say, *It's none of your business,* but he didn't have the confidence. 'My mother is sleeping,' he said. 'It isn't convenient.'

'Mmm.'

He was cool. When he looked Yiannis in the eye the effect was unnerving. Had he done the right thing? Ahmet Öden wasn't some kid he could enchant, some visitor with half-remembered impressions of the house in his mind. Öden, if he was telling the truth, remembered it all, and in spite of what Hakkı always maintained, he'd seen something.

'Get here before midday and I'll let you in,' Yiannis said.

'I'll think about it.'

The coolness made him angry. As the property developer pushed a button to raise his car window, Yiannis yelled into the contracting space, 'You'd better! Because it's going to be the last chance you ever get!'

Hürrem Teker had hoped, in a way, that the erotic photographs of Ahmet Öden and Ayşel Ocal had been Photoshopped. Dealing with people like him was always a nightmare. But they hadn't been. In the opinion of the photographic expert who had looked at them, they were genuine. Öden had had an affair with the woman she now knew was also called Gülizar.

She knew why he'd lied about it. Öden was famous for his piety, his devotion to his Down's syndrome daughter and his espousal of family values. Fucking a gypsy woman didn't fit in with that. Briefly she thought about her own officer, Süleyman, in thrall to a gypsy. Then she looked at the photographic report again. There was no getting around it. Öden had been with the woman, he may even have bought the apartment for her. It was in her name, but where would a stripper in low-rent clubs have got enough money to buy an apartment in Moda for cash?

The neighbours said that a man did visit, but none of them knew who he was. Those who had seen him said he always wore an overcoat and a fedora hat, whatever the weather. And he always turned his face away from anyone he met on the stairs. Clearly he didn't want to be recognised. And that would fit with Öden very well. But what the neighbours had also said was that the kapıcı had been seen talking to the man. The kapıcı who, again according to the neighbours, was somewhere in Gezi Park.

What was certain now was that Ahmet Öden had lied. He'd been having an affair with Ayşel Ocal – at some point – and he'd denied it. And in the absence of final results from forensic tests on the body and the apartment, he was the only subject in the frame.

'But he was in his daughter's bedroom all night,' Süleyman said when Teker called him to give him the photographic expert's opinion. 'The nanny said he didn't leave. She was awake all night.'

'Maybe the nanny lied,' Teker said. 'Maybe she's in love with Öden and wants to protect him.'

She heard Süleyman sigh. 'One thing I have been told is that the connection between Öden and Inspector İkmen's hippodrome victim was more visceral and more pertinent than we thought.'

'How so?'

'According to one of the Gizlitepe rubbish pickers Çetin Bey interviewed, Dr Savva knew that Öden had a mistress. She didn't tell this Nurettin who she was or where she lived. But it's possible she tried to use that knowledge to blackmail Öden.'

'For money?'

'Çetin Bey thinks it more likely she was trying to force Öden to rehouse the rubbish pickers.'

'How noble.'

She hadn't meant it to sound sarcastic, but that was how Süleyman took it.

'I think so,' he said.

'Yes, and so do I,' Teker said. 'I wasn't being . . . Look, Süleyman, what we need to do before we go back to Öden is to re-interview the nanny. Get her in here to make a formal statement and impress upon her the full, shall we say, force of Turkish law.'

'Madam?'

'She's British,' Teker said. 'She's not young and so I'm pretty sure she has seen that ghastly old film, *Midnight Express*.'

'Oh the one—'

'Where the nasty Turks rape and murder everything that moves,' she said. 'Don't lay a finger on her but play up to it.'

'Play—'

'Oh use your imagination, Süleyman,' Teker said. 'Walk her past the cells. They're busy at the moment.'

Still full of protesters from the very first few days of Gezi.

'Throw some old cigarette ends around in one of the older interview rooms and break a chair. You have my permission. Tell her,' Teker said, 'just how long it can take to bring a case to court in this country and just where people are held while they are waiting.'

No blood was visible. The floor of what the Erol girls had called the outhouse was covered in oil, faeces and probably, from the smell of it, urine. Blood was almost certainly there. The whole area would need to be treated with luminol. Not that, apart from providing support to the girls' story, blood was needed. A DNA swab had already been taken from inside the child's mouth which would be compared to Ariadne Savva's results. Maternity would be proven, or otherwise, in a few days.

Kerim Gürsel showed his ID to the constables at the entrance and joined his boss. 'This used to be a garage,' he said.

'Did it belong to the house next door?' İkmen asked.

'Yes.'

The old wooden house on the right was derelict.

'A Jewish family lived there until about ten years ago, when

226

they moved to Israel,' Kerim said. 'They had one of those old American cars they used to keep in here.'

'Did the bakkal owner know who owns the house now?' İkmen asked.

Across the road from the outhouse was a neighbourhood grocery store or bakkal. People who ran such places generally knew everything about their local area.

'He says he thinks it's the original family. They had money, apparently, and when they went to Israel they just left the house to rot,' Kerim said.

'Get a name?'

'Yes, sir. Nabarro. Recep Bey, in the bakkal, says that kids are always having to be chased out of this place and the house. He also said that working girls ply their trade here.'

One of the reasons İkmen had chosen Kerim to be his sergeant was because he always spoke about everyone with respect. Most officers he knew would have described the prostitutes who worked the area as 'whores' or 'slags'. But not Kerim. Then perhaps now he knew why.

'So we mustn't get too excited,' İkmen said. 'The child could belong to almost anyone.'

'But he is the right sort of age, sir.'

'Indeed. And I will inform Mr Savva that a child has been found. But I will impress upon him the possibility of disappointment.' He looked around the building. 'I wonder how many other children have been conceived, born or dumped in this place.'

'And I wonder what the Erol sisters and their grandmother thought they were going to do with the child,' Kerim said.

İkmen had briefly been to see the grandmother before he arrived at the crime scene. A more outspoken old secular republican woman it would have been hard to imagine. But then that

227

made sense. In the cities it was generally the under-sixties who were religious. The old people had seen that long ago and rejected it.

'The old woman just wanted to save a prostitute's baby,' İkmen said. 'Wanted to try and bring it up without, as she put it "stigma and superstition".'

'Sounds very liberal.'

'She is,' İkmen said.

'Obviously her granddaughters don't take after her.'

İkmen laughed. 'Oh, don't you be so sure. And don't be fooled by the covering. Muslims Against Capitalism, the group they belong to, want to completely change society. And they embrace all colours, races and creeds. They are radical people. The Erols' grandmother must be proud.' Then he turned towards a group of officers who had been waiting patiently at the back of the old garage. 'OK, the scene is yours.' He said to Kerim, 'Let's go and look at the sphendone again.'

The forensic team began setting up their equipment as İkmen and Kerim Gürsel walked out into the sunshine.

İkmen lit a cigarette. 'I noticed that Mr Öden wasn't outside the Negroponte House when I drove past,' he said. 'Maybe his more recent travails are taking up his time.'

'With Inspector Süleyman?'

'Yes.'

They walked the short distance to the sphendone in silence. It was very close. A baby could easily have been taken from the ancient Hippodrome and placed in the Jewish family's outhouse. For someone light on their feet, it was the work of seconds. On the other hand, lack of any further evidence in the sphendone was underlining İkmen's growing belief that Ariadne had given birth elsewhere, before she had entered the ancient space.

Still cordoned off, the sphendone was guarded by a constable who asked İkmen if he wanted to go inside. He said no. He'd seen what he needed to see.

İkmen and Kerim walked back to their cars in silence, İkmen thinking about the short conversation he'd had with his cousin Samsun early that morning. Breathless and overcome with excitement, she'd said, 'Oh Çetin, I promised not to tell, but I just can't keep it to myself any longer! I went to Gezi and I met this lovely trans girl called Rita, American. Well, she introduced me to this other trans girl who is having a thing with your Sergeant Gürsel!'

İkmen hadn't been shocked but he had been surprised. 'Kerim is married,' he'd said.

'To a lesbian, yes,' Samsun had replied. 'Çetin, the wife is a beard! A disguise to hide what your sergeant really is. He likes chicks with dicks, Çetin, trust me, and his "wife" – ill little thing – well, she likes girls. Now you won't tell him I told you, will you? I promised his lover that I wouldn't tell anyone, so she mustn't find out I've told you.'

Then she'd put the phone down.

İkmen looked at Kerim as he got into his car. 'See you back at the station.'

'Yes, sir.'

When Kerim had driven off, İkmen sat quietly for a moment, thinking. Samsun had a lot of faults but lying wasn't one of them, and so he had no doubt whoever these people she'd met in Gezi were, she had believed them. İkmen had personally never met Kerim's wife. She had rheumatoid arthritis and was an invalid. Was she also a lesbian? It wasn't his business, unless for some reason Kerim's unusual lifestyle – if in fact he had one – impacted on his work. But İkmen knew that it could. Some officers were very punitive when it came to transgendered people and would arrest them for the slightest infraction of the law, real or imagined.

He wouldn't tell Kerim what he knew – yet. But if he needed to some time in the future, in order to protect him, he would break Samsun's confidence. But then, for all her protestations, İkmen knew that she had to know that.

Being back in Dr İnçi's dental surgery a second time was unnerving. Just sitting in the waiting room made Ömer Mungun wonder whether that dull ache he had at the back of his mouth was a sign that one of his teeth was rotting. Then she called him in.

They shook hands.

'Thank you for coming,' she said. 'It's so difficult for me to find a few free minutes.'

'It's no problem.'

'Please sit down.' She directed him to a stool at a bench in front of a light box. She sat down next to him and then clipped an X-ray slide in front of the light box.

'This is the X-ray of your Galatasaray victim's mouth that was taken by your forensic people,' she said.

He was familiar with it. 'Yes.'

She took the slide down. 'The plate I'm going to show you now was loose in a drawer so I don't know who it might have belonged to. We'll talk about that in a moment,' she said. 'But it is the closest match I've found to your X-ray.'

She held an old glass X-ray plate up to the light box and then clipped the new X-ray back to the box. 'You see this molar here has been crowned, and there's a bridge across from the right central incisor, across the gap where the maxillary right lateral incisor should be, to the maxillary right canine. You may also notice that the bridge unit is canted slightly to the left.'

Ömer couldn't really see it. Mouths were mouths and the old plate was very hard to decipher.

'However, I've also done some measurement comparisons and looked specifically at distances between teeth. And fillings. I can't say for certain, because as I said, I don't have a name here, but I think this plate probably relates to your Galatasaray man's dental work. Now, with regard to identification, you will see something in the top left-hand corner.'

There was what looked like a series of scratches and a smudge. Ömer narrowed his eyes. He heard her laugh.

'Oh, don't even try to see what it is,' she said. 'I've had it under my most powerful microscope and I can't see a thing.'

He looked up.

'But,' she said, 'I have an idea.'

'Which is?'

'Your forensic people,' she said. 'I don't know whether their equipment will be able to find something I can't but I think you should give it a try.'

Ömer put the plate carefully into a storage box Dr İnçi let him have. He made a note of the resolution of the dentist's microscope and left.

Süleyman finally got Mary Cox into police headquarters at seven o'clock in the evening. She'd been out with her charge, Kelime, all day, and because Ahmet Öden had been elsewhere, organising care for the young girl had taken time.

He took her into a room just like the one Teker had described. He'd enjoyed smoking in an interview room again. He'd appreciated smashing up a few chairs even more. Her face as she walked in front of him quickly showed her disgust. She said, 'In here?'

'Sit down,' he said.

A female constable, large and expressionless, walked in behind

231

him. He knew her name, Özal, but not much else except that she boxed. She also very easily elicited fear. When Mary Cox saw Özal her eyes visibly widened.

'Stand at the door,' Süleyman said to Özal.

'Sir.'

He sat down opposite Mary Cox and lit a cigarette. 'Mary,' he said. 'Miss Cox.'

'Yes.'

'Citizen of Great Britain, fifty years old. Single.'

'Yes.'

He said nothing. He didn't even look at her, not directly.

She said, 'What do you want, Inspector Süleyman?'

'You have a permit to work in Turkey?'

'Yes,' she said. 'You have that. You have my passport too.'

He'd taken her British passport from her when she'd arrived. Foreign nationals always felt vulnerable without their passports, particularly the British.

'Do I need to contact someone from my consulate?' she asked.

Although the grim surroundings were clearly not to her taste, she seemed to be adapting and was showing very little fear.

'I want you to tell me what happened the night before last,' he said.

'I told you, Kelime was ill, Mr Öden stayed with her. All night.'

'During which time you didn't sleep once.'

'I told you, I—'

'I don't believe you,' he said. 'Why stay awake all night if the father of the child is sleeping in her room? Do you not trust Mr Öden with his daughter?'

Her face flushed. 'What do you mean?'

'Do you think Mr Öden is some kind of idiot that he can't look after his own child?'

232

'No!'

'Then why stay awake?'

Her eyes moved very quickly from his face, to the floor, to the filthy table.

Süleyman dropped cigarette ash on the floor.

Mary Cox sniffed. 'Do you mind . . .?'

'No. No I don't mind, Miss Cox, at all,' he said. 'And now I say again, why stay awake? Is there something you wish to tell me about your employer and the sexual abuse of his daughter?'

'No. No! Mr Öden would never do anything like that,' Mary said. 'He's a good man, a moral man.'

'With a mistress who used to take her clothes off for men to look at her body,' Süleyman said. 'We have photographs of him with this woman.'

'They are entirely fake,' she said.

Süleyman looked at her. There was possibly something more in that rebuttal than just admiration.

'Did he tell you that?' Süleyman asked.

'No. I haven't spoken to Mr Öden about any of this,' she said.

'He must have spoken to you about what you said to us.'

She looked a little confused for a moment, then she said, 'Well, yes, I suppose so.'

'Did you or didn't you?'

'Yes!'

'So?'

'So what? I told Mr Öden I'd told you the truth, which is that I was awake all night,' she said. 'I didn't see Mr Öden or anyone else leave the house.'

He sat back in his chair and crossed his arms. 'You would have me believe that you sat up all night when the sick child

233

in your care was peacefully asleep and with her loving father. What did you have to worry about under such circumstances?'

'I wanted to be available in case Mr Öden needed help.'

'What help would he need? The child wasn't seriously ill. Some minor sickness. According to you and Mr Öden, she asked for her father to sleep in her room. The impression I have been given is that Kelime Öden is somewhat spoilt.'

'She is Mr Öden's only child.'

'Who has Down's syndrome—'

'Yes, which is all the more reason to monitor her health very carefully.'

'I do not know about that.'

'Well, it—'

He held up a hand to silence her. 'Miss Cox, whatever, er, implications that may have, I am still not satisfied that you remained awake all night for no reason. I am not happy that Mr Öden slept, alone, in his daughter's bedroom.'

Her face went purple. 'He'd never do anything like that to Kelime! He's a good man!'

'A good man who uses a prostitute,' Süleyman said. 'A good man who may have a secret life of vice. I can accept that you didn't know about his mistress but I cannot believe that you were happy about his presence in Kelime's room if you really didn't take a sleeping tablet. I looked at your tablets myself and you have many. They are prescribed for every night. You clearly have a problem. You must have to take sleep whenever you can, whenever you don't have to watch Kelime Öden. On the night in question you didn't take a pill, which has to mean that you felt that you couldn't. I am asking you why.'

She didn't reply.

'Miss Cox, the law here works, in some ways, just like it does in Britain. If someone has to wait to be tried for a crime they are kept in prison until their court appearance. That includes assisting a criminal. What is different here, according to my understanding of your prisons, is that ours are much more . . . mmm . . . old-fashioned. Life is hard if you don't have someone outside to bring in proper food for you. There is a system of barter amongst prisoners and guards can be . . . ah . . . Well, I'm sure you have heard how guards can be.'

Mary Cox still said nothing. He hoped she had not just tuned out and was actually thinking through her options.

'Whatever you may feel for a person, if they have broken the law you must forget that.'

She took in a deep breath. 'I feel nothing for Mr Öden but respect.'

Süleyman knew he hadn't done what Teker had asked him to. He hadn't screamed at her or evoked visceral terror. Once inside the interview room it hadn't felt right, for her. Maybe it was because her response to her surroundings had been muted. She was tougher than she looked. Only one thing might get through to her and he raised that issue again.

'I wish I could agree with you,' he said. 'But I can't. Miss Cox, I am not happy with your explanation about the events of that night. And although it does not make me happy to have to do this, I feel I must speak to Kelime Öden.'

This time her skin went white. 'Kelime! But she's just a child!'

'Yes,' he said. 'A child who it is my duty as a police officer to protect.'

'Mr Öden wouldn't abuse Kelime! He wouldn't!' She got to her feet. 'Why are you trying to accuse him of doing things he hasn't done?'

'Sit down.'

She didn't. Constable Özal began to move towards her. Mary Cox sat.

'Listen to me, Miss Cox,' Süleyman said, 'A woman is dead. A woman who was Mr Öden's mistress. We don't know whether he killed her or not. But at the moment he has an alibi. You. Now in my judgement, there is something wrong in the stories I have been told. One of them is definitely wrong. Mr Öden told me he didn't know the dead woman when he did. He told me he was in his daughter's room all night. So I am thinking, is he lying about that? Are you lying about that? And if you are not, why did you stay awake? If you stayed awake.'

'I did!'

He shrugged. 'Then if that is the case, I will have to speak to Kelime Öden.'

'No! You'll frighten her!'

Süleyman leaned across the dirty table towards her and said, 'Then I suggest we take you home and you think about your options tonight. It's late now. We will start our conversation again in the morning when maybe you will have slept and maybe you will not.'

Chapter 19

Aylın Akyıldız looked down at the partial skeleton she and Ariadne Savva had called Palaiologos and said, 'Thank you for letting me see him.'

Professor Bozdağ shrugged. 'He's still yours,' he said. 'Once I'd got over not being told, I realised that.'

'Thank you.'

The broken sword was at his side; robbed of its jewels, it looked violated. But it still dazzled her. Its provenance was still a mystery – like the body. Maybe it would remain a mystery forever.

'What about the threats? To you?' Professor Bozdağ asked.

She looked up. 'Oh, they still keep coming,' she said.

'Do the police have any idea where they're coming from?'

'No. Their experts think that whoever is sending them is routeing them though servers they've hijacked. Abroad.'

'And the letters?'

'Nothing,' she said. 'No identifying features found so far. They know what they're doing.'

'But it seems that, if they're still sending you threats, they don't know that our friend is here.'

They both looked down at the skeleton.

'Which is the way we have to keep it,' Aylın said. 'Can you imagine what people like that would do to him?'

The professor shook his head. 'And yet, who is he? Are you

sure Dr Savva never told you who she was going to attempt the DNA comparison with?'

'I'm certain,' she said. 'And believe me, I've looked at every item of documentation that passed between us. There's nothing.'

'They're sick. Measles.'

Süleyman looked at the man who said he was a doctor and then asked to see his ID card.

'Mr Öden called me this morning,' the man who was indeed Dr Akurgal said. 'This now explains why Kelime Öden was sick two days ago.'

'Does it?'

'Yes.'

He looked at Ömer Mungun, who, he noticed, had an expression of cynicism on his face which pleased him. The boy was learning.

'Well, I need to speak to Mary Cox,' Süleyman said.

'Mary Hanım is too ill to speak to anyone and this house in quarantined.'

'I've had measles,' Süleyman said. 'Sergeant Mungun?'

'Oh, I've had it too, sir.'

He looked at the doctor. 'Step aside, sir.'

And then Ahmet Öden appeared.

'What do you want this time, Süleyman?' he said. 'You bullied my nanny last night, now you come back to do it all over again. Well, she's sick and so is my daughter. Miss Cox told you what she knows last night, and by the way if you do want to talk to my daughter you will have to do so in the presence of Dr Akurgal and my lawyer. And only when she is better. If you want to speak to Miss Cox again then I suggest you charge her with something. I've already spoken to the British Consulate on her behalf this morning. I expect that Commissioner Teker will be hearing from them very soon.'

Teker, who had ordered him to get tough with Mary Cox. Süleyman felt himself deflate.

Together with Ömer Mungun he'd driven out to Bebek because Mary Cox hadn't arrived at the station at nine a.m. as agreed. All attempts at calling her had failed, and now this. Thwarted on Öden's doorstep.

'Miss Cox didn't have any sort of rash I could discern yesterday evening,' Süleyman said.

'It came on overnight,' the doctor said.

Between them, Öden and this doctor had and would have answers to every objection Süleyman might make.

'I was here all night when that woman died in Moda,' Öden said. 'Just like Mary Cox said. Just like my daughter would tell you, if I ever let you near her, which I will not. And don't think that those disgusting suggestions you made to Mary will be forgotten, because they won't. Now go away and allow me to look after my sick child in peace.'

They left. For a minute or so Süleyman drove in silence, then he pulled the car over into an unmade rural lane, put his head back and closed his eyes.

'Bloody bastard.'

Ömer Mungun, accustomed to the occasional outburst from his superior, could nevertheless understand this one. 'His fingerprints are all over that apartment, we know he lied about knowing that woman,' he said.

Süleyman opened his window and lit a cigarette. 'But did he kill her? In a way, knowing that he was having a relationship with her for certain isn't helping. When he does confess to his affair with Mrs Ocal, which he will, he'll say he was there off and on all the time. He will do anything to save his own skin in the end. Miss Mary, on the other hand, will I believe do anything she has to, to help him.'

'Why?'

'Why do you think? He's a good-looking man and so she's convinced herself she believes his holy man act.'

'Oh.'

Süleyman smoked. 'Ah, but Miss Mary and the girl can't be ill forever.'

'You think they're really ill?'

'No. But it's a clever delaying tactic and involving the British Consulate was smart. As if these people didn't have enough pull already with those at the top of the food chain.' He shook his head. 'You know, Ömer, I look at this city and—'

'Öden!'

Ömer pointed to his right.

'What?'

'That was Öden's car, just went towards the city,' Ömer said.

Süleyman started his engine and roared out on to the road ahead. 'You sure?' The driver of a Porsche slammed on his brakes, narrowly missing a shunt from a Mercedes behind.

'As much as I can be.'

A Land Rover was three cars in front of them but neither of them could see the licence plate. They followed, Ömer Mungun trying to find some vantage point that would allow him to see the back of the Land Rover properly. But this didn't happen until they reached a set of traffic lights. Süleyman stopped the car and Ömer jumped out.

Seconds later he was back inside Süleyman's BMW again and he was smiling. 'It's definitely him, sir.'

Süleyman shook his head. 'What a caring father he is, eh?'

Fatma had gone to pray at that space behind Aya Sofya again and so İkmen was in a bad mood.

'Why do you want to pray amongst lunatics?' he'd asked her

before he'd left the house that morning. 'You know the people who go there only do it to piss off the Christians, don't you?'

'No, they don't,' she'd said. 'They are sincerely religious men and woman.'

'Oh yes,' he'd retorted, 'the type of "sincerely religious men and women" who like to make big shows of themselves dressed for the desert that we don't, you might have noticed, live in. They're bigots and fanatics, and if I were in any way like one of their men I'd forbid you from going there.'

Fatma had just laughed.

'And your laughter at such an absurd idea just goes to prove my point,' İkmen had said. 'I'm not like them and you couldn't cope with me if I was. Fanatical religion is all very well and good as a notion, Fatma. But at heart, you're just too liberal. If you're not I don't know why we're still married.'

Then he'd slammed the apartment door behind him. But the altercation, plus lack of sleep, had left him agitated. Now that Gezi had moved far beyond Taksim and out to every open space across the city, the police had been ordered to move in again. There had been altercations in the night and Çetin and Fatma's son Kemal hadn't got home until the early hours of the morning. He'd had a bruise on his back the size of a dessert plate. Çetin didn't ask him who had made it. He knew a plastic bullet bruise when he saw one. All he'd done was tell the boy to go to the doctor to get it checked. But Kemal had said, 'There's loads of doctors at Gezi, Dad. I've already had it looked at. It's fine.'

But it wasn't. Çetin had hoped that maybe the younger children would grow up in a country not plagued by factional violence. Now that military coups were a thing of the past that should be possible. But clearly it wasn't. Gezi was an amazing phenomenon and he could only applaud its liberal, ecumenical spirit, but he feared for it and everyone associated with it.

He switched his computer on and looked through his e-mails. Another request from Mr Savva to take his daughter's body back to Greece. He'd only spoken to him the previous day to tell him about the baby the Erol girls had found. His response had been one of pessimism, which was probably for the best. Results from the IT investigators were inconclusive on the source of Aylın Akyıldız's threatening e-mails. And then there was one from Professor Bozdağ at the museum. It just said, 'Re your looking for as yet undiscovered Byzantine structures in the Old City. Shows where some of the old tunnels might be.'

There was an attachment which when opened revealed a map of Sultanahmet. Hand-drawn, indistinct and small, it was written in French and was dated 1895.

They tried to stall him by first offering him lemonade in that hot, ikon-stuffed salon of theirs and then they took him upstairs to go into the old woman's bedroom. He didn't want to see her. He could hear her breathing and he wished she wouldn't. With her gone it would be so much easier. But standing by her bedside table, full of her brushes, her pills and her very modest bits and pieces was a good opportunity and one he hadn't imagined he would get. He'd never dreamed they would let him see her.

Then he said, 'I want to go downstairs. You must know that.'

'I offered you a tour of my house and so that's what you'll get.'

Yiannis Negroponte was enjoying making him wait. He knew what was down there and so did that old Hakkı who followed him everywhere like a dog.

Three more bedrooms, a hamam and old man Negroponte's study had to be gone through before they descended to the basement. Then it was the toilet, a cupboard full of jars of preserved fruits and vegetables from decades back, and then, finally, they walked into the kitchen.

242

Ahmet Öden held his breath. For a moment he couldn't move his head at all. Frozen in a forwards position, even his eyes couldn't move from a scene that was entirely not as he had remembered it. And then when he could move, what he saw was even more alien. Where had the great stone blocks in the walls gone? Where was the entrance arch on the left? The step down just in front of it, the door that had been made out of rough plasterboard, just open enough for him to see . . .

'Where is it?' he said.

'Where's what?' Yiannis replied.

'You know!'

He saw Yiannis and the old man exchange the quickest of glances and for a moment he felt his head swim. 'I don't have to tell you! You know!' he roared.

'Know what? This is my kitchen, which you wanted to see. I'm showing it to you.'

He put a hand up to the wall and scratched it with his fingers. Yiannis Negroponte pulled his hand away. 'Please don't damage my kitchen, Mr Öden.'

Ahmet paced. Backwards two steps, forwards, sideways. Whichever way he moved, it was still the same. It wasn't right.

'What have you done?' he hissed. 'Have you destroyed it yourselves? Have you covered it up somehow? Where have you hidden it?'

'Hidden what?'

His blood pressure had to be through the roof. He *knew* they knew, even if they wouldn't say it. And he couldn't. The words were in his head but they just wouldn't come out of his mouth. He leapt forwards to grab that faux Greek's neck, but he side-stepped him.

'What have you done?' he said. 'How have you concealed it? Is it one of your tricks? An illusion? Or have you truly bewitched me with your ungodly magic? If you have bewitched me, I will make sure that you are pursued to your death as a false prophet!'

'I have neither . . .'

He sweated. They were laughing at him. Like a pair of hook-nosed demons. Ahmet wanted to kill them.

'Whatever you thought you were going to find in my kitchen isn't here,' Yiannis said.

'Which implies you *know* . . .'

'I don't know anything. My kitchen is my kitchen. As it is, as it always has been.'

'This is true,' the old man said.

Was he going mad or were they really toying with him? The fact that the faux Greek had invited him in at all had to indicate the latter. But what could he do about it?

'I'm sorry my kitchen hasn't lived up to your standards,' Yiannis said. 'But then you don't have to buy the house. It's not even for sale. There's no obligation.'

He wanted to throw himself on the man and rip his heart out. But he couldn't move again. Instead he spoke, 'Well, don't get too comfortable, "Yiannis",' he said. 'Because in a few days' time I will know exactly who you are and so will everyone else.'

For the first time Yiannis Negroponte's face tensed. 'I am Yiannis Negroponte, I am—'

'Remember that night we talked sitting outside your gate?' Ahmet said. 'When I took your hand and dug my fingers into your flesh?'

Yiannis didn't reply, but he had to remember it.

'You probably thought that was just spite, but you were wrong,' Ahmet said. 'I took your blood and the flesh that was inside my fingernails and I sent it off for DNA analysis. You know

244

they can tell everything these days from DNA. They can even tell what race you belong to.'

Was it just his imagination or did the room move just a little then? But Ahmet Öden didn't stop to find out. He turned away from Yiannis and the old man and he left.

'He came out half an hour later,' Süleyman said.

'Then what did he do?'

'Got in his car and drove off towards Sirkeci.'

Süleyman and Ömer Mungun were in Çetin İkmen's office with the inspector and Kerim Gürsel.

'You didn't follow him?' İkmen said.

'I'd had a call from Teker by then,' Süleyman said. 'The biggest "back off" I can recall.'

'He's an important man,' Kerim said.

'Who lies!' Süleyman shrugged his shoulders. 'When we left him he was so worried about his daughter he implied he could barely leave her side. But within minutes he's on his way to the Negroponte House.'

'Who let him in?' İkmen said.

'A middle-aged man. Sallow, unhealthy looking.'

'Yiannis, Madam's son.' İkmen frowned. 'Why?

'You mean because they're at odds,' Süleyman said. 'I've no idea.'

'I'll call them,' İkmen said. 'Yiannis knows we're watching his house and Öden. What did Öden look like when he came out? Did he look pleased? Defeated?'

'Angry, I'd say,' Ömer Mungun said. 'His face was red, and when he got into his car, he slammed the door behind him.'

İkmen put his phone on speaker so they could all hear the conversation and dialled the Negropontes' number. Yiannis answered.

'Yiannis, it's Inspector İkmen. Noticed that Ahmet Öden was at your house this morning. Is everything all right?'

'Oh, yes,' he said. 'Fine.'

'Just a little curious as to why he would be *inside* your house,' İkmen said. 'Did he pressure you to let him in?'

'No.'

'Then . . .'

'You know how much in need of repair this place is, Çetin Bey,' Yiannis said. 'He's been offering such enormous sums of money I thought that if he saw the state of the place he might go off the idea.'

'And did he?'

'No.' He sighed.

'It's the location, Yiannis. In the heart of the Old City,' İkmen said.

'I know. I know.'

'But you and Madam and Hakkı are all right?'

'Oh, yes,' he said. 'Mr Öden came, he saw and he still wanted to buy and I still turned him down. He wasn't happy when he left here.'

'Let me know if he comes back and if you need help,' İkmen said.

'Thank you, Çetin Bey.'

İkmen put the phone down. 'He appears to be in good spirits.'

'Öden was in his domain,' Süleyman said. 'Whatever designs he may have on that house, it belongs to Yiannis and his mother and they have the power.'

'That's true.'

'Öden however had the power when Ömer and I went to see him this morning,' Süleyman said.

'About his dead mistress in Moda?'

'Indirectly.'

246

'We think that his alibi for that night is unsound,' Ömer Mungun said.

'Who or what is his alibi?'

'His daughter's nanny,' Süleyman said. 'I have an unpleasant notion that she may be in love with him.'

İkmen shook his head. 'It never ceases to amaze me the people other people fall in love with,' he said.

Süleyman looked away.

'I even wonder whether Öden could be the father of Ariadne Savva's child,' İkmen said. 'She was supposedly his enemy but I don't see any other men in her life and, if that did happen, she wouldn't be the first woman to fall in love with a man she thinks she hates.'

'Maybe he raped her,' Kerim said.

'That too is possible.' He turned to Süleyman. 'I imagine you've heard that we've found a baby boy who may or may not be Dr Savva's child. DNA and time will tell. What would also be useful is a sample from Mr Öden.'

Süleyman grimaced. 'Ah.'

İkmen shook his head. 'Yes, of course you haven't been allowed to get that far, have you? Any forensics from other people possibly at the scene?'

'One partial fingerprint, not on our records, and some as yet unidentified hair strands. But they could be Öden's.'

'Which means you'll have to take DNA eventually.'

'When I'm allowed, yes.'

İkmen nodded. 'I think that we both need to go and see the Commissioner to make our need for Mr Öden's compliance known,' he said. 'Not that I think for a moment she isn't aware of it. I'm sure she is, and I'm also sure that she has already done everything those above her are permitting her to do. We've always lived in strange times because this is Turkey and strange is what we do. But I must admit that much of what is happening now makes me more fearful for the future than I have ever been. And yet the nation has never been so economically powerful.' He smiled. 'Is it the country or me who is wrong, do you think?'

Ahmet Öden put his phone down and walked out of his office, down a flight of stairs and into his kitchen. His cook, a Chechen, looked at him with expressionless eyes.

'Cook for Miss Mary and my daughter as usual tonight,' he said. 'But not for me. I'm eating out.'

'Yes, Ahmet Bey.'

He left. On the stairs back to the first floor he met Mary Cox. He noticed that she blushed.

'Ah, Mr Öden . . .'

'Mary.'

'I've, er, Kelime is watching TV and wants some ice cream. I've come down to, er . . .'

'Oh, please . . .'

He stepped out of her way.

Mary moved past him.

He said, 'You know I can't tell you how much I appreciate what you're doing for me and for Kelime, Mary. I am sure that your consulate will complain about Inspector Süleyman in the strongest terms.'

She looked up at him and smiled. 'It's nothing,' she said. 'You're innocent. You told me where you were the night that woman died, Mr Öden, and I believe you. But I also understand why you can't say any of that to the police. I couldn't believe how set against you they are.'

'I am successful and I am a man of faith,' he said. 'The old police guard don't like that. But times are changing. The police are changing.' He began to walk away. 'Oh, and thank you for having measles for me.'

'It's no problem. I know you'll do right by me, Mr Öden. Always.'

'Of course.'

He saw her smile and he smiled back.

But once back in his office, Ahmet Öden's smile faded. Could he trust her? Probably, she was besotted with him. But what had she meant by "always"?

Chapter 20

The dervish was slim and tall and so he was probably young. He wore a gas mask which covered his head and face, shrouding his identity. But it was his entari, the wide-skirted robe that all Mevlevi dervishes wore, that was most dramatic. Unlike the traditional white entari, this one was green and made of velvet, and as he turned in the dying evening light he was followed by an ever growing crowd of photographers, grizzled academics, children, students – and Samsun Bajraktar, Çetin İkmen's cousin.

Earlier in the day she'd met up with İkmen's youngest son, Kemal, who had showed her the deep bruising on his back due to a police issue plastic bullet. Knowing that Çetin's wife Fatma had to be losing her mind at the thought of what the boy was doing, she'd tried to persuade him to go home. It wouldn't be long before the police moved in again and she wanted Kemal to be safe. But he wouldn't go. He'd hung around with her all day, getting ice creams, finding water and talking to her friend Madonna about politics. In her previous incarnation as a bookish young man called Hakan, Madonna had been a student of political science at Boğaziçi University. That had been back in the 1980s, before Hakan had discovered men and drag and become the lady Madonna beloved of several thousand clubbers across İstanbul.

'He's a lovely movement there,' Madonna said as they followed the dervish as he whirled across Taksim Square.

'Yes, but he's probably very religious so don't get your hopes up,' Samsun said.

'I think it's amazing the way people from all across the religious secular divide have come here to do this,' Kemal said. 'That's why I keep on coming back. I wish Mum would come. If she would she'd be able to see that no one here is anti-religion.'

'Except her,' Samsun said, pointing to Madonna.

'I'm not anti,' Madonna said. She lit a cigarette and took a swig from a can of coke. 'People can believe whatever they like. Just don't try and get me to believe it too. Because I won't.'

The dervish stayed in one place, whirling on the spot, his head turned towards heaven, the wide skirt of his entari putting space between himself and those who watched him, ensuring his privacy as he communed with God. And although his performance wasn't accompanied by music, it was hypnotic. Samsun had even heard somewhere that watching dervishes dance lowered your blood pressure. She hoped so, because hers had been right up for the last few days.

One of the things that had led up to Gezi had been the issue of lesbian, gay, transgendered and bisexual rights. A lot of people wanted to extend them, and this included elements within the government. But the more conservative members of parliament had been against it and they were in the majority. Samsun didn't know whether Gezi would help the community to achieve more equality or not, but she feared that if the protest was crushed, the hope of more parity would be destroyed along with it.

As the sun went down, the three of them watched the young dervish dance and felt better for doing so. Arm in arm, the young man with one middle-aged and one old transsexual woman on each side.

*　　*　　*

The journey took forever. What with the clubs that lined the Bosphorus, the Gezi Park protest, and all the other, smaller demonstrations all over the city, traffic going into the centre of İstanbul was at times gridlocked.

When the taxi got to Ortaköy, where there were a lot of clubs, it stopped for over half an hour. Ahmet Öden was glad he'd left so much time to get to his assignation. He looked out of the cab window at a group of barely clad girls waiting for their friends outside a club called 'Machine'. To him they summed up the complacency and corruption of the secular elite. Much as he disagreed with the kids in Gezi Park, at least they were there for a reason, albeit a misguided one.

He gave the cab driver an extra twenty lira and told him to try the backstreets when he could. He did, but it didn't improve things. It still took over an hour to get to Sultanahmet.

The Hippodrome was dark and almost deserted. What tourists there were wandered in ones and twos and there were no police on duty at all. Ahmet sat down on a bench and looked at the Egyptian obelisk. He found it confusing, always had. When he'd been alive his father had hated it. There were carvings down the four sides that represented false gods. But his grandfather had loved it. His father and his grandfather had not got on. His grandfather had always believed that his father had been converted to an extreme religious ideology by a group of Arabs he'd met just after the Second World War. Refugees from Syria who had come across the Turkish border looking for work, they'd been full of fear and hatred for all the Jews that had been arriving in Palestine. Ahmet could remember his father railing against the Jews when he was a child. He wouldn't even believe that the Holocaust had taken place at all – a view which, at the time, was considered irrational and mad. Now it was common. Ahmet knew several otherwise sensible people who subscribed to it. He couldn't. The Jews had died in those camps. Surely people who denied it had to know there was no way the Holocaust could have been a figment of the imagination. Surely even his father had to have known that?

The old man had been dead for nearly twenty years, but Ahmet still felt compelled to please him. He'd wanted the Negroponte House and its secret ever since Ahmet could remember. But that had been after 1955, when everyone had become nervous about Greeks and what happened to them in the city. In the twenty-first century things were different again.

Ahmet wanted a cigarette. It was the first time he'd thought about them for years. As a young man he'd hidden his smoking from his father, who didn't approve of any sort of addiction. Now in his exalted position as one of İstanbul's most successful property developers and as a pillar of the community, smoking wasn't appropriate. Just as having a mistress hadn't been appropriate, either.

'Ahmet Bey.'

And here, at last, was the man he had come to meet. Old and arthritic, he walked a lot more slowly out in the open than he did in the house.

'Good evening, Hakkı Bey,' he said. 'I'm glad you've come to your senses.'

The Great Palace of the Byzantines was what had stood on the Sultanahmet peninsula before the Turkish invasion of 1453. Together with Aya Sofya, it was a complex of buildings rather than just one vast palace. It meant that in one relatively small area, the Byzantine emperors and their families could live, work, worship and even watch games at the Hippodrome. But because assassination was a real possibility for so many Byzantine rulers, tunnels were dug that led between significant parts of the

253

complex. That way the emperor and his family could pass from building to building in safety.

The map Professor Bozdağ had e-mailed him, originally drawn by a Monsieur René Goudeket, was small and hard to read. But Goudeket had clearly been very interested in mapping sites of Byzantine structures. Some were known, like Aya Sofya and Aya Irene, but back in those days only fragments of the Great Palace had been excavated. Not a great deal had changed in the intervening time, but what was thought to be the Palace Library had been discovered on a site next to the Four Seasons Hotel, and a few small chapels had been located in Cankurtaran.

It was nearly midnight but Professor Bozdağ had told İkmen to call him if he wanted any more information or had questions. Whether he, like İkmen, was still in his office, was open to question, but he answered his mobile phone immediately. He was even jovial. Maybe he was lonely?

'Rene Goudeket wasn't a Byzantine scholar, just an amateur enthusiast,' he said. 'You know rich people from Western Europe – Britain, France, Germany – used to do what they called The Grand Tour? This was a trip into antique, usually poor lands like Italy, Greece and parts of the Ottoman Empire, generally Constantinople, Egypt and Palestine. For almost nothing they could travel in style and eat like kings while fooling themselves they were becoming very cultured. Most of them just got sunburn and food poisoning, but a few fell in love with this part of the world. Goudeket was one of them. Spent his life walking the streets of Sultanahmet looking for signs of the Great Palace. He never found it, of course.'

'So his map is speculative?'

'In part. The Sultanahmet Jail, now the Four Seasons Hotel, hadn't been built then. But Goudeket does place what we think is the Great Library in roughly the same area as the structure we are gradually unearthing today. But most of the palace, the great reception halls, the baths, the university, the private royal quarters remain underground. Some we think we know about which, again, roughly relate to Goudeket's map, while other parts of the building seem to have disappeared even from the consciousness of the old Byzantine families who remain in the city.'

'Including the tunnels.'

'Yes,' he said. 'We know they're there. We know it's all there, somewhere. But where?'

'Do you think that Dr Savva found a Byzantine building no one had ever discovered before?'

'She found a Byzantine skeleton that could be significant. Who knows?' He sighed. 'I should have kept a closer watch on Ariadne. I didn't know how secretive she was. We all suffer from professional jealousy from time to time, but I like to think that my team share information freely. To be honest with you, Inspector, the fact that she didn't share is hurtful. It shows a lack of care for the team. In retrospect I feel as if I never really knew Dr Savva at all.'

'No.'

There was a pause and then the professor said, 'I don't suppose you know about the child . . .'

'Not yet, sir, no,' İkmen said. 'As you know, unlike in the movies and on TV, DNA tests take time.'

'Of course.'

Professor Bozdağ guided İkmen through the main features of Goudeket's map.

'We can't be sure exactly how the Great Palace Goudeket drew relates to the modern city now, but I think you will be able to see roughly where the buildings he is speculating about might be. Of course many of the street names are different now. Back in Ottoman times a lot of small thoroughfares weren't named at all. And of course Goudeket was French and so he may have misinterpreted names.'

'Of course. Thank you.'

İkmen carried on looking at the map through a magnifying glass once the call was over. It looked to him as if the Sultanahmet Blue Mosque was right on top of what had been the private quarters of the Byzantine imperial family. So that would never be excavated. But part of the road behind the mosque had been redeveloped in recent years. Kabasakal Caddesi only had three large houses left intact now. One of them was the Negroponte House.

Hakkı led him down the stone stairs from the garden and through the back door into the kitchen. When he'd been inside the building before, the kitchen could only be accessed from the entrance inside the house. The back door had been blocked then. And now everything was different. Though not exactly the way he remembered it, Ahmet could now see the arch right in front of him, the small tunnel and the tiny door at the end of it. The one he'd slipped through all those years ago.

He turned to the old man. 'How did he do it? Yiannis?'

'It's one of his illusions,' Hakkı said. He half smiled. 'If I told you, I'd have to kill you.'

It had to be, in part at least, a change in vantage point. But he'd felt odd too. When he'd lost his temper it had felt as if he was shouting through wool. That was his memory of it.

'Did he hypnotise me too?' he asked the old man.

Hakkı shrugged.

'What does that mean?'

'It means if you want them upstairs not to know about this, you'll have to keep your voice down.'

Hakkı hadn't betrayed his master and mistress out of Muslim Turkish solidarity as Ahmet had hoped. He'd asked for money and Ahmet had given him half. It was nothing, but the greed made him angry.

'Do you want to go in?' Hakkı said.

'Yes.'

'See your "wonderful things".'

He was mocking him. When Ahmet had told Hakkı what he'd seen all those years ago when the kitchen door had been left unlocked and he had gone inside, he'd quoted the words of the archaeologist Howard Carter who, when he had discovered the tomb of Tutankhamun, had seen 'wonderful things'.

'I'm going to take photographs. For proof,' Ahmet said.

The old man shrugged. 'Be quick.'

Ahmet walked towards the archway and into the small tunnel. He had to ignore the fact that the old man was a mercenary bastard for the moment. He had to get some good shots, so he could prove that it existed and that he knew about it. Once copies were in Yiannis' hands he'd have to stop playing games and sell or be reported to the Ministry of Culture and Tourism. The house would be dismantled to make way for a very lucrative archaeological site. Except that it wouldn't, because Yiannis would sell to him rather than be compulsorily purchased by the State. And then the site would be destroyed – by Ahmet.

The small metal door scraped against the stone floor as he pushed it. It was dark inside. Ahmet no longer carried a lighter.

'Don't you have a candle?' he asked.

'Yes.'

He looked back into the kitchen, but the old man hadn't moved.

'Well bring it!'

He looked into the gloom again, waiting. As soon as it was illuminated it would spring out at him as it had done that first time, like a massive, hidden jewel.

He heard the old man move towards him and so on one level he was excited, but there was something else close to him too now. Something in the shadows that he couldn't see, hear or dare move his hand to touch.

'Are you sure we're alone?' he said to the old man as the light from the candle behind him began to ooze into the darkness. For a second there was a colour of blood on the floor and Ahmet smiled.

So it came as a shock when Hakkı said, 'No.'

His heart had only just begun to hammer in his chest when there was a terrible pain in his head and everything went dark and silent.

Chapter 21

Getting out of bed was a slow business for Mehmet Süleyman. Gonca's entire family had decamped to Gezi Park and tent-dwelling the previous day and for the first time in years he had spent a quiet night alone with his gypsy lover. It had been blissful. She'd cooked, they'd eaten alone outside in the garden, then they'd made love and gone to sleep in each other's arms. In the calmness he seemed to have fallen in love all over again. He looked at her sleeping and smiled.

After he'd showered and shaved, Süleyman dressed quietly, careful not to wake her. But she was already stirring. Looking at him through half-closed eyes and a curtain of hair she said, 'Is it time to go already?'

'Yes,' he said. 'Go back to sleep.'

But she hauled herself up on her elbows. 'I must cook,' she said.

'Cook?'

'If everyone is going to stay in Gezi, they'll need to eat,' she said. 'The adults can fend for themselves but the little ones and my father have to be properly fed.'

He shook his head but he didn't say anything. There was no point. Gonca would look after her endless stream of relatives, usually at her own expense, whatever he said. But her devotion did irritate him. Her work suffered and so did their relationship. That had been proven the previous night. Without the Şekeroğlus in tow, he didn't think about anyone but Gonca. Well, he did, but only in a casual, looking at women in the street sort of way. He kissed her and left. On his way down the hill to his car he saw a lot of covered women and one girl in a tiny summer dress with flowers in her hair. She carried a rainbow flag and had the word 'Gezi' written on her forehead in what looked like lipstick. She was very young and very beautiful and she smiled openly at him.

His head was sore but there was something else too – a chemical taste in his mouth and a feeling of his head being full. He'd been in that room, alone, and then someone had come . . . Had it just been the old man? He'd lost consciousness and now he was here. Which was terrifying because here was small. Unable to sit or lie down, he was propped like a plank of wood between two serpentine porphyry walls of amazing beauty. A large candle, like those the Christians had in churches, sat in a saucer at his feet, ensuring he could see everything.

In front were bricks. Modern and rough with mortar in between. Turning his head so he could see what was behind his back, he saw a jug of water on a porphyry shelf. That, like the candle, was large. Ahmet Öden wanted to think that he was dreaming. But he wasn't. He pushed the mortar between the bricks with one finger. It was still wet and for a few seconds that gave him hope. But even if he wiggled his finger almost all the way through the mortar, he couldn't get to whatever was on the other side. The bricks stayed where they were. Probably because something outside was holding them in.

He put his hand in his pocket to find his phone. But it wasn't there. A chill rose from his feet to his head and he shuddered.

'Things are going to get rough.'

Çetin İkmen looked up at his superior. Standing in front of his office window, Commissioner Teker flicked ash from her cigarette out into the car park. He flicked his into an old saucer he'd brought from home.

'Gezi Park cannot be occupied forever,' Teker continued. 'The politicians won't have it.'

'We won't have it, I take it,' İkmen said.

'No. So you'd better get your son out of there before the sky falls in,' she said.

İkmen shook his head. 'He loves it.'

'He may do, but there are officers on the ground who are just gagging to have a go. You know it and I know it. Half of them come from places nobody's ever heard of where women never leave the house and everybody is related. This is exciting for them.'

He looked up at her. 'Isn't there anything you can do?'

'If I'm ordered to move in, we move in,' she said. 'That's my job, it's what I do. I'm not political and I've come to you only because I know that your son is one of the protesters.'

'A lot of people have relatives at Gezi . . .'

'Yes, and I've told Sergeant Mungun to warn his sister.'

'You know, if it hadn't been for Gezi and Mungun's sister we would never have found that baby,' İkmen said.

'That's not a reason to believe that everyone in Gezi Park is perfect.'

'I know that.'

She put her cigarette out. 'Whatever we may think about the current situation, it isn't sustainable,' she said. 'One way or another it has to be resolved. And as servants of the State we will be asked to do that. Even if it goes against every personal belief we possess.'

Briefly she put a hand on his shoulder and then she left.

İkmen lit another cigarette. If anyone reported him for smoking indoors he'd just own up and take his punishment – with the requisite amount of resentment. What was he going to say to Kemal? And would it even make any difference? He was at Gezi every day now, along with his Auntie Samsun.

And why was he worrying about the kid so much anyway? He was young, fit, he'd done his army service and knew how to handle himself. Was İkmen just absorbing Fatma's excessive concern for their youngest child? She wanted to keep that boy at home and a 'baby' forever and it wasn't healthy. But then the kid very readily took the free board and lodging he had right in the middle of what had become one of the world's most vibrant cities.

He knew he should really be more worried about Samsun. She knew some very tough trans women who could handle themselves far more effectively than Kemal, but Samsun herself was old and weak. She had an arthritic knee, diabetes and vertigo to his know-ledge and yet he knew that if things got rough she'd throw herself into any sort of action, however dangerous, to protect Kemal. İkmen's mother's family were an odd lot. Albanian by birth, most of them, including Samsun, and for much of the time very 'foreign' to İkmen, they nevertheless cared about him and his family. Maybe Kemal would stop going to Gezi if he explained to him that he could be putting his auntie at increased risk of harm? Young policemen, like young men everywhere, tended to target people like themselves. You could have a good scrap with an equal opponent. Would Kemal buy it? He didn't know.

İkmen switched on his computer and went into his mail programme. There was a message from Mr Savva, asking about when his daughter's body might be released, asking about the child. He'd had to tell him but he didn't feel good about it. The Greek was, in spite of what he'd said at the start, pinning his hopes on the Erol sisters' baby. It was natural he wanted to believe that something remained of his dead daughter, but it was more than possible that it didn't, and there was nothing İkmen could do to hurry the DNA test results.

In the meantime, whoever may have killed Ariadne Savva was still free. And much as he wanted to believe it was Ahmet Öden, there was no evidence to connect him to her death.

The first Mary had heard about Mr Öden's absence had been at the dinner table the previous evening. The Chechen cook had said that 'Ahmet Bey' had given him instructions only to make dinner for Miss Mary and Kelime Hanım. She'd thought that he had probably gone out to dinner with business associates. But now it was lunchtime and he still wasn't home. Also, why were all of his cars still on the drive? Mr Öden didn't drink and so there could have been no reason for not driving himself. Unless someone had given him a lift?

'Where's Daddy?'

Kelime was asking every five minutes, or so it seemed, and it was driving Mary crazy. She didn't know! But she, unlike the girl, couldn't express her agitation. Mr Öden was her employer and so to be overly concerned about him would be unseemly.

'He's at work, Kelime,' Mary said.

'When's he coming home?'

The poor kid looked like a massive pink curtain in the voluminous party frock she'd wanted to wear that day. 'Soon,' Mary said.

'Is he? Can I have an ice cream now?'

'After your lunch.'

Kelime put her head down on her chest. Lunch, which was an over-large portion of mantı with salad, sat in front of her, untouched – and, Mary knew, hated. As she did every day, Kelime had started hassling for chocolate, ice cream and cake almost as soon as she'd woken up. And Mary had allowed her to have some. Now she was digging her heels in.

'Eat your mantı, Kelime,' Mary said. There was nothing new in the fact that Mary was at odds with the girl over food. But she was aware of a tension that wasn't usually present. It was because Mr Öden wasn't at home. And because he'd been out all night. Did he have another mistress? Already? In her head she could admit to his weaknesses and the reality of how bitter they made her feel. How could he have taken a dirty gypsy into his bed? How could he? Mary smoothed her pencil skirt down over her thighs and nibbled at the tiny ravioli. Kelime watched her from underneath knitted, resentful brows. She wondered how the inevitable tantrum would take her.

'Kelime, my pumpkin!'

At first Mary thought it was her employer. But it was only Semih, his brother. Mary felt her body slump.

'Look what I've got for you!'

The young man had a bar of chocolate behind his back.

'Is it sweeties? Is it sweeties?'

'Kelime needs to finish her lunch before she can have sweets, Mr Öden,' Mary told him.

'Oh Miss Mary, she doesn't like her lunch,' Semih said.

'Yes, but . . .'

Kelime jumped off her chair and barrelled into her uncle's tight torso.

'Please give me sweeties, Uncle Semih! Please, please, please!'

Semih Öden looked at Mary in a way she interpreted as triumphalist and then gave the girl the chocolate. Kelime ran away into the TV room, giggling.

'I suppose you think I shouldn't have done that, Miss Mary,' Semih said as he sat down at the table and began eating Kelime's mantı.

'What I may think is irrelevant,' Mary said stiffly.

He smiled. 'But you think that my niece should be saved from her appetites, don't you?'

'I . . .'

'What else does she have? Eh?' He ate. 'You know we say such damaged children are blessed by Allah? And you know why? Because they will always be children.'

Mary also imagined that he believed they would be devoid of sexual desire. A common, patronising misconception.

'Her father is diabetic,' Mary said. 'I fear that if Kelime goes on eating in the way she does, she too may develop the disease.'

'Do you know where my brother is?'

The question caught her unawares. When Semih Öden had come in, apart from being annoyed at how he had undermined her with Kelime, Mary had thought that at least she might now find out where Ahmet Öden was.

'No, don't you—'

'We have a meeting here at midday,' he said. 'I'm a little late but . . .' He took his mobile phone out of his pocket and dialled. Mary heard the call go straight to voicemail. Semih shrugged.

'Mr Öden went out last night,' Mary said. 'Cook told me.'

'Where?'

'I don't know.'

He frowned. 'The police didn't take him, did they?'

She hadn't thought of that. Mary felt her heart jolt. 'No. But he didn't drive.'

'That's why I was surprised when I realised he was out,' Semih said.

'You have no idea where he might be, Mr Öden?'

'No.' He put Kelime's fork down and stopped eating. 'Maybe I'll make some calls to his contacts. He might be at the site. We had some trouble there the other day.'

265

'What kind of trouble?'

'Vandalism,' he said and then he got up and left the table.

Mary, alone, began to feel sick.

When the old woman woke she noticed the change in the air almost immediately. Like the tiny ripple in the atmosphere that some say always precedes an earthquake, she caught it just as Yiannis entered her room with her lunch.

'Mama . . .'

She looked into his eyes and he stopped talking, stranded with her plate of börek in his hands.

'What . . . is happening?'

His eyes moved in that way that they did when people wanted to escape. She was a long-time student of human behaviour.

He put her food down on her bedside table. 'There are still protests in Gezi Park. The Prime Minister is still out of the country.'

'In this house.'

He took a step away. 'Nothing.'

Yiannis lied fluently and well. It was an everyday occurrence and she was used to it. But this was different. A unique lie. It interested her.

'Eat your börek while it's warm.' He smiled and then he left.

But Anastasia Negroponte wouldn't eat her börek. What little appetite she had left had gone with his guilty eyes.

İkmen could see the attraction. Gezi was like a festival. There was music, food and drink, people wearing colourful clothes, free talk about everything imaginable, dancing and even one man reciting poetry to the trees. It was very much like a festival his eldest son Selim had been to and told him about some years back, in England. Glastonbury.

'Çetin, dear, of course I will help you get the boy out of here, but I'm not going anywhere,' Samsun said.

He'd found her, surrounded by trans women in evening wear listening to the tree poet, and had taken her to one side. Kemal had apparently gone off in search of food.

'But you know we're all aware of the fact that the police won't hold off for much longer,' she said. 'I think there are very few people here who are roaming around with stars in their eyes. We're not about to storm the Bastille or take over the battleship *Potemkin*.'

İkmen looked up into the night sky; a few fireworks joyfully illuminated the old Ataturk Centre.

'I'm more worried you'll all be cut down like rows of tulips,' he said. 'Which, Samsun, forces me to be blunt. I want to get Kemal home as soon as I can, but I also want you to go home too.'

'Not a chance.'

'I have to try,' İkmen said. 'You're not as young as you were and with all the stress and the erratic eating . . .'

'I've been feeding myself very well since I've been here, thank you, Çetin,' she said. But then she frowned. 'Not that I don't appreciate your concern. I know I'm old and weaker these days but you know that if there is an attack I won't hold back. I've still got balls, even if I haven't got testicles.'

İkmen smiled.

'Dad!'

Kemal was like a plastic bag packhorse. Some contained bottles of fizzy drinks while others were full of bread, hummus and other vegetable-based meze food. He'd been flirting with the idea of becoming a vegetarian for about a year which had panicked Fatma, who feared he might also be gay.

The two men embraced. 'What are you doing here?'

'What do you think?'

The young man put his bags down on the ground. 'Mum.'

'She's worried,' İkmen said. 'She's not happy and she's nagging me into an early grave. What can I say?'

Kemal sighed. 'She's *so* with this government, Dad. And I just can't be. Because they say they're religious, she thinks they can't do anything wrong. But all this building and knocking stuff down they do is not something I can support. I can't accept how they are with gay and trans people either.' He looked at Samsun and smiled. 'How can I not support my own auntie?'

Samsun put an arthritic, heavily ringed hand on his arm and said, 'Darling, you're a good boy, but I can look after myself.'

'I know!'

'Kemal, my love, you should go home for a little while now,' she said. 'So your poor mother can sleep in peace.'

'Yeah, but—'

'Come back tomorrow,' she said. 'We all know that you support what is happening here. You are a Gezi hooligan – one of the best!'

He smiled.

'But your mother, whatever you think about her politics, is a good woman and so you must be a good son too.'

İkmen's phone rang. He walked away from the group to answer it.

'İkmen?'

'Sir.' It was Kerim.

'Yes?'

'Sir, we've had a call from the brother of Ahmet Öden. Nobody knows where he is.'

Chapter 22

It wasn't easy for Yiannis Negroponte to take his eyes off Hakkı. He was just peeling onions in the sink, but he was doing it in such a state of measured calm, Yiannis wondered about his sanity.

His legs shaking, Yiannis sat down at the kitchen table and lit a cigarette. He tried not to look at the entrance to that terrible room behind him, but he felt it. It made his back bend under the weight of its age, its purpose and what had been done in it. He hated it.

'She knows,' he said.

Hakkı shrugged.

'Her eyes looked right into my soul,' Yiannis said. 'I can't go into her room again, you'll have to.'

'I will.'

Yiannis pulled on his cigarette. 'How can you be so calm?'

Before Ahmet Öden had arrived Hakkı had calmly gathered bricks from the building site at the end of the road, prepared the cavity and its contents and brought a wardrobe down from one of the guest bedrooms on his back. Made from solid oak, it stood guard over Ahmet Öden's death chamber, stopping the bricks and stone he'd mortared together in the cavity from collapsing. Until the mortar hardened it would have to stay.

'He would never have stopped,' Hakkı said.

'Oh, so now we just wait for his company to take over where he left off! I shouldn't have listened to you! Every time I listen to you—'

'I sort things out.' Hakkı walked over to the table and pointed at Yiannis with the vegetable knife. 'I have saved your skin and, more importantly, Madam's.'

Yiannis looked down at the table. 'But she knows. I can't meet her eyes. She knows everything in the world.'

'No, she doesn't. And don't meet her eyes. Stop being pathetic.' Hakkı returned to the sink and began peeling again. 'I will feed and take care of her. I always have.'

Yiannis looked at the old man's back and was glad he wasn't the one wielding the vegetable knife. Why had he lived so long? Was it just to punish him?

'She won't know what has been done,' Hakkı said. 'She lost her ability to distinguish between what was really happening and what was not in 1955.'

'What do you mean?'

But Yiannis knew. Hakkı turned and looked at him without speaking. It was Yiannis who dropped his gaze first.

He looked at his fingernails. 'What are you cooking?'

'Moussaka.'

Yiannis didn't care. His stomach had tied itself into a confused washing bundle and he felt certain that he'd never eat again.

Eventually when he could speak, all he could talk about was the man in the room at his back. The one they had both bricked up like a nun who had broken her vows or like a cruel Byzantine princess who had tried to take power by killing her own brother. 'Do you think he can hear us?' Yiannis whispered.

'I don't know where my brother was yesterday,' Semih Öden told Çetin İkmen. 'He went out in the morning.'

'Where?'

'I told you, I don't know.'

İkmen and Süleyman looked at each other. They knew that

Ahmet Öden had been at the Negroponte House, which he had left at around lunchtime in a very agitated mood.

'But he came home from that appointment?'

'His child's nanny and the cook say he did.'

'Can we speak to Miss Mary Cox, the nanny?' Süleyman asked.

'No. She's sick.'

'Oh, yes of course, measles.'

Semih Öden glared at him. 'How do you know?'

'I wanted to talk to her when I came here yesterday,' Süleyman said. 'But your brother denied me and my sergeant access.'

'Oh. Did he?' He looked away.

'Yes, and then he went to the Negroponte House in Sultanahmet. You know, I assume, that he's interested in purchasing a house in Sultanahmet?'

But Semih Öden was lost in his own thoughts.

'My sergeant and I followed him there,' Süleyman continued. 'He went inside.'

Semih Öden looked shocked. 'I don't know anything about that.'

'But he came home?' İkmen said. 'Afterwards?'

'He must've done. The cook and Miss Mary saw him and spoke to him. You can speak to the cook if you don't believe me.'

'We will.'

'Ahmet didn't say where he was going to anyone,' Semih said. 'And there's nothing in his diary.'

'Do you have any idea why he didn't take a car?' İkmen asked.

'No. But sometimes we all take taxis, Ahmet included. The traffic is so stressful and you can usually just hail a cab outside the front gates.'

What he didn't add was that for people like them cost was

immaterial. Last time İkmen had had to hire a cab he'd feared he might have to sell his apartment to pay the fare.

'My brother would have called by now, whatever he was doing,' Semih said. 'My niece, his daughter, she has er . . . she . . .'

'The young lady has Down's syndrome, yes,' İkmen said.

'If he doesn't call her, Kelime becomes agitated,' Semih said. 'And I've tried contacting him on his mobile and it just goes straight to voicemail. Something has happened to him.'

'What do you imagine that might be?' Süleyman asked.

Semih flung his arms in the air. 'I don't know! We're property developers, people don't always like us.'

'Anyone in particular?'

'What, apart from that weird man in the Negroponte House?' He shrugged. 'The site over at Gizlitepe has been repeatedly vandalised ever since we started work there. But if he'd been over there, Ahmet would definitely have taken his car. It's not safe there at night.'

'So where could he have gone?' İkmen asked. 'I believe your parents are both dead. But what about other relatives, friends, business associates . . .' he paused for a moment and then he added, 'mistresses?'

Semih Öden looked at him with disgust. 'My brother is a moral man, he doesn't have mistresses.'

'Any more,' Süleyman said.

The young man ignored him.

'Anyone I know of would have got in touch if Ahmet had been with them and unable to communicate for any reason,' he said. 'He's Type One diabetic and so he has to inject himself with insulin. If he doesn't he gets sick. My brother is missing. Someone has taken him or harmed him and I want him found.'

When they left the ugly, expensive house in Bebek, İkmen

and Süleyman both lit up. İkmen started his car. 'So where's he gone then, do you think?'

'Well, the last place he was seen alive, apart from his home, was the Negroponte House. But I saw him leave there,' Süleyman said. 'We need to appeal for information from taxi drivers.'

'Yes.'

'But I think, if I'm honest, that he's done a disappearing act. I don't know whether his brother, Mary Cox or anyone else is in on it too, but I think that it's all got a bit too hot for him lately. What with the dead mistress, and the dead academic who opposed him.'

'Could be,' İkmen said. 'Although I had him pegged as more of a fighter than that. These conservative types are quite aggressive these days. They've got a lot of money and power now.'

'Ah, but maybe the events in Gezi Park have spooked him. I mean, we don't know what's going to happen there, do we? What if the protests spread still further and this government falls? What will happen to people like Ahmet Öden then?'

'I don't know,' İkmen said. 'But then I don't think we'll find out, because I don't believe that the government will fall.'

'Don't you think there's enough public support for the protests?'

'I think it's extensive,' İkmen said. 'But it's almost exclusively in the cities. Think how big Anatolia is by contrast and how many people live in villages where a conservative lifestyle that was derided for decades is now held up as something virtuous by this government. Whatever the reason for Öden's disappearance might be, I don't believe it has anything to do with Gezi Park.'

'He's back.'

Peri Mungun frowned.

'The Prime Minister,' Iris said. 'From his north African visit. Just read it on Twitter. He's at Ataturk airport. Met by a huge crowd.' She looked back down at her iPad. 'Oh my God, they're chanting "Give us the way, we'll crush Taksim".'

'Who are?'

'His supporters.' Iris shook her dreadlocks. 'Bastards!'

Iris had built a fire when darkness fell which had attracted a group of very diverse people, including an elderly communist, a covered woman, a boy dressed as a clown and a tiny woman Peri had discovered was the wife of one of her brother's colleagues, Kerim Gürsel. Unable to walk or stand, Sinem Gürsel was being cared for by a transsexual called Pembe who was roasting marshmallows over Iris's fire.

'Let them come,' the clown boy said. 'We can deal with them.'

The old communist shook his head. 'Have you seen any hard-line government supporters lately, Murad Bey?' he said. 'I fought in Cyprus in 'seventy-four and I'd rather take on the Greek army than tangle with that lot. What are you going to do? Fire your water pistol at them? Hope that when your trousers fall down it frightens them away?'

The covered woman laughed. It was deep, dirty and unexpected and it made Peri smile.

'They'll hide behind the police,' the old man said. 'Those bastards'll get stuck in first and only then will the brainwashed masses come along to mop up what's left of us.'

Peri saw Sinem Gürsel look away. Like her, she found it hard to hear about possible police brutality. She'd never been able to square the image of her gentle brother with stories about torture in police cells and miscarriages of justice.

'But if they're all fired up to come now . . .' Pembe said.

Iris looked at her iPad. The sound was muted, but Peri could hear a sort of general hubbub.

'Who knows?' Iris said. 'I expect we'll see some of them. The total crazies.'

The old man shook his head, 'It'll be like 1905 all over again.'

'1905?'

'When the ordinary people of St Petersburg were massacred on the Tsar's orders outside the Winter Palace.'

They all looked at each other. That was too much even for Iris. 'Rauf Bey,' she said, 'we're not underfed Russian peasants whose lives can just be snuffed out. We have social media . . .'

'Much good that did the Persians who tried to assert their rights last year,' Rauf Bey said.

'This is not Iran.'

They all turned to look at Sinem. 'Whatever we may think about what's going on here, this isn't Iran,' she said. 'Women don't have to cover and we do still have Gay Pride . . .'

'For the moment,' the old man said. 'For the moment.'

And then the party round the fire went quiet. Iris put away her iPad and Pembe gave out marshmallows in silence. Ömer had told Peri she should leave the park, but she couldn't. Word had come from on high that the police were not going to hold off for much longer. When it came, the attack would be bad. Not quite along the lines of the Winter Palace massacre of 1905 but it wouldn't be easy. Peri thought – as Ömer had asked her to – of her parents. If she got killed or even injured, they would be distraught. And they were far too old for that.

She contemplated leaving, for her parents' sake, but time passed, marshmallows were eaten, the fire died down and eventually she found herself going to sleep beside Pembe. The dry Gezi grass underneath her body was strangely comfortable.

Hakkı brought her food, a small bowl of moussaka that joined the uneaten börek on her bedside table. He looked at the cold pastry and said, 'You must eat.'

She looked into his eyes. Yiannis had said she knew something

275

and Hakkı was aware that starving herself was the only weapon she had left. And she knew that he feared it.

'What have you done?' she said.

'Nothing.'

She looked into his eyes again. Speaking was so tiring. She knew he understood her eyes and what lay behind them.

'There is nothing for you to worry about,' he said.

He made to go. Her mouth moved without sound. Then it came. 'You . . . killed,' she said. There was a long pause. He started walking. 'Again.'

Hakkı stopped.

'Again.'

His eyes darted around, sliding over her face, but they didn't rest anywhere. 'No.'

'Yes.' She switched to Greek. She hadn't done that for decades. But it was appropriate and she saw Hakkı shudder.

'Now,' she said, counting on her shaking fingers, 'the girl . . . 1955 . . .'

He put a hand out to steady himself against the end of the bed. She'd never, ever said the name of that year to him before. Never.

'I had no choice.'

'You . . . you stop,' she said.

His face was usually pale but now it was grey. It frightened her. She wondered whether she should go on.

He said nothing. Could he speak?

'I am ordering . . .'

'I can't,' he said. Holding on to the bed, he knelt down beside her. 'We are at risk again, Madam. These people, now, they're like . . .' he stopped.

He couldn't say it and so she said it for him. ''Fifty-five. You saved . . . me.'

'Yes, I saved you.' His hands kneaded her ancient fraying counterpane.

She put a hand on his head. Over the years she'd wondered if he'd thought she was dead when he'd lifted her out of that devils' orgy on İstiklal Caddesi. He had definitely thought she was unconscious. But one eye had been open, just a crack. She'd seen his tears as he'd looked into her face. She stroked his hair.

He took her withered hand and kissed it. Although he was almost as old as she, his eyes were clear, which gave her a sure and uncommon view of the passion that he always hid from everyone except the two of them.

She couldn't say the words. But in her head she knew that finally the time had come for her to move on. She had never thought that she would.

Eventually she said, 'It . . . must . . . stop.'

He cried. All the time he looked away from her saying, 'No! No! No! No!'

And she wondered whether after all these decades he was going to finally defy her. And the thought of it made her want to take her own life.

If he managed to reach the water, the cavity was so narrow he risked spilling it over himself or, even more frighteningly, the candle. He'd had to pee three times and so there was already liquid on the floor. It, and he, stank. Eventually he'd need to defecate. He didn't dare think about that.

The old man, may God curse him, couldn't have done this to him on his own. Negroponte had to have helped him. They'd tricked him and he hadn't even had the wit to see it coming. He'd so wanted to believe the old man, he'd completely blinded himself to the truth. Why would Hakkı betray the Negropontes after so many years of faithful service? What he'd done for the old woman in 1955 had to have bound him to her forever. To betray her would negate his entire existence. Ahmet had that from his father and so it had to be true.

But he'd so wanted to get into that room. There had been stories when he'd been a child. His grandfather had seen it and had described it to his father as a marvel. A blood-red room where dynasties were born, where those who had once ruled the city performed their rites of succession – where those that remained could perform them again.

Ahmet hit one of his red prison walls with his fist. Blood ran down his knuckles. He winced, stuck his fist in his mouth and choked back tears. The salty taste of blood made him want to gag. Was it a sin to drink one's own body fluids?

He'd been careful not to put the blood he'd collected underneath his fingernails from Yiannis Negroponte's hand anywhere near his mouth. Were the results of the DNA test he'd had performed on that sample back? Would he ever know?

His instinct told Ahmet that he should hammer on the walls, but his mind told him it was pointless. In hour after hour of stuffy silence he hadn't once heard anything from outside the tiny chamber. And where was he in the room? He didn't remember any small cavities like this when he'd first stepped into the Red Room all those years ago. There had just been wonder, horror and awe, plus a feeling of being in a place of great evil.

Now he was going to die in it and he knew that however hard he shouted, however loudly he screamed, there was nothing he could do to change that. He hadn't eaten for many hours and he'd left his house without his insulin. He'd fit, lose his mind and then die in a coma. Ahmet knew that scenario backwards.

Chapter 23

Gonca pulled him out of bed by his hair.

'My family are being slaughtered!' she screamed.

He hit the cold early morning floor with first his naked side, then his head.

'What?'

Dressed in a transparent black chiffon kaftan, Gonca shouted through her thick grey hair. 'You, the police, in Gezi Park! My father says you're firing on the people! Get up!'

He sat up. Looking around the bedroom lit by the harsh neon light she favoured, he felt disorientated.

'Get up! Get up!'

She threw a dress on over the kaftan and began to lift him to his feet.

Her family were all at Gezi Park, protesting and, no doubt, doing a bit of business too. Commissioner Teker had said that the government wouldn't let them do it forever. He pulled his clothes on. He didn't know what he could do.

'How do you know? What happened?'

'My father called,' she said. 'You, the police—'

'Will you stop—'

'Well you are the police, aren't you?'

He said nothing.

'You, the police, said that you were just going to clear Taksim for traffic. Then suddenly there's Molotov cocktails in the air!'

'From—'

'Oh, from the fucking police, of course! Provoking! Then plastic bullets! Now who knows what!'

She picked up a bag and stuffed a packet of 200 cigarettes inside. 'Come on!'

He'd only just put his shoes on when she pulled him out of her bedroom door and into the garden.

Not even food could distract her. Kelime had begun weeping in the afternoon and she was still crying the following morning. Mary didn't know what to do. Semih Bey had stayed over in one of the guest rooms but he'd made it clear he didn't want to be disturbed unless his brother was found or his niece became ill. And although Kelime was distressed, she wasn't sick. The lack of endless treats could even be doing her good, physically.

'Where's Daddy? Why doesn't he come?' she sobbed. 'What have I done wrong, Miss Mary?'

'Nothing, dear. Nothing.'

Mary held her. Even though he gave her everything and called her his princess, Ahmet Öden had still managed to instil a sense of guilt in his daughter. She blamed herself for his absence and it was biting at her heart.

Mary knew that Ahmet Öden wasn't the man she wanted him to be. Vain and hypocritical, he didn't worship God, but money. God just helped him get where he wanted to go. However, Mary had believed the high moral act with all her heart. So the appearance of the gypsy hooker when she'd first seen her with him months ago had been a shock. The Ödens had been on holiday at Ahmet's villa in Marmaris when it had happened. It was Mary's day off and Semih Öden had taken Kelime to the beach for the day. Mary had planned to drive to the ruins at Knidos for the day but then she'd felt sick in the heat and had returned to the villa. She'd almost walked in on them. Later she'd discovered that the woman lived in Moda, later still that she lived there at Ahmet Öden's expense.

Kelime cried, smearing snot all over Mary's nightdress. She'd tried to get her to use tissues, but she wouldn't. It didn't matter. Mary smoothed the girl's hair. 'Sssh. Sssh,' she said. 'Daddy will be home when he can, Kelime. Daddy loves you so much. You know that, don't you?'

The girl just carried on crying.

And at the bottom of her soul, Mary didn't know whether she was giving Kelime, or herself, false hopes. Mr Öden, Ahmet, was involved in a business known for its controversy. That's what all the mad Gezi nonsense was about. She pictured Öden in her mind's eye. When she'd been a girl she'd dreamed of a man like him. She'd become a nanny so she could find some dark, exotic man straight out of a romance novel. But then she'd discovered that all such men ever wanted was sex. She'd never consented to it. She'd lost jobs because of it. And then she had got old.

Even in her darkest moments, Mary hadn't been able to accept that the reason Ahmet Öden had never touched her was because he didn't want her. If she closed her eyes to the gypsy mistress – and now that she was dead that was easier to do – she knew he'd want a pure virgin like her, whatever her age. Good men did. Except that he wasn't a good man . . .

Silently, Mary started to cry. She'd waited all her life for someone like Ahmet Öden and just as she had finally begun to get him where she wanted him to be, he'd gone. Who, she wondered, had taken him from her?

'Go on! Kick it down, you cowardly bastard!'

Samsun flicked her front teeth with a polished thumbnail and

281

called the man in full riot gear the worst name she could think of.

'You started this, you shits!' Madonna screamed.

Another officer joined the one kicking the tent down. They stamped on the women's food.

'You have alcohol in there,' one of them said in order to justify his actions.

'No, but I wish I did,' Samsun said. 'I could do with a rakı now. But actually I wouldn't drink it, I'd throw it at you. Then I'd use this.'

She clicked her cigarette lighter.

He caught her round the side of her head with his riot shield and laid her out cold.

Madonna screamed. 'Samsun!' She ran to the body stretched out next to the ruined tent.

Someone laughed.

Madonna put a hand on Samsun's throat. She still had a pulse, but the old girl was not well at the best of times. She looked up and saw even more police pouring into the park. Where those Molotov cocktails had come from, she didn't know. But she couldn't believe it was from any of the protesters. This was provocation, it had to be!

A bearded man in şalvar trousers ran over to her and said, 'I saw what happened. Is she breathing?'

'Yes.'

He turned to the officers. 'That was a cowardly act,' he said. 'Unworthy of a Muslim!'

They said nothing.

'You should be ashamed!'

One grabbed his arm and pulled him behind a tree where two more officers beat him until he was just a motionless bloodied figure on the ground. Then they left.

Madonna pulled Samsun up into a sitting position and slapped her rapidly swelling face. First she made a groaning noise and then she very slowly opened her eyes.

'Oh, my God, you're conscious!' Madonna said.

'Takesh . . .' Samsun took the bottom set of her false teeth out so that she could talk. 'Takes more than a riot shield to put me down,' she said.

The bearded man on the ground began to whimper.

Madonna looked at him nervously. 'We can't leave him,' she said. 'He tried to protect you.'

Çetin İkmen flung the laboratory report across his desk and then tried his son's mobile again. Gezi had exploded and Kemal was missing. He'd left Fatma at home, virtually prostrate. But whoever else was missing or dead or unknown, Commissioner Teker was leaning on him to find Ahmet Öden. Semih Öden had threatened to involve the Prime Minister himself if his brother wasn't found soon. The bastard was probably already in a diabetic coma, but İkmen knew he had to do something.

He put out an information request to taxi drivers, which he left in the hands of Kerim Gürsel. Then he got in his car and called Mehmet Süleyman. He thought it was going to ring out. Then a breathless voice said, 'Çetin?'

İkmen turned the key in the car's ignition. 'Where are you? Why are you out of breath?'

He instantly regretted his allusion to breath.

But Süleyman said, 'The police have moved in on Gezi. Something about the protesters throwing Molotov cocktails. We've just managed to get Gonca's father and two of her daughters out.'

'I heard they'd gone in,' İkmen said. 'Mehmet, you haven't seen Kemal, have you?'

More breathlessness and then, 'No. I'm sorry, Çetin, it's chaos. That we managed to find anyone in that madness is a miracle. Do you want me to . . .?'

'No, no. Just if you do see him, tell him to go home. You can imagine how Fatma is.'

'Yes.'

'Get out of there if you can,' İkmen said. Then he ended the call.

When he arrived at the Negroponte House, all its windows were shuttered. It was early for anyone not involved in Gezi and so he decided to wait a while before he rang the bell. With the exception of his own house, this was the last place Ahmet Öden had been seen before he disappeared. And, according to Süleyman, it had been a stressful encounter. At least for Öden.

Twenty minutes passed before he saw old Hakkı walk into the garden and light a cigarette. İkmen got out of his car and walked towards the house.

'Good morning, Hakkı Bey.'

At first he frowned. Then he squinted. He didn't see so well any more. Eventually he smiled. 'Ah, Çetin Bey. What brings you out on the streets so early today? Is it the madness we hear about in Gezi Park?'

'No,' İkmen said. 'Do you have time to talk?'

'Of course.' Hakkı unlocked the front gate and let him in. 'Would you like tea, Çetin Bey? Some breakfast?'

'No thank you, Hakkı Bey.'

'I have just cooked for Madam and Yiannis, it's no problem,' he said.

They walked into the house via the French windows which led into the salon. Yiannis Negroponte, still in his pyjamas, was sitting at the dining table eating menemen. The omelette was deep and luscious and, had he been in the mood to eat, İkmen could have demolished the lot. But his stomach, as it was so often, was as tight as a hazelnut.

'Mr Negroponte . . .'

'Oh . . . Oh, good morning, Çetin Bey. To what do we owe the pleasure of your company? Please do sit down.'

'I will bring you tea,' Hakkı said and left the room.

İkmen didn't really want any tea but he knew the rules of Turkish hospitality and so tea would probably be accompanied by a freshly cooked omelette in spite of his earlier protestations.

Until the old man returned, İkmen and Yiannis talked of Gezi, of the weather and of how the city had changed so rapidly in recent years.

'When I first returned from Germany in the early nineties, all of the historical buildings in Sultanahmet could be seen unimpeded against the skyline,' Yiannis said. 'Now, from almost every angle, you can see tower blocks heading into the sky behind Aya Sofya, Topkapı and the rest. I think it's a shame. The city is poorer for it.'

İkmen agreed and not just to placate Yiannis Negroponte. He hated the way the skyline had become compromised over the years.

Hakkı returned, with tea and, predictably, an omelette.

'Ah, Hakkı Bey, you—'

'All your life you've been far too thin, Çetin Bey,' the old man said. 'Even as a child. You need feeding.' He put the plate down on the dining table. 'Come. Eat. If you can't finish, it's no matter.'

İkmen did as he was told. In most Turkish households resistance to middle-aged mothers and old men, particularly when it came to food, was useless. And so he ate, drank and complimented the old man on his culinary skills. Then he said, 'Hakkı

Bey, Yiannis Bey, the reason I'm here this morning is about Ahmet Öden.'

'What about him?'

Öden's disappearance wasn't common knowledge yet, but İkmen was surprised that neither of the men asked him whether Öden was outside. As they well knew, İkmen's presence couldn't stop that.

'He's missing,' İkmen said.

'Missing?'

'The day before yesterday, he went out in the evening and never returned.'

Yiannis shrugged. 'If he is really missing, I'm sorry for his family. But why are you talking to us about it?'

'Because he came here the day he went missing,' İkmen said. 'One of my colleagues saw him enter this house mid-morning and leave about an hour later, in what appeared to be a furious state.'

'Yes, he was here,' Yiannis said. 'I won't deny it. I had him in here so that he could see the state of this place he so wants to buy. I wanted him to see the rotten plumbing and the subsidence cracks for himself.'

'He wants to knock it down to build a hotel, doesn't he?' İkmen said. 'Why would the state of this place worry him?'

'If this house has subsidence then so will his hotel,' Yiannis said. 'Anyway, he left in a temper because I still refused to sell. This is my home.'

'And that is your right,' İkmen said.

'So did Öden go missing after he was here?' Hakkı asked.

İkmen took another spoonful of menemen. It was delicious but he was full, even though he'd only eaten a third of it. 'No, he went to his home and then went out again later on that evening without telling anyone where he was going.'

286

Yiannis shrugged. 'He didn't come here, if that's what you want to know. When he left in the morning, our business was concluded.'

'He didn't tell you, maybe while making small talk, about where he might be going that evening?'

'Öden never made small talk with me,' Yiannis said. 'I told him he couldn't buy the house and he left in a fury. If one of your colleagues was following him, why doesn't he know where he's gone?'

'He wasn't following him, he saw him,' İkmen said. 'As I've told you before, Mr Negroponte, we can't ban Mr Öden from this area. The way he pesters to buy this house is annoying and, to my mind, borders on coercion, but I can't stop him doing it.'

'Well, wherever he's gone, he can stay there,' Hakkı said and he laughed.

But Yiannis didn't. And neither did İkmen. Being in that house again brought back the same feelings of disconnection that he'd experienced the last time he'd visited. Again, he was accompanied when he went downstairs to the bathroom. This time, though, the kitchen door was closed and when he finally left the house he heard Madam Anastasia calling and was shocked by the way that both Hakkı and Yiannis ignored her.

Kerim Gürsel was trying to stave off the evil moment when he had to call Dr Savva's father in Greece. He didn't have good news and so he carried on contacting cab companies in the city. But so far nobody had picked up anyone answering Ahmet Öden's description in Bebek the night before last. Not that most of the cab office controllers really gave his request too much attention. Half of them didn't even bother to get back to him. Then his mother rang.

'Is Sinem all right?' she asked. 'I've been calling and calling and she doesn't answer the phone.'

'She must be out,' he said. He didn't tell her that Sinem was at Gezi. Fortunately his mother didn't have his wife's mobile number. Sinem was with Pembe and that American, Rita, and, last he heard, they were leaving the park and heading off to the Sugar and Spice cafe on İstiklal Caddesi – provided that hadn't been attacked. Gay venues were, Kerim imagined, prime targets for his colleagues while Gezi was being battered.

'Out? Out where?' his mother said. 'The woman's a cripple! You chose to marry a cripple who never gets pregnant and will never get pregnant.'

'I love—'

'Yes, I know, you love her,' his mother said. 'But it's not enough, Kerim. Your brother has children and your sister, ten years younger than you. It's shameful. You must divorce her.'

It was a conversation he had with his mother a lot. She wanted grandchildren. She'd always said that her sick daughter-in-law would never get pregnant and she'd been right. But not for the reasons she supposed. Maybe Sinem could have become pregnant had she and Kerim ever had sex, but they hadn't.

'Um . . .'

Kerim looked up and saw Süleyman's sergeant, Ömer Mungun, at his office door. He beckoned him in. 'I have to go now, Mother,' he said into the phone. 'Sinem is fine, I'm sure.'

His mother said something else but he put the phone down. 'Ömer Bey.'

Ömer Mungun had one of those sharp eastern faces and slanted eyes that Kerim always associated with the very few Syriani boys who had been at his school. Ömer – like his sister, whom Kerim had met in the grounds of the Aya Triada Orthodox church – was all angles and bones. In fact the sister probably looked the more masculine of the two.

Ömer sat down in what was usually İkmen's chair. 'Kerim

288

Bey,' he said, 'you're working on the disappearance of Ahmet Öden, aren't you?'

'Yes. Amongst other things.' He still had to call Mr Savva. His heart beat a little faster.

'So you know about his dead mistress . . .'

'Yes.'

'We've a lot of forensic material from the crime scene which, so far, matches with no one on record,' Ömer said. 'Because Öden was undoubtedly her lover, we need samples from him. I know he's missing, but there must be hairs in his brushes, on his clothes – you know what I'm saying.'

'DNA.'

'I know we've all had to be very hands off with Öden. But now he's missing, surely if we can get a DNA sample it will help us match that with any possible samples we may find.'

'Where?'

'I don't know. Didn't he take a taxi when he disappeared? If a cab driver says he was in his cab . . .'

'Mmm. It's a thought.'

'It can help both of us,' Ömer said. 'And if the request comes from this office then I can't see how the family can object.'

'No. Was this your idea or—'

'Yes, it was mine. Inspector Süleyman is on his way in. He's been to Gezi Park this morning.'

'What for?'

Ömer shrugged. 'I don't know. We're not involved, although . . .' He shrugged again. 'What can you say about Gezi?'

His face crumpled a little. Kerim wondered whether his sister was still in the park. After a short silence he asked him.

'As far as I know, yes,' Ömer said.

A longer silence followed until Kerim said, 'Are you worried?'

'Wouldn't you be?'

289

Kerim knew that if he said 'no' he would be lying. But it was different for him. His own sister was a virtual prisoner in a smart gated community in Göktürk. Sinem, his wife, was either still in Gezi or in a gay cafe with his lover, Pembe. And yes, he was worried about them.

'Yes,' he said. 'What will you do?'

'What can I do?' Ömer said. 'My sister is older than I am and she's a nurse, and she's always telling me to mind my own business.'

Kerim smiled. Peri Mungun had come across to him as a feisty woman.

'But that's beside the point,' Ömer said. 'Will you ask Çetin Bey about the DNA?'

'I will.'

'The family can't object.'

'No, it's a good idea.'

'Thanks.'

Ömer walked back to the office door. Then he turned. 'Oh, have you heard anything about that child those two girls found in an outhouse?'

Kerim shook his head. 'Sadly, yes.'

'And? It's not your dead woman's child?'

'No, it isn't. We don't know who it belongs to, but it isn't the late Dr Savva. And now I have to tell her father.'

Ömer Mungun shook his head. 'Tough day.'

'Help me. Help me! Help *me*! *Help me!*'

He tried different tones, emphases, even accents. Because although he couldn't hear anything through the dark red walls, he couldn't be absolutely sure that he couldn't be heard. Sound was organised in frequencies which, although he didn't under-stand what they were, he gathered could be heard by different

290

species and sometimes different people according to their age, health and hearing ability.

There were other sorts of frequencies too. Hitting wood with a hammer would be one, while bashing away at metal, another. He experimented. God knew he had time. God knew he had to so the madness and the panic didn't overwhelm him. Light tapping on the stone with his knuckles, clanking the water jug – being careful not to break it – against the wall, kicking, stamping, slapping his trousers against the stone. They'd had to go when he'd finally been unable to stop himself defecating any longer. Heavy with urine, he used them to beat time in between smashing a shoe on the ceiling and screaming long, senseless vowel sounds.

For a while, before he'd eventually slept, his head slumped down on his chest, smelling his own piss-stained crotch, he'd managed to fool himself with the idea of rescue. Eventually someone would come and let him out and take Negroponte and the old man away and put them in prison. Or maybe Negroponte himself would change his mind about what he'd done and let him out.

But what if Negroponte didn't know? What if the old man had put him in there on his own? But how could he? He was old and weak. No, Negroponte had to know. But no one else did. The old man had told him to come alone and tell no one and so he had, because he had wanted so badly to be exactly where he was now. In the Red Room.

Chapter 24

Her eyes couldn't take any more. One more exposure to gas and she was sure they'd melt, even though she knew that wasn't possible. Trying to see anything was painful and terrifying and, as Peri staggered forwards, she tripped over something that could have been a bundle of someone's possessions or another human being. As far as she knew it hadn't made a sound as if it were hurt.

Dull thuds on the ground signalled the coming back to earth of spent tear gas canisters – almost a cause for joy when they didn't hit some poor soul on the head or gouge an eye out. The assault on the park had grown during the day, as had the level of resistance. People were pouring in from all over the city and beyond. But Peri had had enough. Exhausted, sick and sore from the tear gas, she staggered off in what she hoped was the direction of her apartment.

Even the noises got to her now. She had thought that she'd become inured to the scream of sirens in the past couple of days, but now they made her head ache. That and the screaming. That was almost organic, seeming to rise up from the earth rather than from people. What fanciful, magical thinking! Peri chided herself for it. People in İstanbul didn't want to hear what they would class 'nonsense'. That she'd seen – actually seen – the great Sharmeran snake goddess walk the Mesopotamian Plain as she held her parents' hands at dawn as a very young child, was a fact. But then again it wasn't. As Ömer always said, it 'depends on who you're telling'.

An explosion to her right had Peri hurling herself to the left. Someone screamed and she tried not to imagine what was happening to that person. Had he or she been shot? A combination of darkness and streaming eyes meant that she couldn't see much and so was incapable of helping.

Eventually the screaming subsided and Peri picked herself up and continued on her way. All she could think of now was her home, her parents and her goddess walking the silent plains of Mesopotamia. All she wanted to do was join her.

'If the boy says he's OK then we have to believe him,' İkmen said.

Fatma paced the living room, stopping only occasionally to look at some dating show on the television. 'But I could hear screaming and shouting in the background!' she said. 'He was still at Gezi! After everything you said to him! Or said you said to him.'

Kemal had finally answered his phone to let his parents know that he was unhurt.

'I told him to come home and so did Samsun,' İkmen said.

She shook her head. 'But he's still there! With all that going on!'

'No he isn't, he's leaving. And all what?'

He knew, but he wondered how she did. There'd been a news blackout on television.

'All the violence in Gezi Park,' she said. 'If you go out on to the balcony at the back you can hear it. And Deniz Hanım's son is there too. But he's in opposition to the protest. He's a sensible boy.'

'He's a little thug,' İkmen said.

'Çetin!'

'Any twenty year old who goes around accosting young women in short skirts to tell them how immoral they are, needs some serious watching,' İkmen said. 'What does he take his frustrations out on, eh? What's his nasty little vice?'

'Oh, he doesn't have one,' Fatma said. 'Why do you always think that people who publicly espouse morality and modesty have secret vices?'

'Because they usually do,' he said. 'And my job means I have to be a student of human nature which, Fatma dear, is largely governed by hormones and greed.'

'No it isn't!'

She flung herself down in a chair and stared at the television, but without really seeing it. 'I wish Kemal would come home.'

Nothing İkmen could say would make her feel any better and so he stayed silent. His son had sounded as if he was perfectly in control of his situation in Gezi Park and had even teamed up with a group of other young people, including a couple of girls. With any luck he'd be violently attracted to one of them, date and eventually marry her. He was a good kid, with a kind heart, but İkmen had been raising children for forty years and he wanted some peace – at least in his apartment if not in his mind.

Whether Yiannis Negroponte knew anything about the disappearance of Ahmet Öden was a good question which İkmen couldn't answer. If Yiannis had somehow had the property developer spirited away, while İkmen could imagine why, he couldn't see how. The Negropontes were broke, and to really get rid of someone, permanently, took money. What was undeniable was the feeling of unease he got in that house. When he'd gone there as a child, he'd loved it because Madam Negroponte had let him play wherever he liked. Now her son followed him and if the place could not be proven to be filled with ghosts, it was definitely infected with Yiannis' paranoia. İkmen wondered whether this stemmed from the possibility that he wasn't really Madam Anastasia's son. Did Yiannis himself even know that? İkmen had no idea, but he doubted that old Hakkı really believed in him.

'Fatma, you must remember the Negroponte House when you were growing up?' he said.

'What?' She looked away from the television. 'Why do you ask me about that now? Our son is—'

'Kemal said that he and his friends were heading for one of the boys' apartments in Cihangir,' İkmen said. 'He's leaving Gezi, Fatma. He'll be safe.'

'With anarchists and communists? I don't think so!'

He shook his head. 'Let the boy grow up,' he said. 'Let him have his own opinions.

'Your—'

'I'm not getting into an argument about how I have indoctrinated our children – again,' he said. 'I'm sorry, for your sake, that none of our children hold their religion very dear but that has been their choice. Now, Fatma, the Negroponte House. What do you remember?'

There was a moment when she could have carried on arguing with him, but it was late and she was tired. 'You knew it better than I did,' she said. 'You went there.'

'Your father knew Hakkı Bey. You must have heard stories.'

She sighed. 'Why—'

'Just answer the question, will you?'

There was a pause, then she said, 'I don't remember a lot beyond Hakkı Bey and my father in the old coffee house that used to be on İshak Paşa Caddesi. They used to meet there. A couple of times I took tobacco to my father and they let me sit and watch them play tavla. But I don't remember Hakkı Bey talking about Madam Negroponte. He's always been very loyal, I do know that. He rescued her from that disgusting mob who attacked the Greeks in 1955. Her husband died and her child . . .' She shrugged.

'Do you believe that Yiannis Negroponte is Madam Anastasia's son?'

'I don't know him, so how can I tell? Hakkı Bey stays. He must believe, don't you think? When I saw him with his son Lokman and his children I thought how much more appropriate it would be for Hakkı Bey to live with them now he's so old. But he continues to work in that house and keep the apartment he's had for years. As for stories . . . Well, all I have, Çetin, is one memory and that's hazy after fifty-plus years.'

İkmen leaned forwards in his chair. 'Which is?'

'Hakkı Bey told my father there were ghosts. This was after Madam's husband was killed. He said that the old emperors of Byzantium were angry with the city and that they'd come back, through the house, to get their revenge.'

He saw her shudder. He felt a chill pass down his back too. And then he remembered something from almost sixty years ago.

When he could finally focus, Özgür Koç found himself looking at a group of completely unfamiliar faces. Some young, some older, but all, apparently, were heavily painted. There was also a lot of jewellery.

'Don't try to get up,' some red lips said.

'What's your name, love?' Another, deeper voice from behind his head.

'Özgür . . .'

He was on a floor inside a building that smelt of cigarette smoke.

'Where am I?' he asked.

There was a pause. Odd, almost cartoon-like faces looked at each other and then someone said, 'I've got aspirin and paracetamol and I know Samsun's got codeine if your head hurts. Which it must.'

'When those bastards kick you, you know you've been kicked.'

The speaker was a drag queen. Özgür had seen them. He'd always tried to avoid them. What was he doing here with them?

'Do you want water? Or a cigarette?'

A disgruntled voice said, 'He won't want a cigarette! Don't be fucking stupid!'

He'd tried to rescue some drag queens. Now it came back. The police had moved in on them like wolves and it wasn't right. It wasn't Islamic. He'd reminded them of that and they'd beaten him. Now he was . . .

'Where am I?'

'You're at the Sugar and Spice.' The smiling face was vaguely familiar and really quite old. 'I know it's not your sort of place . . .'

'Not many here but us fairies,' a very deep voice said. There was laughter.

'But you are safe here and that's important, because you saved my life earlier today.' A gnarled, heavily jewelled hand reached out towards Özgür and, although he never usually shook hands with anyone, much less a transsexual, he took it. 'I'm Samsun.'

'Özgür.'

'Yes. Would you like a drink and some tablets?' Samsun said. 'By drink I mean some water or . . .'

'Water would be good, thank you.' He sat up.

It was a cafe or bar of some sort. Very plainly decorated in contrast to its many flamboyant patrons. Özgür rubbed his head.

It ached even though that was the only place the police hadn't hit him. He looked down at his shirt, which was covered in blood.

'I couldn't find any broken bones,' a young man said.

'Oh.'

He knelt down beside Özgür. 'I'm a doctor,' he said. 'You've been in and out of consciousness for some hours. You probably don't remember. I've got nothing with me to help you but if you take some paracetamol that will improve any headache you may have.'

Samsun gave the doctor a glass of water which he passed to Özgür. Someone produced paracetamol.

'How did I get here?'

'We carried you,' Samsun said.

'You?'

'Me and Madonna and my nephew Kemal and his, er, his friends,' she said. A young man in some very bloodied blue jeans waved at him.

One of the young man's friends said, 'Are you one of the Muslims Against Capitalism?'

'No,' Özgür said.

'Oh.' He looked down at his nails in what, to Özgür, was a dismissive fashion. He was very effeminate even if he dressed as a man.

'I'm just a Muslim worried about my country,' Özgür said. 'To not respect nature is un-Islamic, to hurt trees and plants and people is a negation of everything that is good. I can't let it go.'

'Well good for you,' Samsun said. 'And thank you. Oh, and welcome to the Sugar and Spice. It's a very gay place but we're all very inclusive here and you're really welcome, Özgür.'

He wasn't comfortable but Özgür wasn't miserable either.

And he was alive, which was his fate, but which was also amazing.

Those first months after she'd left hospital had been times of pain, confusion and grief. She hadn't known what had been in her mind or what the drugs she'd been given had made her experience. All of it had been frightening. But more terrifying than anything else had been the idea that her husband was buried alive. She'd never been able to articulate that to anyone else. Most of the time she blocked it out. But the last time she'd seen Nikos was on the back of a man whose face she couldn't make out, who had carried him from their shop on İstiklal Caddesi. Bloodied, his face swollen and distorted from the kicking and stamping he'd endured, as Nikos was taken away, she saw one eye open. And although she'd been told that he had been buried some time after the riots – she'd even seen what was purported to be his grave in the churchyard in Şişli – she couldn't shift it from her mind that while she'd been fighting for her life, Nikos had been put into the ground, somewhere, alive.

For years she'd heard him scratching. At night, whether she was awake or asleep, he called to her to let him out. She could never move. She could never tell anyone. She especially couldn't speak of it to Sırma Hanım. Anastasia would have died without the care Hakkı Bey's wife had given her. When she needed medicine, Sırma would give it to her; Sırma washed her, dressed her and gave her back something that passed for life while she waited for her son to return to her. She'd seen the face of the woman who had taken him. She could have described it in every detail but by the time she could speak just a little again, 1955 had become 1956 and the world had moved on from the September riots.

Still Nikos had scratched. There was crying too. It stopped only when Yiannis returned, when she had thought herself mad. He had saved her. But now it was back and this time it wasn't Nikos. This time something terrible had been done and Hakkı and Yiannis existed in grey rain clouds of guilt.

A creature was buried, alive, just like her husband had been. She could hear his fingernails scratching her walls; his sobs echoed through the house like tolling bells. And they were getting louder.

If someone other than Çetin İkmen had called him, Mehmet Süleyman would just have let his phone ring. It was after midnight and he was exhausted. But when he saw Çetin's name appear on the screen, he picked up. Half an hour later he was sitting in İkmen's car opposite the Negroponte House.

'There was a chamber or a room or something,' the older man said. 'It was down on the same level as the kitchen, down a corridor. I never went into it but I do remember a door and, more pertinently, a doorway, which was old.'

'How old?'

'Ottoman? Byzantine? Who knows? It was a long time ago,' İkmen said. 'But significantly, on the two occasions I've been to the house recently, I haven't seen anything like that. On the first occasion I actually saw into the kitchen from the bathroom. The second time the door to the kitchen was closed with Yiannis Negroponte standing in front of it. I knew that something was different, wrong.'

'But you still don't really know what, do you?' Süleyman said. 'Or what it means. What do you think it means?'

'I don't know.' İkmen flicked his cigarette ash out of his car window and listened, for a moment, to the sounds of distant voices from Gezi Park.

'But I'm thinking that my dead academic, Ariadne Savva, claimed to have found an as yet undiscovered Byzantine structure. However, apart from being Greek, what connection is there between her and the Negropontes? Aside from a tentative link through Ahmet Öden, I can't find any.'

'And from what I've heard, wasn't she a bit of a fantasist? Claiming she could positively identify that skeleton she found?'

'Constantine Palaiologos. Is it a fantasy? They have him at the museum now,' İkmen said. 'Someone was threatening Dr Akyıldız the forensic archaeologist, trying to stop her working on the skeleton. So someone believes he's real.'

'Or chooses to. You know how fanatics are,' Süleyman said. 'Can't have a Byzantine emperor turning up on the eve, some hope, of Aya Sofya being turned back into a mosque. Bad omen.'

İkmen smiled. He was still no less angry with Süleyman for his treatment of the late Ayşe Farsakoğlu, but he was also glad to be able to share ideas with him again.

'So what is the significance of your disappearing space in the Negropontes' house? Do you think that they've put Ahmet Öden in there?' Süleyman asked.

'I don't know. I didn't pass through that archway and open that door even as a child, and on the last few occasions I went to the house, I didn't see it at all. I've no reason to suppose that either Yiannis Negroponte or Hakkı Bey have done anything wrong and I know that my memory could be false. When you get to my age a lot of them are.'

Süleyman smiled. 'But you're uneasy and, false memory or no false memory, I have learned to trust your instincts, Çetin. And so have you.'

He shrugged.

'Come on.'

Süleyman got out of the car. When İkmen didn't move he said, 'Let's get them up.'

Even with two of them on the job, the wardrobe didn't move easily. Once he'd shifted it out of the way, Hakkı touched the wall behind. For a few moments he said nothing, until Yiannis prompted him, 'Well?'

'It's set.' He bent down and slowly scooped a handful of pink dust off the floor and smeared it over the small section of wall that was brick, dressed with porphyry stone. 'There, good as new.'

But it wasn't entirely soundproof. Now he was close to the cavity, Yiannis could hear slight tapping inside – and what could be sobbing.

'What did you do with his phone?' he asked.

'Dropped it in the Bosphorus.'

'I don't feel good about this.'

'A lot of things in life don't make you feel good,' Hakkı said.

'You've done . . . For me . . .'

'I've done what I've done for Madam,' the old man said. 'You?' He shrugged. 'What are you?'

He turned away and walked slowly back through the arch and into the kitchen.

Yiannis stared after him. He should hate him so much that killing him should be just like putting down a rabbit or a chicken. But he couldn't. He owed him too much, even if the old man had done nothing out of love or even liking for him.

'Come on, you need to get some rest,' Hakkı said.

Something that could have been a voice, an unintelligible word, came from behind the wall he'd built with Hakkı, but he couldn't imagine what it was.

He walked back into the kitchen, just as the front doorbell rang.

He'd heard voices. He'd shouted inasmuch as he could. He'd drunk all the water and now his throat was dry and so shouting was difficult. He'd stamped his feet, but that too had been a puny effort. He was weakening. His head was spinning, as what one part of his mind recognised as hypoglycaemia began to take over.

Sometimes people who were in danger of death offered something to God in exchange for their lives. He'd read lots of stories where people were saved from certain death in exchange for offering to perform Haj, give up alcohol and women or promise that their daughters would cover. What could he give up? He'd been on the Haj twice, his woman, Gülizar, was dead and Kelime would soon cover anyway. He could always give money but he was already doing that. What was left he needed for Kelime. She would never marry; she'd need his money to be able to be cared for as she grew up and then grew old.

There was, however, one sacrifice he could make that would be pleasing to God. It was something he knew he would have to do anyway. Ahmet Öden began to shiver. Then he vomited.

He'd die soon. And nobody would ever know how.

The kitchen looked exactly the same as it had the last time.

'Cooker,' Yiannis pointed to it. 'Fridge, cupboards, sink. I don't know what else I can show you.'

İkmen walked over to the sink and looked out of the window into the dark garden. Süleyman, in the kitchen doorway, watched Yiannis Negroponte and the old man.

'When I was a child I remember an archway,' İkmen said, 'and a door.'

'A door to where?'

'I don't know. I never went through it.'

'I think it was a door in your mind, Çetin Bey,' Hakkı said. 'Children invent worlds that don't exist when they are little. And you were a very imaginative child.'

That was true.

'There's nothing here,' Hakkı said. 'And even if there was, what of it?'

He didn't want to say that he feared that Ahmet Öden might be dead inside some secret room he'd never seen. İkmen had asked his brother Halil if he remembered anything about an archway and a door leading off from the Negropontes' kitchen, but he'd had a problem even recalling the house.

When they left the house, İkmen lit a cigarette and told Süleyman that he felt stupid. 'The place was the same. It was the same!' he said. 'What can I say?'

Süleyman lit up too. He was frowning. 'Ah, but I wonder,' he said. 'Did you see how they moved?'

'Yiannis and Hakkı?'

'When you moved so did they. Not mirroring your movements, I don't mean that.'

'Then what?'

'I don't know. But it was odd, an unnatural movement. I don't think they always needed to move.'

'Then what were they doing?'

Süleyman shrugged.

They were walking back to the car when İkmen suddenly clicked his fingers. He looked at Süleyman and smiled.

'Çetin?'

'Yiannis,' İkmen said, 'is a magician.'

The sword, although missing what must have been some enormous precious or semi-precious stones, did have the double-headed eagle of the Byzantine emperors carved into its hilt. But as Professor Bozdağ looked at the fragments of skeleton that lay beside the weapon he wondered if the two were connected. Ariadne Savva had come to the museum with excellent academic references. She'd known her subject and had been an asset to the department. But, since her death, he'd learned that she'd been a fantasist too. How could anyone who believed that a direct descendant of the Palaiologi dynasty still existed be anything but a fantasist?

He knew the few grand old Byzantine families that still existed in the city and none of them, however much they might desire royal blood, could claim any. Blood was one of the great paradoxes. The purer or more inbred it was, the more dangerous it became to the dynasty that cultivated it. The old Byzantine families had been forced to marry out over the centuries in order to survive. If they hadn't they would have become diseased, weak and distorted. He'd seen people like that in some of the tiny, isolated villages in the east he'd marched through as a conscript back in the 1970s. If a descendant of the Palaiologi were to exist, he or she would probably be mad and sterile. How could Ariadne have got access to someone like that? Had she met a rubbish picker with delusions of grandeur over in

Gizlitepe? There had always been oddities in İstanbul. In spite of a political shift to conform to conservative values, the city still asserted its individuality. Gezi Park was a case in point. There was always a surprise around the corner in İstanbul. Had he missed one?

'No, no, it's not convenient now,' Yiannis said.

İkmen, this time accompanied by Süleyman, Kerim Gürsel and two uniformed officers, said, 'I have a warrant to search this house.'

There was a silence. Hakkı Bey, who had been weeding in the front garden, stopped.

'Then I'll need to make the place—'

'Now, Mr Negroponte,' İkmen said. 'I've a warrant to search right now.'

'Why? What are you looking for?'

İkmen held what had been a hastily acquired and hard won document up to Yiannis' face and moved past him into the house.

'You can't—'

'Inspector Süleyman, would you and your officers like to secure the kitchen and the basement while I go and inform Madam Negroponte,' İkmen said. 'Kerim, come with me.'

Yiannis Negroponte raced them to the stairs. 'My mother is sick, you—'

'Please get out of the way, Mr Negroponte,' İkmen said.

But Yiannis was already halfway up the staircase. Hakkı, now in the house, attempted to push past Süleyman but was held back. İkmen saw Yiannis look at the old man and then turn away.

Anastasia Negroponte was still in bed but she was awake. İkmen saw her head turn as her son ran to her and knelt beside her bed. 'Mama, Çetin Bey and his police have to spend some time in the house so it might be a little noisy,' he said.

'Why?'

İkmen looked into her eyes, which were afraid.

'They think that workmen on the site next door might be stealing building materials,' Yiannis said. 'They want to use this house to observe them.'

It was quick thinking. İkmen was impressed.

'We will try to be as quick and discreet as we can, Madam Negroponte,' he said. 'I can only apologise for the inconvenience.'

When they left the bedroom, İkmen heard Yiannis calm his mother, who was crying. Once she spoke, but he couldn't hear what she said. Now intent upon getting down to the kitchen, he ran with Kerim at his back and found Süleyman and one of the uniforms standing where he had stood the night before. Hakkı was in his previous position too. The only difference was that the second uniformed officer was walking in through another door that led out to a stone staircase up to the garden. It had been locked, but he'd just kicked it in. And when he saw what was in front of him, he frowned.

The government media outlets were reporting that the Gezi protesters had thrown Molotov cocktails at the police. But Peri could only remember the tear gas. She had to get to work by lunchtime but her eyes were so sore and her sight so hazy that it was going to be hard for her to leave her apartment.

Ömer had called three times in the last hour but she still hadn't answered him. He'd left two messages, one telling her he was going out to Bebek for some reason and another reminding her that she should call their parents to let them know she was all right. Although quite what news had got through to her isolated, computer illiterate parents in Mardin, Peri didn't know. It was quite possible that they didn't know anything about the İstanbul protests. She hoped they didn't.

She washed her eyes again and wondered what had happened to her Gezi friends – Iris and the transsexuals, the Muslims Against Capitalism and the gay boys. When the police moved in, everyone had scattered. Where once there'd been flowers, trees and tents, a chaos of gas and plastic bullets had taken hold. Before she'd been gassed, Peri had seen gypsy boys hurling themselves in front of their female relatives as they tried to protect them from the police.

Peri felt sad more than anything else. When her brother had joined the police a lot of people back home had been surprised, and some, angry too. Whether one was Turkish or Kurdish, the police and the gendarmerie were, in the east, the enemy, with a reputation for corruption and brutality. When Peri and Ömer had been growing up people had always kept away from officers of the law. Then Turkey had got serious about its bid to join the European Union and standards had been imposed from Brussels. Things had improved. Which was why Ömer had joined.

Now all of that was disappearing into a slurry of violence. Men who looked like Robocop walked the streets of İstanbul as if they owned them and the rhetoric coming out of the government was, to Peri, shrill and unhinged. There had been talk about an 'interest rate lobby' being behind the protests, whatever that was. If Peri understood correctly it was something to do with foreigners being jealous of Turkey's economic success. Someone in power had even named the German airline, Lufthansa. It was crazy. Why would Lufthansa or any other foreign company want to bring Turkey's economy to its knees? The German staff at the hospital were furious.

Peri had to go to work. But when her shift was over, would

she go back to Gezi Park? She'd have to think very carefully about it before she made a decision. And see what was left of the protest camp.

Çetin İkmen walked into a room that, illuminated by candles, was every shade of purple. It wasn't large but it did contain a raised slab of porphyry stone and it was a 'red' room similar to the one that Ariadne Savva had described in her notebook. At first he thought that the only real difference was that it didn't have windows. But it did, or rather it had. Now the small slits that had once passed for windows were blocked off to stop earth from outside coming in. Where the level of the land had risen over the centuries, so the room had slowly descended into the ground.

He walked back into the kitchen.

Yiannis Negroponte swallowed. 'We . . . You know what happened to my parents in 1955, Çetin Bey,' he said. 'We had to keep it secret.'

'You employed very simple illusion,' İkmen said. 'Why did you open up the door to the garden? And why didn't you just close this room up? What exactly is it, by the way?'

Yiannis put his head down. 'If I may, I'll tell you when we're alone.'

'If you wish.'

'Nobody comes here, or came here,' Yiannis said.

İkmen walked towards him. 'I will need to get a forensic team into that room.'

'Why?' He looked up.

'Mr Negroponte, have you ever met a woman called Ariadne Savva?' İkmen said. 'Think carefully before you answer.'

The house had become very quiet. The police had to be watching the building site. But in the silence would they hear the tapping

309

on the walls and the sobbing of a dead man too? Even if she strained to hear it, she couldn't grasp those sounds any more. Had a terrible thing been done, just as it had been done to her husband?

Who had been the man who had taken Nikos away? Who had buried him alive? In her mind she'd tried to make his attacker turn so that she could see his face but her mind always went black.

Why had the Turks turned on them like that? They had been their neighbours. And yet her father had always known. As children she and Nikos had wanted to bring their friends to see the fabulous red room underneath the house. But her father and Nikos' father, her uncle, had forbidden it. 'As Greeks we were the enemy, we remain the enemy and we will be the enemy in the future,' her father had said. And he had been right.

The tapping began again.

'Where have you found these samples that could have come from my brother?'

'I can't tell you because, as yet, I don't know,' Ömer Mungun said. 'But if we have your brother's DNA . . .'

'I don't like it,' Semih Öden said. 'But I don't suppose I have a choice, do I?'

He was already looking very comfortable at his brother's desk.

'I can get a warrant.'

Semih shook his head. 'What do you need?'

'A strand of hair, from a brush or a comb for preference.'

Ahmet Öden's desk was covered in paperwork, mainly architectural drawings. 'My brother's bedroom is down the corridor, first on the left,' Semih said. 'There's an en-suite bathroom. I believe there are brushes and combs . . .'

'Would you like to accompany . . .'

310

'No.' He waved a dismissive hand while he looked down at the plans. 'If you steal anything I'll have your job. So don't. I know what you people can be like.'

Ömer was way beyond what his darkness and his sharp eastern features made people think he was. They thought he was a Muslim Kurd or an Arab. They'd never guess what he really was. People were stupid . . .

The corridor was carpeted with something cheap looking in pink. Öden's daughter liked pink. It had no doubt been very expensive. The door first on the left was open when he got there. In front of him was a king-sized bed with a figure lying on it. For just a moment, Ömer thought that miraculously Öden had returned. But then he saw it was a woman.

When she became aware of him, Mary Cox, Öden's nanny, sat up and wiped a hand across her eyes. They were red. But her skin was clear.

'Miss Cox . . .'

She turned her face away.

'I'm sorry,' Ömer said. 'I didn't know you were in here. Mr Semih Öden gave me permission to look for something. I understand you're ill . . .'

'Yes.'

'Sorry.'

As she shuffled off the bed, he looked away. She put a hand up to her face and then she left. Not a measles spot in sight. Süleyman would be interested.

Ömer went into the en-suite bathroom and looked around. It was full of bottles and jars, male grooming products at their most excessive. Ahmet Öden was a good-looking man. He wanted to keep himself that way. Ömer picked up a basket of bath salts and saw that they came from Paris.

Mary Cox had to be at least five years older than Ahmet

Öden. In a timid sort of a way she was attractive but there was also a stiff, unhappy quality about her. Had she been crying on Öden's bed because she missed him? It was very unlikely that Öden had been having an affair with her as well as with the gypsy in Moda. But Ömer wondered whether, in Miss Cox's head, their relationship was more than just employer/employee? If it was, then what could that say about her testimony with regard to Öden's whereabouts the night his mistress died?

Ömer found the brushes and combs on top of one of the bathroom cabinets. There wasn't much hair on any of them but he did manage to find a strand with a follicle and put it in an evidence bag. As he left the room he had a quick look in the small rubbish bin, which was where he found something that surprised him. It was an empty packet of medication. On the side was the legend 'Viagra'.

'I don't have to tell you what my reasons are for wishing to have that room forensically examined, Mr Negroponte,' İkmen said. 'But I can ask you again whether the name Ariadne Savva means anything to you.'

'And I'll tell you again that it doesn't,' Yiannis said.

'She was Greek, she was an archaeologist and we have reason to believe that she discovered a Byzantine structure that could be the room under this house. If you'd read a paper lately or watched TV you'd have to know that her dead body was found in the sphendone of the Hippodrome and that she'd not long before given birth. She may have been murdered, Mr Negroponte, and so we need to find her killer, and possibly her baby too. If it's still alive.'

'I don't know anything about any of it.'

Three men in white overalls entered the front door and Süleyman led them down the stairs towards the kitchen.

'Who are they?'

'They are forensic investigators,' İkmen said.

'There's nothing down there! What is there for them to investigate?'

'That's what we'll find out,' İkmen said.

Yiannis stood up. 'I'd better go down. In case they need me.' İkmen put a hand on his arm. 'They won't.'

'Yes, but—'

'You can't go down there. Not now.'

Yiannis' voice became hoarse. 'Why not?'

'Because it could be a crime scene,' İkmen said. 'If you go in, you may taint it.'

Yiannis didn't speak for some time. Then he said, 'But what if something goes wrong, Inspector?'

'Wrong?'

'What if a pipe bursts or there's a fire?'

He said it slowly and a bit dreamily. İkmen felt very cold.

'But nothing will happen, Mr Negroponte,' he said. 'Don't worry. And if it does, the forensic investigators will deal with it. You don't need to be in that room now. You can leave it to them. Did you know Ariadne Savva?'

'No.'

'Are you sure? There's an infant involved. We need to find it.'

'No!' Yiannis turned his whole body away, like a petulant child.

İkmen knew nothing of Yiannis Negroponte's early life in Germany. But he did know that, as a middle-aged man, he'd led a cloistered, rarefied life with two old people, one of whom was brain damaged while the other, İkmen suspected, didn't believe Yiannis was who he claimed to be. His only pleasure seemed to be performing magic tricks for children – and simple illusions, it would seem, for adults.

313

'Why did you seek to keep that room a secret?' İkmen asked.

'Because it's ours. Because this is our home, not a tourist attraction.'

'If you were so worried, why didn't you wall it up completely then?'

Yiannis coloured. 'Because, as I said, it's ours! Our heritage. Why should we wall it up?'

'To keep it secret—'

'I go down there, all right? I like it down there.'

'It could be significant. You know that the Great Palace of the Byzantines was built in this area . . .'

'You think I don't know that?' Yiannis said. 'My family are Byzantine. It's ours. Take Aya Sofya if you want, you've taken everything else. But leave us this.'

'So it is Byzantine?'

'Yes.'

'Do other İstanbul Greeks know about it?'

'No.'

'Then how can you say you're claiming it for your community?'

'I didn't. I'm claiming it for my family,' Yiannis said.

'Mr Negroponte, what is that room? You said you'd tell me when we were alone. We're alone now. What is it?'

'It's Byzantine.'

'Yes, we know that,' İkmen said. 'What was it for?'

Yiannis shrugged.

'You don't know or you won't say?'

'I don't know. Nobody does.'

'What about your mother? She's lived here all her life. I imagine your family must have had some stories, even if they weren't true, about such a significant monument.'

There was a pause and then Yiannis said, 'My mother knows

314

nothing. Not any more. You know that, Çetin Bey. Not since 1955.'

'She knows you.'

They looked at each other. It was only when Süleyman came up from the kitchen that the spell between them broke.

'May I have a word please, Inspector?' he said.

'Of course.' He said to Yiannis, 'I'll be back, Mr Negroponte.'

They moved into the salon. 'The large, I don't know what one would call it, the thing that looks like a porphyry sarcophagus in the middle of the room is luminol positive,' Süleyman said.

'Is it.' İkmen wished he'd been down in that room to see it. There was nothing, in his opinion, as eerie as the deep blue glow that emanated from even invisible blood traces when treated with the forensic chemical luminol. Every time he saw it, it thrilled him.

'Over a large area,' Süleyman said. 'Very faint, because it has been comprehensively scrubbed.'

'Can forensics get samples?' İkmen asked.

'Don't know. We're just talking trace at the moment. But don't hope too hard. As I said, the place has been scrubbed. What does Mr Negroponte have to say for himself?'

'Knows the room is Byzantine, doesn't know what it is and claims its existence isn't any of our business.'

'So why hide it?'

'Exactly. Says he's never heard of Ariadne Savva.'

'Do you think he knows what a coincidence is?'

İkmen smiled. 'Oh I know he does,' he said. And then his face fell again. 'Yiannis Negroponte, I think, knows a lot of things. But he isn't telling any of them.'

'So?'

'I think a trip down to the station,' İkmen said. 'For Yiannis and for Hakkı Bey.'

315

'And the old woman?'

İkmen frowned. If neither Hakkı nor Yiannis were in the house to look after her, there was no knowing how she would react. She was very old. She might even die.

'I'll just take Yiannis,' he said. 'For the time being.'

'OK.'

'Can I leave you in charge of forensic?'

'Of course.'

İkmen returned to the hall and Yiannis Negroponte.

'We will need to take a trip to police headquarters, Mr Negroponte.'

Yiannis' face whitened. 'Why?'

İkmen put a hand on his shoulder. 'I'll tell you when we get there,' he said.

Chapter 26

Peri's phone just went straight to voicemail every time he called and so, in the end, Ömer gave up. She was thin but she was tough and she was a nurse, so people would protect her. She could save their lives.

He was just about to put his phone back in his pocket when it rang.

'Sergeant Mungun?'

'Yes?'

'Hello. My name is Barçın Şişko, I work at the forensic institute. You left an old dental X-ray for us to try and identify. There's what might be a name written on one corner.'

'Oh yes,' Ömer said. The old plate that Dr İnçi had managed to find for him.

'I wish I could say that I've managed to decipher it for you, but I can't,' she said. 'Or rather only partially.'

'It's better than nothing.'

'I'll send you an e-mail with a photo attached but what we've managed to pick out are the following letters. So we've a capital *n*, then another capital *n* then a gap, *o*, *p*, *o* and then *t* and *e*. Don't know if that means anything to you?'

Hakkı came and gave her a drink. She knew he'd put something in it to make her sleep but she didn't say anything. The tapping and the breathing and the crying were driving her mad.

She gave him back the empty glass just as a very handsome man appeared in her bedroom doorway. Tall, dark and slim, he had a wounded gravity around his dark eyes that reminded her of Nikos.

'Sleep now, Madam,' Hakkı said. 'The police will not disturb you. When they find the thieving builders they will take them away and then we'll be alone again. There's nothing to worry about.'

Why did he say those words? Didn't he recall he'd said them to her when he'd taken her out of that hell on İstiklal Caddesi all those years ago? Hour after hour, or so it had seemed, he had told her that everything was going to be all right, that there was nothing to worry about. He even tried to soothe her as he slit the throat of a man, a Turk, who offered him money for her.

The feelings never went away. The loss of her child, the loss of Nikos with his one live eye, the knowledge that she'd never do anything for herself again. And the images. A woman raped, right in front of her face, in the street, a priest with his beard torn out bleeding into a drain, faces stretched into caricatures of hatred.

Her body wanted to sleep but as she looked at the handsome man in her doorway, her mind again tried to reach for who had carried her husband to his premature grave. But as he always did, he went as soon as she felt she was just about to see him. Getting smaller and smaller and further and further away as he broke away from her into the past.

Anastasia Negroponte slept, watched by Hakkı and Mehmet Süleyman.

'You will have to come down to the station some time, Hakkı Bey,' Süleyman said. 'And then you'll have to leave her.'

The old man, without looking up at him, simply said, 'No.'

'It's animal blood,' Yiannis said. 'When Hakkı's son Lokman came from the east he brought a goat as a present.'

'Alive?'

'Yes.'

'How'd he get it here?'

'He has a truck,' Yiannis said. 'Hakkı and I slaughtered and dismembered it on the slab in the room. It's cool in there. I've used it many times over the years.'

He may have done. İkmen wouldn't know for some time whether the blood traces that had been found on the slab could be subjected to further analysis.

'What is the thing you call the slab?'

'I don't know.'

'It looks like a sarcophagus to me,' İkmen said.

Yiannis Negroponte said nothing.

İkmen hadn't chosen to speak to him in one of the smallest and darkest interview rooms in police headquarters. It had just worked out that way. And Kerim Gürsel, as well as Yiannis Negroponte, was sweating.

İkmen passed a photograph across the table. 'You know who this is?'

Yiannis Negroponte looked down at a smiling photograph of Ariadne Savva without emotion. 'No. Should I?'

'Ariadne Savva—'

'Not this again!'

'She worked at the Archaeological Museum,' İkmen said. 'She was an expert on Byzantine history. Yours is the sort of family she would have been interested in; your house would have been the type of house she would have wanted to explore.'

'But she didn't.'

'Didn't she?' İkmen took Ariadne Savva's photograph back and replaced it with a photocopy of some text. 'I assume you read Greek.'

Yiannis Negroponte looked at it.

'I am told by our translator,' İkmen said, 'that this, a photocopy of two pages from Dr Savva's private notebook, refers to a new and unknown Byzantine structure she calls only "red".'

Yiannis appeared to be reading it but İkmen couldn't be sure. Maybe he was just making sure that their eyes didn't meet.

'Now it is possible that Dr Savva, an enthusiast for her subject, was also a fantasist . . .'

'I think so.'

'But then maybe she wasn't,' İkmen said. 'Because, as we know, you, Mr Negroponte, do have a red room, don't you? And Dr Savva, when she was found, had a piece of porphyry stone in her left hand and as you may or may not know, there was none of that in the sphendone of the Hippodrome where her body was discovered.'

Yiannis put the photocopy down. 'I didn't know this woman.'

'Then you'll be happy for us to do further tests on the blood traces we found in your red room,' İkmen said.

'Do I have a choice?'

'No.'

'Then why ask?'

'Courtesy.' He smiled. 'I want to get this over with as soon as possible, Mr Negroponte. But mainly I want to find Dr Savva's child if I can. So if you do know anything about her or the child I must urge you to tell me. Whatever has been done by you or by others, it will go better for you if you tell me about that baby.'

'I know nothing about it.'

'You are sure about that?'

'Yes.'

İkmen sighed. Maybe Yiannis didn't know anything about Ariadne Savva. Perhaps his room and the academic's 'find' were not one and the same. There was no evidence, so far, that Yiannis had even met the woman.

320

'Then we'll have to wait and see what else our forensic team can find,' İkmen said.

It could be 'N Negroponte', but with the missing letters it could also be *N N* almost anything, foreign or domestic. Ömer couldn't think of anything but he was sure that some other name had to fit. He just thought it was unlikely. But *N* Negroponte? Who was that? As far as he knew, N. Negroponte was Nikos Negroponte, Madam Anastasia's late husband. And he was buried in the Greek cemetery in Şişli.

Ömer's phone rang. It was the front desk.

'There's a woman here wants to see you. A foreigner.'

Mary Cox entered the office Ömer shared with Süleyman as if she were approaching the gates of hell. Sweating and hollow-eyed, she looked at him round the door and said, 'Can I come in?'

'Yes.'

He stood up.

'I don't have measles.'

'I know.'

She widened her eyes as if he'd just told her something almost unbelievable.

Ömer offered her a chair. 'What can I do for you, Miss Cox? Would you rather speak in English? I can do that if it's easier for you.'

'No . . .' She sat and looked down at her hands. 'I lied to you, about where Mr Öden was the night that woman in Moda died,' she said. 'I said he was with his daughter all night.'

'And he wasn't?'

'No.'

'Where was he?'

She looked up. 'I don't know. He told me he was looking at a new development site somewhere in the Belgrade Forest.'

321

'But you didn't believe him.'

'I don't know,' she said. 'But if he did go there then maybe he went again and that's where he is now. He said that homeless people live in the forest and I'm afraid they might have hurt him. He could be lying injured in the forest now. I had to tell you.'

Ömer sat back in his chair. Her passion for Öden was strong. It had overcome her fear of, possibly, implicating him in Gülizar the gypsy's murder. 'Does Mr Semih Öden know you're here?'

'No. He took Kelime, Mr Öden's—'

'I know who Kelime is.'

'He took her to his sister's apartment in Nişantaşı. I came here. I can't bear to think that Mr Öden's life may be in danger while I know something that might help.'

'Why did you lie about Mr Öden's whereabouts the night his mistress was murdered?'

He saw her cringe. She knew he knew why. It wasn't difficult. But he helped her. 'Because you're in love with him,' Ömer said. 'It's all right, you don't have to answer, I know.'

'He couldn't have killed that woman,' Mary said. 'He couldn't kill anyone.'

'Why not? He was out somewhere the night she died. You don't really know where . . .'

'Look in the forest! He could be injured or even dead!'

'Oh, I will,' Ömer said. 'I will also tell Inspector Süleyman that Ahmet Öden no longer has an alibi for the murder of his mistress.'

'Oh, just find him, will you? Find him! He could be in a coma now! He could be dead!'

She began to cry. Ömer Mungun watched her without emotion. Why did some people fall in love with characters who were so obviously complete bastards? This woman had got herself in trouble in a country that wasn't her own for a man who probably didn't even look at her from one year's end to the next.

He called Süleyman and told him.

'Keep her there until I arrive,' he said.

'Yes, sir.'

'Inspector İkmen is releasing Yiannis Negroponte so he can care for his mother until we have more forensic evidence,' Süleyman said. 'Mary Cox pathetically in love with Öden, is she?'

Ömer looked at the woman who, he was sure, had heard what Süleyman had said. 'Yes, sir.'

'Some of the Taksim Solidarity people are going to go to Ankara for talks with the Prime Minister,' Kemal said.

'Oh, really.' Samsun flicked her cigarette ash on a dead tear gas canister and then kicked it away. 'You think he'll listen to a load of students, hippies and faggots?'

'Well, we have to—'

'Forget all this bullshit,' Samsun said, waving a hand at what remained of the protest camp. 'You're young. Leave it to the old warhorses now. If they kill us, then so what? We've lived. And believe me, kid, arthritis, vertigo and all the other age-related shit old bastards like me have to put up with are no fun. Go home, hug your mother, then take your father to one side and tell him you're gay.'

Kemal blinked. Then his mouth opened.

'I've suspected for years,' Samsun said. 'Then when I saw you in Sugar and Spice with all those little faggots, I knew.'

'Oh.'

'And no, I won't tell your mother, mainly because I don't think I can stand the histrionics. But you must tell Çetin. Your father will protect you. Any marriage nonsense your mother may have in mind will be aced, you understand?'

He said he did, although whether he'd actually come out to his father was open to question. Kemal had to know how liberal Çetin was but it was still a big deal for the boy, and then there was his mother to contend with.

'Anyway, you stink,' Samsun said. 'Go home and have a shower.'

'Stink?' Kemal sniffed his armpits. 'I've been using deodorant all the time, and aftershave.'

'Yes, which covers the sweat up beautifully and then turns sour,' Samsun said. 'Go home, wash and then get some sleep.' She put a hand on his shoulder. 'I know it's all very exciting discovering your sexuality, but even faggots with nice bums like yours have to sleep.'

'Auntie? Do I have a nice . . .?'

'Samsun Hanım!'

'Özgür Bey!'

It was the elderly Muslim they'd all helped to rescue from a police kicking, the one they'd taken to Sugar and Spice.

Samsun smiled. 'I hope we didn't shock you too much, Özgür Bey. I know you're not used to—'

'You saved my life.' He took her hand. His type didn't, usually. Samsun, uncomfortable, forced a smile. 'Thanks to you and to God, I live to one day see my grandchildren grow up,' he said. 'If it please God.'

'I can't think why it wouldn't,' Samsun said.

'Would you – and your nephew, is it?'

'Yes.'

'Would you like to accompany me to a little cafe I know? It's a short walk up İstiklal. It is my son's.'

'Oh, er . . .' It felt odd standing behind a man in such simple, pious garb when she was wearing red stilettos and cubic zirconias the size of quails' eggs hanging off her earlobes.

'I'm afraid it doesn't sell alcohol,' Özgür said. 'But I'd love to treat you both to coffee and a meal. It really is the least I can do. We must fortify ourselves for the battle I'm sure is still to come.'

'You're staying in Gezi?' Samsun asked.

'Of course!' he said. 'We can't give up now.' And then he turned to Kemal. 'Can we, my boy?'

And Kemal, who smelt like a dirty brothel's bathroom, smiled and said, 'No sir, we can't.'

The old woman was still sleeping. Çetin İkmen left her son and Hakkı Bey with her and went down to the basement.

The head of the forensic team, Ali Bey, had come outside the red room and was leaning on one of the kitchen cupboards. When he saw İkmen he said, 'Where do you find them eh, Çetin Bey?'

'Find who?'

'These oddities,' he said. 'As soon as Süleyman left, that old man was down here yelling at us all to stop what we were doing.'

'What? Hakkı Bey?'

'If that's the ancient's name, yes.'

'What did you do?'

'What, apart from telling him to fuck off . . .' He shrugged.

'So how's it going?'

İkmen lit a cigarette. Both Yiannis and Hakkı smoked in the house and there was a half-full ashtray on the cooker. He dragged it towards him.

'We've some hair, a lot of dust, much of it red.'

'It would be.'

'There are some areas where the stone has been damaged and replaced over the years. Can't find any cavities yet. Stone's difficult. You can't get much from tapping it like an ordinary wall. You have to take it down. I'd say it's Byzantine. You told the Archaeology Museum yet?'

'No.' He knew he'd have to but he also knew that as soon as the 'find' became common knowledge it would pass, to some extent, out of his control. 'What about the blood on the slab?'

Ali shook his head. 'As I've said, trace. Bit on the floor too. But scrubbed almost invisible.'

'The owner of the house says that he slaughtered a goat on the slab.'

'Maybe he did.'

'Will you be able to tell whether or not it's animal blood?'

Ali Bey sighed. 'There's no real sample,' he said. 'Just a trace, a ghost of past blood. And apart from that, the luminol process does damage. You know that.'

'Yeah.'

Ali Bey went off to the toilet.

Alone, İkmen faced the possibility of leaving the Negroponte House as he had found it. None the wiser and with only the Archaeological Museum getting any benefit from the operation. Yiannis Negroponte was adamant that he'd never known Ariadne Savva and İkmen couldn't prove him wrong. No one who had known Dr Savva had ever mentioned any man in her life.

İkmen's phone rang. It was Süleyman.

'Çetin, two things,' he said. 'Firstly I've just spoken to Ahmet Öden's nanny.'

'Mary Cox.'

'Yes. Significantly not suffering from measles and now saying that Öden did go out the night his mistress died.'

'Ah. Where?'

'He spun her a story about surveying a new development site in the Belgrade Forest which I think is probably nonsense – why would Öden take a taxi to somewhere like that? He'd drive. But I've despatched a team. Puts him back in the frame for Gülizar's murder, especially in light of his disappearing act.'

'Indeed.'

'Second thing involves the Negropontes,' he said. 'You know that a body was found in the grounds of the Lise. Middle-aged man, been in the ground for fifty-odd years.'

'Yes.'

'Long story short, Ömer found old dental X-rays that fit. Only problem is that, as far as we can make out – time's passed and the labelling is unclear – they belong to an N. Negroponte. Wasn't the old lady's husband called Nikos and isn't he buried in Şişli Greek cemetery?'

'Yes, he is.'

'Then it has to be another N. Negroponte,' Süleyman said. 'Can you ask Madam Anastasia if she knows who that might be? If she can remember.'

'When she wakes up, I will.' İkmen ended the call.

He felt cold, but it didn't stop him walking slowly into the red room. Two forensic investigators were very carefully dusting a wall. Now that the candles Yiannis Negroponte had used had been replaced by arc lights, the room looked much less impressive. Strong white light leeched something important from the stone which made it look dead. İkmen turned to leave. He couldn't remember any other male Negroponte with the initial N. Madam's father's name had been Alexis, her father-in-law and uncle had been Konstantine. Had she had any brothers? Had her husband?

İkmen took a step. Then he stopped. 'Did you say anything?' he said to the two forensic investigators.

'No, Çetin Bey.'

'No.'

'Mmm.'

He went on his way. A voice, just a whisper, had come to him. What it said, he didn't know. No, more a sibilance than a voice. Like a snake.

327

Mad people heard things that weren't there. He'd read some-where that as the body died, it went mad. Especially the diabetic body. Ahmet Öden put his ear to the wall. Tapping.

Who was tapping and why? Were they, Negroponte and the old man, tapping to hasten his insanity? Ahmet cringed away from the wall and whispered, 'Stop it!'

But the tapping went on.

Should he scream? If he did, would it only give them pleasure? Make them laugh? His father had said they were inhuman. Their priests were rapists and their men were cheats and swindlers. How some of his own people could have protected them was unfathomable. But his father had said they had. Army officers included. And Hakkı. His father hadn't thought he would, but he had. He'd taken Anastasia Negroponte out of Beyoğlu and put her back in her house, this house. Where he'd worshipped her.

'Stop it.'

But they didn't. Would they come and look at him after he had died? Or would they just leave him undisturbed forever? Hakkı, as a Muslim, would know that a body not buried in the ground would result in the soul being in torment. Was he capable of doing such a thing? Even to an enemy?

'No.'

His hands shook. The candle flame shimmered. It was almost done.

'No,' he whispered again. Shaking, he felt sick.

Then he'd be in the sort of darkness where it is impossible to know whether your eyes are open or shut.

And still the tiny noises from his tormenters ticked against the side of his brain.

Chapter 27

Apart from the toilet, the basement was out of use. Police officers made sure nobody crossed the 'Crime Scene' tape slung across both kitchen doors. As he had always done, Hakkı Bey organised the practicalities. A local tea garden provided drinks while his landlady came with food that no one ate.

Anastasia Negroponte had been asleep for many hours. İkmen suspected that either her son or her servant had given her a sleeping pill or a tranquilliser. Old people, in his experience, rarely slept for such long and concentrated periods of time. One needed less sleep if anything as one aged. Unless one were dying . . .

'Will you go when you've spoken to my mother, Çetin Bey?' Yiannis asked.

The one newspaper İkmen had been able to find – courtesy of a particularly slack-jawed constable – was full of superstitious rubbish. It was a relief to put it down. 'Yes,' he said.

'You know she isn't always lucid.'

'Yes.'

'Can you not ask us whatever it is you want to know, Çetin Bey?' Hakkı said.

'No.'

Outside the sky was dark. The Taksim Solidarity group had left to go to Ankara for talks with the Prime Minister and yet again, the city was tense. But at least İkmen could bask in the knowledge that Kemal was at home. Dusty and, to his mother's horror, smelly, the boy had returned mid-afternoon and was now sleeping. By way of celebration, Fatma had baked for several hours and had then begun work on a new knitted jumper. She was so easily pleased.

His phone rang. It was Süleyman. İkmen walked out of the salon and into the hall.

'Mehmet?'

'Without digging it up I can't be sure that Ahmet Öden isn't lurking somewhere in the Belgrade Forest, but there's no obvious sign of anything untoward happening up there so far. And we traced his phone to Tophane, probably in the Bosphorus,' he said. 'Ömer's been in touch with the airports and coastguards since the start and nothing's come to light from that direction either. Do you think he's killed himself?'

'No,' İkmen said. 'Unless he's suddenly decided to do jihad, then as a good Muslim he can't.'

'He's not got his insulin with him. Could be doing it that way?'

'I don't get that he'd kill himself,' İkmen said. 'Even if he did murder his mistress. He's a daughter who needs him and more money than is decent. He went out intending to return. That's my belief. And that's why he didn't take his insulin with him.'

'Did I tell you Ömer found an empty box of Viagra in his bathroom?'

'No. Was it prescribed?'

'No.'

İkmen shook his head. Getting any sort of decent painkiller over the counter at pharmacies was like looking for Atlantis but Viagra was on sale, loud and proud, everywhere. 'Well if he takes that stuff maybe he's lying in some hooker's bed after a stroke,' he said.

330

'Have you spoken to Madam Negroponte yet?'

'No, she's still asleep.' He lowered his voice. 'I think she's probably been tranquillised. I'm staying until she wakes.'

'What about Yiannis and Hakkı Bey?'

'Oh, they periodically ask me why I want to speak to Madam and I don't tell them. I know she's slow and confused but I also know she remembers the past. Until Yiannis reappeared in the early nineties, it was all she had.'

When he'd finished the call, İkmen went back into the salon where Hakkı and Yiannis were in close, whispered conversation. When they saw him they fell silent, but İkmen noticed that Yiannis looked angry. 'Everything all right?' he asked.

'Yes,' Hakkı said before Yiannis could open his mouth. 'Everything is fine. But I think I may go and check on Madam.'

'Take her dirty washing out of her room,' Yiannis said. 'It smells.'

There were generally a few shabby tents in the forest, mainly, these days, housing displaced gypsies. Kerim Gürsel knew they were generally gathered around old structures like what remained of the Ottoman aqueduct system and the reservoirs. But apart from a couple of alcoholics collapsed in the picnic area, the forest, so far, was empty.

'All the filth has washed up in Taksim,' one young constable said.

His colleagues laughed.

'So are you saying that this is not a free country?' Kerim said.

'Sergeant?' The boy still had acne spots. He was very young. Kerim had to remind himself of that.

'In a free country people are allowed to demonstrate,' Kerim said.

'Oh yeah, well, they can demonstrate but—'

'But what?'

'Not if they're doing it for bad reasons.'

'Like what?'

Part of one of the Ottoman aqueducts loomed out of the darkness.

'Something against Islam,' one of the other young constables said. 'Or supporting perversion.'

'I don't think the Gezi protesters are against Islam, are they?' Kerim said. 'They're against the government—'

'Which is Islamic—'

'Is it?' Something on the ground caught Kerim's eye and he bent down to look at it. An old tin can. 'Surely the government of Turkey is supposed to be secular.'

'Er, well, yes it is. But the Party—'

'The party, whichever one it is, is not the government,' Kerim said. 'Or it shouldn't be.'

He looked at the boys and smiled. They glanced at each other nervously. Were they members of the ruling party? Probably. And if they weren't, then their fathers were. Kerim wondered what they'd do if they knew his wife was a lesbian, his lover, a transsexual. All life was in wicked old İstanbul and at that moment much of it was in Gezi Park, colourful, loud, proud and threatened. Kerim hoped that Sinem and Pembe were safe. He'd never seen his wife look so well as she had since the protests had begun. Together with Pembe and Madame Edith, she was out every day and the movement and the air were definitely enlivening her. Possibly if the talks went well between the Taksim Solidarity group and the Prime Minister, the camp wouldn't be attacked again and maybe Sinem might meet a nice woman in amongst the trees. As it was, love and sex were the last thing on the minds of most people in Gezi Park. Tear gas and batons tended to focus the attention of the majority on simple survival.

Kerim said, 'I don't think we're going to find Mr Öden tonight.'

One of the young men shook his head sadly.

Anastasia Negroponte opened her eyes and saw a tangle of her own grey hair. She could see her room easily through it now that her hair was so old and thin – the yellow curtains her mother had made up back in the 1930s, the purple Hereke rug that a hunched figure was walking slowly across.

A man, he was moving away from her, his back slightly stooped under a sack. It reminded her of that other man, the one who had taken Nikos and buried him still alive. Who had he been? Why had he done that? And why was she the only one who knew that Nikos had not been buried in Şişli?

Because he had told her. The man without a face had said, 'I will bury him for you.' And because she couldn't speak, she couldn't tell him that her husband was still alive. And then later, Hakkı had come . . .

The figure on the Hereke rug stopped. Was this part of a dream?

He turned. He looked over his left shoulder.

She froze.

Then she screamed.

'What's going on?' Çetin İkmen said.

Yiannis Negroponte sprang to his feet. 'My mother. You wait here!'

He ran out of the salon and up the stairs.

İkmen started to follow, but Yiannis turned. 'I said stay here!' he said. 'She's probably had a bad dream!'

He heard Yiannis and the old man try to calm her down. But

she screamed again and then she whimpered. There were so few İstanbul Greeks who remembered 1955 left in the city. Most of them had gone away or died. He wondered what her damaged mind saw and whether whatever it was reflected the reality of what had happened to her.

He remembered his Uncle Vahan, Arto Sarkissian's father, talking to his father about it. He'd been a surgeon and had been called on to try and save the lives of some of the 1955 riot victims. But not Nikos Negroponte. And he'd not been the only one. Vahan Sarkissian had run along İstiklal, leaving the dead, tending to the dying, falling over on the blood that coated the road surface. Çetin's father, Timur, had been so ashamed of his own people that he'd apologised to every Greek he knew.

He could hear the old woman crying now. How could he ask her questions?

Yiannis ran down the stairs. 'I'm sorry, Çetin Bey, my mother has had a bad dream and so she's distressed. Can you leave asking her anything until tomorrow?'

The basement was a suspected crime scene and so officers would be on site until the investigation was complete.

'I know we can't leave the house . . .'

'No, you can't.'

'I won't.'

İkmen left the Negroponte house and strolled along slowly, cigarette in hand, feeling tired and emotionally empty. Could he, even if he tried, remember that red room from his childhood? When he'd first revisited the Negroponte House he'd felt that something was different. But was it that? He didn't know. Something had been wrong in that house but he felt that it still was wrong even with the room fully exposed.

Had Ahmet Öden, somehow, known about the red room? He had been so adamant about having the Negroponte House. İkmen had just thought that he was simply conforming to the arrogant way property developers behaved when they wanted a site. But was he? And how had he known if Yiannis had kept the room a secret? If he had. How had Ariadne Savva known about it? If she had.

And whose blood was that on the porphyry slab in the red room?

When he got home he had his dinner and then spent some time with the small box that contained all that remained to him of his mother's possessions. This included her tarot cards, hand-painted by her grandfather, which expressed the universal principles of love, death, and destruction in terms of a rural Albania Çetin had never seen. They also gave him a good idea.

'Do you know why she's so bad?' Yiannis said.

Hakkı shook his head. He was grey and breathless. They'd both had to hold Anastasia down when Yiannis had given her another pill. It had taken it out of the old man. Now her eyes were closed again he sat down by the door. Yiannis joined him.

'What happened? How did it start?'

'I don't know. I thought she was asleep, I was leaving.'

'So she must've woken and seen you. Thought you were an intruder? Did she seem to be stuck in a nightmare?'

'I don't know! I don't know!'

She stirred.

'Keep your voice down!' Yiannis whispered.

'But what I do know is I don't think she should see Çetin Bey tomorrow. I think we should tell him she is too ill,' Hakkı said.

He looked over at the bed and frowned. 'Because you think she is?'

'Partly.' He tipped his head to one side.

'Well?'

'I don't know what she knows,' Hakkı said. 'She lies up here year in and year out but what she knows . . .' He shrugged.

'She can hardly talk!' Yiannis hissed. 'Her brain is damaged. Where's the harm?'

Hakkı looked over at her bed now and said, 'I don't know. But if we are to keep this house we mustn't leave anything to chance. She can't talk to him, Yiannis. Ever.'

Yiannis paused and then he nodded his head. 'I'll talk to her.'

There was a subdued feeling in Gezi Park. Protest representatives had gone to Ankara at the request of the government and so all anyone could do was wait and see what happened. For the time being the police had pulled back. Peri walked past tents and fires, makeshift shops and even an outdoor library. The protest was still vibrant, but it was also tense.

'Hey! You!'

Peri looked around. Was someone calling her?

'Nurse!'

Possibly. 'Yes?'

A long brown hand on her shoulder made her turn. She recognised the face. It was that amazing, fierce gypsy woman, the lover of Ömer's boss, Mehmet Süleyman.

'Gonca Hanım.'

'You are Sergeant Mungun's sister,' Gonca said.

'Yes.'

'From the east.'

'Yes.'

Gonca took Peri's hand. 'You must come with me.'

'Where? What . . .'

Gonca was strong, but Peri was stronger. She pulled her hand away. 'Hanım?'

336

Gonca put her hands on her hips. 'I need a nurse,' she said. 'Don't usually need one. But now . . .' She shrugged.

'A nurse for . . .'

'One of my daughters is having a baby and I think it's premature,' she said.

'What, your daughter's having a baby here? In Gezi Park?'

'That tent.' She pointed to a conical military style tent. 'She didn't know she was pregnant until her pains started this morning. Neither did I.'

'Does your daughter know how many months she's been pregnant?'

'No. She says not,' Gonca said. 'The boy, the father, has been sniffing around my house for months. I've told her, when I see him I'll beat him. Then we'll have a wedding.'

She lived in what some would consider 'sin' with Süleyman and yet clearly her children were expected to be more conventional.

Peri looked inside the tent and saw a girl sweating on a blanket on the ground, surrounded by women who covered their faces when her eyes caught theirs.

'Will you help us?' Gonca asked.

Peri opened her bag and took out a pair of latex gloves. 'If the baby's tiny or distressed I'll take it to hospital,' she said. 'No arguments.'

'None from me,' Gonca replied.

Chapter 28

There were few silences between the wittering, stammering, senseless jabberings in his head. And when they did come, he shook, because he was in darkness now. The candle had gone out at some time he couldn't name. He moved his eyes to prove to himself that he was still alive. A nibbling sound made him try to move his body, but he couldn't. Had rats invaded his chamber? Had the old man and Negroponte sent them in to eat him alive?

He hadn't injected himself for – how long? He should be in a coma. Maybe he was? Perhaps that was what being in this place was all about? He wasn't there at all. He was in a hospital somewhere, in a diabetic coma. He hoped the family hadn't brought Kelime to see him. She'd be so frightened! He was all she had. If anything happened to him, what would become of her? Semih loved her but he wouldn't want her in his life when he eventually married and had children of his own. His sisters tolerated her. Kelime would end up in a home. A very expensive home, but not a place where she'd be loved. She wouldn't be indulged and so she'd scream and then they, the people at the home, would beat her. Because that was what people who ran homes for children like her did.

Ahmet Öden's eyes leaked. He couldn't cry, he wasn't strong enough. For himself he wanted to die. He'd already pissed and defecated all over himself. What was next? When hunger came again, would he start to eat his own flesh? Death had to be preferable to that and yet if he died all hope for Kelime would be lost.

He wasn't being rational. How could something that didn't exist, be lost? Kelime had gone. She'd gone into a home already and he was going to die.

Why was he dying so painfully? Hadn't he been a good man? He'd always done whatever those who were senior to him had asked. From his father onwards. What was wrong with that?

A voice answered him. 'Oh everything's wrong with that,' it said. 'You stupid fucking puppet.'

Ah, Gülizar. His gypsy lover. He thought he felt his face smile. If he hadn't gone out to get Viagra from that discreet little pharmacist in Yeniköy the night she had died how would that have worked out? But he'd had to go in the night. That night. In spite of Kelime and her sickness. He'd been out of the drug and he'd been aching to see Gülizar as soon as he was able.

'Yes, I brought a goat for my father,' Lokman Atasu said.

'OK.'

Kerim Gürsel had grown up in İstanbul but he knew how country people were because in recent years so many of them had moved to the city. Even if they only had a small flat, sometimes they had their most valuable animals with them. And when relatives visited they often brought a celebratory goat or a lamb to slaughter when they arrived. Hakkı Atasu's son was no exception.

'Where do you live, Mr Atasu?' Kerim asked.

A dour man in his fifties, Lokman had a wonderful face for suspicion. 'Why do you want to know?'

'I'm a police officer,' Kerim said, 'just answer the question.'

It wasn't like him to pull rank, but sometimes that was the only way.

'I live on my father-in-law's farm just outside Van.'

Very far east. Kerim looked around the small, dark room that, apart from a tiny kitchen and a very basic bathroom, was Hakkı Atasu's only accommodation. Lokman's three children, one of which was a baby, grizzled miserably in the morning heat while his wife, a covered woman with the eyes of a child, stared helplessly at the floor. Too tired to care.

'Did you slaughter the goat or did your father?'

'He did,' Lokman said. 'With Yiannis Bey.'

'Where?'

'At the Negroponte House. There's no room here.'

He was right.

'Do you know where in the Negroponte House your father and Yiannis Bey killed it?'

'No.'

Yiannis Negroponte had said that he often used the porphyry slab that he and Hakkı had slaughtered the goat on.

'My father cooked the goat in a tandır in the garden. We went for the feast later in the evening,' Lokman said. 'Madam Negroponte doesn't like people in the house.'

'Must've been difficult with the children.'

'We stayed in the garden,' he said.

'So you didn't see Madam Negroponte?' Kerim asked.

'I haven't seen Madam for years,' he said.

Just for a moment the child-eyed wife looked up at her husband. Her gaze was unreadable. But Kerim noted it. Then she went back to bottle-feeding the baby.

Nestor Negroponte had been a male version of those unmarried, impoverished aunts aristocratic and middle-class families had always had. There had been a woman of that sort in Mehmet Süleyman's family, although she had had a flat of her own, which was unusual. Nestor Negroponte was much more typical.

A cousin from an aunt who İkmen suspected had become pregnant out of wedlock, he had stayed in the house until 1955. Then he'd disappeared. He hadn't been involved, as far as anyone knew, in any of the violence in Beyoğlu. He'd just walked out of the door one day and never come back.

'He was . . . simple,' the old woman said. 'Child.'

The photograph on her bedroom wall showed a man, probably in his forties, wearing a light coloured suit and a panama hat. Unsmiling, he looked confused.

Yiannis Negroponte had stayed until İkmen had asked him to go. He'd said he was afraid to leave his mother in case İkmen's questions upset her. But eventually she'd waved him away.

'You never saw Nestor again?'

She shook her head.

'Since 1955?'

'No . . .' She beckoned him to her. As İkmen got closer he saw that her eyes were wet. Was she still suffering from the effects of the bad dream she'd had that night?

He walked over to her bed and sat down. She looked into his eyes. When she was young, she'd been incredibly beautiful. İkmen's mother had always said that the world was in love with Madam Negroponte, and if the world constituted the men of İstanbul, that had been true. Nikos Negroponte had always had to keep close to his wife whenever they went to parties. Otherwise she'd be bothered by their unwanted advances. Even just with himself and his brother in the house, İkmen could remember how Nikos Bey always held his wife's arm.

'Madam Anastasia, what's wrong?' İkmen said. 'I am not my

mother, but I do have some of her sensitivity to atmosphere. There's something not right in this house. Tell me what it is?'

Slowly, she moved her eyes away.

'I know about the red room,' İkmen said. 'I think I saw it when I was a child. Do you know why Yiannis has been trying to hide it in recent years?'

She said nothing.

'Was it to stop the archaeologists moving in? Preferable to property developers, I think,' İkmen said. And then he stopped making what he considered chit-chat. 'Madam Anastasia, a young woman died in a room made of porphyry. We found her body in the sphendone of the Hippodrome, but that is not somewhere dressed with porphyry and so we don't think she was murdered there.'

She looked at him.

'Yes, murdered. That had happened in a red place,' he said. 'She gave birth to a child and then, we think, she was slaughtered. I want to know where the child is. I want to know if it's dead like its mother or like your cousin Nestor . . .'

'Mmm.'

She'd begun to hum. Her body shook.

'Madam, I know that something . . .'

She wept, humming, her voice rising, her tears spilling over her eyelids and falling down her cheeks.

'Madam, I don't want to upset you,' İkmen said. 'But I know something isn't right and . . .' He put a hand in his pocket and took out his mother's old tarot cards. 'Remember these?'

He heard heavy footsteps approaching from the stairs.

'They were my mother's. Remember Ayşe İkmen? The witch?' he smiled.

A thin, twisted hand took the pack from his fingers and the humming stopped.

'Maybe if you can use these cards to show me . . .'

The bedroom door slammed open. 'What's going on?'

'I've been asking your mother some questions . . .'

'I heard her whimpering.' Yiannis Negroponte went straight to his mother and put an arm around her shoulders. 'What are these?'

'Tarot cards,' İkmen said. 'They were my mother's. She used to read them for Madam Negroponte before you were born.'

Yiannis made to grab them, but his mother pulled the pack to her chest, cradling them against her thin breastbone.

'I brought them for her,' İkmen said.

'I know I perform "magic" but that's just—'

'I don't know what I think about it either, Mr Negroponte,' İkmen said. 'But these are hand-painted Albanian tarot cards. They're works of art.'

The old woman looked up into her son's face. 'You want them, Mama?'

'Yes . . .'

He smiled. Then he looked at İkmen, 'So now you know about Nestor Negroponte . . .'

İkmen's phone rang. He excused himself and left the room. It was Ali Bey from forensic.

'Can't give you anything on the blood we found at the Negroponte House,' he said, 'except a small quantity on the floor of that room was definitely not human. Anything the luminol threw up was trace. Sorry.'

İkmen shook his head. 'What can you do?'

'Do? Nothing. We've found nothing of any forensic value. Take the tapes down and move out.'

'I know,' İkmen said. He sighed.

'But you're still not happy.'

'There's something wrong here,' İkmen said. 'And I don't know what it is.'

'I don't get anything from that house at all,' Ali Bey said. 'But we all know how you are, Çetin Bey.'

Did he mean 'weirdly insightful' or just nuts? Did İkmen even care? He ended the call. It was then that he saw Yiannis Negroponte looking at him. He'd heard everything.

'I take it you and your men will be leaving,' he said. Then he went back into his mother's room and closed the door behind him.

They insisted on calling the baby Peri. Or rather Gonca did.

Like a lot of gypsies, her daughter hadn't wanted to have her baby in a hospital. So the little girl had been born in their tent in Gezi Park under constant threat of attack from the police. But Peri Mungun had stayed with her all the time. Together with her mother and other female relatives, she'd soothed the girl and reassured her and, when her time was near, she'd told her what to do. And although little Peri was small, she wasn't as small as big Peri had feared. She also appeared to be healthy.

Once mother and baby were settled, Gonca and Peri stepped out of the tent for a smoke. A boy juggling a diabolo ran past, laughing.

'I've heard the Prime Minister has walked out on the Taksim representatives,' Gonca said.

'That's not good.'

'It's a disaster,' she said. 'If he won't even listen, what are people supposed to do? How can you live in a place where you don't know what will be demolished next?'

'I don't know,' Peri said.

They smoked in silence and then Gonca said, 'You know one of these property developers has gone missing?'

'Yes.'

'Ahmet Öden. Your brother—'

'I've not seen my brother lately, but I've no doubt he's doing his best to find this man.'

'Well I hope he isn't,' Gonca said. 'Öden killed a woman I know. I hope he's dead.'

Peri looked at her. 'Killed a woman? Are you sure?'

'She was a gypsy and he's one of those pious hypocrites that use women like her. The ones that get rich all the time now. I hope he's dead and I hope it hurt.'

Peri knew all about passion but Gonca took it to another level.

'Have you told Mehmet Bey about this?'

'And why would I do that? Eh? Gülizar was a good woman and they are worth a thousand men. If Ahmet Öden is lying injured somewhere, the slower my Mehmet finds out the better.'

'Çetin Bey.'

Commissioner Teker had come into his office, apparently noiselessly. Her predecessor Ardıç, though a big man, had also possessed that skill. Did it go with the job?

İkmen looked up. 'I've received orders to attack Gezi Park at seventeen-thirty,' she said. 'I wanted you to know.'

She shut his office door and sat down. 'I've run out of cigarettes.' İkmen handed over his packet. 'You've drawn a blank at the Negroponte House.'

'Yes.' He lit her cigarette and then opened his window. 'Not happy but . . .'

'Why not?'

He shrugged. 'I feel the Negropontes and Mr Atasu know more than they're saying. But I can't prove it. Short of digging up their garden to look for Öden's body there's nothing more we can do.'

'Then dig it,' Teker said.

'Seriously?' He frowned.

'People way, way up the line, almost as far as the ones who want us to attack Gezi, want Öden found,' she said. 'You can get a warrant this afternoon, dig first thing tomorrow.'

'Tomorrow? Why not get it over with now if it has to be done?'

'Because if a senior detective like you has a major investigation to pursue in the morning, I can't very well deploy you to Gezi Park today,' she said. 'Some of the officers already at the site haven't had leave for days. The protesters have been feeding and watering a good proportion of them. We need fresh blood up there. Or rather they do.'

'They?'

She looked around before she answered. 'I think we both know where we stand with Gezi, İkmen,' she said. 'I can't get out of it, attacking Gezi is my job. But if I can make sure that you don't have to, I'll still not be able to sleep at night, but I may be able to live with myself.' She paused, smoked. 'I should resign. But I can't.'

'Madam—'

'Get a warrant, go in the morning,' she said. 'Take your sergeant and try and find some other bodies to do the labouring. Normally you could have five or six constables . . .' She shrugged. 'Your boy out of the park now?'

'Yes,' İkmen said. 'But I have a cousin there and Sergeant Mungun's sister has remained.'

'The demonstrators have been told that seventeen-thirty is the deadline,' Teker said. 'Anyone found in the park after that time will be treated as a terrorist. There are officers out there who haven't slept for three days. What they'll do . . .' She shrugged again. 'My orders are to deploy them.'

'Then maybe I should go,' İkmen said. 'Possibly they'll listen to me . . .'

'What, functionally illiterate farm kids from Anatolia? I come from Urfa, I worked in Gaziantep. Luckily for me my parents had money so I had an education. But I went out to the villages, saw the kids with genetic defects because of inbreeding, saw the women beaten black and blue by illiterate husbands who see women as their possessions. Why do you think I never married? They won't listen to you, İkmen. You, and I, are anathema to them.' She stood up. 'Obtain your warrant and go home. Tell Sergeant Gürsel to go home too. And make sure he stays indoors. He lives in Tarlabaşı, doesn't he?'

'Yes.'

'I'd recommend he keeps his windows closed,' she said and then she left.

Çetin İkmen allowed himself a moment of grief for his country and then he called Samsun.

Chapter 29

Madonna wasn't even in the park. She'd decided to leave with Madame Edith, who felt she was too old for an all-out police offensive. They got as far as the Church of St Antoine before they were grabbed by men in riot gear and beaten. Edith, in full Piaf get-up, was kicked between the legs so hard she felt her testicles would burst. There were teeth on the ground that Madonna realised were hers.

Some of them dragged Edith off but others carried on kicking Madonna until they got bored. However, when they left, others came in their place and they punched her. One of them threatened to fuck her and a young girl who had just appeared at her side. Through broken teeth, Madonna managed to shout, 'Fuck me? You'll be lucky, bastard!' That got her a punch to the kidneys. But she heard the young girl say, 'If you like, sir.'

Members of the press corps, plus Samsun Bajraktar, had taken refuge in the Divan Hotel. People were sneezing and vomiting from the effects of tear gas and pepper spray and when she arrived, the whole of the reception area was covered in sick. Just the look of it made her heave.

'Are you OK?'

A smart woman in her forties took Samsun's arm and led her to a chair.

'Yeah.' She was. Her eyes stung from the effects of the gas

but she hadn't been sick and she could speak. The main thing that was upsetting her was that the police had burned the Gezi Wish Tree.

'The Gezi Wish Tree?'

'It's where we put all our hopes on little bits of paper,' Samsun told the woman. 'They burned it. They burned our future.'

And then she cried.

No local TV station even referred to Gezi. Kemal İkmen alternated between BBC World and CNN.

'I should be with them,' he said to his father.

Çetin İkmen looked like a ghost. White and unfed. 'I promised your mother I'd keep you home,' he said.

Fatma İkmen had gone over to his sister's apartment in Gaziosmanpaşa earlier in the day and was unable to get back. Çetin had brought cakes home for his and Kemal's dinner, but he hadn't eaten any.

'They're mad with tiredness and hunger,' İkmen said, pointing at the baton-wielding officers on the screen. 'And they come from places in Anatolia that don't have names. It's like letting a pack of wild dogs loose.'

Kemal said, 'I should still be there. Auntie Samsun's there.'

'I know. I don't like that either, Kemal, and I can understand why you want to be in Gezi now. But what good will it do?'

'Why aren't you there, Dad? CNN said that the police had deployed every available officer.'

İkmen shook his head. 'I got lucky,' he said. 'I have a good boss.'

'Teker excused you?'

'She assigned a job to Sergeant Gürsel and me at first light . . .'

'What, at Gezi?'

'No. Nothing to do with that. I don't have anything to do

with that, Kemal. Whether that's a good or a bad thing . . .' He shrugged.

In Tarlabaşı, Sergeant Kerim Gürsel looked out of his firmly closed window. The streets below were alive with his neighbours banging pots and pans in protest while plastic bullets flew through the air. Two officers grabbed a man and hauled him into a custody vehicle. One of them raced after a woman who tried to run away but he brought her down and then carried her to the van as well. As he put her inside he punched her.

Sinem was asleep on the sofa with BBC World blaring out on the TV. Episodes of old British sitcoms were interspersed with scenes from Gezi that looked like something Dante might have dreamed up. Kerim lit a cigarette. He didn't usually smoke but Pembe was still somewhere in the park and the last time he'd heard from her she'd said that if they, the police, were going to kill her, she was going to take a few of them out first. And because he loved her so much, he had wanted to tell her just to come back and not put herself at risk. But he couldn't. It was what she wanted to do and if he really loved her, he'd let her.

What she'd had for her supper was now not even a memory. But Anastasia Negroponte remembered Ayşe İkmen. A tiny dark witch with a weird foreign accent and always accompanied by her two sons – one tall and blond, the other small and dark and quick as a firecracker. She looked at the strange, frightening cards he'd given her. Their names were written in Albanian so she couldn't always tell what they were. An image of a man looking up at the stars, his clothes tattered, one shoe being eaten by a goat, was, she thought, the Fool. But that wasn't appropriate.

She slowly moved the cards in her hands. Swords were scimitars and empresses veiled. Because Albania had become a communist country after the Second World War people had forgotten it had once been a Muslim enclave in Europe. It had been an Ottoman province. The Magician followed the Tower, which had peasants and kaftan-clad nobles falling from its battlements. And then there was Shaitan. She knew that he was right. The Devil. A djinn made of smoke whispering into the chests of veiled women, suggesting sin. Ayşe İkmen had always interpreted this card as indicative of slavery and bondage. When it had arisen, she had asked her what things in her life were oppressing or trapping her. In those days there had only been her father. Now there was so much. It had to end.

But would the witch's small, firecracker son understand?

Anastasia put her feet to the floor for the first time that week. She couldn't walk. But if she held on to furniture she could pull herself short distances. She put the Devil between her teeth and put her hand out to the sideboard beside the window. She'd asked Yiannis to open it so that she could get some fresh air. He'd argued, saying that there was a pall of tear gas over the city because of the protests in Gezi Park. Yiannis was agitated because the police had called to tell him they were coming back. But she'd insisted. The window was only open a little but it would be enough. In the morning Çetin Bey and his men would arrive and find it. Hopefully he would understand. Then she knew that snake in her house would run away. What else could he do? Because if he'd buried a man alive once before, Hakkı Bey could do it again. And he had. Anastasia could hear him crying.

She dropped the tarot card into the mulberry bush a second before Yiannis came into her bedroom.

'What are you doing, Mother?'

But he didn't wait for her to even try to form a reply. He picked her up and put her back to bed. Then he closed the window.

Ömer had begged Peri not to stay in the park, but she'd ignored him. She'd stayed with the gypsies until they'd all left to take their children away. Gonca had said she'd come back and so Peri had remained in their tent where she'd been joined by a group of Sufis. Now they too had moved on and it was just her and a big man in full riot gear.

For a moment they just stared at each other. She couldn't see his eyes, which were hidden behind a black visor. But she could see his mouth, which smiled.

'A nurse,' she heard him say. His accent was rough and eastern and it reminded her of the worst, most notorious families back in Mardin. 'I've always wanted to have a nurse.'

He was going to rape her. Peri said the first thing that came into her head. 'I've got chlamydia,' she said.

'What?' He grabbed her arm with one of his great, gloved hands.

He didn't know what chlamydia was. Which could mean that he had it.

Although every part of her body shook with fear, Peri landed a punch on his jaw. It did nothing but infuriate him.

'Whore!'

She tried to twist out of his grasp, but she couldn't. He put his other hand inside his trousers and pulled out his cock. Peri screamed. She'd seen plenty of those before, but she'd never had one used against her in anger until now.

She shouted, 'Rape!'

'If you're lucky,' her attacker said.

Peri kicked out at him, but she missed. He punched her in

the face and the world exploded into a million stars. Then he kicked her in the stomach. She'd seen her brother in those boots. Suddenly she wanted to cry.

'Donkey fucker!' she rasped. 'Son of an infected whore!'

The old oaths she'd learned as a child who had spent her time with the rough country kids who roamed the Mesopotamian Plain came back to her.

He pushed her to the ground and stuck his hand roughly up her skirt. Then he took his helmet off. Did he do it because he wanted to delight in her discomfort? He was ugly and he had to know it. He looked like a frog.

Peri crossed her legs. He slapped her. 'Bitch!'

Her face was swelling where he'd punched her and so Peri could only see properly out of one eye. It was a shock to her when he fell on top of her without pushing himself inside her. For a moment she just lay underneath him without moving. Then she turned her head.

A tiny covered woman was standing behind the fallen man holding a frying pan. She said, 'Push him off, get up and then let's get out of here.'

'Thank you—'

'No time for that, sister,' the little woman said. 'We have to get away.'

'My husband's in Gezi Park.'

Aylın Akyıldız put her hand near to but not on the bones of the man with the double-headed eagle sword.

'Shouldn't you go home? It's terrible in the park. He might need you,' Professor Bozdağ said.

'He won't.' She looked down at the body again. 'But *he* might.'

'Him? You're not still receiving threats, are you?'

'No,' she said. 'But we'd be fooling ourselves if we thought that he was safe.'

'Dr Akyıldız—'

'Ariadne knew,' she said. 'In her bones. She knew he was Greek and she knew he was special. Professor, if these protests are quashed, those who don't want to acknowledge anything except our Ottoman past will destroy him.'

'No, I don't—'

'No, you don't understand,' she said. 'I've thought and thought and thought it over and I can only come to one conclusion, which is that Ariadne told someone else about him. Someone who hates him.'

'Whoever he is,' the professor said. 'Really, Dr Akyıldız, his identity is entirely speculative . . .'

'I don't think it is, though! I think that Ariadne knew it and I think she told someone she shouldn't. Maybe the father of her child. And then he killed her.'

Exhausted, she sat down.

'I don't think she told him where Palaiologos was,' she continued. 'But it wouldn't have been difficult for him to work it out, especially if they were lovers.'

'This is all speculation. I think you should go home.'

'I want to stay here.'

She put a hand on the table where the body lay. Dr Savva's death had affected everyone who had known her, badly. But Aylın Akyıldız had suffered more than most. It had been Aylın who had kept Palaiologos secret, then received death threats. Finally she'd had to hand him over to the museum. Now in a city beyond boiling point she feared he would be looted by the same people who wanted to turn Aya Sofya back into a mosque.

The professor thought that was a remote possibility. But he didn't try to convince her. She was in the grip of a fear that

354

almost amounted to an obsession. Also, given the chaos in Taksim, would she even be able to get home? He knew he wasn't going to risk it.

After a moment he said, 'Well, I have work to do and so I imagine I will be here all night. I have tea and börek which you're welcome to share.'

At first she didn't appear to have heard him, but then he saw her smile.

Chapter 30

A boy wearing expensive sports kit and trainers that probably cost a month's wages casually kicked a gravestone. He didn't even look at it. Had he done so he would have seen the tall, slim man standing beside it. This man grabbed the boy's arm.

'Why did you kick that gravestone?' Mehmet Süleyman asked.

The boy shrugged. 'Don't know.'

'Would you have kicked it if it had been your grandfather's? Or your mother's? Or any member of your family? Would you have kicked it if it hadn't been Greek?'

'No! And what's it to you? Who are you?'

'I'm a police officer,' Süleyman said. 'We received reports that this place was being vandalised. Was it you?'

'No!'

'Thinking you're on some sort of jihad . . .'

'I'm Jewish. Why would I go on jihad?'

And then the Star of David round the boy's neck suddenly looked very obvious.

He waved him away.

Now he'd stopped trying to clean up after the excesses of some of his fellow officers, Mehmet Süleyman was finally tired. Fifteen minutes before, he'd received a call to say that some gravestones in Şişli Greek Cemetery had been desecrated. He'd checked, it was true, he'd spoken to one of the priests, but there wasn't much he could do. Another example of insanity in a city that had lost its mind. He sat down next to a broken monument and lit a cigarette.

He hadn't done his job. Teker had sent him into Gezi to be a police officer and do what he was told. But he'd spent all his time helping people get to the doctors who were trying to treat the people his fellows had injured. Some of them had gone to the Divan Hotel where thugs in uniform threw tear gas canisters in after them. Later he'd found Peri Mungun crouched behind a tree, shaking. She couldn't speak.

He'd picked her up and carried her to her apartment. Her brother was somewhere in Beyoğlu, but he couldn't raise him. He'd made Peri a glass of tea and she'd smoked five of his cigarettes before she'd said, 'A police officer tried to rape me.'

She'd described some half-evolved monster from the east. She'd not got his number. But she had been rescued by a tiny girl in a headscarf who'd had a good way with a frying pan. When Ömer found out he'd want to give the little girl a medal and kill the gorilla who had tried to rape his sister.

'I know I'm a grown woman and so rather me than some little virgin girl,' Peri had said. 'But policemen shouldn't behave like that, Mehmet Bey. I know they did in the past, but not now.'

She was right. Whatever one felt about the current government, police accountability had improved. Now it seemed all that had disappeared in one night of awful violence. There had been a build-up, for weeks. But what he'd seen and heard during that night and on into the early morning, made Mehmet Süleyman want to howl with despair.

It was Father's Day and people were going to the shops wearing gas masks even when they were many kilometres away from Gezi Park. As Çetin İkmen left his apartment, his son Kemal put his head round his bedroom door and mumbled, 'Think you're great, Dad.'

He smiled. That was better than any present the kid could have got him.

İkmen met Kerim Gürsel and the squad of uniformed officers he'd asked for outside the Negroponte House. The constables carried shovels and rakes and one of them held a battering ram.

İkmen wished them all a good morning and then he rang the bell on the Negropontes' gate. He'd seen a flash of face at one window already and so he knew they were in. And where, after all, would or could Madam Negroponte go?

He rang again and then he called out, 'Open up, Mr Negroponte, it's the police. I gave you fair warning.'

İkmen had a warrant and so he could force entry to the premises if he needed to. He didn't want to. But as time passed he felt that he may well have to resort to force. Then Yiannis Negroponte walked out of his front door.

'I've a warrant to search your garden, Mr Negroponte.' İkmen held the document up for him to see.

'You've searched already.'

'Not the garden,' İkmen said. 'We've a warrant to dig it up.'

Yiannis still didn't move towards the gate. 'Why? What are you looking for?'

'I've a warrant,' İkmen said again. 'Open the gate, Mr Negroponte, or I'll have to break it down.'

'Yes, but . . .'

İkmen looked at the constable with the battering ram. 'Yıldız . . .'

'All right! All right!' Yiannis ran up to the gate and unlocked it.

İkmen presented him with the warrant. 'We won't come into the house, Yiannis. But we have to do this.'

'Why?'

'Dr Ariadne Savva's child is still missing.'

'I don't know anything about that!' Yiannis said. 'I told you!'

Hakkı Bey watched them from the front door, frowning.

İkmen looked at him as well as at Yiannis Negroponte as he spoke. 'Yes, you told me, sir. But a man's word is sadly not proof.'

He pushed past Yiannis and called to Kerim, 'Sergeant Mungun, bring the men in.'

'Sir.'

Anastasia recognised İkmen's voice even if she couldn't hear what he was saying. He'd come back, as she'd known he would, because he too knew that something was wrong. First the young woman had disappeared, then the property developer had given up, and now she knew what Hakkı was, she felt unsafe.

He'd tried to come into her room but she'd screamed and although he'd begged and pleaded, he'd had to go. Yiannis had been in the bathroom and hadn't heard. But even if he'd been there she couldn't have formed the words she needed to make him understand. Now she just had to hope that the Albanian witch's son would find his mother's tarot card and understand what it meant. The breathing coming from the walls was very shallow now, the scratching non-existent. Time was short.

Pembe had found Madonna weeping and bleeding outside the Divan Hotel. She'd taken refuge in there with a journalist but then the police had tear-gassed the hotel. She'd had to get out to breathe. She'd been sick twice on the short journey to Sinem and Kerim's apartment.

Once indoors, Madonna went straight to the bathroom.

'She's lost her front teeth,' Pembe said. She shook her head. 'Bastards!'

Apart from a big tear in her top and some very matted hair, Pembe looked all right. Uncharitably, Sinem wondered if she'd holed up somewhere until the worst of the violence had passed. Even though she didn't have, and didn't want, a sexual relationship with her husband, Sinem still resented Pembe at times.

'They took Madame Edith away.'

'Where to?'

Pembe shrugged. 'Who knows? Where's Kerim?'

'At work,' Sinem said. 'Not Gezi, somewhere in Sultanahmet.'

'You should call him, ask him where Madame Edith is.'

'I can't do that,' Sinem said. 'He won't know. He's digging a garden trying to find the body of this missing baby.'

Pembe curled her lip. 'He might know.'

'He won't.'

She put her hand out. 'Oh, give me your phone and I'll call him. Come on.'

Pembe wouldn't call from her own phone because Kerim had said right from the start that he would never answer her calls when he was at work.

'No.' Sinem held her phone close to her chest.

'Why not?'

'Because he's at work. Because I don't want to worry him.'

Pembe's face reddened.

'I'm his wife,' Sinem said. 'I care about—'

'You're only his wife in name,' Pembe snapped. 'Anyway, what are you getting all protective about Kerim for? You don't even like cock.'

Sinem looked down. 'Kerim is my best friend,' she said. 'We've known each other since we were children.'

This time Pembe looked away. She was right. Sinem and Kerim had grown up together and there was a love between them that went beyond sex. It was something Pembe knew she

360

couldn't reach. She also knew that if Kerim were to have to make a choice between her and Sinem, she would be the one to go.

'All right,' she said. She looked at Sinem. Shrunken and twisted, she was in the kind of pain not even the Oramorph could touch. How could she even think about being jealous of a crippled woman who was also a lesbian? 'I'm sorry, Sinem.'

'It's OK.'

Madonna walked into the room and lisped, 'What am I going to do about my teeth?'

The guilt was bad but it was also useless. Pembe couldn't undo the fact she'd spent the night with a butch gold dealer in some part of Tarlabaşı even she'd never seen before. They'd done an awful lot of poppers but she'd needed to. The gold dealer had been a brute.

Pembe went over to Madonna and kissed her on the cheek. 'We'll get you implants,' she said.

Madonna sat down next to Sinem who put a hand on her knee. 'Yes.'

'How?'

'I dunno,' Pembe said. 'Maybe I'll go to that government rally this afternoon and demand compensation.'

'What government rally? Where?'

'Over in the Old City somewhere,' Pembe said. 'The unions are calling for a general strike and so the State has to rally its forces. It'll be full of men baying for the blood of perverts.'

'Us.'

'Yeah.'

'Well, they won't give you any money for my teeth,' Madonna said.

Pembe sighed. 'I was being ironic,' she said. 'I'd be lucky if those people just threw shit at me.'

It was her day off and so Mary Cox had decided to make the long journey from Bebek to Kazlıçeşme for the government rally. It was what Ahmet Bey would have done. But he couldn't. As she covered her hair with the scarf he'd given her for her last birthday, she cried. Where was he? Was he even alive? She had felt that she had finally managed to manoeuvre her way into his affections and then he'd disappeared. People meant him harm. It was the same with all men of vision. She'd seen those awful slums Ahmet Bey had redeveloped and so she knew how much he'd improved those areas. Why did people think that was a bad thing?

If Ahmet Bey had met an untimely end, would the family keep her on to look after Kelime? No one would want the child. Her mother was dead and Ahmet Bey's siblings would probably want to sell his house to pay for Kelime to be put into a home. She couldn't argue with them.

Mary took a plain brown coat out of her wardrobe and put it on. It was going to be hot outside but if she didn't dress modestly she'd never get in to the rally. Also, she knew that Ahmet Bey preferred women to be modest. She didn't care what people said about his mistress in Moda. She had been a one-off. And Mary didn't believe he'd run away because he'd killed that women either. He hadn't, she was sure of it.

She put on a pair of flat shoes and went out of the house to get the bus to Beşiktaş. Then she'd change on to a tram. Given the traffic and all the detritus from the rioting, it would take her a few hours to get to the Old City. Once there, however, she'd feel, she hoped, a little closer to Ahmet Bey. They were his people and she admired them. Mary hoped her Turkish was good enough for her to be able to follow the speeches.

*　　*　　*

'Don't cut that down, you moron!'

Çetin İkmen grabbed the constable's arm and pulled it and the machete it held away from the mulberry bush.

'That's an ancient mulberry,' he said. 'You don't chop the thing up!'

'But how do we dig the garden if we can't knock it all down?' the man said.

İkmen raised his eyes to heaven. Then he pointed to the gnarled trunk of the bush and its deeply embedded roots. 'I challenge you, Constable Baran,' he said, 'to find a way of burying a baby underneath this bush without damaging its root system. We're looking for disturbed ground. Get it? Disturbed ground.'

'All right.' He went to the flower bed beside the bush and started to dig.

'Thank you.' İkmen lit a cigarette. Kerim Gürsel, who had watched the altercation, came over.

'Nothing so far, sir?'

'Just morons who think that it's possible to bury the body of a baby underneath a bush without disturbing the soil,' he said. 'Where do they find them these days? Baran's not a child and yet he shows no common sense at all.'

'I think sometimes, sir, that a lot of city boys these days just don't have any contact with agriculture. They all live in apartments, without gardens.'

İkmen sighed. 'Yes, of course, you're right,' he said. 'Poor stupid bastard's probably only ever left his concrete hell to do his military service.'

'And that was probably in some—'

'End of the world shithole that's off the map,' İkmen said. 'I take your point, Kerim. There's no excuse for my middle-class ravings. I'm not even middle-class—'

'Aaaaggghh!'

Constable Baran was holding one hand up as if it were hurt or poisoned.

İkmen said, 'Have you injured yourself?'

But he just screamed again.

İkmen walked around the mulberry bush to the flower bed Baran had been digging. 'What the hell is it, man?'

Kerim followed.

Baran pointed at something on the ground, his eyes wide with fear.

'What is it?' İkmen asked.

Kerim Gürsel saw it first. 'This,' he said as he leaned forward to pick something up.

'Don't touch it, sir!' Baran flinched away. 'It's witchcraft!'

'Oh, don't be so—'

And then İkmen saw what Kerim had in his hand. It was the Devil, more specifically it was his mother's Devil tarot card. He looked up at the front of the Negroponte House and noticed that Madam Anastasia's window was directly above.

Chapter 31

'This is a sign, for me, isn't it?' İkmen said.

The old woman nodded her head.

There was no way Anastasia would have dropped one of Ayşe İkmen's precious tarot cards out of her bedroom window unless she had a purpose.

İkmen took one of her skinny brown and purple hands in his. 'I know it's hard for you to talk—'

'Then leave her alone!'

İkmen turned and looked at Yiannis Negroponte, who stood in the doorway to his mother's bedroom.

'She's demented,' he said. 'She can't do anything. She probably threw the card out without even knowing what she was doing.'

İkmen looked at Kerim Gürsel. 'Get him out please, Sergeant.'

'Yes. Sir.'

Yiannis Negroponte had already been warned when he'd tried to stop İkmen entering his mother's bedroom. Now he screamed, 'No!'

Kerim enlisted the help of one of the constables and took Yiannis out of the room.

İkmen looked into the old woman's deep black eyes. 'I know it's hard for you to speak,' he said. 'And I know that I should understand what the message you have sent me means. But you're going to have to help me.' He smiled. 'I'm not my mother, I can't read people's minds.'

She smiled back.

'Madam, if I remember correctly, the Devil in the tarot deck indicates deception.'

'In . . . part . . .'

'So someone is deceiving. You?'

She said nothing. Her injuries all those years ago had rendered her functional only at times. İkmen looked down at the Devil card again.

'Scapegoat.'

He looked up into her eyes again. 'Yes, that's another interpretation,' he said. 'The fact that the Devil has the hooves of a goat means we can make him the reason why we do bad things rather than taking responsibility for ourselves.'

She grimaced. In the few audiences he'd had with Madam Anastasia, İkmen had recognised when she was straining to say something. Frustrated, she beckoned him forwards. İkmen put his face close to hers and she scratched his cheek, lightly, with one twisted finger.

He shook his head. 'What do you mean?'

He could hear Yiannis arguing with Kerim outside. He heard Kerim say, 'If you want to get arrested, carry on!'

She heard it too. İkmen saw the panic enter her eyes and then she took a deep breath in. 'Prisoner,' she said.

'Prisoner? Where?'

'Here.'

'In this house?'

She scratched his face again and said, 'The walls . . .'

Professor Bozdağ put a hand on his chest.

'It's the Red Room,' he said.

366

'Yes,' İkmen said, 'I know.'

'I don't think you do,' the professor said. 'What do you mean when you say the words "red room"?'

'A rather extraordinary, in my opinion, Byzantine room made entirely of porphyry,' İkmen said. He touched the stone as if to make his point.

Professor Bozdağ had to be in late middle-age and yet he ran around that room like a child. 'Yes, but it's also *the* Red Room,' he said.

'Yes?' İkmen really wanted to get on with the process of somehow dismantling the walls. That was why he'd called the museum, so it could be done under academic supervision. If possible. Because if someone was trapped behind the tonnes of porphyry in the walls, he'd have to prioritise that person's survival whatever objections Professor Bozdağ might make. A forensic team already had a listening device normally used after earthquakes, slowly moving across the surfaces.

'The Red Room, the only entirely porphyry dressed room in the whole empire, was where Byzantine empresses gave birth to future rulers,' Bozdağ said. 'That is what being "born to the purple" means. When one was "born to the purple" one wasn't just royal, one was also born in this room. Arguably it was the most important room in the Great Palace. And one of the reasons why women could sometimes rule the empire unopposed was because they were born in this room. Dr Savva's favourite study, Empress Zoe, was born here. This is the Byzantine archaeological find of the century. You do know this?'

'Professor, I've reason to believe that someone is being held hostage behind one of these walls,' İkmen said. 'I'm very impressed with what you've told me, I'm amazed actually, but I have to get this person out. I asked you here to advise how we might do this without wrecking the place.'

'I accept you need to find where this person is,' Bozdağ said. 'But I do hope you won't just break these precious walls down without—'

'That's why we've got the listening equipment. It picks up noises the human ear can't,' İkmen said. 'If the team hear anything they think might be signs of life, I will have to give the order to break down whatever conceals it.'

'Smash up the walls.'

İkmen saw him shudder. 'Unless we can get it off in blocks or sheets. I know nothing about it. How thick is it? Do you know?'

'Porphyry was very expensive,' Bozdağ said. 'It comes from Egypt and so it had to be mined, transported and then fashioned by expert craftsmen. In Aya Sofya, which is all I have to measure this amazing place by, the stone literally dresses the walls. It was rendered into thin slivers using silk as a cutting tool. Absolutely niche technology. Brilliant!'

'You imagine this stone will be thin like that?'

'There will be brick or ordinary, non-decorative stone blocks behind it, I imagine. The porphyry will have been fixed to that with mortar and so immense care will have to be taken when loosening it. If, as I suspect, these sheets of porphyry are thin, then you risk cracking them if you try to wrench them off. I can't stress more forcefully—'

'Inspector İkmen!'

'What?'

Ali Bey, head of the forensic team, held the headphones he had been wearing out to İkmen. 'May be rats but I can hear something.'

'And there's something here that could be a cavity.' His partner, a female officer, looked into İkmen's eyes. 'It's only small.'

İkmen took the headphones and listened. For a moment he heard nothing and when something did come it wasn't much more than a click. Which could have been anything. He gave the headphones back. Then he turned to Kerim Gürsel. 'Get Hakkı Bey and Mr Negroponte down here.'

'Yes, sir.'

'What are you going to do?' Professor Bozdağ asked.

İkmen said to Ali Bey, 'Could that sound be human? Given your experience with this equipment?'

Ali Bey put his head on one side. He wasn't sure.

Professor Bozdağ said, 'If there's any doubt . . .'

'Well?' İkmen said.

Ali Bey sighed. 'Given what I've heard through this device before, I'd say it's a, well, a being,' he said. 'I think I got breathing. But as I say, it could be a rat or a bat or . . .'

'What are you going to do?' Professor Bozdağ said.

İkmen stayed silent. Kerim Gürsel and two constables escorted Yiannis Negroponte and Hakkı Bey into the Red Room.

'All right, no time to waste,' İkmen said. He put his hand on the wall. 'This is hollow and we can hear some sounds that might be human. Last chance. Do you know if anyone is imprisoned behind these walls?'

He'd asked them separately when he'd first worked out what Madam Anastasia had been saying to him. They had both said the same thing: they didn't know what he was talking about. This time they said nothing.

İkmen walked up to Yiannis. 'I know what this room is now,' he said. 'It must be very special to you.'

Yiannis turned his head away.

'But I'm going to have to break down that wall,' İkmen said. 'I'm going to have to damage the Red Room . . .'

He heard Professor Bozdağ say, 'Oh, my God.'

'And because we think a person might be trapped behind that wall, we're just going to have to smash our way in there,' İkmen continued.

369

He studied both their faces.

'And if we do find someone in there, we are going to talk again.'

Neither of them so much as flinched. İkmen told Kerim to take them away.

Professor Bozdağ grabbed İkmen's arm. 'For the love of God, you can't just smash your way in, man! This room is priceless!'

İkmen patted the professor's hand. 'We'll do our best,' he said. 'But if a human being is in these walls . . .'

'But why would that be?' Bozdağ said. He knew very little of the background to what was about to happen, so of course he was confused. 'Because an old lady says she can hear scratching sounds?'

'There's more to it than that,' İkmen said. 'All I will say is that the Negropontes have enemies. Now I'm going to have to request a team to come and get this wall down.'

Professor Bozdağ began to cry.

Once İkmen had called for technical assistance he phoned Mehmet Süleyman.

There was such a simplicity in the faith of the people around her that it made Mary want to weep. Women of all ages – she was only surrounded by women – looked up to the Prime Minister, who smiled at them and told them that everything was going to be all right. Gezi Park was under control now and he would personally make sure that anyone who had damaged property or injured police officers would be brought to justice.

A lot of people waved banners. One said 'Let's ruin this big plot!' In spite of trying to keep abreast of recent political developments, Mary had been distracted by the disappearance of Ahmet Öden, so she wasn't entirely sure what the reasons behind the Gezi protests were. She asked a woman next to her.

'Oh, it's a secular plot, that is,' the woman said. 'Those old generals who used to run the country want to do so again. But we won't let them.'

'No.'

She'd heard Mr Öden talk about 'them' – the secular opposition – his voice full of contempt. He'd told her once that when he was a child and the army ruled the country there had been curfews, religious people had been put in prison for no other reason than their faith and some of them had subsequently disappeared. The AK Parti had redressed the balance.

Mary felt inspired. The women around her were tactile and friendly and they shared their food and drink with her and with each other. These were good, kind people. Why had anyone ever wanted to hurt them? One woman explained, 'It's because there are more of us than them,' she said. 'If God wills, we have more children and we bring them up to be good Muslims. And that is a much more powerful thing to be than a godless soldier.'

'Yes.'

Everyone had come to hear the Prime Minister speak, which he did at length. And with passion. Some men in the crowd shouted out their desire to go to Gezi and finish off the traitors in the park. Mary, brought to tears by the ardour people were exhibiting, screamed her desire to join them.

Professor Bozdağ had gone into the garden. Kerim Gürsel had taken him out at İkmen's request. As soon as the stone cutters had arrived, he'd tried to get involved, so he'd had to go. But as the professor had predicted, the porphyry in the Red Room was thin. Underneath it was undressed stone, and below that were bricks.

İkmen joined Süleyman in the Negropontes' kitchen.

Süleyman offered him a cigarette. 'Why do you think that Madam Anastasia's imprisoned individual is down here?'

İkmen took the cigarette and lit up. 'Because of the tapping in the walls,' he said. 'The house is largely wooden. Where could you imprison someone in a structure with such a thin skin?'

'Who do you think is in there? Öden?'

İkmen shrugged. 'He's still missing.'

Stone cutting began again in the Red Room. When the technicians stopped to clear the detritus away, İkmen said, 'You know, that room in there is the Red Room where only true Byzantine emperors and empresses were born. It was part of the Great Palace.'

'Why's it under this house?'

'The Negropontes have lived on this site forever,' İkmen said. 'They must have taken it upon themselves to preserve it. I imagine that when the city was first conquered, people knew where the Red Room was. Land levels rise over time, so after a while it got lost.'

'Do you think that Ariadne Savva found it?'

'I don't know. But if she did then I wonder whether she found it with or without Yiannis Negroponte's knowledge.'

'You're thinking he might have killed her? Because she knew about this place?'

'You know the lengths he went to, to protect this place,' İkmen said. 'All those optical illusions. This place means something to these people that we can only glimpse. History is always written by the victors, isn't it? We forget about the losers and what was important and sacred to them. We throw their magic into the dustbin of history.'

'Inspector İkmen! You need to see this! Now!'

The voice came from the Red Room. İkmen looked at Süleyman. They both got up and walked into the dark porphyry space together.

Chapter 32

He'd been almost dead. He still was, in spite of the machinery that was keeping him alive. Ahmet Öden was a Type 1 diabetic and he hadn't eaten anything since he'd disappeared. He was also dehydrated, unconscious and, when he'd been found, covered in his own excrement. The only things that had been discovered with him in the cavity where he'd been bricked up were an empty jug of water and the remains of a candle. How long he'd been in complete darkness was unknown. But whoever had put him there had done so with his suffering in mind.

'I can understand why you hate Mr Öden,' İkmen said to Yiannis Negroponte. 'Especially now I know how important your home is to you. How'd you do it, Mr Negroponte? How'd you get Öden to come to the house without any of his people? Was it at night?'

Yiannis Negroponte said nothing. He'd declined the offer of a lawyer, opting instead for silence.

İkmen ploughed on. 'Do you even know? Or did Hakkı Bey do it all? He's done most things for your family over the years. Not now, though. Now he's with Inspector Süleyman, and I believe he's talking.'

He wasn't, but it was never a bad idea to put doubts into a suspect's mind about his fellows. Yiannis Negroponte didn't react. He stared at the table in front of him in the same way he'd done ever since he'd entered the interview room.

İkmen looked at Kerim Gürsel and shrugged. 'Well, Sergeant, tell me what I can do? I have a man here who won't talk about another man who was imprisoned in his house.'

'Can't see that you can avoid charging him with imprisonment and attempted murder, sir,' Kerim Gürsel said.

'Or maybe actual murder,' İkmen said.

Yiannis looked up.

'He could die, Yiannis.'

He looked down again and then he said, 'Who is looking after my mother?'

'We're looking for Hakkı Bey's son Lokman,' İkmen said. 'She knows him. In the meantime social services have become involved.'

'She's not to go into an old age home.'

'If we find Lokman and he agrees to care for Madam Anastasia for the time being, she won't,' İkmen said. 'If not, I don't know.'

'There's her priest, Father Diogenes,' Yiannis said. 'At the Aya Triada. Why can't I go home?'

'I've told you,' İkmen said, 'you are here because we found an almost deceased missing person, Ahmet Öden, imprisoned in your house.'

'Has Öden said I put him there?'

'No. He can't speak, he's in a coma. He may never speak again, but hopefully we'll be able to recover enough evidence from the scene and beyond to be able to convict someone.' He leaned on the table. 'Tell us what you know, Yiannis. This terrible thing happened in your house, you must know something. The Red Room is the most precious part of your home. You know everything that goes on in it.'

Yiannis Negroponte closed his eyes and went silent again.

'I could have you beaten so hard your kidneys explode.'

The old man looked at Mehmet Süleyman without emotion.

'We're looking for your son. When I get hold of him, I could do what I want with him too. He lives in the east, I could charge him with terrorist offences.'

'Do what you will, Mehmet Bey,' Hakkı said. 'I can't tell you anything about the Öden man.'

Mehmet Süleyman sat down. Then he put his legs on the table in front of Hakkı Bey and lit a cigarette. 'You've worked for the Negropontes all your life,' he said. 'Why?'

'My father worked for them, and his father.'

'Why?'

'Madam's grandfather, Bacchus Bey, he took my grandfather in.'

'Why?'

'He was a hamal,' the old man said. 'Carrying things for rich people. Bacchus Bey wanted him to take a bed from Sirkeci Station to his house. My grandfather did it, but when he got to the house he was exhausted. He'd been wounded in the war against the Arabs. One of his legs was twisted and partially paralysed. Bacchus Bey gave him a job in his garden and my grandmother a job in the house. When my father grew up, Bacchus Bey gave him work too. Madam's father continued the tradition. Then Madam.'

'And what about your son? What about Lokman? Will he work in the Negroponte House when you die?'

'No. It's different times now. He works for his father-in-law on his farm. He has another life.'

Süleyman smoked. 'Mmm. I suppose the Negropontes must be running out of money now,' he said. 'Mind you, should they decide to exhibit the Red Room . . . I do know what it is, you realise, Hakkı Bey. I know how important it is too.'

'You are an educated man.'

'It's where the Byzantine emperors were born. Being born in that room meant that you were automatically "born to the purple" and so could legitimately rule the Byzantine Empire. When Ahmet Öden was pressing Mr Negroponte to buy the house, did he know about the Red Room?'

'We have always kept it to ourselves,' Hakkı said.

'Yes, but did he know about it, somehow?'

'We kept it to ourselves,' he reiterated. 'Why?'

'I think I ask the questions,' Süleyman said.

'Yes, Mehmet Süleyman Bey—'

'But I'll take it.' He took his feet off the table. 'You ask why. Because anyone would have to be either truly full of hatred or fearful almost beyond reason to do what has been done to Mr Öden. Walling a person up is mediaeval-style torture. In fact I think the Byzantine emperors did it to their enemies. Whoever did it to Mr Öden wanted him to die but they also wanted him to suffer. He knew about the Red Room, didn't he? He knew about it and had plans for it you and Mr Negroponte didn't like.'

Hakkı said nothing.

'We'll find out,' Süleyman said. 'Whether Mr Öden is able to talk to us eventually or whether he is left without speech or dies is irrelevant to us. Hakkı Bey, I know that the Negropontes are your employers, that you feel grateful to them, that there is a connection between you, but—'

'Mehmet Bey, what of Madam Anastasia?'

The sudden change of subject, briefly, threw him. 'What?'

'Madam. Who is looking after her? She can't be in that house on her own. She can't feed herself.'

He'd tried to get to the old woman when he was arrested. He'd begged to see her and Çetin İkmen had asked Madam Anastasia if she wanted to see the old man before he left the

376

house. But she had been very firm that she didn't. She'd seen Yiannis, but not Hakkı. And yet his eyes were filling with tears when he spoke about her.

'Madam Negroponte isn't your concern,' Süleyman said.

'Yes, she is!'

'No, she isn't. She rejected you. Remember? She saw her son, but not you. I know you think you're part of the family but you're not. You're just a servant. They know it and so should you.'

Hakkı Bey began to cry.

'Oh for God's sake!' Süleyman stood up and paced the room impatiently. 'Ahmet Öden's argument, if you can even call it that, was with the Negropontes, not with you! If Yiannis Negroponte walled Öden up in the Red Room then it's your duty to inform on him. You owe him nothing! Did he threaten you? Make you help him entomb Öden?'

Hakkı didn't speak.

Süleyman shook his head and sat down again. 'You're a sad man, Hakkı Bey,' he said. 'A man who has lost his identity, who doesn't know his place. You've been with the Negropontes for so long, you think you're one of them. You're not. They have abandoned you. Reclaim yourself now and tell me what you know.'

Again, Hakkı said nothing.

'When people's backs are against the wall, Hakkı Bey, people tend to protect their own. And these people are not your own.'

Hakkı, no longer crying, raised his head. 'Ah well, that's where you're wrong, Mehmet Süleyman Bey.'

Lale Hanım, Ahmet Öden's eldest sister, was one of those very stylish covered women. Her scarves were Hermès and she wore a pair of the prettiest, tiniest Jimmy Choo shoes that Mary had

377

ever seen. Compared to Lale Hanım, she felt like a bag lady. Not that it mattered. Just one room away, Ahmet Öden lay on a bed, on life support, fighting for his life. She'd been told that those Greeks he'd been dealing with had tried to kill him by burying him alive behind a wall. The things people did!

Mary looked at Kelime. Happily playing with her Barbie house on the floor, she seemed to have lost not only much of her anxiety about her father in recent days, but also any real notion of his existence. She had been fed – Semih Bey, Ahmet Bey's brother, had said she was to be given everything and anything she wanted – she had her toys and her television. Now she was chattering away to herself and even laughing.

A doctor entered. Semih Öden stood up.

'Are you Mr Öden's next of kin?' the doctor said.

Mary felt her heart squeeze with anxiety.

'Yes,' Semih said. 'But you can say anything you need to, to all of us.'

The doctor looked around the small, stuffy room with emotionless eyes.

'Ahmet Bey is suffering from a condition called diabetic ketoacidosis. It's serious.'

'We know,' Semih said. 'What are you doing about it?'

His tone was aggressive. Mary wondered whether it was just because he was so worried about his brother or because the hospital and its staff were foreign. There was a rumour going round that the Germans were behind the Gezi protests and this was a German hospital. It was also one of the best in the city.

'Mr Öden has some swelling of the brain tissue,' the doctor said. 'We are trying to reduce that. Also the kidneys have been compromised and so we are giving him dialysis.'

Lale Hanım looked confused. Her brother looked as if he was about to explain when the doctor said, 'Due to the insulin deficit that he suffered, his body is breaking down. We are trying to arrest this process.'

'So will he be—'

'If he survives, I cannot say what his prognosis might be,' the doctor said. 'When the brain swells there is always damage. Time will tell.'

Kelime, in her own little world of Barbie, chuckled.

The doctor left and Mary went to the toilet so she could cry her heart out on her own.

'When we find Hakkı's son, who is probably in some goat-fucking settlement with a broken gearbox, we will ask him what he knows,' İkmen said. 'But it's intriguing.'

He lit Süleyman's cigarette and then his own. Other guilty smokers also haunted the car park, looking shifty. İkmen always made sure that he didn't look in the least bit guilty and smoked openly and effusively.

'When Hakkı's grandfather went to work at the Negroponte House, he brought his wife with him,' Süleyman said. 'The couple were childless which, Hakkı claims, was down to his grandfather. Following this logic, when Bacchus Bey had an affair with Hakkı's grandmother, she got pregnant.'

'With Hakkı's father.'

'Yes.'

'Did he say any more than that?' İkmen said.

'Said he was one of the family and then he clammed up,' Süleyman said. 'If he is a member of the Negroponte family he won't say anything against them, will he?'

'No. But Mehmet, the fact remains that we found Öden in that house, in a room the Negropontes have kept secret, one way or another, for possibly centuries. Who else could have put him there? And have some faith in the forensics. There will be evidence of Yiannis or Hakkı, or both, inside that – what did you call it?'

'Burial chamber.'

'Death niche.'

'You didn't find forensic evidence for any Negroponte involvement with Dr Ariadne Savva,' Süleyman said.

'No. But then maybe they didn't know her,' İkmen said. 'Maybe there's some other porphyry room hidden somewhere in this city that only she knew about. This is İstanbul, Mehmet, anything is possible. You know Professor Bozdağ told me that there are more classical Greek ruins in Turkey than there are in Greece?'

'How was Professor Bozdağ when you left him?'

'Like an excited five year old. I did think I'd have to tie him down or put him in a cell to stop him telling the world about the Red Room.'

Süleyman smiled. 'How did you persuade him?'

'I told him that if he started telling everyone about it, they'd want to see it, and he'd have to beat them off with a stick to get to it. Not that I think that's true.'

'You don't?'

'I think that some people may well want to see it but others won't. The turn-Aya-Sofya-back-into-a-mosque mob certainly won't. If Ahmet Öden didn't know about the Red Room he was going to get a nasty shock when he eventually bought the Negroponte House. Not that I think he didn't know.'

'You don't?'

'No. For all his talk about the need for a truly luxury hotel in the Old City, with the Four Seasons just down the road, what was he trying to prove? And why the Negroponte House – why not the Alans' place next door or as well as? Hakkı Bey himself told me that Öden's father Taha was fanatically xenophobic.

Ahmet's not exactly on board with multiculturalism, is he? I know he's an Aya-Sofya-must-be-a-mosque nut.' He frowned. 'You know some of them pray behind Aya Sofya?'

'Yes.'

'Tell no one, but my wife included,' İkmen said. He rolled his eyes. 'She saw Hakkı Bey and his son on her way there the other day. She said she thought he was going to pray somewhere.'

'He's a Muslim, of course,' Süleyman said. 'His antecedents have been kept secret.'

'Ah, secrets, yes,' İkmen said. 'What damage they do, eh?'

'We all have them, Çetin. Sometimes for very good reasons.'

'I know.' İkmen still had a few, he'd once had a lot more. His sergeant had a big secret. He'd have to talk to him about that one day. He cleared his throat. 'So Hakkı Bey is a Negroponte and we therefore have to assume that he won't give us Yiannis.'

'Ah, but wasn't there something about Yiannis Negroponte being an imposter?'

'Years ago, yes,' İkmen said. 'And I thought that Hakkı was suspicious of him. I think he may still be. But the other aspect to consider here is Hakkı's feelings for Madam Anastasia. He loves her, she loves Yiannis. He won't betray someone she loves.'

'He loves her?'

'He rescued her from the mob in 1955 and he's looked after her ever since,' İkmen said. 'I'd say that was love. And she was very beautiful. I remember her well.'

'And they are related.'

'They are connected,' İkmen said. 'The only thing that I find truly odd is the way she refused to see Hakkı when we left the house. He's been her right hand for almost sixty years. Why would she turn on him now?'

* * *

A doctor came to take something called DNA. He was an odd little man with that pale red hair typical of some of the south eastern Kurds. Hakkı let him take mouth swabs and a blood sample. The doctor explained that the DNA would tell the police everything they wanted to know about him, including his ethnic background.

He didn't care. So they'd find out he was Greek? So what? He knew that anyway. He'd not been as Greek as Nikos Bey, which was why Madam had rejected him. But that didn't matter any more.

The doctor left. Then he heard another door open somewhere outside. For a while there was no sound but then he heard raised voices. He thought one of them belonged to Yiannis, but he couldn't work out what he was saying. Or even if it was him. The cells were full of protesters from Gezi Park, the place was full to bursting. Alone, all he could think about was why Madam had suddenly rejected him.

Chapter 33

Ahmet had hundreds of e-mails. Semih would require help to answer them. But initially he needed to separate the urgent post from the trash. For some reason there was a load of stuff about Byzantine emperors, specifically about the last one, Constantine Palaiologos. Why? Had the end of Byzantium also been part of his brother's obsession with the wretched Negroponte family and their room? He discarded it all. When he first saw the e-mail from *dNa Search Team*, he thought it was rubbish too. But then he opened it. He wished that he hadn't.

He'd understood and gone along with Ahmet's plans for the Negroponte House for years. In a way he'd agreed with them. But he'd also known what they were based upon and he'd never been comfortable with that. Semih only just remembered his father, Taha, as a man who had been short on patience and would quickly resort to violence if his children disobeyed him.

The story with the Negropontes was that Semih's grandfather Resat had been offered a job by the then head of the family, Bacchus Negroponte. Resat had been a builder and the job he had been promised was gardening, but work of any sort was hard to come by at the time. However, this offer was suddenly withdrawn and the job given to Hakkı Bey's grandfather. Why it happened was a mystery, but Resat Öden had accepted it as the will of God and never bore the Negropontes any ill will. Unlike his father. Years of poverty had followed the loss of that job, which Taha never forgot. And in 1955 he'd paid back all and any Greeks he could get his hands on, in blood. He'd also held in his mind what his father had said about a secret Byzantine room in the Negroponte House. It was, the old man had told him, a great marvel he must never tell anyone about. The last great Byzantine relic. But Taha had told Ahmet, who had seen the famous room and promised his father that one day he would destroy it. Which was exactly what Taha had wanted. It was great revenge.

And now here was a report on what was described as a 'very small' blood sample taken from someone his brother had described as 'male, allegedly ethnically Greek'. Who else could it be except Yiannis Negroponte? How had Ahmet got his blood?

Semih Öden read it and then he read it again. Yiannis Negroponte had been arrested, along with Hakkı Bey, for the attempted killing of his brother. Soon one or both of them would almost certainly be charged with his murder. A phone call from the ward doctor that morning had let Semih know that his brother was fitting. The swelling in the brain, in spite of their best efforts, hadn't reduced and the doctor wanted to know if he could administer diamorphine to alleviate Ahmet's distress. Semih knew what that meant. Once he was on regular doses of morphine, the end wouldn't be far away. Lale and his other sister Rabia were at the hospital all the time. Semih wanted to be, but someone had to run the company and he'd have to get used to it.

What he'd also have to get used to was not having to do as his brother told him. On the one hand this made Semih want to cry, but on the other it placed a piece of steel in his soul. He'd never wanted the Negroponte House. There were so many better places the company could build a hotel. So those Greeks had the Red Room of the Byzantine emperors? Good luck to them. His grandfather Resat had always had a great affection for that family. The bad blood raised by his father had only served to make Ahmet crazy and bring about this tragedy he was sure Yiannis Negroponte hadn't sought. He could even see, now, why he'd tried to kill Ahmet. He also decided that it wasn't his place to tell the police about that. They'd find out in time. They performed DNA tests themselves.

Semih deleted the e-mail.

Pale and hollow-eyed was how Çetin İkmen would have described Kerim Gürsel. Without looking up from his paperwork, he said, 'Events in Beyoğlu keep you awake last night, Kerim?'

After the government rally in Kazlıçeşme, police action in the Beyoğlu area had increased. A lot more people had been injured, including some of the doctors and nurses who'd gone to Gezi to treat the wounded. Samsun Bajraktar, ever the fount of all knowledge, had phoned İkmen at two a.m. to tell him that, 'Your lot are punching medics now!'

İkmen knew he needed to speak to Kerim. Yiannis Negroponte, who had refused to give a DNA sample the previous evening, was apparently having his breakfast in his cell and wasn't due to come before İkmen and Dr Selim for a second, hopefully less fraught, attempt at DNA testing for another half an hour. But how to start? For a few minutes he thought about all sorts of things he could say to introduce the subject of Kerim's sexuality without causing the young man to panic. But he couldn't.

'Kerim?'

He looked up. 'Sir?'

'Kerim, what I'm about to say to you is said out of concern and not prejudice or accusation.'

The pale face became still paler. 'Sir?'

'Kerim, I know that your marriage is one of convenience. I know your wife is not, unlike you, a lover of men.'

He saw Kerim's head sink slowly down into his shoulders. 'Oh, God. How do you know?'

The way he didn't even try to deny it made İkmen admire him.

'It's not important, and it isn't a problem,' İkmen said. 'Not for me. But—'

'But you want me to resign because of other people.'

'No. Oh, no, no, no, no, no!' İkmen stood up and paced his office. Then he opened his window and lit a cigarette. 'No, Kerim, I don't. That's the last thing I want. After the death of Sergeant Farsakoğlu, well, you've, you've . . .'

Kerim had made him feel something like himself again.

'Kerim, I want you to know that I will always, *always* fight your corner. And for what it's worth, I don't believe you'll have any problems with Commissioner Teker either. But we live in what the Chinese call "interesting times", which means we have some real challenges in our lives now. I want to tell you to be careful.'

'Yes, sir.'

'There's nothing I'd like more than to see you at the World Aids Day march. I go every year with my cousin who lost a partner to Aids. But you must be careful. You're still a young man at the beginning of your career and—'

'Sir, you don't have to—'

'You have not replaced Ayşe. I still miss her,' İkmen said. 'I always will. But I'd miss you too. Selfishly, I don't want to go through that again. Kerim, you can be open with me and you must.'

There was a lot of noise coming from somewhere. İkmen shook his head. 'Why do we have cells creaking under the weight of protesters? See what I mean about interesting times?'

His office door flew open and smashed against the wall.

Commissioner Teker, her hair unusually loose and tangled, put a bloodstained hand on the door frame. İkmen shot to his feet.

'Down to the cells. Now!' she said.

The pistol lay two metres away from the body which lay face down underneath the cell window.

'How did he get it?' İkmen said.

'He asked for tea,' Teker said. 'Sergeant Korkmaz brought it to him.'

İkmen had seen custody sergeant Korkmaz weeping.

'He didn't know it had gone,' Teker said. 'Not even when he heard the shot.'

'He was a stage magician,' İkmen said. 'They can take your balls without your knowledge.'

He put a hand up to his head. Yiannis Negroponte had fought to refuse a DNA test the previous evening. Now they could take as much of his blood as they wanted, but he'd blown a hole in his skull, and so whatever the results, they would never be able to ask him what those results might mean.

'God.'

A crowd of officers stood behind him, jostling for position, trying to have a look. İkmen, annoyed by their prurience, elbowed one in the stomach.

'Dr Sarkissian is on his way,' Teker said.

Voices from other cells demanded to know what was going on and who had been shot. Someone shouted, 'Fucking shut up!'

İkmen moved away from the cell.

Looking at the weeping Korkmaz, he felt nothing but rage. He'd told the custody officers, including Korkmaz, that Yiannis Negroponte was a tricksy fellow who had been a stage magician back in Germany. 'Didn't you listen to what I said about that man?' he asked.

Korkmaz cried harder.

'It's no good fucking crying now!' He turned to the other officers. 'And someone check on the old man Hakkı Bey! If he decides to top himself we'll never know what happened.'

'Sir, there is the victim . . .' Kerim began.

'Oh, God! What? You believe in miracles now, do you, Sergeant Gürsel? Give me strength!' He walked away. 'If anyone wants me I'll be smoking myself to death in the car park.'

Lokman Atasu and his family had only got as far as Kayseri in their ancient truck. Although the gearbox hadn't broken, as Çetin İkmen had predicted, the exhaust had blown and the local police had eventually found him at a breaker's yard looking for a cheap replacement.

When he heard what had happened to his father, he agreed to go back to İstanbul. He took his wife and children with him. They arrived at Hakkı's flat in the afternoon, then Lokman went to see Madam Anastasia.

It was odd seeing police officers stationed outside the gate to the Negroponte House. A covered woman who said she worked for social services took him into the salon where he met a smart police officer called Süleyman. He asked Lokman to sit down, which he was reluctant to do because he knew he had some oil on his clothes. He put some newspaper down and then he sat.

'I'm afraid I have some bad news for you,' Süleyman began.

'Dad?'

'No. Your father is still in custody, but he's all right. No, I'm afraid that not only is the man we found imprisoned in this house, Ahmet Öden, dead but Mr Yiannis Negroponte is dead too. He committed suicide.'

Lokman began to shake. Yiannis Negroponte had been in

police custody and everyone knew what happened to people in cells. Everyone knew that 'suicide' could be a euphemism.

'Does Madam Negroponte know?'

'No.'

The officer was looking at him in a way that seemed to suggest he wanted Lokman to tell her.

'She's an old lady and very fragile,' Süleyman said.

'Dad'll have to tell her. She might be all right if he does it.'

'Madam Negroponte won't see your father,' Süleyman said.

That didn't make sense. 'Why not?'

'We don't know. We thought that maybe you could tell us?'

'No.'

Süleyman leaned forwards. 'Your father has told us that he, and so you, are related to the Negroponte family through your grandfather.'

He'd never been comfortable with that. He wasn't ashamed. In fact he was proud. But he'd always felt it undermined what he considered his identity. 'Yes.'

'An illicit connection but valid.'

'I don't know much about it,' Lokman said. 'Dad never behaved as anything more than a servant. He didn't abuse it. What happened between his grandmother and Bacchus Bey was wrong. But we are who we are. Our blood isn't pure.'

'Unlike Madam's.'

'No.'

'Lokman, what do you know about the Red Room?'

He knew they'd found it. The police in Kayseri said that the property developer, Ahmet Öden, had been found walled up down there. They'd said his father had done it. Lokman knew nothing about that. What he did know about was bad enough, but he didn't know about that.

'It's where the Byzantine emperors were born,' he said. 'The

Negropontes and us protected it. It's all part of the Greek past. Christian. But it's also part of me, you know?'

'Did you feel that Mr Yiannis Negroponte was "part of you" too?' Süleyman asked. 'It's thought that your father has always been suspicious about his origins.'

'Yeah. When he first came, we were. But Madam said she recognised him immediately. I think Dad thought he was not trustworthy because of the magic. And he couldn't believe that the baby Yiannis had survived.'

'What do you think?'

He shrugged. 'Don't know. I wasn't born in 1955. Story was that a Turkish woman stole the baby from the back of the Negropontes' shop. Madam said she saw her. Dad's always had his doubts.'

'Lokman, we have taken samples from Yiannis Negroponte for DNA analysis. You know what that is?'

'Yes. It's to find out who someone's related to.'

'Yes. So in order to find out if Yiannis was Madam's son, we need to compare his samples to hers. It means taking blood from her. This is obviously a delicate matter and normally we'd ask your father to help persuade her, but . . .'

'She's got a doctor. You could ask him.'

'We could but we think that . . . Lokman, someone will have to tell Madam that Yiannis is dead and—'

'I can't do it! I can't!'

'But who else can? If we tell her the shock may be too great. You are at least a relative of—'

'Call her doctor! I don't know how she'll take it! We were never close, not like her and Dad. Why won't she speak to him?'

'I don't know.'

'Does he?'

'He won't say.'

Lokman shook his head.

'I'd ask you to speak to him, but—'

'No. No, I'll see him but I can't make him say what he won't. I can't make him do anything. I never have. He's always only thought about her, Madam. I don't matter, Inspector. Not really.'

The smart policeman sighed. 'Well, Lokman, then can you tell what, if anything, you know about a woman called Ariadne Savva?'

Lokman felt bile rise in his throat. It made his denial sound fuzzy.

'Are you sure you've not heard that name? From your father or from Yiannis Negroponte?'

'No.'

It wasn't cold in that room but Lokman felt chilled. And he had to wait a long time for the policeman to stop looking at him, which was hard. But eventually Inspector Süleyman said, 'OK. Now are you all right looking after Madam for the time being?'

'As long as I don't have to be the one to tell her that Yiannis is dead, yes,' Lokman said.

'I understand.'

Did the policeman see that his brow was slathered in cold sweat?

Mary had to tell Kelime that her father had died. She had to explain what death meant. But the girl didn't understand. In the end her Uncle Semih told her that Ahmet had gone away on business. She wouldn't see the funeral, none of the women in the family would. It wasn't done in pious circles.

Mary cried. Kelime's aunts watched with dead eyes as the girl played while she went to her room and wept into her pillows. Semih Bey had said that she could stay on as Kelime's nanny for as long as the house remained under Öden family ownership. He'd have to discuss what would happen next with his sisters after the funeral. But for Mary every light had gone out of her life. Ahmet Bey had gone and all she was left with was hate for that awful family who had killed him. Why Semih Bey had decided not to buy and then knock down that wretched house, she couldn't imagine. But he'd sent a letter to the old woman whose terrible son had killed Ahmet Bey, telling her that he didn't want to buy her home any more. Why had he done that?

Mary couldn't understand why he didn't go there and kill her.

It was difficult to see how the old woman took the news. Speech was so difficult for her. Only her eyes showed her pain, which was dry and without hope. Her doctor, an Armenian called Zakaryan, held her hand. He spoke to her in Greek, which Süleyman only partly understood. He told her that Yiannis had died and asked her if she wanted to see Hakkı, but she shook her head. How Zakaryan persuaded her to let him take some blood, Süleyman couldn't work out, but he did. Lokman watched from the hall outside.

When the doctor had gone, Süleyman asked Madam Negroponte if she wanted anything and told her that Lokman, who had gone to the kitchen, would soon be bringing her a drink. But she wouldn't let him go. She pulled his sleeve, remarkably forcefully.

For a while they just looked at each other and, although he was tempted to speak, Süleyman didn't. In the end she said, 'Hakkı . . . buried Nikos.'

'Your husband is buried in Şişli, yes,' he said. 'Hakkı Bey rescued you.'

She clenched her teeth. 'He . . . killed . . .' She coughed, clenched her teeth again. 'He killed one Turk. Then . . . killed . . . my husband.'

Her brain was damaged and she'd just had a shock. But she'd accepted Yiannis' death, as far as Süleyman could tell.

He asked, 'How?'

'Again. Buried . . . alive.'

'In this house?'

He looked around the room, he didn't know why. What did he expect to see? A ghost? But his whole body was cold now.

'N-no . . .'

'Madam Anastasia, your husband Nikos Bey died in 1955. He's buried in Şişli Cemetery. I really don't understand. How could he have been buried alive?'

And then she sat up, suddenly and very quickly, and she said, in perfect Turkish, 'Because I saw Hakkı carry Nikos' body away. I watched him and his eyes sprang open. I heard him trying to get out for years.' She screamed. Süleyman heard Lokman run up the stairs. 'I remembered. I remembered.'

Chapter 34

It was the dead time of the morning. A day of strikes by five trade unions in support of the Gezi protests had failed to bring the country to a standstill and İstanbul's police cells were still full of demonstrators. Old Hakkı Bey remained incarcerated too. But at least he was in the relatively sanitary surroundings of an interview room. He'd asked to be there and he'd asked for İkmen and Süleyman very shortly after he'd been told of Yiannis Negroponte's death.

'I killed Ahmet Öden,' he said. 'I lured him to the house, disabled him and then buried him behind a false wall. Yiannis had nothing to do with it.'

'Why did you do it?' İkmen asked.

'To stop him. He wanted the house. He wasn't going to be dissuaded.'

'And why wasn't he going to be dissuaded, Hakkı Bey? Was it because he knew about the Red Room and he wanted it?'

'He knew about it. His grandfather had seen it. He saw it too. He was just a builder years ago. He and some others came to the house to do some work. The family always tried to give the Ödens work because of what Bacchus Bey did.'

'By letting your grandfather have the gardening job?'

'Yes. Although I never told Yiannis that. He would've gone mad. It was all wrong. Bacchus Bey was sorry for my grandfather, but it was when he saw my grandmother who came to give him his lunch that he made up his mind. He wanted her and he had her. You know the rest. Taha Öden, Ahmet's father, always bore ill will to the Negropontes. He was a bigot and a racist. I know that Ahmet Öden wanted to destroy the Red Room and I am glad he's dead so he can't do that.'

'You confess to his murder?' Süleyman said.

'Yes. Me alone,' he said.

'Oh come on, Hakkı Bey!'

'Me, alone!' He raised a finger. 'Not Yiannis, me. Do you want a confession or don't you, Çetin Bey?'

'I want the truth.'

'The truth is, I killed Öden and I killed his mistress too,' Hakkı said.

'Aysel Ocal or Gülizar?'

'When Öden began persecuting us, I began to study his habits. I waited for him to go out one night and then I went to Moda and I killed her. I knew that eventually you'd point the finger at Öden. I thought that would stop him.'

İkmen frowned. 'How did you know that Öden had a mistress in Moda?'

'As I told you, I watched him.'

'Yes, but—'

'I killed her! Write it down. I confess. You're Turkish policemen, aren't you? Don't you like confessions?'

'We like the truth.'

'And that is what it is.'

The two men looked at each other for a moment. Then İkmen said, 'And Dr Ariadne Savva?'

'I don't know who that is,' he said.

'You're sure?'

'I'm certain.'

İkmen, who was as stiff as a tree after a long, hot day punctuated by corpses and his colleagues' incompetence, said, 'And what about Nikos Negroponte? Did you kill him?'

The old man's face flushed. 'What?'

'Nikos Bey, your old employer,' İkmen said. 'Did you kill him during the 1955 riots? I know, and I'm not alone in this, that you have loved Madam Anastasia all your life. I can imagine how galling it must have been to you, to all intents and purposes a relative just like Nikos, to have not even been considered as marriage material. Did you think that if you killed him in the madness of the riots you could have Anastasia for yourself?'

For over a minute, no words were spoken. The old man sat with his mouth open, his breathing coming short and ragged. His throat full of phlegm, he said, 'I would never have killed Nikos Bey. Never! Madam loved him! Where did you get such an idea?'

'From Madam Anastasia,' Süleyman said. 'She finally remembered.'

'Madam . . .'

'You had to kill a Turk to protect her. But before you took her out of the shop on İstiklal Caddesi, you removed Nikos Bey.'

'Yes . . .'

'You threw him over your shoulder like an old sack, like something discarded, that you had no care for.'

'I did care for him! I took him out of there and I buried him—'

'Alive!' Süleyman said. 'You buried him alive!'

For a moment it was as if he didn't understand. Then he said, 'Those animals were burning the dead, violating them. I ran with his body to the school and I covered him with earth to protect him from them.'

'His eyes were open,' İkmen said. 'Madam Anastasia saw

them open as you lifted him on to your back. You buried him alive so you could have her for yourself!'

'No. No!' He stood up.

'Sit down, Hakkı Bey!'

'No!' He walked over to İkmen.

Süleyman stood.

'No, Çetin Bey, Madam is wrong.'

'She remembered when she saw you walking out of her bedroom two days ago,' İkmen said. 'Your back bent, your—'

'No! He was dead! If his eyes came open it was because that is what happens with corpses sometimes, you must know that! He was dead. I took him to the school then I came back for her and I took her to the hospital. But her mind had gone. I was too late . . .' He walked back to his chair and sat down again. 'I went back later and I buried him properly. He was dead.'

'In the Galatasaray grounds?'

'Yes.'

'So who is buried in Nikos Negroponte's grave in Şişli?'

'I don't know,' he said. 'There were dead bodies everywhere. Madmen were ripping the faces from them. It could have been anyone.'

'So why didn't you tell the authorities where Nikos Negroponte was buried after the riots were over?' Süleyman asked.

'As a Turk? They were all very sorry for the Greeks by that time. They would have said that I had killed him. I had to leave him where he was.'

'You know that he was found, don't you?' Süleyman said. 'I've seen him. A skeleton with very complicated dental work.'

'Nikos Bey always had bad teeth. He liked cakes too much . . .'

İkmen looked down at his notes. 'Madam Negroponte says

that she heard her husband trying to free himself from his premature grave.'

'She couldn't have!'

'No,' he said. 'And we have to accept that the poor lady is brain damaged, but Hakkı Bey, we also have to find the truth.'

'I've told you the truth! I didn't kill Nikos Bey!'

'And yet you have loved Madam Anastasia all your life, haven't you?'

His face fell and he cried. 'Of course I have,' he said. 'I would do anything for that woman. She is my blood. I would even let an imposter into her life, if it made her happy.'

'Are we,' İkmen said, 'talking about Yiannis Negroponte, her son?'

'One day he came from Germany with little Turkish and no name,' Hakkı said. 'But he made her smile and he loved her more than his own life. How will she live without him now, Çetin Bey?'

He just stood. A young man in casual clothes, in Taksim Square in front of the Ataturk Centre, facing the portrait of the great leader. Hands in his pockets, he contemplated the features of the man who had brought the Ottoman Empire to an end and moved Turkey into the modern world. Soon others joined him.

'He's just standing, they can't do anything to him for that,' Samsun said. She took Madame Edith's arm and began to move her towards the man. 'Let's join him.'

Madame Edith moved with difficulty. Her ribs had been broken and she was always in pain.

Pembe Hanım said, 'Edith, I've got some morphine if you want some.'

'No, no.' Edith waved a hand. 'That's Sinem's. I don't want to deprive her.'

'She's OK at the moment and Kerim is getting some more from the pharmacy tonight.'

'No. No.'

'Come on, you silly bunch of old fruits,' Samsun said. 'Look at all these people joining the standing man.'

A lot of people had joined the man, silently. Only the small group of transsexuals were making any noise.

A young man in front of them turned. Fearing he'd disapprove of the commotion they were making, Samsun said, 'Sssh!'

But the young man smiled. 'Auntie Samsun?'

'Kemal?'

Kemal İkmen came and joined them. 'What do you think of this, eh?'

'Well, I preferred the carnival atmosphere of the old Gezi,' Samsun said, 'but I have to admit that, as an act of defiance, this is genius.'

'Passive resistance. What's to attack?'

'Passive?' Madame Edith grimaced. 'I went that route and look what happened to me.'

'You were on your own,' Pembe said.

'So was he. Once.'

'But not any more.'

'I wonder when we'll be able to stand and get people to join us,' Madonna said. 'I wonder when people will come out on the streets for chicks with dicks.'

'They have. They did,' Samsun said. 'I don't know whether this is all over and done with now, but I do know that this is a good country with a lot of good people. If we haven't got what we want this time then we will next time or the time after that.'

'I don't know.'

'Well I do, Lady Madonna,' she said. 'Have faith.'

'In what?'

'In whatever you like, but mostly have faith in this country. Anywhere that can produce someone like him,' she pointed at the big portrait of Ataturk, 'can't be all bad. Now Kemal, dear, have you told your father you're a gay boy yet?'

Kemal, ashamed, put his head down. 'He's been busy . . .'

'And you've been cowardly.' Samsun lit a cigarette. 'Get it done.'

'Yes, Auntie.'

Someone in front said, 'Sssh!'

'Sorry!'

Madame Edith held on tight to Pembe's arm and whispered, 'Will you be with Kerim tonight, dear?'

'No, he's spending some time with his wife,' she whispered back. She clearly forced herself to smile. 'Why?'

'Well, can I come home with you then? I'm so frightened by just about anything these days.'

Pembe put a hand on her shoulder. 'Of course you can. Stay as long as you like.'

'Thank you, dear,' Edith said. 'You are a love.'

Two Weeks Later

'My cousin and my son are in there somewhere,' Çetin İkmen said as he finished his glass of beer and called for another.

He and Mehmet Süleyman had a good view of İstanbul's Gay Pride march from their vantage point outside a small cafe on Zambak Sokak.

'I'm just glad it seems to be going off without incident,' Süleyman said. 'Given recent events. How is Fatma Hanım about Kemal's, er, sexuality?'

'Entirely ignorant,' İkmen said. The waiter brought his beer and he took a sip. 'Which is best for all concerned.'

'Ah, but Çetin, secrets fester.'

'You refer to the Negropontes,' he said. 'I wonder who Yiannis Negroponte really was?'

'Well, no relation to Madam Anastasia, that's for sure.'

'I wonder how he found out about the family? And where the real Yiannis Negroponte is? Or even if he survived the events of 1955?'

'Who knows? But the fake Yiannis was a magician, remember.' Süleyman smiled. 'Those people know things.'

'They do.' He lit a cigarette. 'You must be pleased to know who your body in the garden of the Lise is.'

'I am. But who is in Nikos Negroponte's grave at the moment, eh?'

'A homeless person? An unfortunate tourist?'

A group of boys dressed in rainbow coloured tutus ran into Zambak Sokak and performed a small spontaneous ballet. Everyone eating and drinking outside clapped.

'We still don't know who killed Ariadne Savva or where her baby is,' İkmen said. 'That Greek tragedy continues. That makes me sad. You know, Professor Bozdağ now thinks that the skeleton she thought was the last Byzantine emperor is actually too modern. The sword, on the other hand . . .'

'Could be genuine.'

'Could be. But he's just happy to have the Red Room all to himself.'

'Is Madam Negroponte all right with that?'

'Now she's got Lokman and his family looking after her, she's happy for the archaeologists to have their fun. She's changed her will to leave it all to Lokman, you know.'

'Well, he is family, I suppose. Do you think the Red Room will ever be opened to the public?'

İkmen shrugged. 'If Aya Sofya becomes a mosque again, probably not,' he said. 'But what do I know? It's easy to judge conservative people and put them all in the same box with those who believe in djinn, celestial virgins and holy death. But look at Semih Öden – just made peace with Madam Negroponte, said he'd leave her alone, even wished her well.'

'I wonder if his brother killed Ariadne Savva?'

'I wish I knew,' İkmen said. 'Maybe it would give her family some peace. I think that Ahmet had more contact with Ariadne than he said. I think she may have tried to barter the body of Palaiologos for homes for the Gizlitepe rubbish pickers. If he didn't send those threatening letters to the forensic lab, I can't think who did. I mean, she can't have really believed that a Byzantine prince still lived in this city, can she? But I do wonder where her porphyry room was. Red. If it wasn't *the*

Red Room, underneath the Negropontes' house, then where the hell was it?'

The little girl gurgled when she saw the old lady. Madam Anastasia gently stroked her face.

Lokman took the baby from her old, purple hands. 'Come on, little Zoe,' he said. 'Time to leave Grandmama to rest.'

'She . . . so . . .'

The old woman's eyes moistened. 'She has Yiannis Bey's mouth,' Lokman said. 'And his eyes.'

'Yes, but his m-m-m . . .'

'Sssh! Sssh!' Lokman rocked the baby on his knee. 'Madam, Dr Ariadne didn't suffer, honestly! Dad said that when she'd had the baby she got up too quickly. She fell down and hit her head on the edge of the birthing platform. It was an accident. It was stupid not just to get the police then but—'

'Centuries of . . . secrets . . .'

'Yes.'

The baby gurgled.

'And another one here,' Lokman said. 'Daughter of a Negroponte, born to the Purple.'

'With royal blood . . .' The old woman smiled.

'Through her mother. Yes,' Lokman said. 'The first Byzantine princess born to the Purple for over five hundred years.'

'And she will . . . she will rule again,' Madam Anastasia Negroponte said with pride.

But Lokman just smiled. Then he took Yiannis Negroponte and Ariadne Savva's baby back to his wife.

Acknowledgements

Grateful thanks go to Ruth, Pat and Elsie as well as to everyone else who added their valuable insights into the events of summer 2013.

Author Q&A

What inspired you to start writing the İkmen series?

When I first started writing there were very few books set in Istanbul – let alone crime fiction novels. Knowing the fabulous city as well as I did, I found this hard to understand. So I decided to do something about it. I also had a very stressful job at the time, so I wrote to relax. I know that 'relaxing' into murder is probably a bit odd, but that's how it was.

What do you enjoy most about setting your writing in Turkey?

Turkey is a very dynamic and vibrant place. Not only does it have a rich and diverse history and culture, it is always changing and so getting bored is impossible. There's really not much I like better than exploring obscure and forgotten parts of the country. And of course, Turkish people are some of the most welcoming folk in the world.

How does the writing process work for you?

Getting ideas about a place like Turkey is easy. There's almost too much material. Marshalling these ideas into a plot that will be tight, tense and, hopefully, fascinating is where the work really begins. I always produce a synopsis for every new book. But it is a little bit elastic to allow for things to just happen without conscious intervention from me. Sometimes this can mean whole new sub-plots or even some new characters. I like to leave the door open to spontaneous creativity.

Which characters do you most enjoy creating and why?

Flawed types. And villains. I think I'm a little in love with Çetin İkmen because he's flawed. He's certainly no looker, but he is bright and he questions and he wrestles with himself and his vices all the time. As for villains? They're just fascinating which-ever way you swing it. I mean why would anyone kill? Just that fact makes them irresistibly interesting.

What and who are some of your favourite books and authors?

I recently went back and re-read one of my all-time favourites *London Dust* by Lee Jackson. It didn't disappoint. I also love Phil Rickman's Merrily Watkins series. I'm just getting into Colette McBeth's *The Life I Left Behind* which is excellent. However my absolute favourite book is not crime fiction. It is *The Alexandria Quartet* by Lawrence Durrell. It's about Egypt but parts of it could be about the Turkey I remember from my youth. Pure poetry.

What was the last really good book that you read?

Midnight at the Pera Palas by Charles King. A brilliant account of Istanbul life in the jazz age.

If Land of the Blind was turned into a movie, who would you choose to play the lead characters?

It would have to be the wonderful and very handsome Aiden Turner (*Being Human*) for Suleyman. Mark Strong (*Our Friends in the North*) would do a good job with İkmen I think, in spite of being too tall and not thin enough. Mind you, who would be thin enough? Commissioner Hurrem Teker would be a great challenge for Miranda Richardson but I'm sure she'd do a brilliant job.

Can you tell us a little about what is coming next in this series?

Without giving too much away, the next İkmen book will see poor Çetin completely out of his depth in the burgeoning world of Turkish gastronomy. Research into that could have a few little perks for me, however!

THRILLINGLY GOOD BOOKS
FROM CRIMINALLY
GOOD WRITERS

CRIME FILES BRINGS YOU THE LATEST RELEASES FROM
TOP CRIME AND THRILLER AUTHORS.

SIGN UP ONLINE FOR OUR MONTHLY NEWSLETTER AND BE THE FIRST
TO KNOW ABOUT OUR COMPETITIONS, NEW BOOKS AND MORE.

VISIT OUR WEBSITE: WWW.CRIMEFILES.CO.UK
LIKE US ON FACEBOOK: FACEBOOK.COM/CRIMEFILES
FOLLOW US ON TWITTER: @CRIMEFILESBOOKS